THE SPIRITUALIST

Also by Lex Sinclair

Abducted
Diadem Books 2016
ISBN 13: 978-1326541200

Don't Fear the Reaper Part 1
Diadem Books 2016
ISBN: 978-1-326-77008-2

Don't Fear the Reaper Part 2
Diadem Books 2016
ISBN: 978-1-326-91503-2

Don't Fear the Reaper Part 3
Diadem Books 2017
ISBN: 978-1-326-99163-0

The Hunt is On
Diadem Books 2017
ISBN: 978-0-244-05210-2

Passion for Christ
Diadem Books 2018
ISBN: 978-0-244-35210-3

The One-Eyed Monster
Diadem Books 2018
ISBN: 978-0-244-99618-5

The Slime
Diadem Books 2018
ISBN: 978-0-244-69893-5

The Holy Son
Diadem Books 2018
ISBN: 978- 0-244-71771-1

I Wish
Diadem Books 2019
ISBN: 978-0-24418192-5

Star
Diadem Books 2019
ISBN: 978-0-24450382-6

THE SPIRITUALIST

by

Lex Sinclair

DIADEM BOOKS

THE SPIRITUALIST

All Rights Reserved. Copyright © 2020 **Lex Sinclair**

No part of this book may be reproduced or transmitted in any form or by any means, graphic, electronic, or mechanical, including photocopying, recording, taping or by any information storage or retrieval system, without the permission in writing from the copyright holder.

The right of Lex Sinclair to be identified as the author of this work has been asserted in accordance with the Copyright, Designs and Patents Act 1988 sections 77 and 78.
Published by Diadem Books

For information, please contact:
Diadem Books
8 South Green Drive
Airth, Falkirk
FK2 8JP Scotland UK

www.diadembooks.com

The views expressed in this work are solely those of the author and do not necessarily reflect the views of the publisher, and the publisher hereby disclaims any responsibility for them.

This is a work of fiction. Names, characters and incidents are products of the author's imagination. Any resemblance to persons living or dead is entirely coincidental.

ISBN: 9798694371100

Dedicated to

Stephen King

&

Dean Koontz

PART ONE

1.

SATURDAY was an overcast day. Toby Jones sat in the passenger of his mother's Volvo. The drizzle had ceased but the battleship grey clouds still hung ominously overhead. Toby gazed out the window and watched the world go by. He loved going for a drive in the car with his mum, Abigail. They only went for a drive now if they were going someplace since petrol prices had soared.

Today they were headed to the cinema now that the weekly shopping had been done. Toby loved going to the pictures. The experience of sitting in the pitch-dark theatre with surround sound and no talking engaged him wholly and completely. His mother enjoyed it too, just not to the extent that her only child did. They didn't go often as Abigail was a single parent. Toby's father, Ian, had departed a few years back. He had packed up his cherished belongings and left without an explanation or a goodbye. To say that Toby and Abigail were shocked to the core didn't do their emotions justice.

As he got older it dawned on him that his childhood was over and the time had come to face the fact that he was the man of the house. He got a job from the local sweet shop, delivering newspapers for twenty-five pounds for five days' work. It made him feel important, bringing home money to give to his mother who worked full-time in the leisure centre as a cleaner. Ian had left two hundred pounds behind when he left and Abigail took the money out of the pot and deposited it into her bank account.

They went without a TV at first, which was hard. However, they would take books out of the library and sit on the sofa and take it in turns to read to each other. It was fun. And Toby had bonded with his mother on a much closer level than most boys his age. He laid the table when it was time for food and did the dishes afterwards.

They worked together and didn't talk about Ian as a father or a husband. Together they were a rock that the other could lean on for support… and it worked.

'Mum, can I have a Diet Coke, please?'
''Course you can my love,' Abigail said.
'Thanks.'

Once they got their drinks, Abigail handed the usher the tickets over and then made her way down the red carpeted corridor to the correct cinema. The darkness engulfed them and Toby got frightened for about two seconds. Then his mother put a hand over her shoulder and guided him to the steps which led up to the top of the stairs where they eventually found their seats. They sat down and got comfortable and relaxed. The film was *Terminator Genisys*, starring Arnold Schwarzenegger and Emilia Clarke. Toby had his eyes glued to the screen and was totally entranced. When the ending passed over to the end credit sequence Toby blinked as the lights came on overhead. As he followed his mum down the steps, Toby saw a tall gentleman cut across him and head down the steps. Toby kept his eye on his mum and followed behind the man who overtook Abigail and headed down the hallway. Toby thought the man rude in the manner he walked. His mum turned and caught hold of his hand and guided him back out into the spacious hallway.

'That was a good film, Mum,' Toby said. He still thought it a bit odd having to hold his mother's hand but as he did he felt his mum relax a little. There was no telling what she would do without him. Having lost her husband out of the blue was bad enough but when she couldn't see her son or didn't know where he was, she started to panic right away without having any control over herself whatsoever. Toby understood this and that was the only reason he stayed close to her at all times.

'I'm just going to the boys' room to go for a wee,' he said.

'Okay,' Abigail replied.

He let go of her hand and pushed the heavy gents' room door open. The rude man was standing at the urinal, doing his business. He finished using the facilities and whirled around. As he did this he smacked right into Toby who felt the blow. There came a brilliant flash as they collided that Toby had no control over whatsoever. He hit the floor on the seat of his trousers. The back of his head nearly hit the floor and his head started vibrating violently. The man knelt down and rested a hand on Toby's shoulder, not that he could feel it.

'Hey kid! You all right?'

Toby blinked and he saw stars twinkling around his eyes as if he'd just had a seizure or an epileptic fit. He grabbed the man's arm and went into another seizure, this time even more violently. Then he stopped and opened his eyes wide. 'You shouldn't have killed her,' he said.

The man recoiled. 'What did you say?'

'You shouldn't have killed that young girl last week.'

The man rose, the colour draining from his face. He couldn't stop staring for a few moments. Then he whirled around, threw the door open and darted outside.

Toby lay down, supine. The shaking ceased in two hard judders. As he lay there the fluorescents shone deeply in his eyes. He rolled over and heaved himself up, feeling light headed and shaky. He coughed twice, hard. He buried his head in the washing basin and splashed water onto his face. He cleaned up with the paper towels, dried his hands, checked himself in the mirror and headed outside to see his mum.

She was standing there looking concerned. And Toby thought for a split second that he somehow looked entirely different to when he'd entered the restroom. But as he drew closer she gave him a smile and Toby said, 'Sorry I took so long.'

They walked down the corridor and exited the building out into the car park. Driving home, Toby did his utmost not to think about the incident, but there it was. Furthermore, he was amazed at how quickly he had recovered. It nagged him that he couldn't get it out of his head. He knew better than to tell his mum about the incident. So he just sat there with the mystery playing over and over again in his mind.

When they arrived home, Toby went upstairs and sat in his room. He got into bed and pulled the covers over himself. As he lay there, Toby replayed the incident that had befallen him. How did he know what the man had done? He closed his eyes and a vision showed him an image in graphic detail of a man carrying a corpse in a translucent body bag down the narrow stairs and resting it on the floor.

Toby opened his eyes and exhaled deeply.

He got up and headed down the stairs and gasped.

At the bottom of the stairs he saw a body bag lying on the floor, translucent with drops of blood on it. He blinked and the body bag was gone.

'Whew! Jeez!'

'What was that?' Abigail called out, attuned to everything so it seemed.

'Nothing, Mum.' He got to the bottom of the stairs and entered the living room. He picked up the *Radio Times* magazine and flicked through it. Nothing good on. May as well go upstairs and read before dinner was served. 'What's food Mum?'

'Pizza.'

'Cool.'

'Be ready in about ten minutes.'

Toby poured himself a glass of lemonade.

He sat down at the dining table and gazed out the window.

*

The man Toby had grabbed after getting knocked over had fled the cinema, got into his Ford and drove back to his flat in Sketty. His hands couldn't stop trembling. He turned the radio on to give himself a distraction from what had occurred in the male toilets. He thought the boy was going to die. Instead something far worse from his own perspective transpired. He gritted his teeth in vexation. The boy had said in a hollow, yet strong, voice what he had done. If the boy told his legal guardian and they took it to the local constabulary and they investigated further he might have the crime brought to his front door. However, the boy was in shock and was delirious. Also, he had only stared at the boy for a few seconds. His short black hair was neatly trimmed and stood up on its strong roots. He had shaved and changed his appearance to the week before when he had killed a young woman.

He indicated left at the traffic lights and got into the appropriate lane to perform this manoeuvre. It seemed like memory was doing the driving for him while he mused over the incident with the young boy.

Behind him the car blasted its horn in protest. The man snapped out of his reverie and ascended the steep hill past the university sport centre and the hospital on the right and continued straight on at the first roundabout.

The murder had been planned. There had been no witnesses. Just himself and the victim. So how the hell did that boy know what he had done?

He felt like turning around, slamming his foot onto the accelerator and speeding back towards the Odeon cinema in an attempt to find the boy so he could choke him to death. In fact, in his mind's eye he could see and almost feel himself doing this very act there on the floor of the restroom.

As he turned off down the street where two blocks of flats were situated the man cussed violently and struck the steering wheel and smashed his clenched right hand against the driver's door.

After parking the vehicle the man killed the motor and sighed. His shoulders finally slumped into a natural posture. He could feel the weight of the incident depart from him. Yet the memory had already embedded itself into the deepest recesses of his mind and could not be erased.

He got out of the car, locked it and crossed the parking bay to the entrance. He used his ID card and four-digit pin number that permitted him access. Once inside the man wasted no time climbing the stairs. He leapt up the floors like a wild, lithe animal. He arrived at his flat out of breath but grateful for the exercise. He let himself in, locked the door behind him, tossed his coat onto its hanger and collapsed on the sofa to finally relax, knowing he was safe and out-of-the-way from the suspecting eyes of the world.

The boy or anyone else for that matter couldn't touch him now. He was safe. He grabbed the remote control from the arm and turned the TV on. It was almost ten o'clock. The national and local news would soon be on.

Since killing the young woman last week there had been only one brief report that Danielle Thompson had been reported missing from her home in Morriston.

The man had lived like a hermit for the best part of the week, anxious about the police, who would no doubt be putting on an investigation team to get to the bottom of case of the missing woman who had disappeared without trace and totally against her nature.

The weekend before, the man, whose name was Ian Cravis, had been standing outside a bar on Wind Street in Swansea, finishing off his beer when Danielle and two of her pals had been looking over their shoulders at him and then giggling like little girls. Ian got nervous around attractive women. He had no experience other than when he had been studying plastering in college when he shagged his friend from school one night when a group of friends had gone camping. However, since then, Ian had got a job as a taxi driver and worked long hours well into the night.

He had been awarded fourteen days off work by his manager since he hadn't had a day off in three whole years. It was against the law. Ian didn't want to lose his job… and only after much persuasion did he agree to take some annual leave.

The job had cost him a lot of friendships due to the unsociable hours. Ian had gone out just to get out of the flat and into the company of merry folks.

Danielle turned as Ian was walking in her direction, to order another beer. She said, 'Hi.' Then she went on to introduce herself. Ian reciprocated and they shook hands and kissed each other on the cheek. She was very attractive and had smooth, tawny skin that clung to her silk black dress, provocatively highlighting her sensual figure. She held his nervous gaze for a few seconds and then broke into a warm smile.

'Can I get you anything?' Ian asked, standing side on.

'I'll have a shandy,' Danielle said.

'I'll be back now,' Ian said and made a beeline for the bar to order the drinks.

As Ian glanced over his shoulder, he saw Danielle turn in the direction of her friends and give them the "thumbs up" gesture, meaning all was good. He noticed her finely-shaped bum and grew hot in the face at the thought of laying his hands on it and caressing her. Full of lust, Ian ordered the drinks and when the barman returned after giving him his change, Ian made his way carefully back to Danielle and handed her the glass of Shandy.

'Those your friends?' Ian asked, already aware that they were. Danielle told him that indeed they were. Then they got to chatting about Danielle's career as a finance director for a local building firm. Ian's eyebrows shot up, impressed. He told her he was a taxi driver and worked long into the night and slept until lunch.

They chatted about the weather and then the football. And although they ran out of things to say they both still felt comfortable in each other's company.

'What do you like doing in your spare time, Ian?'

'I go to the movies.'

'Oh cool.'

Danielle drank the last of her drink. 'What films do you like?'

'Action films mostly. I love the eighties era. You know, films with Arnold Schwarzenegger and Sly Stallone.'

'Okay. Well, I like films like *Pretty Woman*.'

'That's with... Julia Roberts, right?'

Danielle nodded a yes.

'Danielle?'

'Yes.'

'Would you like my mobile number? I'd like to see you again, if you'd like?'

'Of course,' she said in an upbeat tone. 'I'll also give you my number. But please don't call me in the week. My job is very demanding and I can get quite snappy when I'm stressed out.'

Ian laughed a little at that comment. 'I'll remember that,' he said with a smile of his own. 'Well, the weather is supposed to be nice tomorrow. How 'bout I give you a call in the morning and we can go out for a meal and a walk around the pond in Llansamlet afterwards?'

'Where do you live?'

'Neath Abbey. Up the mountain, towards the suburbs called "The Highlands". Maybe I'll show you my place.'

Beaming with excitement, Danielle said that would be great. She typed Ian's number into her phone, took his mobile off him and inserted her number. She kissed him twice on the cheek and once, quickly on the lips. 'See you tomorrow then.'

'You will,' Ian had said. Then he watched her make her way through the crowd back to her friends.

2.

TOBY finished his pizza and took the empty plate back downstairs to the kitchen sink for washing later on. Abigail was finishing off a glass of Strongbow cider. She gulped down the drink and offered her son a broad smile.

'What've you been up to, Toby?'

'Nothing much. Just a bit tired. Might get dressed for bed now and watch a film.'

'*Another* film?' Abigail said, quietly astonished.

'Yeah.'

'You know you can hang out with friends from school, if you want? It might be good for you in the long haul. It's been my fault really. I'm a bit clingy at times. But you're all I've got in this world worth living for. But I know you need time apart from me to learn to grow into a boy who has a happy childhood. Have you got a best friend?'

'You're my best friend in the world, Mum.'

'Oh, that's sweet, little one. That really is.'

Toby watched his mum's face closely. He enjoyed spending time with her. However, there were times when he saw boys and girls his own age doing some exciting stuff, like going to Laser Dome. Abigail was only on one meagre wage and they struggled to get by. They had to give up the TV for a couple of years and resorted to going to the local library, getting a few books out and took it in turns to read to one another.

Things like that Toby never forgot. 'When I'm older Mum, I'm gonna get a good job and provide for you the way you've provided for me.'

'You're the sweetest boy ever… and you're my son.'

They embraced for a hug and then parted again.

Then Toby exited the kitchen and sauntered back upstairs to his cosy bedroom. The walls were painted sky-blue. The beige carpet was clean and refurbished. There was an air freshener in one of the sockets that gave off a tropical fruit aroma. Toby

grew to like after the first two days when the scent made him sneeze something awful.
He got down on his hands and knees and pulled out some of his DVDs. As he was doing this an electrical blue light sliced across his immediate vision which caused him to wince and slap a hand over both eyes as if stung by an angry wasp. He recoiled and dropped the handful of DVDs in his hands. The retinas in his eyes transformed into forked lightening behind the lids and Toby's breathing accelerated as did his jackhammer heartbeat. He made it to his bed and crawled inside, still covering his eyes, doing all he could to stop this unimaginable assault that he had no defence against.

*

Ian sat behind the wheel of his car and turned the volume down on his radio so he could talk to Danielle. She wore a very bright red outfit and white stilettos. Ian had told her that he was going to take her to his home before going to a pub he knew in Ystalefera
'At least it's stopped raining now,' Ian said.
Danielle agreed and continued to gaze out the window.
Ian noticed the palpable difference in this beautiful lady now that she was not in the company of her friends. She was very quiet and polite.
'I forgot to tell you how amazing you look in that dress.'
'Oh, thank you, Ian. You look nice too.'
Ian laughed. 'I had a shower and a shave. I think I look better – younger, at least, - when I've shaved than I do when I've got stubble.'
'You do!'
They arrived at Ian's residence and slowed to a stop on the paved driveway. 'Here we are,' he announced.
'It's a nice bungalow,' Danielle said, observing the white pebble-dash façade and neatly trimmed front lawn.
'It's not big,' Ian said, taking the key out of the ignition, 'but it is ideal for me, as I live on my own.'
They got out of the car and went inside.

Ian went and poured them both a glass of red wine. Then they talked about each other's background and interests more deeply than when they had been standing together in a loud bar on Wind Street. This, Ian decided, was much better. At least they could hear each other clearly without having to yell into each other's ear to be heard.

'Can I kiss you?' Ian asked.

'Okay.'

Ian moved in and cupped Danielle's full lips with his own. She kissed him back and together they made out with both lust and passion. He pulled away and Danielle caught her breath. 'Would you like to go further?'

Danielle didn't have to ask what Ian meant by that comment. She simply nodded, taken aback by the intensity of kissing. She accepted Ian's hand and followed him to his bedroom where he closed the door shut.

In less than an hour of copulating, Danielle emerged and Ian pulled his trousers up. They left the bungalow and headed out for the pub as they were both now ravenously hungry.

After food, Ian told Danielle that he had to pop home before dropping her off because he needed to get his spare key. Danielle thanked him sincerely for taking her out for food and in private for making her have a wonderful orgasm. When they arrived back at the bungalow, Ian offered Danielle a drink. She agreed to a can of Pepsi Max. Ian poured the can into a glass and dropped some powder into it from the cabinet to the right and above the sink. He handed her the drink and surreptitiously watched her make light work of the drink. He finished his own can and put them in the white rubbish bag that he left outside for the rubbish men to collect the day after tomorrow. Then he came back and sat down next Danielle and proceeded to kiss her neck and face. She moaned in pleasure, recalling the intercourse earlier and started kissing him back. They copulated on the sofa in the living room, passionately and quickly.

'I'm tired,' Danielle said ten minutes later, feeling woozy and light-headed.

'Just rest here,' Ian told her, taking her long, slender legs and propping them up on the other end and then carefully placing a woolly blanket on top of her.

Danielle drifted away in minutes.

Ian made his way to the shed out the back door and took out a long, serrated army knife. He entered the bungalow through the back door and rested the blade on the proffered neck of the woman he has just had sex with and slit her open with one quick, silent slash…

*

The quilt was drawn up to his neck and his head was propped up on his pillow. Toby lay in his bed, mouth wide open in the shape of an O, witnessing the death of the beautiful woman wearing a black silk dress. A strangled cry escaped the confines of his mouth. His eyes were wide open. They kept opening and closing all the time without his consent. The visions he was receiving were vivid in detail with graphic horror.

The woman had shot up in an instant, slapping her hands over her fatal wound, falling off the sofa and looking at the perpetrator of this heinous act. Her mind was in utter turmoil. Her head reeled at seeing her lover standing there in the living room holding the weapon that dripped blood on the patterned carpet.

She was on all fours, looking up in shock and fear as the blood bled profusely through her trembling fingers until she tottered sideways, lost her balance and collapsed on her side and waited for the warm hands of death to overcome her and remove her from this misery and her life forever…

Toby was shaking from head-to-toe and couldn't control the seizure that started in his brain and rapidly inflicted his whole body. He grasped the ends of his quilt and muffled his cries of anguish at seeing this event that he had no business knowing in the first place.

His head started vibrating and for a few moments in absolute mercy of this infliction, Toby truly believed that whoever that woman was dying, he would soon follow into the endless chasm of death.

He resurfaced an hour or so later, a film of sweat dampening his brow, the memory of those images like a film reel in his poisoned mind. Toby stayed exactly where he was grateful that the day had succumbed to night. He believed he ought to have been grateful for the sleep he'd had, but frightened of the explicit vision he had been forced to witness. He exhaled and took his glass of lemonade from the bedside cabinet and finished it with a small burp.

Toby put the TV on purely for company and distraction. However, his mind refused to cooperate with his sensible plans and resurfaced. This time his eyelids felt like two heavy dumbbells and gave him no power to keep them open and on the illuminated TV screen.

This time the man was dragging the woman (who was now dead) across the stained carpet into the kitchen where her exposed wound redecorated the tiled flooring. The killer cussed at the mess and wasted no time using a household appliance to clean the carpet, removing the stains while they were still fresh to prevent them from being soaked and stained permanently for anyone to see.

He spent a good twenty minutes scrubbing the carpet until he was satisfied the carpet was clean. Then he wiped the tiled flooring in the kitchen and wrapped Danielle's body in a transparent plastic bag to stop the wound from leaking out again in any other part of his bungalow.

Toby blinked. His eyes opened and he caught a flicker of the TV before his eyes snapped shut again...

This time the killer was carrying the dead woman out the door at night and dumping her in the boot of his car, slamming the lid and driving off to a destination somewhere that wouldn't be linked back to him in any way whatsoever.

What Toby didn't understand (even in his profound fear) was why the man had committed this crime. It didn't make sense... at all. The man had had a great day. He was attracted to this woman. He had enjoyed the highest pleasures lovers can only share intimately. Shared a splendid meal with her and then did something that was completely out of this world and unthinkable, let alone doable. He could have had that gorgeous woman for the rest of his life if he treated her well.

So why? Why did he kill her?

The Llansamlet pond and walk-path area was deserted. It was late night when the man drove his car into the parking bay and killed the motor. He checked all around him before getting out of the car, opening the boot and carrying the dead body down the slope where during the day fishermen used and hurled Danielle into the murky water.

Satisfied that he had managed not to been seen by any motorists or pedestrians, Ian made his way back to the car and drove home as if nothing had happened that day.

Toby's head started vibrating again. If it continued it could cause him a brain haemorrhage. Yet as much as he tried to stop it, he found that he was helpless and had no choice but to endure this bodily attack induced by his own senses...

3.

ABIGAIL watched the news and weather on TV before killing the power with the remote control. She finished her glass of Strongbow and headed into the kitchen. She switched off all the lights on the ground floor before ascending the staircase. As she climbed she thought it strange how silent the house was, as though she was living on her own.

She turned at the top of the stairs toward her son's bedroom and knocked gently before pushing the door open. Darkness engulfed everything.

'Toby?' she said. 'Are you all right?'

Silence...

She stood at the threshold, attempting to see through the pitch darkness and focus on her son's bed. This proved to be impossible so she flicked on the switch and as the sudden radiance blinded her she saw her son lying on his side, trembling uncontrollably, foam escaping his mouth and running off his chin onto the sheets.

'Ohmigod!'

Abigail darted to the bed and cradled Toby's lulling head upright, squeezing him tight to stop the body quake. She failed at this miserably. Toby was not responsive to her shrieks of fear and desperation. Her mind was buzzed and electrified by a myriad of wild questions.

'Sweetheart! Sweetheart! Wake up! Wake up, my love.'

She continued this panicky and soothing voice for ten minutes before she rested her son's head down on the pillow. She hurried across the landing, burst through her bedroom and snatched the wireless phone out of its cradle and dialled 999.

Then she hurried back to Toby and waited to be put through to the emergency services. The woman on the other end asked how she could help. Abigail blurted out that Toby was having a seizure of some kind and was not epileptic or had any other seizures before in his life. Then she gave the woman the house and street name and number as she contacted and dispatched an ambulance to her right away. However, Abigail had not expected the woman to stay on the line. The woman told her to feel for Toby's pulse. Abigail did that and told her she could feel a rapid pulse in Toby's neck and that he'd stopped dribbling but was still unconscious.

The woman then advised Abigail to speak to Toby in his ear on the chance that he might still be able to hear her familiar voice. Abigail did that and before long there was a loud knock on the front door. She flew down the stairs, tore the door open and told the paramedics to follow her.

When the paramedics came into Toby's bedroom they could see how serious the situation was and that it had palpably affected the anxious mother. Abigail stood to the side, giving them room to lift Toby off the bed and onto a stretcher. They placed a head support around Toby's head and strapped him to the stretcher and carefully carried him down the stairs.

Abigail asked what hospital the paramedics were taking him to so she could follow them.

'Morriston Hospital,' the blonde haired, female paramedic said. She then added, 'Bring some clothes and toiletries down with you in a bag. He'll be taken to the ICU in the first instance but if he comes around tonight he might be moved onto a ward thereafter.'

Abigail watched her precious child being carried into the back of the ambulance and then she rushed back indoors to get some essentials for Toby, hoping and silently praying to a God she'd never spoken to until now, begging Him to let Toby make a full recovery and never suffer from anything like this ever again.

She got a bag, slammed the front door behind her and made her way to her Volvo. She started the engine and then all of a sudden exhaled, only then realising how long she'd been holding her breath, running up and down the stairs to and fro without pausing to regain some composure. This was followed by a powerful rack of shudders and then tears.

She thought about Toby as a baby. She had just given birth to him and was cradling his tiny form in a white woolly blanket. That day had been the best day of her life. And since then Toby had lived a life of such pure kindness and gentleness that she couldn't have wished for more. Toby was Abigail's miracle. He had the wisdom and calmness of an old man in the body not yet reaching its full physical prime. The world was his oyster. Toby could achieve anything he wanted if he put his mind to it. Abigail hated her husband for walking out and leaving her and Toby to defend for themselves. If she lost Toby now then there was no turning back. The blackness of her soul caused by a very strict and tough upbringing and being abandoned by the man she believed was her soul mate would swallow her completely if anything happened to Toby.

'Come on!' she shouted. 'Get going, girl.'

She had to dig deep to get herself out of her melancholy and pulled away from the kerb and headed toward Morriston Hospital to be there for her son.

*

Toby was wheeled into ER to be treated without delay. A Pakistani doctor and two young nurses assisted the boy whose face had turned hollow and pallid in complexion. Nevertheless his heart was beating very strongly and he'd stopped shaking and foaming at the mouth. Now he laid supine, unconscious.

The doctor glanced back and forth from the heart monitor and the boy whose eyes began rolling beneath the lids. The two nurses stood either side of Toby, ready to carry out the doctor's instructions.

The doctor was about to speak when without any sign or forewarning, Toby burst out of his catatonic state and shot upright, eyes blinking open, shock painted across his features, eyes wide and scanning the room.

The hospital staff all recoiled in fright and then bringing their senses to the sudden and unexpected reaction of the patient drew closer, holding him and speaking in soothing tones, explaining what had happened and where he was.

Toby settled his gaze on the nurse in a blue uniform that clung to her, revealing her comely assets. She took Toby's clammy hand in her own and placed her left arm around him.

'Hospital?' Toby said, clearly confused.

The nurse told Toby again what had befallen him.

'What's the last thing you remember?' the doctor said, taking a pen and small notepad from his tunic pocket.

Toby's brow was drenched in sweat and as he caught his breath, he focused on the Pakistani doctor to answer him clearly. 'He killed Danielle...'

The doctor and the two nurses glanced at each other, confusion and fear masking their faces at what Toby had just said.

'Who's Danielle?' the doctor asked, curious.

'He met her on a night out,' Toby said, his eyes distant and far away from ER. 'She liked him the moment she saw him. He fancied her too. They had sex. Then he spiked her drink, which made her unconscious and then killed her.'

'When did this happen?' the nurse with gorgeous blonde hair and a desirable figure asked.

'Last weekend,' Toby said with no hesitation.

'You saw it?' the nurse asked, incredulous.

Toby turned his head to look at her directly. 'I have the gift of Second Sight.'

No one spoke for a minute. Toby watched them process all he had said before coming to terms with the information and making any plans from that moment on.

'I need to talk to the police,' Toby said.

The doctor noticed that the boy's face had already started to go pink as blood rushed through his veins, bringing him back with renewed vigour and life.

'How do you know this for sure though?' the other nurse asked, baffled and unsure that the boy was talking complete nonsense.

'I literally bumped into him in the cinema. There was a flash behind my eyes. Then I saw what had happened in my room with my eyes closed, like it was a film being played in my mind.'

'Where did he kill this woman?' the doctor asked. He was now focused entirely on the boy, believing that the sudden seizure was the root cause of his ability and that it had nothing to do with physical or mental health at all.

Toby met his gaze. 'He killed her in his bungalow, in the Highlands, Neath Abbey, but dumped the body on Sunday night at the lake on Siemens Way. I know where exactly. That's why I need to prove to myself whether or not I'd had merely a detailed vision or if I do possess certain powers. I do hope I'm wrong though.'

'Me too,' the nurse holding his hand said.

*

The hospital staff moved Toby onto a ward. The doctor had gone to talk to Abigail, who arrived shortly afterwards, about Toby's miraculous recovery and what he'd told them. Toby's bed was the last one on the right. He had forgotten all about his mother. He desperately needed to talk to the police to see if he had been right about everything that he'd felt and seen.

Within an hour, Toby reiterated his incredible story to his mother and a uniformed police officer.

'How could you possibly know this though?' Officer Darny asked, incredulous.

Toby shrugged. 'Your guess is as good as mine,' he said. 'But I know it like the way you know the route home at the end of the day. As soon as the doctors and nurses realise I am no longer in need to be in hospital and discharge me, I will escort you to the exact location of the victim's remains.'

Officer Darny exhaled deeply. He could tell by Toby's demeanour that the boy believed everything he'd said to be true. Furthermore, there were no indications that would make this nice and polite boy tell such a detailed lie. However, he did remind Toby that what he was saying was very serious and if he was lying then he ought to say so before he was taken to be serious.

Toby assured him that unless he'd literally lost his mind then this was the location of Danielle that would give the local constabulary a reason to follow up on this deed and finally catch the perpetrator that had committed this heinous crime.

Toby glanced at his mother. Abigail could do nothing to hide her emotions. Toby could tell before she even opened her mouth that she was deeply concerned and didn't want to believe what he'd told the police. 'But you can't know for sure, love,' she said in her soothing, motherly voice. 'You've never had a fit before until today.'

Toby shook his head, both in disagreement and disdain. 'I had my first fit when I went to the men's toilet in the Odeon in Swansea when I got knocked over by Ian Cravis. That's why I took so long. But I made a full recovery and didn't tell you 'cause I know how much you worry.'

'Who's Ian Cravis?' Officer Darny asked, perplexed.

'That's the name of the killer,' Toby said, not missing a beat.

'What I can't understand,' Officer Darny said aloud, 'is why he killed Danielle in the first instance.'

'That's why you need to find the body of Danielle and question Ian Cravis, who lives in Sketty and is either in his late thirties or early forties.'

Darny caressed his brow, turned and headed to the entrance of the ward to confer with his partner.

Abigail didn't need a second to use this chance to try and talk sense into her son. She was grateful that Toby was wide awake and alert. What she couldn't understand was how he'd managed to spin such an intricate yarn that was "supposedly" factual.

'It's gonna be all right, Mum.'

'If you're wrong about this,' Abigail said, deliberately ignoring what her son just said, 'there could be serious ramifications brought against you. So now is the chance to tell me the truth. If you don't know for real that this is what's happened to two complete strangers then you must tell the officer. Your head is recovering from an injury that almost killed you tonight. Your brain is getting all kinds of messages. You're most likely hallucinating.'

Toby leaned back on the upright pillows and sighed. 'And what if I'm not?'

Abigail didn't – couldn't – answer that question. In truth she hadn't even considered it in her mind. All she was concerned about was her son's wellbeing and not being troubled by the police for giving them false information regarding a crime which Toby only saw in his own mind while suffering with a life-threatening seizure.

Darny returned ten minutes later and stood at Toby's bedside. 'I just spoke to my superintendent about what you told me. You'll be discharged tomorrow morning according to your doctor. I will come by in the morning. Is half past ten okay with you, Toby?'

Toby nodded. 'Fine.'

'I'll take you to the lake and you can show the detectives where exactly you believe that woman's body is. We're running a check through our database for an Ian Cravis. Try to get some sleep tonight. Tomorrow will be a big day for you. Are you sure you're up for it?'

Toby nodded again.

'Then I'll bid you a goodnight and will see you in the morning.' With that said, officer Darny turned on his heel and exited the ward out of sight.

'I don't know what to say,' Abigail blurted out, shaking her head in utter disbelief.

Toby rested his left hand on top of his mother's bowed head. 'Don't worry, Mum. Once tomorrow is out of the way we can go home and pretend that nothing happened and go back to our normal lives.'

Abigail nodded then raised her head. 'I don't know what to hope for,' she said, her emotions overwhelming her. 'If your story proves to be wrong the police will probably charge you for wasting their time. On the other hand, if you're telling the truth, that means you have a very special gift that will take up most of your time for the rest of your life, which you have yet to live.'

Toby absorbed his mother's words. After a minute he replied thoughtfully. 'Mum, I do hope I'm wrong, in some ways. I'd like to believe that there is no body to be found and that if these folks do exist then they are either happy together as a couple or alive and well as single. But I've never felt so much power charging through me that I can't put a label on it.

'Go home. Sleep,' he added. 'I'm fine. I'll see you tomorrow. There's no point racking your brain in a hope to find an agreeable notion. What'll be will be.'

Abigail leaned over and kissed Toby's head. She grabbed her handbag and asked if he wanted anything before she took her leave. Toby assured her he was fine and didn't want her assistance for anything; that she ought to go now to beat the traffic.

He watched her leave with a pang in his heart…

'Please be wrong, Toby,' Toby whispered to himself and closed his eyes…

4.

THE SUNLIGHT slipped through the parted curtains and spilled its warmth and radiance onto Toby's unblemished face. He stirred awake after rolling onto his side and blinked his eyes open. He narrowed his eyes in the full glare. He got his bearings after a minute of coming to properly. The clock on the wall at the far end above the doorway told him it was half past eight. Officer Darny would arrive in an hour and a half to take him to the lake. Toby climbed out of his hospital bed and got dressed into his jogger bottoms and long-sleeved Addidas T-shirt. His mother had brought some clothes down and placed them on a chair.

There was a transparent bag on the bedside table containing his toiletries. Bag in hand, Toby tip-toed out of the room and down the corridor towards the vacant bathroom and went through his morning ritual wake-up routine.

Once he had achieved this task, Toby slipped out and back into the ward and sat on the unyielding mattress, gazing out the window. The connections in his brain were highly wired to be ready and alert for Officer Darny. He wasn't anxious in the slightest, but his hands trembled in his lap.

A young, blonde-haired nurse approached him and Toby was taken aback by her beauty. He could tell that this lovely, kind hearted nurse would have trouble fighting the boys off. According to her tag the nurse's name was Jules.

'Is everything all right, my darling?' she asked in a soothing voice.

Toby nodded and gave her a big, cheery smile. 'I'm just waiting for the police officer to come get me. We have to go someplace to find out if something bad has happened.'

Jules sat next to him and wrapped her arm around his shoulders. 'I know, love. But I'm more concerned about your well-being. Did you get adequate sleep last night? You were quite early getting up.'

'I slept for nine hours, which for me is very good,' Toby said, loving the warmth and comfort Jules gave him. 'Its just today is a big day in my life. There's no easy way out of this situation. I want to be right, but at the same time I want to be wrong.'

'What'll be will be, sweetheart,' Jules said and kissed him on the top of his head. 'Would you like me to stay with you until the policeman arrives? I can talk to him.'

Toby gazed longingly into Jules' eyes. 'That would be lovely. Thank you.'

'You're more than welcome,' she said.

They sat on the mattress gazing out the window at the azure sky and resplendent sunshine. Seagulls squawked loudly as they perched on the chimney stacks.

When Officer Darny arrived, Jules gently ushered him to one side and grabbed his full and undivided attention.

'Be gentle with him, please,' Jules said, glancing at Toby who was still mesmerised by what was happening outside on the tiled rooftops.

'What d'you mean?' Officer Darny said, somewhat perplexed.

'He doesn't know if he is right or not… and is not sure which'll be best for him. This is a huge turning point in his life. If he is right then he's psychic. If he's wrong however he's worried that he'll get into trouble.'

Officer Darny took a deliberate step back and looked at Jules. He was seeing someone, but in that brief moment he wanted to hold Jules and grope her all over before making love to her. However, Jules held his gaze and the aura emanating from her demanded his attention to be professional and nothing more for the sake of the young boy, who he could tell she really cared for.

'Okay,' he whispered.

'Thank you,' Jules said.

She went back to Toby and helped him put his belongings into a plastic carrier bag, kissed him again on the cheek and wished him well. Then she turned to Darny and said, 'Like I said, be gentle.'

Officer Darny heeded her advice and escorted Toby out of the ward, into the lift and out of the hospital grounds.

*

Officer Darny had made light conversation with Toby who opted to sit in the back seat heading towards the lake. When it came into view, Toby's hands started shaking again and his mouth went dry. He wanted to flee the patrol car and be with his mother.

The policeman flicked the turn signal up to show the surrounding traffic that he intended to slow down and take the next right into the parking bay where he spotted the detective.

They rolled to a halt approaching the group of swans that had just emerged from the lake itself. Toby unfastened his safety harness. Darny did the same, got out and opened the rear side door, permitting Toby to step out. Then together they crossed the concrete parking bay toward the detective seated on the bonnet of a navy BMW, smoking a cigarette.

Officer Darny shook hands and turned to Toby. 'This is Detective Inspector Sark. He'll ask you some questions before we proceed. But do you know exactly in the lake where the body was disposed of?'

Toby didn't hesitate. A blanket of warmth, love and comfort overcame him as he pointed his index finger in the direction where the path narrowed and where the recycling bins were situated. 'Beyond those trees, he dumped her body where the fishermen go. Her dead weight has kept her beneath the surface.'

DI Sark and Officer Darny exchanged a baffled look.

'This boy is serious,' Sark said, his voice filled with astonishment. He had heard from his colleagues that Toby had gone into two seizures ever since the man known as Ian Cravis had killed and disposed of Danielle a few nights ago.

'There is a man by the name of Ian Cravis residing in Sketty,' DI Sark said, still in disbelief, regardless of the fact that according to the rumour, the boy might be super-psychic.

'Show us where,' DI Sark said.

Toby moved forward with a purpose. The shaking had ceased all of a sudden and his gift took over. DI Sark and Officer Darny followed in perfect silence.

The young boy stopped and stooped down, and gently raked his fingers across the silk surface causing a beautiful ripple. He stared at the water and could just make out the rocks at the bottom. Tangled in the undergrowth was a pale white leg with a twinkling gold bracelet.

Without any forewarning, Toby swung his right leg over the embankment and his left leg trailed him. The lower half of his body was submerged. He bent down and dipped under the surface. When his head broke the surface moments later the two officers of the law retreated, unnerved and proud of the young boy who now held the dead woman up and into the world once more to be taken to the morgue to be examined and identified.

DI Sark snapped out of his shock and cussed automatically. Officer Darny literally had to blink a couple of times to believe what he was seeing right before him.

Toby stood still in the lake and wept uncontrollably. He wept for Danielle who had died an awful death. And he cried for himself, knowing that there would be no normality for him or his loving mother ever again…

*

The body was dragged over the lip of the embankment. Toby got out of the cold water and accepted the proffered hand of the uniformed police officer. DI Sark looked at Toby with a whole new expression. He was in shock at what he'd just witnessed and in complete awe of the boy's amazing talent. Although talent might not have been the right word. Nevertheless, without Toby's precognition, or whatever the hell you called it, they would never have found the remains of Danielle Thompson and what was most likely her murderer, Ian Cravis, who resided in Sketty.

'Jesus kid,' DI Sark said in a gasp. 'What world you from?'

Toby glanced at him for a moment then climbed the bank to the footpath. He squeezed his tracksuit bottoms in his fists and water spilled out. He did this for a good ten minutes until the he got most of the water out. Yet he was still desperate to get out of his clothes and into the shower before changing into clean, dry clothes for the remainder of the day.

DI Sark dug into his trouser pocket and fished out a mobile phone. He turned away from Officer Darny who climbed the bank to assist this amazing boy.

'You all right, Toby?' he asked, reaching the path and looking at the boy who seemed distraught.

Toby shrugged. 'At least I'm not in trouble with the law for lying,' he said in a frustrated tone. 'Can I please use your phone to call my mum to come pick me up before I catch pneumonia?'

'I'll call her now,' Officer Darny said unclipping his phone from his yellow glow-in-the-dark jacket.

Toby gave him his house phone number and the policeman waited for an answer. Then he glanced over his shoulder at the family of swans swimming idly by, not a care in the world. Toby envied them more than he could put into words.

Officer Darny finished the conversation and then switched his mobile off and hooked it back onto his uniform vest. 'She's on her way,' he told Toby, shifting from one foot to the other. His lips looked dry and crinkly.

'What's wrong?' Toby asked.

'You do realise that from this moment on your life is gonna change drastically, don't you?'

Toby nodded.

'That's why you were crying?'

'I was crying for Danielle. Crying for my mum. And I was crying because I was right and am frightened of what happened to me when the killer literally bumped into me in the Men's Room in the cinema. People can be so cruel. I'm thirteen years old for God's sake. What the hell am I doing digging dead women up from obscurity? I should be out on a push bike, exploring, or playing PS3 in my bedroom. Instead of that I nearly die from powerful seizures. Is this how it's gonna be for me for the rest of my life? I hope not. Can you blame me?'

Officer Darny didn't reply. He had no idea what to say or if there was anything his brain could conjure up so he could offer this young boy reassurance. Toby was right. He had nearly died. However, according to the doctor and the nurses, the boy's amazing resuscitation to recover in a second without any injuries, physical or mental, was a miracle in itself.

'You have something inside you that is very powerful,' Darny said. 'You just brought a grieving family peace and an opportunity to bury their child and a killer to justice before anything like this happens again. To Danielle and the Thompson family, you are worth more than any amount of money... and to other young women and their families you have named the culprit so he can be arrested and placed into custody for this heinous crime.'

Reluctantly, Toby nodded. 'Yeah, all right,' he said, with effort.

DI Sark walked over and whispered something into Darny's ear. Then he turned to Toby and said how proud he was of him.

'I'm just gonna wait for my mum over there,' Toby said, pointing at the entrance where a concrete wall offered an ideal place to sit.

DI Sark informed Darny that more police officers were coming to cordon the area while they waited for emergency services prior to taking the deceased to the morgue.

'What's wrong with him?' DI Sark asked. 'He sounds really ticked off.'

'Can you blame him? He's a kid and now he'll be famous for being psychic, or whatever he is, and solving a murder crime. He had two massive seizures that nearly killed him and then seconds later came to with not a trace of pain or damage. I think it's a bit much for him.'

'Well, least he'll be famous for something good, anyway,' DI Sark said. 'He'll have no trouble finding a girlfriend once this hits the nationwide news, that's for certain. The boy's a goddamn hero.'

DI Sark and Officer Darny went and stood where Toby was and told him all this in an attempt to cheer him up and prepare him for what was about to come. Toby did smile, but it seemed to be forced. However, when DI Sark mentioned the part about girls, Toby chuckled and playfully rolled his eyes.

As his mum's car slowed and approached the parking bay, Toby shook hands with Officer Darny and DI Sark. They both thanked him and Toby felt their true affection and gratitude towards him.

'Hey kid!' DI Sark called out as Toby crossed the parking bay to his mum's car.

Toby stopped and turned around.

'Ever fancy working for the police force?'

Toby shrugged. The thought had never crossed his mind.

'We could use someone with your gift. You think about that on your way home.'

Toby nodded and smiled at the same time. Then he got in the car and slammed the door.

'Great kid,' DI Sark said, as the first siren started wailing in the distance, growing louder the closer to the crime scene where they now stood.

'He'd make a great detective,' Officer Darny said, watching Abigail turn the Volvo around and exit the lakeside.

'No,' DI Sark said. 'Better than that. If he is precognitive, then he can predict murders before they even happen.'

'Guess we'll have to wait and see,' Officer Darny said.

5.

TWO WEEKS LATER

THE DAY was overcast and had been drizzling steadily in the morning. Then the clouds dispersed, leaving patches of blue and the hidden glow of the sun.

A new, red Ford Focus pulled up alongside the kerb on the street, deserted of people and covered with scattered autumn leaves. A man with curly, gelled hair got out of the car after killing the motor and waited for his auburn-haired assistant to come round the parked vehicle before they opened the small black gate and headed down the path, arriving at the front door.

'Ready?' the woman asked her partner.

'Readier than I'll ever be,' he replied, carrying his brown briefcase containing all his documents and other necessities.

The woman rapped quite hard on the door and then stepped back and waited. They listened attentively and finally heard a door closing from inside. The door opened and Abigail Jones poked her head through the aperture, looking harried.

'Yes? What is it? What d'you want?'

The man stepped forward, facing Abigail directly so that there was nothing else to look at beyond the entrance. 'We're journalists,' he started, clearing his throat as he sounded groggy. 'There's been a lot of media attention in regards the Danielle Thompson murder and the arrest of one Ian Cravis; the case your young son solved by informing the authorities what happened and where to look. Then a day later, telling the police to check the woman's private parts for the killer's semen. They did. It matched Ian Cravis. If we can, we'd like to talk with Toby to get his story out in the public view. We want the exclusive.'

Abigail visibly frowned. Her eyes narrowed. Evidently, she was contemplating what the journalist had just said and let the silence envelope them in a difficult and awkward situation. 'My son is thirteen years old. Early next year he'll be fourteen. Yes, it is true that he solved a crime. It is true that because of my son, that young woman's family now have her body to bury instead of wondering what the hell happened to her for the rest of their lives. It is true that the culprit will almost certainly spend the next ten years in prison for murder. But what you fail to understand is that my son almost died twice from massive seizures. He's still recovering. Don't you get it? The seizure was caused by brain trauma. He's in his bedroom, catching up on his schoolwork. If I disturb him now to do some interview it'd likely add to his stress and put him in a perilous state where he might become unwell again. Now I know you have a job to do. I do actually respect that. Honest, I do. But could you live with yourselves if anything untoward befell my son due to being reminded of those terrifying moments all over again? Could you?'

The female journalist, Sue Bassy, looked away then turned back to Abigail. 'I can assure you that's the last thing we want. But we'll be gentle with him. We know he's been through an ordeal. If there are any questions or parts of the crime he feels uncomfortable about then we'll avoid that. Your son, Toby – he's amazing.'

Abigail shook her head in defiance. 'Thank you for your kind words, but really, as a caring mother, I have to close the door on you literally and to your work.'

'How does ten grand sound?' Sue blurted out.

The front door that was about to close opened again, enough to permit Abigail to stare out at them both with raised eyebrows.

'One condition,' Abigail said, eyeing them both carefully.

'Name it,' Sue said.

'I get to sit in on the interview; to make sure Toby is all right.'

'Deal…'

*

Sue and Barry had set up a camera on a stand, laid out a silver Dictaphone and waited with their notepads for Toby to join them in the living room. After ten minutes they both heard two pairs of footfalls descending the staircase. The living room door opened and in walked Toby, followed by his mother, Abigail.

Sue and Barry rose to their feet from the comfortable sofa and proffered their hands to the young boy, who appeared nervous and twitchy now that he took in the equipment and the journalists.

'Nice to meet you,' Sue and Barry said simultaneously.

They all sat down and Toby tried to relax. His shoulders slumped and he looked exhausted.

'How are you doing, Toby?'

'All right,' he responded.

'Good. That's what I like to hear,' Barry said. 'Shall we begin?'

Toby nodded. He wanted this interview to be over the minute it had commenced. He had slept well. However, he'd taken a Diazepam and was still feeling groggy and weak.

Barry went through some routine questions. Name. Age. Birthplace. That sort of thing. Then Sue finished what she jotted down on her A4 notepad and turned the Dictaphone on.

'Tell us about the incident at the Odeon Cinema,' she said. 'Had you been feeling funny or unwell prior to going to see a film with your mother?'

'I was feeling great,' Toby said. 'Anytime I get to spend with my mum is a blessing. My father walked out on us during a drinking binge and we were given no warning or hint that this was gonna be the case. For awhile we lived in deep despair and fear that someone had done something bad and that my dad was involved. But then mum caught a glimpse of him in Neath town centre, holding hands with a scraggy, eighteen-year-old girl, sharing a bottle of cider and a rolled-up fag.'

'I bet that must've upset you,' Sue said.

Toby shook his head. 'No. Not really. I was relieved that my dad was alive and doing well. But as I got older I came to realise that his disappearing act had taken its toll on my mum. To witness her husband, father to her only child, literally walk out on us to consume himself with alcohol and drugs was a disgrace and pitiful. I'd sit in my bedroom sometimes and wonder what it was that I or/and my mum had done to him that made him flee without any explanation as to where he was going and what his feelings were. There were no debts to pay. He had a job as a driver for the Royal Mail that lasted the best part of twenty years. He'd take us out for drives in the Brecon Beacons and west Wales when the weather was nice. He loved football, and every once in a blue moon, he'd take me to the Liberty Stadium to watch the Swans.

'Life was good and kind to him,' Toby went on. 'So you see, his sudden departure hit us for six. No one could ever have predicted it. There were no shouting matches or lengthy arguments. At that time, I'd say he was a good father and a devoted husband.'

'Do you think that your father's abrupt disappearance had done something to you that might explain the psychic abilities and seizures that aided in the capture of a murderer?'

Toby leaned back in the armchair and gazed at the groove-patterned ceiling. 'All experiences in life are linked,' he said, emanating the aura of someone who is very wise and prudent. 'The shock of not seeing my dad for so long has obviously impacted me. My mum thinks because I'm so sensitive that this might be the reason why I'm able to experience these phenomena. Had I been a happier child with both parents then perhaps I wouldn't be able to see these visions and flashbacks. It's really too hard to say for sure.'

'How did you know for sure?' Barry asked.

Toby regarded him. 'I didn't... at least not at first. I doubted myself. But I also knew, somewhere deep inside me, that I'd had those visions to help aid the police to finding the victim's body and know the murderer's name and where he lived.'

'How's school been?' Barry asked, leaning forward.

'I haven't been back. My mum goes to school to pick up the coursework for all the subjects. The headmaster told my mum that I could take as long as I want and should not feel pressured into coming back before I am ready. I have seen some friends from school when I go shopping with my mum and although they're saying nice things to and about me, it can often get too intense. I know they don't mean to overwhelm me, calling me a "hero" and suchlike; it's just that I need more time to process this. I'm sleeping a lot now. And I'm slowly getting back my strength and vigour for life like it was before the incident.'

'Do you feel like a "hero", Toby?' Sue asked.

Toby shrugged. 'I dunno,' he said. 'I guess not. I feel like anyone else who has been through what I have seen and witnessed. I'm just glad that I was able to find the dead body and aid the police in arresting the guy before he even thought of doing the same thing ever again. Anyone else would have felt the same way.'

'I think you're a hero…' Barry said.

Toby chuckled. 'Well, that's up to you.'

'The local authorities have declared that if something like this ever happens again then you could work for the police and continue to aid them in other homicidal cases. Is that something you'd be inspired to do? Or do you have other plans for your future?'

'If something like this happens again, the seizures I have will most likely kill me before I reach anyone. You see, I was busy minding my own business when I first started having these lifelike visions. It was as if something had taken over my whole being and decided to show me all that I've told the police. It's not funny, not in the slightest. It's really scary. I thought I was gonna die. Thankfully I didn't. But what if I hadn't bolted upright in ER and had knowledge of the case? What if my body was unable to reach the surface of being awake? It's nice when my schoolmates and other members of the public smile at me and insist I'm a godsend, but they only know the best part. No one can identify with what I went through. If that's how it's gonna be for the rest of my life then I'm already as good as dead.'

'Toby!' Abigail said in loud protest.

'Sorry,' he said. 'But you see my dilemma.'

Both Sue and Barry nodded.

'Do you think you suffer with any illnesses, like schizophrenia?' Barry asked, liking Toby more and more as he listened to the wise, eloquent boy.

'I wouldn't say I suffer from a treatable illness,' Toby said. 'But I do think that I suffered those seizures due to brain trauma.'

Sue exhaled deeply.

'What did it feel like though when the police informed you that there was DNA found inside Danielle Thompson that matched the name of the man you'd given the authorities?'

'Like electricity charging through my veins,' Toby said, not missing a beat.

'What's the plan for you next?' Barry asked, transfixed by the affable young boy.

'Well, hopefully I can do well in school and go on to college. Hopefully the events we have discussed will never return. If they do, I can't see there being much of a life for me. I just cross my fingers and hope I can return to living a normal life again, that's all.'

Barry nodded. 'The more I listen to you, the more I understand. Before we came here most people thought you had a very powerful gift. But now you've discussed the seizures and the trauma in your brain I don't think you'll have to worry about others being envious of you. I hope for your sake nothing like this happens to you ever again. Old news dies to new news. Give it time and you'll be left alone. You are a very down to earth boy. Your life, I hope, will find its normal tracks again; you've just got to give it a chance.

'Anyway, thanks for meeting with us today and talking about the incidents of the harrowing events and how it's affected you. If you don't mind, we just want to take a portrait photograph of you, Toby, to go in the paper. Is that all right?'

The two journalists were very genial and honest, Toby decided. He had been lukewarm to meet anyone, especially folks who worked in the media. However, he was now glad that he'd been able to get his emotions off his chest and out into the open so everyone could understand that he wasn't a celebrity but just a normal boy who sought a normal life.

Once the picture had been taken, Toby rose from the armchair, shook hands with Barry and Sue, handed the bundle of cash over to his mother and waved them off at the front door.

6.

TWO YEARS LATER

TOBY had grown four inches in height and had started doing running and weightlifting. When he first returned to school to sit his exams he was stopped every five minutes by both staff and pupils, who took pictures of him with them on their mobile phones. At first he didn't mind the attention, but then as time passed Toby learned to say a curt "hello" before moving on to his next destination.

It was Wednesday afternoon and Toby had just completed his English exam that lasted for approximately two hours. Exhaustion had seeped into his bones and brain leaving him tired. He was at his locker, tidying his class files and taking his running shoes out when in his peripheral sight he saw Jenny approach her locker alongside him.

Jenny had long blonde hair and was a very attractive and alluring woman. She bore no blemishes. Her skin was tawny and flawless, her figure slender and voluptuous at the same time. Her teeth glowed with untainted enamel. She was wearing her black, lycra bottoms that accentuated her gorgeous bum and a brown woolly top. She gave Toby her best smile. He reciprocated the gesture, closed and then locked his locker.

'How's things, Jenny?'

'Good. What did you think of the exam?'

Toby shrugged. 'I wouldn't like to say. I think I did all right. I've been studying at home as well and felt more than capable of answering the questions and writing the thesis. How 'bout you?'

'Oh, I dunno,' she said, and Toby couldn't help admiring her beautiful features.

'Well, I'm sure you did fine,' Toby said, trying to bring back that heart-warming smile to her face again. 'But I think we could both use a break. I'm gonna grab something from the canteen before the bell rings. Care to join me?'

Jenny's eyes widened and twinkled under the fluorescents.

'Okay. That'd be great.'

'Cool.'

Together Toby and Jenny headed to the canteen which was outside and one hundred yards away from the school edifice. They talked amiably and Toby couldn't help feeling taken aback by how effortlessly they both carried themselves and undeniably enjoyed being in each other's company.

They reached the canteen, where the older students had had the same idea, to grab an early lunch before the mad rush. Toby ordered a plate of chips and a bottle of sparkling water. Jenny had chicken and chips and decorated the contents with an ample amount of red sauce. They sat down at an empty table. They continued their chat and Toby felt a nice sensation in his heart that had brought him a sense of comfort and love towards Jenny. He believed that she too was feeling the connection but did not bring it to mind. Sometimes it was better to just go with the flow than discuss the tingling sensation in his beating heart.

'What did you think of the short story we had to write?'

'Oh, I enjoyed that bit very much,' Toby said. 'During my time away from school, my mum enlisted me in the local library. She always said that intelligent people read a lot and that my English would improve vastly if I read a lot. And, in all fairness, she was right.'

Jenny gazed longingly into Toby's eyes. She no longer saw him for the famous boy with such an extraordinary gift, but saw him as a very handsome and kind soul.

'Are you going running after food?' Jenny asked, nodding at his Addidas spikes.

'Not straight away,' Toby said. 'I'm gonna sit on the grass and let my food go down. Then I'll do my four laps before walking home, seeing it's a nice day and all.'

'Do you run fast?'

'I sprint on the home straight,' Toby explained. 'But I'm a bit tired from staying up all night studying. But if I do my four laps and walk home, I should sleep much better tonight. How 'bout you? What're you up to this afternoon?'

Jenny didn't answer right away. All she knew then was how enamoured she was by being in Toby's presence. 'All my friends are going into town to let our hair down. But I'm a bit cream cracked myself. Maybe we could walk home... together... if ya like?'

'Yeah, sure,' Toby said, not thinking to hide his pleasant surprise. 'But what are you gonna do while I do my running?'

This time it was Jenny who shrugged. 'I'll just chill out and watch... if that's all right with you?'

Shit! Is she coming on to me? I don't believe this. This is crazy. I really do like Jenny. It can't be true. Can it? Well, you should know, dipshit. You're the one who's psychic. She's stunning.

'Of course it is,' Toby said, swimming back to the surface before he lost all contact with himself and Jenny. 'Do whatever you want. I won't be long, anyway.'

They finished their food and rose together.

Graham Harris, the school's best rugby player, stared at them, ignoring all his friends. Toby noticed that he was ogling Jenny's curvy bum. Then he met Toby's gaze and glowered at him. Toby did the most sensible thing and averted his gaze before Graham had any chance to express his selfish feelings.

Toby was putting his and Jenny's dirty plates on the stack when he overheard the rugby boys talking about Jenny.

'Oh fuckin' hell,' one of the boys said, following Graham's unblinking gaze. 'I'd love to get my cock up inside her.'

Toby glanced at Jenny's bum and could feel himself becoming aroused. Then he snapped his head back and silently chastised himself for his lustful thoughts. He was only human too. However, to say aloud what you were thinking was going a bit too far, in his opinion. He could also see the problem other boys his age would have with him as he and Jenny were growing closer together in a much more meaningful way.

This was the price to pay for being in Jenny's company. He didn't believe that it was fair. But then from a young age, Toby learned harshly that life wasn't fair at all. The innocent were abused and slain while the arrogance and demanding got whatever they desired.

Shaking his head inwardly, Toby headed back to Jenny who waited for him, and together they exited the canteen, heading for the running track.

Toby didn't waste time. The fact that the best looking girl in school was sitting on the small bank of grass absorbing the sunlight, spurred him on to do better. He ran that much better and that much faster, looking like a pro coming round the bend on the last one hundred yards. After four laps of doing this without stopping, Toby sensibly came off the track and approached Jenny who was beaming and applauding him with genuine admiration.

'My God,' she said. 'You were amazing out there. You should represent the school in competition.'

Out of breath, Toby plonked himself down next to Jenny. 'The headmaster saw me when I came back last year and said the same thing.'

'So why don't you?' Jenny asked.

'I just do it to keep fit and healthy,' Toby explained between breaths. 'Had I not had that spell off school, I would've probably done just that. But it keeps me fit and healthy, plus I was trying to impress you.'

'Well, you certainly did that,' Jenny said and leaned over and laid a kiss on Toby's reddening cheek.

'What was that for?'

'I dunno,' Jenny said, smiling. 'Just did it...'

'Can I kiss you back?'

Jenny shook her head. 'No way, Buster. You're all full of sweat. Take your time to get your breath back and then let's walk home. I'm gonna study out in my back garden.'

They began their walk home, up the long incline, talking about the exams and what they may or may not do regarding their futures. Toby mentioned that he might like to go to college. Jenny didn't quite have as many aspirations as Toby. She said she'd be happy if her mum got her a job at Tesco superstore. She loved going to the movies on the weekend with her mum, and as her best friend was her mum, she'd like to work with her too.

Toby told Jenny that he too was close to his mother, ever since his dad had done the disappearing act and he'd helped the police solve a crime.

'Are you still psychic?' Jenny asked, all of a sudden, remembering seeing Toby on the front page of the national newspapers and news programmes.

'No,' Toby said, sounding relieved. 'That was just a one off. And I'm glad for it. I nearly died for Christ sake.'

Jenny fell silent for a few moments, realising how devastating it had all been for Toby and that he had solved a murder crime and was a bit of a celebrity, but that he was fifteen years old, (nearly sixteen) and had his whole life ahead of him.

'What would you study in college?'

'Either literary English or train to be a gym instructor. Something that I enjoy and is stress free.'

'Cool.'

At the summit the road forked into two distinct pathways. Jenny leaned over and kissed Toby on the cheek unexpectedly, said, 'Goodbye' then took her leave. Toby stood motionless, dazed. He was happy and touched by Jenny's kiss and sudden departure. It took him a minute to snap out of this brief memory and take the alternate route that led to his humble home, wondering if Jenny kissed him purely because he had asked her to earlier as a friendly gesture or if there was something more meaningful behind it. Either way he was taken aback. The thought preoccupied him as he neared home.

When he arrived home Toby poured himself a glass of Pepsi Max and grabbed a mini-sized Mars Bar for a snack. Then he retired to his bedroom to do his homework. Today was Friday. And in order to fully enjoy the weekend break the boy always decided to do the majority – if not all – his homework on Friday to get it out of the way. It was a good strategy, he thought; one that worked well for him since he'd returned to school.

He only had one more exam... and that was on Monday afternoon. Religious Studies. Toby promptly went through his coursework of this subject to remind himself what he'd studied the last year before the exam on Monday. He jotted down some notes that he decided were imperative and would definitely be brought up. Once he had done that Toby logged onto the internet and typed into the Google search engine key questions that related to his coursework to see if there was any difference or if he was indeed not eating from the poison tree.

A couple of hours later the sound of his mother's car slowing and scraping against the kerbside reached Toby. He had finished his work for the evening five minutes ago and was now placing them in order to study and browse over the weekend as a reminder to refresh his memory for Monday afternoon.

Abigail pushed the door open and fought the gale force wind to shut it again before it slammed into the recess wall. She glanced over her shoulder and saw her son descending the staircase to greet her.

'How did the exam go?'

Toby shrugged. 'I thought I did okay, but I don't want to say I did brilliantly and then only get a mediocre result, so we'll have to wait and see, I guess. Just been studying for R.S. on Monday. My head's kinda fried though, to be honest.'

Abigail hung her coat up and swept her long mane back off her brow. 'What time do you want food, my darling?'

'Not for another hour, if that's all right,' Toby said. 'I had a bar of chocolate when I came home. Been busy today. Might just put the TV on in my bedroom and chill for an hour.'

Abigail nodded, fully understanding. 'Just make sure you don't go nodding off before bedtime though, okay?'

Toby assured her he wouldn't.

7.

LATER that Friday night Toby was brushing his teeth in the bathroom and Abigail was downstairs watching the BBC News and sipping a glass of red wine. Toby washed his mouth out and then exited the bathroom, crossed the landing and closed his bedroom door behind him. He browsed his notes that he made of the questions he'd asked the internet and felt satisfied that he'd done enough to prepare for his exam. Then he placed them all in their correct order into a transparent sleeve.

He sprawled across the large bed and let darkness invade his fertile mind. He was soon asleep. Dead to the world.

In front of him, Toby saw a man with a shaven head walking with a purpose down a desolate street on a cold winter morning where the only sound were his footfalls pounding the dampened concrete. The man was young. However, he had a deeply etched crease in his brow and a wide, mirthless smile that made his eyes look evil and manic. He was wearing a blue and yellow Adidas tracksuit, carrying an un-opened can of lager.

A dirty brick building that had two floors and was much larger in width than it was in height that had been abandoned and dilapidated in condition for some years now came into focus. There was a white billboard sign that hung askew and on rusty chains, the weather blotting out what it used to say. The rollers were down and locked.

The young man who walked with a stride in his step cornered the building, fished out a large, metallic key from his tracksuit bottom's pocket, and unlocked a molten steel door. The door opened ajar before jolting to a stop. The young man fished out another key; this one made of brass and fed it into the padlock. Once that was removed the steel door slid open. Cavernous darkness swallowed everything from within. The young man was unaffected by the pitch-black interior. He turned back around and pushed the door a second after Toby managed to float inside with him. The steel bolt was thrown, preventing anyone else from gaining access. Confidant now, the young man ambled to the left-hand side until his fingers found the switch on the wall.

Bright fluorescent light blinked on and the factory was given birth, minus the sewing and textile machines. The chairs which women from the WWII used were stacked against the far, grubby, moss-covered wall. In the centre of the expansive and unused floor space was a steel girder. Around this immovable object, three young women were chained together, beaten, starved and exhausted. They sat in crumpled forms, heads hung low, chins tucked into their chests.

The young man approached them wearing the biggest, most sadistic smile. One of the women who had long, blonde hair that had gone thin and lank due to lack of nourishment raised her head. Her right eye was purple and swollen from the most recent beating she had endured.

'What's the matter, Puss?' the young man said, his words reverberating throughout the factory.

She reached up to him, her hands cupped, begging for food and water.

'Food will be later,' the young man said, as though he was doing them some kind of favour. 'Tomorrow you shall enjoy a cereal breakfast, shower and additional toiletries and make-up ready for your departure.'

This time all three women raised their heads towards him. There was a glimmer of hope in them that had otherwise died, rendering them mere husks, bereft of souls and life.

'You'll be transferred to one of my associates in central London,' the young man continued. 'You won't see me again, that's for sure.' He studied their forlorn faces. 'Oh, come on! As if you'd miss me terribly or just a little. You shall be made into beautiful women once more, but not like your previous lives. You will bring pleasure to many powerful businessmen who will pay you ample amounts of money and safe havens. You shall live like princesses and enjoy the lifestyles more glamorous than singers and Hollywood film stars.'

He studied them, absorbing each face, covered with dirt, dry blood and grazes.

'You may think you've been through a lot since being taken from your old lives but believe me when you see what lies ahead, you'll look back on this day and say, "Gee what a small price to pay for everything in the world and more".'

The kidnapper returned to his full height and posture, shaking his head in disdain at the lack of gratitude from his victims.

*

Toby woke, perspiring like a madman on the run from the police. He sat upright, supported by his arm muscles and blinked purposefully, bringing everything in his bedroom back into focus. The vision was very acute and lifelike. It unnerved him, marking his brain without any forewarning. He didn't like what he saw and heard. He scrunched his face up into one of displeasure and bewilderment. This wasn't fair on him. He was a really nice guy and it felt as though this gift that he found was more like a curse that refused to permit him the peace and quiet he so desperately sought.

'Leave me alone,' he muttered, visibly vexed by the kidnapper and the victims, all waiting for the next stage of their new and now awful lives.

He wanted nothing to do with what he saw, although in the back of his mind where common sense kept order in his brain, Toby was well aware that he had these visions for a reason.

'Why me?' he asked, shaking his head. 'I don't want this. Bugger off.' He cussed God inwardly, balling his hands up into clenched fists and hitting the wall behind the headboard.

His shoulders slumped and he exhaled deeply. Then he got up and hauled himself off his bed and went into the bathroom. In the bathroom, Toby checked his haggard reflection and washed his face with warm water. Then he got dressed into his pyjamas. He dreaded going back to bed in case he started having more visions. He prayed that this latest vision was fiction. Otherwise it would play on his conscience until he went mad like what almost happened the first time.

He fell asleep around half past twelve and enjoyed a dreamless slumber. The break of dawn woke him and Toby rolled over and blinked his eyes open. After going through the usual morning rituals, Toby placed his bowl and glass in the kitchen sink, chatted a while with his mother then went back upstairs to look over his notes ready for Monday.

As he did this, his vision became blurry. His eyes joggled in their sockets, scanning the room, but not seeing it, seeing something else. Toby was nullified. He left his shell and found himself once again seeing beyond the bedroom walls and into the spacious factory where the three women were being held captive.

They were all chained together around a steel pillar, battered and beaten, weary and downtrodden. There was a young woman whose face was a horrible pallid hue, naked from the waist up. He breasts were covered in lashes from a whip where she'd resisted her kidnapper who desperately had the urge to grope and fondle with them. Her nose had been bleeding, the trail running down into her charred lips. She had all but surrendered. She even hoped that death would seize her just so that it would put her out of her misery.

The other three women moaned and groaned as the manacles tightly fitted around their wrists left deep indentations, having prevented them from moving and maybe even from working together in an attempt to break free from this hellhole and escape into the world where they could get help from the police.

Yet they were all still suffering from the physical abuse inflicted upon them, beating them all to their knees and keeping them from rising and standing up for their lives and human rights.

Tears pooled in Toby's protuberant eyes and ran down his quivering cheeks. He found himself back in his bedroom, profoundly affected by the second sight he had the misfortune of seeing what was happening to those broken victims.

'I shouldn't be seeing this,' he croaked. 'This is not my problem. How am I gonna be able to help? This could be taking place anywhere in the world. What's that got to do with me? I'm sorry if this is true, but don't expect me to save the day.'

Toby sat in perfect silence for five minutes and then got up off the bed. He grabbed his jacket off the hanger on the bedroom door, laced up his trainers and headed downstairs. He entered the kitchen where his mother was drinking her coffee.

'I'm just popping out for a short while to get some fresh air.'

Abigail nodded. 'Good idea. Too much studying without respite won't help you pass your exams.'

'Do you want me to get you something while I'm out?'

'No. Thanks love.'

'Be back soon. Okay?'

'Okay.'

Toby stepped outside and got out onto the pavement. He had no idea where he was going. The walk, wherever he wound up, would do him the world of good. As he did this, keeping his head down at all times, he thought about going to his local GP about getting some sleeping tablets or any other type of medication to prevent these intrusive visions that caused Astral Projections. The more he thought about it the more harrowing it seemed. It was far from normal. He didn't want to go through this ritual again. The first time he'd had visions and aided the police in the discovery of the victim had been miraculous. Yet Toby still felt that it was also pure luck. At least that's what he dearly hoped. He had received payment from the national newspapers and found fame, but Toby now remembered all of that as a blur. This he decided was good. Money and fame could affect the mind into making you believe that you were special and better than the average folk. People whom he'd known most of his life looked at him in a certain way, like he was royalty or something. Yet had he simply been a nice kid down the street they would have ignored him or made assumptions and labelled him to satisfy their own minds.

'But is this about you or four women facing unspeakable futures?' Toby asked himself.

What was more important?

He didn't want to do selfies any more with folks he didn't know. He just wanted to study for his exam and chill out and watch a film while saving up enough money for driving lessons.

Toby had been in deep thought for some time now and his brain was running on auto-pilot. All of a sudden he found himself making his way down the steep embankment towards a one-way road. He could never say why, but Toby followed that road under the bridge as if, had he had gone the other way, he would have been heading into the town centre not too far from the school grounds.

The drizzle had ceased. And Toby kept his hands in his jacket pockets and head down, looking depressed and forlorn. The road forked into two directions: One left. One right. Toby chose the left and walked past an old and vandalised payphone. The sound of the river beneath him sounded relentless and noisy.

As he crossed a grey, metallic bridge, the sound of the overflowing river roared. The gushing stream threatened to break its banks and cause flooding for the houses on the other side of the growth of thick foliage.

The young lad felt a shiver go through him. It stopped him momentarily. He glanced back over his shoulder and desired to turn on his heel and head back to the house. Twenty minutes had already lapsed from the time he'd left the house. He didn't want to be out too long in case it started to rain properly.

Nevertheless, he kept going on this narrow path and as the treetops thinned out Toby could see a filthy and dilapidated, red-brick edifice with a grubby chimney at the apex.

As he drew closer, Toby realised he was seeing this warehouse from the rear, hence the ragged mesh-fencing. He took a left turn and headed down a narrow alley between a concrete wall and the warehouse itself. Up ahead, in the distance, Toby saw a rotten steel door hanging off its hinges offering daylight leading to a public road. Relief flooded through him similar to the river below. Toby emerged into the street and cornered the old factory.

A sudden sensation exploded into and out of his brain and mind. Toby gasped at the same, rusting steel door he'd seen vividly in his vision.

'Oh, Jesus Christ!' Toby's left knee buckled and he wobbled before righting himself and his posture again. He cussed under his breath over and over again until the reality of the whole situation kicked in and finally settled into his mind for as long as he lived.

A part of him wanted to turn around and run back home at full pelt, not wanting to have any part in what was now likely happening inside the dilapidated factory.

'Shit! What the hell am I supposed to do now?'

There was a weed-infested concrete-slab path leading to the front steel door that looked as though it was about to give way anytime soon.

Toby braced himself before he chose his reaction to this surreal situation.

This time the stakes were higher. Unless he was mistaken then these three women were alive and being held captive against their wishes, for sale to high businessmen to traffic and fornicate with their associates. If that was true and the kidnapper was also inside, then Toby – who was unarmed – would have to be extremely cautious and brave to achieve what he now resolved to do.

*

The young woman with the straggly blonde mane of hair pulled her legs out from her kneeling position, which she had held for so long and winced in pain. The other two girls had either fallen asleep or passed out due to exhaustion. Initially, she saw this as a good sign. However, what if they never swam back to consciousness again? Perhaps she felt a little jealous of them in some ways. Being awake in the pitch dark had been frightening at first, especially as she was chained to a steel girder and had limited room to manoeuvre herself.

Apparently, their kidnapper had left them for the time being to do whatever he did besides kidnapping and whipping his captives until they bled and finally passed out. He could have easily killed her or one of the other two women, through the beating they endured. Perhaps at first that was the intention. She doubted it. She also doubted that this was his first time seizing young, beautiful women off the street and imprisoning them in warehouses to then be sold off like pieces of meat to the highest bidder.

The woman's name was Carly. Carly lived in Birchgrove with her parents and had been in college studying English

Literature. Carly had fallen in love with books at the age of six and managed to read a book (provided it wasn't a huge tome) in a week. She was a regular at the local library and often bought books from WHSmith and Waterstones in Swansea. Furthermore, she had read the Holy Bible. If a book even mildly interested her (and she was easily impressed and open-minded) then she'd read it.

Carly had a boyfriend a year ago to whom she lost her virginity. However, the relationship did not develop as her boyfriend complained constantly that she made sure she made plenty of time when she wasn't in college or studying at home for reading. He called her a "bookworm", but Carly expected, as Mark was starting to lose his patience calling her a lot worse names aloud and in his mind, that the break-up was inevitable.

Carly didn't care though. Boys weren't her focus of interest as much as they were to her college pals. Super if you met someone who you liked as a person and found them attractive, especially if you had the same interests. But to Carly it hadn't been the end of the world if you didn't find someone.

The idea of being set free from her manacles and chain to be sold at a private auction sent shivers down her spine. The mere thought of having to live a life as a sex slave was now sinking into her brain and taking up all her waking hours. A single fat tear escaped her eye and trickled down her quivering cheek. All her childhood memories came flooding back to her in her mind's eye, as if her whole persona was dying and seeping out of her brain into her bones. It felt as though she was being invaded in her own body and taken over by a foreign entity, if that was at all possible.

In her mind's eye she saw a replay of when she was a child – holding on tight on the roundabout in the small children's park, before losing her grip and sliding off and being struck with an unmerciful blow to the head as her mum bolted out of the bench and rushed over to keep her from harm's way. She remembered the shock and pain that quickly flooded her entire being. That's how she felt now and prayed for a saviour, like her mum or dad.

Carly whimpered and tried her utmost not to let her emotions overwhelm her of the reality of her situation she'd have to face in a foreign country. She was totally innocent. Her biggest crime was a greed for books. When she was sixteen she remembered going to Waterstones and purchasing six Dean Koontz paperbacks. Her mother rebuked her while her laid-back father smirked. He was an avid book reader too and instead of agreeing with his spouse he'd asked his daughter if he could read them too. She had laughed at that, knowing that at least one of her parents had taken her side.

Now all that was a thing of the past. She now faced a situation that was too hard to comprehend, let alone deal with. She liked having sex with Mark the three times they had done so. His manhood was warm and hard. But at the same time she didn't miss it either. Carly would only have sex with a boy if she really liked him and had got to know him and felt safe and comfortable with him. If not, then it was back to her books where she got most of her pleasure.

Being kidnapped and sold to an affluent businessman seemed like something she would read about in a Dean Koontz thriller, not something that actually happens.

The pitch darkness that engulfed her was both comforting and terrifying. What it did mean was that the kidnapper wasn't present and with the other two girls Carly was left alone. However, he would be back sooner or later and tomorrow morning they would be taken from the dilapidated warehouse to an unknown location to be fed, washed and tidied up.

She couldn't even cry. Instead she merely sat there wondering what life would be like never seeing her parents again or having her own freedom to do whatever she pleased. Sooner or later though the authorities would have been notified and be on the lookout for the missing girls.

There was still hope.

And it was that thin string of hope that kept Carly alive…

8.

ABIGAIL was in the kitchen washing the dishes. The soapy water caressed and softened her hands. Once the chore had been completed she used the towel to dry her hands. Then she got the bread out of the basket and proceeded to make Toby's favourite lunch – peanut butter sandwiches ready for when he returned home.

As she busied herself with this small task her mind began to run away with itself. She would never forget the day her husband had gone out one afternoon and decided (without informing her) that he wasn't coming back. He was long gone now. However, it still hurt her deeply, which was why her mind kept bringing it to the surface of her consciousness. Now all of a sudden, a wave threatened to smash straight into her until she was swept out of life by the awesome impact and then finally into darkness.

An intrusive thought broke the dam and she dropped the small knife that she'd been using to spread the peanut butter onto the slice of brown bread. It clattered on the worktop before falling to the tiled floor. Abigail watched the room float in waves as though the devil himself had read her mind and was now trying to drown her in dizziness until she lost consciousness and collapsed in a heap on the floor.

The thought that came to the forefront of her mind was what if Toby had decided to go out for a walk and never came back too?

Don't be silly. Toby would never do that to me. He loves his mum more than anyone else in the whole world. He gave up a normal life, full of friends his own age and girls, to study at home under the tuition of his dear mother.

She used the bread knife to saw through the thick bread and then placed the three sandwiches onto a small china plate and wrapped it in Clingfilm for when he returned.

Abigail brushed the tiny crumbs from her hands into the black bin at the door frame leading into the living room. She lowered herself to the wooden chair around the table and crouched forward, closing her eyes, wondering all the time where Toby was, what he was doing and when he would come through the front door and abolish all her doubts and bring her heart and mind peace and comfort.

She brought to mind the Monday after he had solved the crime of the young woman in the lake in Llansamlet. It was an important day in both her and Toby's life. Abigail had risen early and gently woke her sleeping boy. He got dressed, had some Cheerios and came down the stairs. She waited for him and prayed his day would be easy and kind to him.

Abigail admired his humility. This was something she had never expected of him. Of course, she was fully aware that he was a quiet, shy boy at heart. She worried about him going back to school so soon after the harrowing incident, but relented once he told her that he merely wanted to go back and be like every other kid his age and have a laugh with his pals and pass his exams which would open more doors, full of opportunities for him which included college and then hopefully university.

All of those dreams ready and waiting to be fulfilled was admirable. Of course, they had been to their local GP who ran some tests to find if there was anything awry, typically in the brain area. There was nothing wrong with Toby, the GP said. His brain and the rest of his body were functioning as they ought to. Furthermore, after the GP had spoken to Toby one-on-one and listened to the boy's answers and his own thoughts, he decided that not only was Toby in perfect working condition but also very intelligent and broad minded.

Taken aback somewhat, Abigail willed herself to feel relaxed by the overall summary. However, her mind did wonder how Toby could have known that there was something wrong going on and his acting upon it led to a fact that confirmed that his visions meant that an innocent victim's carcass had been discovered and the perpetrator had been brought to justice.

The GP shrugged inwardly at this notion.

'Is he psychic?' Abigail had asked.

'Well,' the middle aged, grey-haired GP said, 'after speaking with your son and asking him how he managed to act out on an impulse, he said he just knew that there was something not quite right. But, to be perfectly honest, I don't think speculating about it any more than you already have is going to help you or your son. After all, he suffered a great deal of pain and hardship. One wonders if he is fully recovered. After all, the rise in mental health problems in our country in the last four or five years has risen at an alarming rate. My only hope is that he doesn't suffer with seizures again as next time he might not be so lucky. He is still a child. He informed me that it just felt like a moment of luck.'

'Is it a miracle?' Abigail asked, looking up and staring into the GP's eyes.

'It's a miracle he survived...'

Abigail's memory was acutely aware of the events that had happened to her son, who she was deeply concerned about and cherished even more than before.

She had firmly decided that Toby was a miracle.

A lot of other boys would have gone out with a group of pals and experimented with drugs and alcohol. Toby turned his cheek to that sort of behaviour and had taken up cycling.

Abigail planted a kiss on his cheek and wished him well for his first day back. 'And remember,' she said, blocking out all the other students milling around outside, 'if you start feeling not right, you phone me and I'll come and get you. Is that understood?'

Toby dutifully nodded. 'Yes, Mum,' he said in a timid voice.

With that he unbuckled himself and got out of the car and walked through the open gate that led to a cream-coloured stone path. As he reached the steps he turned around and gave his doting mother a farewell wave.

The bell shrilled loud enough for the whole street could hear it over the droning of moving traffic. Toby found himself moving in a wave of school chums towards his first class, which was Maths on the ground floor. It was his most hated subject as he always failed to comprehend the equations and couldn't help but realise that at no point in his life would he ever use Algebra. As far as adding and taking away, he was fairly good, but his concentration only switched on and off at its own volition... so it seemed, anyway.

During class they had to write down what was on the blackboard and were then handed laminated sheets full of equations to be done by the end of the week. There were approximately a hundred of them and they got more complicated as they went on. Toby dreaded taking them home with him and getting a good grade.

His second class was English, which he didn't mind one iota. Because he was an avid reader, Toby's literature skills were above the normal passing-in grade. But as he sat down and looked for grammatical errors in his work he could hear and feel the thunderbolt of his heart. His head buzzed, full of static as though he was an electrical appliance plugged in and turned on up to its full ramp frequency.

He looked up from his notebook and met Jenny's gaze across the room. She gave him a timid smile. Toby reciprocated this kind gesture and then lowered his head back to his work.

I think I love him.

Where did that come from? he wondered.

Then another voice came to him and caused the first flicker of panic.

If only he could concentrate to his full potential then I bet he'd get A grades all the time.

The second voice was his teacher, Mrs Darney. And now that he thought hard about the first voice... it came from Jenny's mind.

Of course he felt a wave of warmth heat his cheeks. He was a bit taken aback by what Jenny had thought. His heart beat slower and measurably with a soothing sensation.

The voices of people's minds caused Toby to start to tremble with anxiety. He focused harder on his work and completed the task before the bell shrilled, announcing the end of class and the beginning of a short interval for some fresh air. However, as Toby had risen from his chair and handed his notepad over to his plump English teacher, he staggered and nearly toppled over. The world from his perspective started simmering and swaying. Toby was aware that he was dancing like a drunkard and had no control of his actions. He heard rather than felt the chair he'd been sitting on for the last hour crash to the floor and tripping him up, which of course made matters worse.

What's wrong with him? Jenny's voice.

Toby reached out for the table to steady himself, slipped, buckled at the knees and then finally fell hard on his bum and lower back. 'I n-n-need my m-mum,' he said and then his eyes closed and Toby's last thought was, *I'm gonna die right here in my favourite class.*

*

Abigail had been by his bedside in Morriston Hospital, holding his hand in her warm grasp and soothing him, gazing upon the only person keeping her alive or from going totally insane. If her one and only child died she'd kill herself, that's how much she loved him. She would rather be dead with him than be alive without him. He was her lifeline, just like she had been when she fell pregnant with him more than a decade ago.

There were so many drugs and medicine in Toby that he now rested, unaware of what was going on around him. His heart was being monitored and doctors suggested that he might be epileptic. His left arm had swollen and had turned a deep purple which would hurt like a bugger when he came to.

Abigail kissed and stroked his injured arm and sung quietly, a lullaby, like she used to every night when he was younger before bed. She never complained like other mothers at the school about how annoying their offspring were for misbehaving and waking them at night. Abigail would go to sleep at night sometimes and wish Toby would wake her because he had a bad dream just so she could be close to him and nurture him.

When it came to Christmas, Toby didn't ask for presents. But one year (the year before his dad had done the disappearing act) she beckoned him downstairs into the living room and cherished the delightful look of heart-warming wonder as he laid huge eyes on a mountain bike. It was an Apollo. It had bullhorn handlebars and thick, treaded tires. She remembered Toby couldn't even move for five minutes until she had gone to him and kissed him on the top of his head and led him towards his present.

'Well, Whatcha think?'

'It's… amazing, Mum.'

She couldn't but laugh at that moment or even smile in the present, grateful for that wonderful memory and hopefully there would be many more.

The streets in the village were dead on Christmas day, so Abigail agreed that as long as he wore a crash hat (another present she bought him) then he could go out for half an hour while she prepared their Turkey dinner.

When he came back his smile was like that of a Cheshire Cat. He told her in no uncertain terms that it was the best Christmas present of all time. Period.

Toby had awoken from his deep sleep and smiled wearily when he saw his mum at his bedside and said under his breath so only his mother could hear, 'I was dreaming of my bike you got me, Mum.'

'So was I, darling. So was I.'

From that moment on, Abigail arranged with his Headmaster that he supply her with the coursework for all his classes, as she was now going to home-school her son. She already knew a lot. Nevertheless, she wanted to prepare Toby with the chance of getting good grades while being safe and not hearing voices in his head that had caused him to collapse and nearly lose his life.

For P.E. Toby trained as a boxer. He read a book a week. Studied maps and History and Religious Studies. And he also became acquainted with Biology and Physics. He did all this at home, where Abigail believed he was most safe from the cruel outside world.

And for many years, she was right.

Then one day during the spring where everyone from school had a week off, Toby studied and had no rest any day of the week. He was becoming more intelligent than even the brainy students due to the fact that he never had a rest except on Sunday afternoons and nights.

Abigail had been strict but fair. She did give him the best schooling she could provide and returned all of Toby's test papers to the comprehensive school much to the teachers' amazement.

He was offered a chance to return… and Toby took it. Most of all to prove to the doubters that he hadn't been given the answers by his mother that he had done it all himself.

Abigail sat alone at the kitchen table. Her coffee had gone cold. A profound sadness overcame her in the midst of the silence.

'Where are you, Toby?' she said aloud.

9.

TOBY stood ramrod straight, deep in thought about his next move. Finally, he snapped out of his options and headed up the worn path to the deserted building with opaque windows, a sense of debilitating dread coursing through his veins like electricity. When he reached the rusty door he braced himself for whatever horrors lay beyond the dark interior, pondering the thought that today could be his last if he was not careful and tuned in to this brand new situation.

The door scraped against the concrete, announcing his arrival. The sound reminded him of fingernails scratching a blackboard in school which caused all students to wince and cringe and turn their undivided attention to their teacher.

Toby sidled up into the narrow hallway, leaving the door ajar, permitting dull grey daylight to dilute the pitch black. He waited for his eyes to adjust to the impenetrable darkness beyond. He moved stealthily into the expansive space, and slowly he could see the other windows on the side of the construction spilling miniscule rays of light. He cussed inwardly for not arriving here with a torch and a weapon. He killed that thought because it would only interfere with the present situation.

The sound of a coarse dry cough from somewhere farther inside alerted him. Toby moved a few steps forward, wondering if it was some kind of trap he was walking into. However, intuition keenly warned him that that wasn't the case.

His right foot came into contact with a brick and Toby stumbled forward before he righted himself.

'Who's there!' he shouted.

Another cough.

'Hello! If there is someone in there cough again if you need help.'

The sound of faint movement reached his ears and Toby wondered why there was such a long pause and why there wasn't such urgency from whoever had heard him and coughed.

A third cough. This time more deliberate and stronger.

Toby edged forward.

'There's a light switch on your left by the fuse box,' a weary female voice told him.

Toby pivoted and ran his hand across the crumbling wall until his fingers eventually found the switch and flicked it.

A single bar of luminescent light blinked on and off until the light finally beat the dark, permitting Toby to see the three female captives and for the captives to see him.

Toby's eyes bulged at the horror before him. The women were chained around a pillar in just their underwear, bruises and whelp marks covering them head-to-toe. Their bodies had been badly damaged due to their stoic refusal to being captured and submitting to the perpetrators sick and twisted desires.

'God in Heaven,' Toby muttered.

Carly tried to smile but her lips were bone dry and cracked.

'What the hell have they done to you?' Toby said rhetorically.

Evidently they had been here in this shithole for more than a day or two. Their wounds were savage and awful. Their hair and bodies were left unwashed. Dried blood on their skin told an untold yarn in Toby's rattled mind. He covered his gaping mouth and moved forward.

'How did you find us?' Carly wanted to know.

Toby blinked and shook his head to aid his mind from being mentally scarred by the abuse these prisoners had endured. 'I'll get to that later,' he said, unable to hide his mortification.

'Are you here to save us?' a woman with short black hair that was coated in plaster and dust asked.

Toby nodded. Then he moved towards them and got down on his haunches and examined the thick grey chain wrapped through their manacles and around the steel pillar.

'I need the key to set you all free,' Toby said.

'He keeps the key on his chain and takes it with him,' Carly croaked, eager to escape and get back home to her doting parents.

'Where is he now?' Toby asked.

The girl whose hair was tangled and grey at the roots tried to smile, and as she did this blood rushed through her crooked and stained teeth down her chin and into her bra.

Toby averted his gaze to the linoleum flooring and exhaled, doing his utmost not to lose his temper at the man who had inflicted this much pain, suffering and lifelong misery. These girls would never be the same ever again. Their vibrancy had been deleted and what was left were scars all over them that would refuse to free them into children of light and innocence. Toby waged that these three girls would think twice about going out down town, drinking, dancing and getting themselves boyfriends and enjoying life's pleasures.

This angered Toby a great deal.

He couldn't touch them, to comfort them, in case he caused them to wince in agony or bleed from another wound.

'When is this nasty piece of work coming back?' he asked, through his gritted teeth.

'Soon,' Carly said. 'He's gone to get us food. Then he's gonna take us to some unknown location to wash and groom us and dress us like we are A-star Hollywood actresses to be auctioned to some of the world's wealthiest confrontational businessmen. We'll be sold to their associates as sex slaves to help negotiations.'

Toby involuntarily shuddered.

*

Toby had found a lump hammer in a dark niche propped up against the far wall of the dilapidated warehouse and tried to break the thick chain keeping the girls trapped around the pillar. He stopped after five minutes or so and exhaled more out of frustration than as a result of his endeavour. As he kneeled there, crying on the inside for the girls, the sound of a motor in a low gear pricked his ears. He cussed then rose. 'Whatever you do don't say a word to him, got that?'

'You're not gonna leave us, are you?' the girl with short black hair moaned.

Toby shook his head. 'No. But I need to hide. Go back to sleep and pretend to be groggy.'

'What're ya gonna do?' the girl with the tangled and dirty blonde hair wanted to know.

'You'll see. But you got to get rid of any hope. If he sees you're awake and alert, he'll know somethin's up. In order to set you all free I need to get him when he least expects it.'

The girls watched the darkness swallow Toby as he walked backwards into the niche where he'd found his weapon.

He got himself into a position where he was out of sight. For the first time in his short life that could end right here, right now, Toby opened his mouth to permit air out into the spacious ground floor that whistled in the gusty wind outside.

Standing there with a lump hammer in his right hand, Toby couldn't help bring to mind the first time he dreaded the dark. He had been about six years of age and was tucked up in his *Thomas The Tank Engine* bed, his head in the crook of his mother's arm listening to one of her stories about a beautiful blonde woman walking in the woods, picking apples when a big bad werewolf sees her and draws close, and instead of screaming and fleeing, having dropped the basket of apples along the way, the young woman smiled at the werewolf and offered him an apple. He was so taken aback by her benevolence that he tentatively approached her and took an apple. He bit into it and chewed loudly and thanked the lovely women who told him that if he ever felt a hunger that gave him the desire to eat people he could come to her house on the fringe of the large woodlands and join her for lunch.

Toby recalled how awestruck he'd been listening to that story conjured up by his dear mum. However, when she had turned off the bedside lamp and closed the door behind her Toby dreamed of a man wielding an axe hammer chasing him down endless corridors that made him feel like he was running blindly in a maze. He didn't know what it meant and to this very day in this very moment he still couldn't fathom it.

He shook his head, doing his best to rid himself of that memory now and to concentrate on the present situation.

Ever since that day, Toby asked and pleaded for his mum to come upstairs and read him a story or tell one of her own (he preferred her stories to the books though). Abigail had the vivid imagination to become a writer. Maybe even a published one at that, he thought.

He smiled to himself in the dark.

Footfalls on concrete drew close and increased in volume with each purposeful step. Toby focused and crouched. The rusted side door scraped against the concrete flooring. Then the footfalls came down the short path and into the factory floor.

The kidnapper crossed the spacious room towards the women with two large suitcases, one in each hand. 'Guess what, girls. I got you some new clothes... and tonight you shall be staying in The Ambassador Hotel where you'll be escorted to your rooms to wash, eat, drink and watch TV while we bring the associates together in an unknown location. Isn't that great? Not only will your pain be taken away but you'll be living and serving powerful men who have access to everything a girl could want in the world.

'I envy you anyway. If a woman wanted to buy me and give me a much better quality of life I'd jump at the chance.'

Toby raised his eyebrows, watching and listening to the kidnapper's words, scarcely believing what he heard. The man was not only insane, but he actually believed that he was doing them a huge favour. Couldn't he see what he had done? He had abused these young women and they wore the scars and contusions. The girls' information about them being sold as sex slaves was not only immoral, it was unthinkable. Wasn't it obvious that what he was doing was despicable, not to mention unlawful?

The girls groaned as though they had dozed off due to their uncomfortable positions, weariness and hurting with the physical pain.

'I got some handcuffs, just in case one of you decides to be brave and run off.' At that Toby watched closely as the kidnapper produced a handgun that was silver and looked from his perspective to be a Revolver. That wasn't a handgun to simply maim, but to actually kill. He had to be very careful about how to proceed now that there was a gun thrown into the mixture.

God, I never should've come down here. You clearly don't like me, do you? My mum'll go mental if I get shot and die.

'I'm gonna release you all from here into handcuffs. You can get up then and walk 'round a bit to get the blood flowing. But remember what I said. This ain't no movie where the kidnapper makes a mistake and the girl runs free and hits the road.'

The man with short, spiked bleached blonde hair put the gun down by his side and fished out a set of keys from his Levis jeans and began to unlock the restraints. He was concentrating on doing this and had no idea that a black shape had detached itself from the far wall.

The blonde-haired woman sighed in relief and exhaustion at having been released from being chained to the pillar for so long without food or water. She got to all fours and coughed, spitting out wads of phlegm and snot.

'N-Need t-t-to d-drink s-s-somethin',' she managed to get out.

The kidnapper shot her a how-dare-you look as though he were a waiter in a luxurious hotel changing her mind about room service after the waiter had ascended to the top floor.

He applied the handcuffs to her. Then he said, 'You are free to get up and use your legs. Water'll be provided in its own time. Don't look at me as though I'm some badass criminal doing wrong to you 'cause I ain't. I'm doing my job 'n doing you all a favour.'

'Trust me you're not,' a male voice said in a rhythmical tone and the kidnapper had no time to turn his head around to face the voice when the lump hammer, swung full pelt, crashed into the criminal's head. The loud crack was the sound of a fractured skull and a broken neck. The man's lifeless body thudded to the concrete.

Toby staggered back and dropped the weapon and swayed.

The blonde girl stared at him, as did the other two girls, perplexed as to why their saviour looked as though he was receiving a ten count after being knocked down by a young Mike Tyson.

'What's wrong?' the blonde girl asked.

Toby shook his head forcefully and then slapped both hands on his face. The surreal situation and the realisation that the man who had kidnapped these young women was now dead by his own hands had stunned him.

I'm a murderer!

The thought sent waves of panic through his brain.

And the first person who came to his frazzled mind was his dear mother. He had lost his innocence.

Shoulda called the police instead.

He managed to steady himself to stop falling down. Once the dizziness abated, Toby got the man's set of keys and went through the slow process of freeing the victims and helping them to their feet.

'What was wrong with you just now?' the blonde asked.

Toby told her.

'But he would've ruined our lives and the lives of our friends and family. You did the right thing.'

'Not in the eyes of the law,' Toby said matter-of-factly.

He helped them to the outside where they made delightful and grateful noises in tremendous approval of being free, even though it was cold. They wore the new clothes that the kidnapper said were for them. And they were ravishing dresses. Silver, black and red dresses from upmarket stores in London.

'There's a house at the end of this street,' Toby said once they had all quietened down. 'In your own time go there and ask to use their phone or get them to call the police and ambulance services for you. Tell them everything you told me. Once in the hospital where your scars and bruises and shock are being tended to, give your statements to the police. But tell them this about me. You didn't see my face. I wore a hooded sweater with the hood over my head and the darkness hid my features. You weren't sure of the accent either, so I could have been European. Tell them that I was the one who killed that piece of shit in there and you were set free. Don't tell them that I'm a hero or anything stupid like that. For God's sake that's all I'll need – is to be famous and in the newspapers.'

'But you *are* a hero though,' the woman with the short black hair said, getting to her feet.

'Don't. Please don't describe my features,' Toby said in a stern voice. 'I can't stop what you think deep down but I really don't want this in the newspaper with my face on the front cover.'

'Just tell us why?' the other girl said who had a swollen lip and a closed eye.

'If my mum found out she'd be terrified. She wouldn't be able to cope. Please. I helped you. Just do this small favour for me and my mum who worries a lot. Okay?'

The three girls nodded solemnly.

'Thank you,' Toby said and gave them a heart-warming smile.

10.

ON HIS WAY HOME, Toby placed his right hand on his thudding heart, doing all he could to sedate himself naturally for when he arrived home and saw his mother. She could sometimes tell just by looking at him that something was amiss. Furthermore, Toby was full of worry and concern. His vision had led him to the exact location where the trouble had occurred. It was uncanny and frightening. He didn't want these graphic visions. He wondered what the damage might be causing his brain as a result. He desired nothing more than peace and quiet, that's all. And yet, once again, he found himself caught up in a deadly serious threat to innocent folks.

As he ambled along, he kept his head down, chin touching his collarbone. He breathed in through his nose and out through his mouth slowly and calmly, trying to steady his nerves and breathing.

It seemed to work, although his mind kept replaying the incident, particularly when he struck the kidnapper a fatal blow to the head so that he slumped to the hard ground in a heap. However, the young women had vocally and mindfully appreciated everything he had done in order to set them free. A small smile quivered on his lips, and a new, fresh thought came to him unburdened that instantly made him feel a hundred times better.

The wind had picked up again and danced in his hair. It reminded him that he needed a haircut. His hair was long and his fringe sometimes flopped and dangled in front of his eyes. Hands, deep in his jacket pockets, Toby increased his half-arsed amble to a strident gait. All of a sudden he wanted to go home and see his mother. The bitter chill of January whipped his face, reddening his cheeks, making his eyes water and numbing his hands.

He got home, unlocked the front door, wiped his feet on the mat and closed the door behind him.

'It's me, Mum,' he called out, as he undid his laces and left his shoes on the wooden rack. 'I'm home now.'

Abigail came through the kitchen doorway and smiled benignly at him. 'I was starting to get worried,' she said, evidently glad that he was home and in her presence once more.

'Sorry about that,' Toby said. 'I lost track of time and stopped to chat to a neighbour. Is everything all right?'

'Oh gosh,' Abigail said, full of relief and love. 'Yes, everything's fine. I'll put your pizza in the oven right now. Why don't you get out of those clothes, take a hot bath and your food shall be done by then?'

Toby breathed a laugh. 'Sounds like a plan,' he said and ascended the staircase to do all that his mother had asked of him.

Dressed in his pyjamas, Toby combed his wet hair and then went downstairs as his mum was about to call for him to come get his meal. He ate the pizza and drained the Coke in the living room. Abigail joined him and put on the evening news on the BBC. They talked amiably for more than twenty minutes. Toby finished his food and put the plate and glass in the kitchen sink.

'You look tired, sweetheart,' she said.

'I am,' Toby said. 'I was gonna do some reading for my exam on Monday but I'm exhausted.'

'You were out walking for quite a long time,' Abigail pointed out. 'No wonder. Why don't you play some PS3 and get to bed early? Tomorrow you should stay in and study and stay indoors. The forecast is snow and ice for tomorrow, so I won't be going out and neither should you. It's too dangerous, anyway.'

Toby nodded in agreement.

'Yeah. I might very well do all that you've said, Mum.' With that he heaved himself off the sofa, kissed Abigail on the brow and said 'Goodnight'.

At 10:50PM Toby killed the game console, switched off the mains and got into bed. Tomorrow was all nicely planned out for him. A sensible thing to do while the weather was cold and the roads and pavements would be slippery underfoot. He closed his eyes and gladly welcomed a deep sleep.

*

Toby found himself walking down a steep road that had been deserted. Cars and vans were parked alongside the road but there were no people. He couldn't place where he was or where he was heading. It was a mystery to him. He turned his head so that he was looking sideways and as the road curved round a bend up into a cul-de-sac he could see all the houses were beige-bricked, except for the black house at the end with a red door and black metallic knocker.

He gasped in surprise as everything else disappeared except for this house. Against his own volition, Toby drifted forward to the black wrought-iron gate and the two-turreted sides crowning the top. The sound of cawing from a single bird reached his ears and from behind him, a crow sailed across his head and soared up again, perching itself on the V-shaped construction.

'There's no need to fear, Toby,' a soothing, croaky voice of an elderly woman said. 'You have a special gift. You and me both. Good luck with your exam on Monday. Come see me the day after – Tuesday during lunchtime and I shall bake you some chocolate chip cookies.'

Toby found his mouth sealed off, leaving him without the power to think or speak; not that he knew what to say or think in that moment.

Now the crow cawed at him three times before taking flight and soared into the azure sky.

*

At 9:34AM Toby blinked his crusty eyes open and scanned the bedroom. He groaned, knowing that it was cold and he wanted to stay under the duvet the whole day. He had an oak writing desk at the window where the sunlight shone down through the gaps in the blinds. Today was the day he studied the topic Physics. He had the whole year's work in a folder that he had to go through, read again and a laptop to watch a couple of YouTube videos on. It was Sunday, and had Toby been a man of faith and attended church, he'd be entitled to the day of rest.

Instead he had a whole day of studying. However, there were some things of Physics that he found intriguing and was most likely why he always did well in class.

At 12:43PM Toby took a break and went downstairs to make himself a peanut butter sandwich. After food he washed his face thoroughly at the bathroom sink before getting his head down to study right the way throughout the entire afternoon.

At 5:36PM Toby had finished his studying and would watch an hour of a YouTube video later on.

He leaned back in his chair and stretched, yawning, (a clear sign of mental fatigue) until he got up and walked out of the room. His mother was downstairs busying herself with her knitting and crossword.

'I need a break,' Toby said.

Abigail looked up and watched her son collapse onto the sofa. 'I was about to say. You've done a heck of a lot today, my dear. You take it easy for awhile. I'll put food on for you once I have finished this part of the scarf, okay?'

'Okay,' Toby said.

*

Toby was wide awake the following morning before eight o'clock. He brushed his teeth, had a quick, relaxing hot shower, got dressed, ate a bowl of cereal and then gave his mum a kiss on the top of her head before departing for school for his final exam.

'Good luck,' she said, smiling warmly at him.

That was always the best thing about his mother, Toby thought as he walked briskly down the tree-lined street toward the main road that turned left up a low incline drive where the comprehensive school stood. His mum never criticized his results. However, in all honesty, and without being the slightest bit egotistical, Toby's schooling was of a high standard. His only subjects were Maths and Chemistry. Everything else was good. He informed his mum of this a couple of years ago, and she was still marvelling over his A in History where he studied D-Day. All she ever said was, "Just do your best". And that was what Toby had done. Perhaps if he had a father figure who was on his back all the time, giving him a hard time by inflicting anxiety and stress, he wouldn't have possessed the drive and determination that he had to not only get good grades but also to please his mother that he was a good boy, worth raising on her lonesome and that there would be a pay-off at the end of it all.

He arrived at the school and signed the register and then made his way to the library as he was still an hour early. He re-read his Physics file, bringing the coursework they had studied for the last two years to the forefront of his consciousness so he wouldn't have to wrack his brain too much during the exam.

The exam was scheduled for 11:00AM and would end at 1:00PM in Room 6. Toby tried to calm his nerves and reminded himself that he was fairly good at this subject and that he had done all he could possibly do to prepare himself for the ordeal of the exam in the next two hours.

'Just do your best,' he whispered to himself.

Then he gathered up his work and made it down the left corridor to the exam room, awaiting his fate.

As soon as the exam began Toby forgot about the world outside beyond the window and immersed himself in the questions, studying them assiduously, making certain that he understood the question and had the correct answers for the solutions. He finished his exam with five minutes to spare and flicked through the pages, confident that he had satisfied the examiner to be awarded a good grade, which would help him in job interviews and more importantly, make his dear mother proud.

The bell chimed at 1:00PM and everyone stopped what they were doing. Mrs Cromwell came around and collected the exam papers that had the pupil's names on the front, and when she had finally collected them all she stood at her oak desk and addressed them all. 'Year 11 students… today, for some of you, this will have been your final exam. Your results will be allocated directly outside the headmaster's office on July 22. I have had the pleasure of teaching many of you and becoming an acquaintance during your years at this school. If I don't see you again, please take your experiences with you into your lives whatever you choose to do from this day forth. It has been an absolute pleasure. I hope you all studied hard and get good grades that will stand well with you as you go to college or into employment. Thank you. You are now free to leave the premises.'

The students stood and looked relieved that it was over. Toby's head was buzzing. He felt lethargic and his stomach grumbled at him. He was fully aware that he needed to meet its requirements and planned on emptying his locker before handing the key over to the prefect in charge.

Toby exited the classroom with his schoolmates and made a beeline for his locker in the main hall. He pushed and sidled his way through the mass of students and finally arrived at his locker, anticipating getting out of the crowd and into the fresh air outside. The sun was shining through big white fluffy clouds, and he desperately wanted to clear the fog in his mind after having been in a bent over posture at a desk for two whole hours without intermission.

A few lockers down on the same row, Jenny unlocked her locker and extracted a pink purse and a bottle of Evian water. Toby tried to meet her gaze in the hope she would see him in her peripheral sight and say "Hello" so they could continue getting to know one another as they had done on Friday. This time, however, Toby could see her cheeks were getting very pink and blotchy, as though she had some kind of reaction to something or was nervous or felt guilty somehow.

'Hi Jenny!' Toby called out.

She flinched but stared into the confines of her locker, closed the door and extracted the key.

'Jenny?' Toby said, totally perplexed.

As Jenny turned around, purposefully ignoring Toby, Graham Harris, the great sport star of the school, came into sight and embraced Jenny. He wrapped his muscular arms around her and gave her a kiss on the cheek.

Toby closed his locker for the last time but couldn't hide his shock at what he was seeing with naked eyes.

'Not here, Graham,' Jenny whispered.

Toby moved back and was swallowed into the crowd. He might not have been totally aware of it at the time, but his heart had been broken irrevocably.

What was Graham Harris doing, kissing and holding Jenny? Boyfriend and girlfriend?

I thought she liked me. She kissed me last Friday. Graham saw us eating in the canteen and watched us leaving together.

Eventually Toby averted his stunned gaze to where he was initially headed.

'You okay, sport?' a student asked.

Toby met the gaze of his fellow student and friend, Matthew.

'Yeah, we're all pretty stunned at how Jenny shagged Graham on the weekend. But there you go. He's got his big house, lots of money and a bodybuilding physique that Frank Zane would be proud of.'

'They had sex?' Toby asked.

Matthew nodded. 'Yeah. Just like that. Her girlfriends and his rugby chums went to that Indian place on the main road. Jenny got drunk and before you know it Graham took her into his tent where he was camping out and shagged her twice.'

'She kissed me on Friday afternoon though,' Toby blurted out.

Matthew turned to him and looked taken aback. 'Aw, dude. That is bad. Try not to take it personally though. But I really thought Jenny was one of those types of girls who got married or into a serious relationship before she started shagging.'

Toby agreed, but not in words. Instead he exhaled, spun on his heel and made his way through the mass of students towards the main entrance.

11.

THE RESPLENDENT SUN warmed Toby as he exited the school grounds and his feet touched the pavement. Still in a state of shock and despondency, he headed to the zebra crossing, looking both ways. Two cars on either side of the road came to a halt, as it was his right of way, and the teenager crossed the road to the other side that led directly to the bridge. Ascending the concrete steps was good exercise, he thought, trying his utmost to delete the scene with Graham Harris and Jenny, who had totally ignored him.

He crossed the bridge and saw one school kid leaning over the side, spitting drool on the passing vehicles going past below. He rolled his eyes. Even when he was young Toby never behaved immaturely. Neither was he ever tempted. Since his own father had got up and departed, Toby, without being told or asked, took up the reigns and steered himself and his frightened mother in the right direction. He had been the one who had spoken to the authorities and got himself a job as a paperboy for the local newsagent until the shop closed.

His main role in life was to make certain that his doting, vulnerable mother felt safe and secure in their home.

As the bridge sloped down on the other side, Toby could see the Morrison superstore in the distance.

He had to be the rock.

His childhood was over... non-existent in a way.

All of this, Toby silently blamed his father for, walking out on them when they desperately needed him. He recalled asking his mother if Dad was coming back and was it his fault that he had left them without a word? Abigail had broken down into a fit of overflowing tears. Toby remembered that he had stood ramrod still at the foot of the stairs seeing his mother like this and vowing never to bring the topic up ever again in case it made his innocent mother cry like that.

If he asked himself honestly how the exam went, Toby would say that he was confident. All the time he had spent studying and revising, he believed, had paid off.

Any ambitions of taking Jenny out on a date had been obliterated. He didn't understand how fast Jenny had forgotten their conversation on Friday to make her lose her virginity to a super star hot-head who only liked her because of her beauty and slender form. Yet Toby did recall Graham's close friends saying how he could get anything he wanted. The academic classes were arduous for him. He lacked the patience and determination for, say English, but not the fervour for making big hits on the rugby field. He could see that Jenny had seen him as a renowned gladiator or hero with his broad shoulders and sculpted physique. But he seemed driven entirely by adrenaline and lust. The body sensations coursed through him and his brain had been left behind.

Toby shook his head, rebuking himself for judging the loudmouthed school rugby legend. The teachers had aided him with some of the non-physical subjects as they were anxious not to fail him after he had been watched and considered by scouts for the under 18 national team.

Good luck to them, I suppose.

And that was that. Now Toby used the pelican crossing and made a beeline for Morrison's. He purchased a bottle of Evian water and browsed the DVD section. Then he decided to go to the market where they sold used paperbacks for fifty pence. Now that all the exams had been done and Jenny was fornicating with Graham, Toby decided he'd treat himself to some books.

Just as he stepped out from under the sloping roof it started to rain. Toby sighed in vexation. Yet he still walked in the direction of the market. He flipped his hooded sweater up over his head and kept his head down to prevent any raindrops hitting his face and eyes.

Before long the big wooden doors invited Toby inside.

The newsagent raised his head from the newspaper he was reading to see if he had a customer. Toby still hadn't removed his hood, but as he did so his eyes met the astonished eye-wide stare of the middle-aged man wearing glasses. 'It's you. Isn't it?'

Toby frowned, clearly not understanding what the newsagent owner had said. The first thought that came to him was, *This guy's drunk.* He stepped back until the glass partition refused to give under this extra weight.

'I'm afraid I don't know what you're talkin' about,' Toby said in a clear, confident voice, feeling sorry for this man who apparently had some serious mental health issues.

The man swept a hand through his thinning black hair and removed his specs. He lifted the newspaper up where there was an etching of a hooded figure. The bold title declared, **HOODED HERO SAVES SEX SLAVES!**

'Oh, Jesus Christ!'

'It *is* you,' the newsagent said.

Toby lied. He shook his head. 'I'm afraid not,' he told the man. 'But at least the front page has some good news for a change.'

The middle-aged man continued to eye him.

Toby wished he didn't. It made him awfully uncomfortable.

A middle-aged woman came around the side of the counter to see what all the fuss was about that had already drawn four people to stop and stare at Toby.

'It's him!' the middle-aged man said in a loud voice.

The woman, who Toby supposed was the man's wife, looked at the front cover of the *Sun* and then at Toby and gasped.

Toby's shoulders slumped in defeat.

'Why did it have to rain?' Toby muttered to himself before turning back the way he came and down the cobbled street and blended in with the other commuters.

*

Toby caught the bus home as the torrential shower did not abate. His hair was soaking wet due to the fact that he had removed the hood so as not to attract any more unwanted and unnecessary attention. It had been a close call and he congratulated himself inwardly for not responding or inviting praise for his deed that he believed anyone would have done if they had come across the harrowing situation.

The 159 took a long route home but Toby cared not. He simply gazed out the window and watched the world go by in front of his eyes, letting his mind switch off from any fear or intrusive thoughts that led down dead end roads.

Jenny was gone...

It wasn't merely the fact that she'd had sex with Graham Harris, (a typical jock, and jerk) but the fact any possible future with her had been deleted like the push of a button.

His future remained unknown.

He supposed that was a good thing. I mean, how could anyone manage or be in control if they already knew their fate in this world? If it was a bad thing that got through to them that they avoided, preventing it from happening in the first place, then he supposed it was good. But Toby believed that you made your own destiny in life by the imperative choices that faced you. He had to self-analyse his thought process when the fact that his father would never return home again sunk in. To be the "man of the house" for want of a better phrase, Toby had to break down his own character, thoughts, feelings and decide who he wanted to be. What type of person did he aspire to be from childhood into adulthood?

At an early age, Toby's childhood came to an abrupt end.

He began doing household chores for his mother. He did his paperboy route five days a week, helped his mother do the weekly shopping at Tesco or Asda, washed his mother's car and studied for good grades that would enable him to get a job with enough income for him and Abigail to live somewhat comfortably. That was the plan anyway.

The bus slowed and then jerked to a halt on the main road. Toby got out of his seat, thanked the driver and headed down the road, turning right until his street came into sight. The rain had reduced to a drizzle. However, it too, was inexorable.

Toby entered his home, wiped his feet, removed his trainers and noticed his mother seated on the sofa reading a newspaper.

His heart jolted.

'Is that you, love?' Abigail called out.

'Yeah. It's me, Mum. You okay?'

'Oh, I'm fine. Just reading the *Post*.'

'I'm going upstairs for a bit,' Toby said, seeing the black and white sketch of a hooded figure that was secretly him once again.

He climbed the staircase and eased into his bedroom and removed his hooded sweater and put on a Nike fleece. He opened his *Total Film* magazine and began reading an article. Consumed by the magazine, an hour passed. Eventually Toby grew weary and finished reading an extensive review before heading downstairs.

Abigail was in the kitchen wiping the worktop when Toby came in through the doorway.

'How did it go?' she asked.

Toby nodded. 'I don't wanna jinx myself or something... but in all fairness, I felt comfortable answering all the questions and providing practical solutions. So, fingers crossed, I did pretty darn good.'

Abigail offered him one of her heart-warming smiles. 'Well, let's hope you are right, shall we?'

Toby nodded again and then noticed the bagels on the small, white china plate.

Abigail let out a breathless laugh. 'Yes... they are for you.'

'Aw good,' Toby said, pulling out the chair and sitting down for his much-needed snack.

Abigail watched her son chomping his way through the bagel and sat down opposite him so they could converse. Toby met her eyes with his own.

'Did you hear of that young man who rescued those three young women in the Abbey just a couple of days ago?'

Toby swallowed the bread with some difficulty, trying not to choke. He poured himself a Diet Coke and washed down his snack. 'No, I didn't,' he answered, somewhat nervous.

Abigail went on praising the unknown hero who had single-handedly saved three beautiful young women from sex trafficking. 'They identified the kidnapper. He is a German-born UK resident, who has escaped arrest for a few months now. He died from severe head trauma. Good enough, I say. The less people like that in the world today is a good thing. Don't you agree?'

Toby shrugged. 'It might have been better for him to have been apprehended.'

'What... and cause the taxpayer more money? No, he already did a turn in prison for smuggling A-class drugs. People like that never change their stripes. They just find another crime so they can get rich quick without having to go to work and perform hard labour. Serves him right. I mean, God knows what would've happened had that young man not been there to save those women. They would be dead... or worse. They'd be sold for sex. I tell you the world's gone crazy. And to think that this all took place a few blocks away from where we are now. I mean, we have a nice, genial neighbourhood. Nice people who warm up by the fire in winter and have barbeques in the summer, who work, pay ever-increasing bills and live quietly, minding their own business.'

Toby gazed at Abigail, feeling the power of her words and morals. 'You're right, Mum.'

'You don't think I'm just some middle-aged woman rambling on about justice, do you? Am I embarrassing you? I know mums who do that to their children.'

Toby offered her a half-hearted smile. 'I think it's great that there was someone there who took the situation into their hands, but it might've been better to have just maimed the kidnapper. Because now the rescuer has blood on his hands.'

Abigail leaned over, closer to Toby and lowered her voice. 'Sometimes people have to do things that go against their morals and conscience in order to get things done. Those girls would have been victims to abuse, rape and discrimination. And when the men who bought them couldn't trust them to go out by themselves, they'd put a bullet in their heads and dumped them somewhere far away so there would be no trace or witnesses. That's how the world works in those circles. The young man did the right thing. He is a hero.'

Toby nodded. Suddenly the urge to tell his mum that it was he who had saved those women was overwhelming. However, he bit down on his lip and suppressed any notion of blurting the truth out. What had transpired in the town centre earlier that day alarmed him to the core of his very existence. He had no aspirations to be famous; that had not been the reason he had done what he had a couple of days before. Of course, that wasn't to say that he regretted any of his actions, but his mum did make him feel better about the kidnapper's fate being sealed not by the axe but his own actions.

'Are you OK?' Abigail asked, eyeing him curiously.

Toby nodded. 'Yeah, just a bit tired from the exam and the walk home. I think I'm gonna watch some X-Files on DVD to relax. Gonna get an early night tonight if I can.'

'I bet you did all right with that exam,' Abigail said, changing the topic. 'All your teachers have remarked how well you're doing all year round. Don't worry about your grade. If it's good – great. If it's bad – we'll figure something out.'

'Thanks, Mum.'

'I'm going over Shirley's house for a coffee, biscuits and a chat. Will you be all right here, on your own?'

Toby nodded. 'No need to worry about me, Mum. I'm just gonna grab a can of Diet Coke and watch my DVD. Make sure you take a key though, in case I fall asleep.'

Abigail rolled her eyes. 'I'll be back in time for supper. I got you a pizza.'

Toby agreed that a pizza was definitely a good choice for him. Then he retired to his bedroom, exhausted and relaxed.

Abigail headed to the bathroom for a pee prior to going over to Shirley's house, and as she was drying her hands on the towel she caught sight of the hamper and checked that Toby had put his clothes in. He had. However, as she grabbed his grey hooded sweater, she saw red splotches down the front. Alarmed and intrigued simultaneously, she pulled the hooded sweater out and held it up in front of her and came to the slow yet undeniable realization that the red splotches were not from drinking wine or paint but were in fact droplets of dry blood.

12.

THE OMINOUS thunderclouds had unleashed their heavy deluge in the southern parts of the United Kingdom all day. Annie Combs sat in her living room with her legs raised on the footstool watching the rivulets chase each other down the double-thick glass pane incessantly. Intuition informed her that Toby had no intention of finding her residence, and if she was being totally honest, she couldn't blame him. Yet he had the "shine" like herself and she desperately needed to talk to him and help guide him in his life before he wasted an opportunity to do great things for which he'd been made.

She had read the *Evening Post* and marvelled at how Toby had concealed his identity in order to avoid the media of unwanted attention. Annie had been taken aback by that fact and the heroic deed which he'd accomplished, saving those young women from a life of torture in a country far away from home and never seeing their loved ones ever again. She believed that there were happenings transpiring in the world that could not go undiscovered from her consciousness.

Furthermore, Annie Combs was getting old and with that came physical weariness high on the Richter scale. She had the ability to talk to another person with the same gift on the opposite side of the world as though they were chatting for real without the use of Facebook or Skype.

She still recalled the murder discovery Toby had solved beyond all doubt when he was younger. He'd been on the front cover of the newspapers and received local fame. However, between that time and now, Toby had gone through a lot of physical and mental changes. He had grown in stature and his mind was purely focused on his exams and other academic concerns. Nevertheless, Annie believed in her heart that although Toby would pass his exams and enlist to go to college to further his studies prior to finding adequate employment he had a special gift that would help and serve mankind in ways beyond imaginable to other folks.

Annie took a sip of her scalding coffee then put it on the coaster on the small table beside her while she watched daytime TV. She couldn't help but feel deflated at the fact that Toby wasn't going to listen to her voice and seek out her red door with the black brass lion's head knocker.

'He's tired,' she croaked to no one.

Annie knew that Toby had the sense of losing someone... and it came to her that this didn't have reference to death, but loss of someone he'd hoped to have a future with.

'A girlfriend... gone. Oh, Toby. My darling. You poor thing.'

And yet fate had struck Toby with a lethal lightening bolt that steered his life in a whole new direction. One he could not have foreseen onto a path of enlightenment.

May the force be with you, she thought and smiled.

Annie had to be told by her dear grandmother when she was a child and always outsmarted her parents that she had the gift of Second Sight and knew precise things when she came into contact with a person. As a child she didn't know any better. She simply discovered things from people she met in person and heard faraway voices and saw visions that no doctor could explain the cause.

She remembered the time that her parents had hidden three chocolate eggs in the front and back garden in Stanley Close, wanting her to keep busy and preoccupied with the search while they "snuggled" beneath the sheets in their bedroom.

'One's in behind the pots of plants in the front garden. There's one in the basket covered with soil in the hanging basket that I can reach but only on tip-toes, and the last one is around the back in the Wendy house behind all the baby toys,' she said at the foot of the bed.

Her parents had stared at her with big, wide eyes of complete astonishment, not really understanding how Annie had come to this conclusion, as they'd not told anyone. And Annie had slept over at her grandmother's last night and had slept during her journey home until sunrise.

Annie decided prudently to keep her knowing things about people and happenings before, during and after they had happened, secret – a knowledge that was clearly impossible because there was no proof and wasn't related to her life in any way, shape or form.

Nevertheless, as she got older and moved out, Annie bought a flat (everything was much cheaper then, she mused) and worked as a Primary school teacher during the day, and on weekends offered her psychic abilities to those who sought out their loved ones—who hoped to find comfort that there was something else that continued after passing away from Earth and proving she was genuine by reciting things no one else would know were in the past. And so she became known well by residents of her small town in Hampshire.

As she got older, Annie became estranged from her family entirely. They had all decided to rest their minds with the fact that she was an "Oddball" and had nothing to do with them. It made the move to Wales much easier, she thought, in hindsight. Had she been close to her parents and aunties and cousins she might have stayed and ignored the voices and visions and continued to pursue what ordinary folks termed "a normal life". Now she was in her fifties and with the aid of technology, Annie did her shopping online, and only went out for a walk for exercise and to the local library. Reading distracted her from her wayward thoughts and bills and anything else that caused her concern.

Now she knew of another who had the "Shine", she couldn't wait to meet him and pass on her knowledge and wisdom in order to assist Toby help those who cried out in their suffering.

Annie was fully aware that this was a tall order and not one that should be entered into lightly. On the contrary, this had to be dealt with gloved hands and astute precaution. This "Shine" after all was a supernatural gift that meant that the receiver's mind would be overtaken by some hidden force that needed addressing for the greater good.

Toby had this gift in spades. Now was the time for him to shine…

*

Toby was lying in bed comfortably watching the X-Files when he started hearing a high-pitched whining. He turned his head towards the window and gazed outside. The gun-ship grey clouds had morphed into a staggering mass growing denser than ever before. Thunder roared like a monstrous lion, preparing to step out of its cage and attack assailants. He watched the end of the episode then turned the DVD player off and killed the TV at the mains to prevent there being a power cut from his appliances, which usually meant that they would take ages to reload and set up properly the next time he turned it on. Something about the massive mushroom, killing the remaining daylight sent an involuntary shudder through him. Then the high-pitched noise ceased and Toby's shoulders slumped in relaxation and relief.

He sat back down on his bed and breathed slowly. The roar of the pending thunder always seemed to frighten him. He never grew out of it, and was ashamed of this emotion. What occurred in its place came the roiling and ever blackening density.

'Toby!'

He leapt up and whirled around at the sound of a female voice saying his name out loud.

'Toby! It's me. Don't be alarmed.'

'Go away,' Toby said, slapping the palms of his hands over his ears in an attempt to block out the voice.

'It's all right, my darling,' Annie said. 'It's me. The woman who lives at the house with the red door. You didn't come to visit me today, so I could introduce myself in person. It would be easier that way.'

Toby's skin crawled with goosepimples.

'Piss off!' Toby said. 'Just piss off! I don't know you. I don't want to know you. Please, for God's sake... leave me alone. This is harassment. I don't know you. I don't want to know you. Just go away!'

'Please listen, love,' Annie said in an apologetic voice. 'You have got a gift that needs to be nurtured by someone who will understand. Come by tomorrow at my house – number five, Bethlehem Road. Can you do that? We speak face-to-face then without having a conversation in our minds.'

Toby was trembling, and he hated Annie for doing this to him. However, he did make a mental note of the woman's voice address.

'Will you come?' Annie asked.

'If I say yes, will this stop?'

'Sort of love,' Annie said, realising and understanding that she had neither the power (any more) nor the intention of communicating like this for very long.

'Come at lunchtime,' she said in a brighter tone of voice. 'I'll make us something nice to eat. I'm not going to hurt you. This isn't a trick. I just need to see you. Don't tell anyone that you're coming to my house. Just say you're gonna give your friend a call. I live locally anyway, so don't worry about it.'

The more he listened – plus the fact that she gave him an actual address – the more Toby realised that the woman actually sounded like a nice genuine person, one who was offering him help.

'Can you make it all go away?' he asked.

'Come by tomorrow,' Annie said.

Then there was nothing…

In the beautiful silence, Toby closed his eyes and wiped his nose. When he looked at his hand, his index and middle fingers were full of fresh blood. He hurried into the bathroom and washed his hands and nose until there was no trace. Then he sauntered back into his bedroom.

*

When Abigail returned home Toby was standing at the kitchen worktop waiting at the microwave to beep to a conclusion. Then he opened the door, squirted brown sauce onto the chips and took his food into the dining room where he devoured the pie and chips. He talked to his mother about the weather. She was rosy red in the face, and Toby could tell without being told that she'd had a great time at her friend's house.

'What're your plans for tomorrow?' Abigail asked.

'I'm going over to my friend's for lunch, but apart from that I'm free. Perhaps help you with the shopping in the morning, if you fancy?'

Abigail shook her head. 'I'm going on Sunday, to ASDA; it's much quieter and less stressful. What friend?'

'Oh, just someone from school,' Toby said in a very convincing way. 'Even though I've seen my friends in school, what with the studying for exams and the exams themselves, we haven't really had a proper catch-up so to speak. So we thought it'd be nice just to hang out for an hour or two.'

'Well, yeah,' Abigail said. 'That sounds cool.'

'Mum, I'm gonna head up to bed and read for awhile before turning in, if you don't mind?'

'No dear,' Abigail said. 'I don't mind. I'm gonna go into the living room and watch Silent Witness. Oh, there is one thing, though.'

'Name it.'

'Could you vacuum your bedroom tomorrow, please?'

'I'll do it first thing,' Toby replied and gave her a heart-warming smile.

*

At sunrise Toby awoke feeling groggy. He lay in bed, awake, for another half an hour, exhausted but feeling fresh doing so. He'd fallen asleep after the news last night. When he finally rolled out of bed, he sat on the edge of the mattress and coughed a few times before going through his morning ritual. Once he had got himself dressed and cleaned, he felt better in himself but still had some anxiety about the meeting with Annie.

He made himself a bowl of cereal for breakfast and chatted with his mum for a while. Abigail left the house at eleven and Toby went for a little stroll up the local park to get some fresh air. He did his best to forget about Annie Combs and what had transpired last night but it persisted in the forefront of his brain, seizing him and overriding every other pleasant thought and tranquillity.

When he returned home, Toby sprayed Lynx under his arms and men's perfume over his face and neck. Then he composed himself and left the house on foot.

Number 5 certainly had a wooden red door. The brand-new beige-bricked exterior and clean white columns gave the front door some shade while the balcony above was in sunshine. Toby hadn't quite expected it to be anything like this. He climbed the two steps and stood at the front door with a black lion's head for the brass knocker. He was about to lift the handle and strike the wood when the door opened and offered him a fresh sight of the staircase and the short woman with lots of deeply-etched facial wrinkles and diamond-blue eyes. She stood smiling at him. Toby immediately liked her and entered the house.

'It's so nice to see you, Toby,' Annie said.

'Okay,' Toby said, feeling a bit uncomfortable and awkward.

'Come, let us go into the kitchen, where I am working.'

Toby followed Annie down the hallway into the kitchen area.

'Take a seat.'

Toby pulled out one of the wooden chairs and parked his arse on it.

'I know you're nervous, pet,' Annie said. 'But, as you can see, I don't offer any harm to you or anyone else for that matter. It is true though that in spite of my expression, I have been given this particular gift. I am sorry for frightening you yesterday. But you need someone to talk to. No doctor or therapist can help you, my dear. This world we live in is a very hostile place. There are so many tragedies in the world today and there's nothing fun about it.'

'Why am I here?' Toby asked, getting straight to the point.

Annie busied herself with the food and placed the pasty and chopped up pork pies and Scotch eggs and laid the plates on the cork mats. She poured him a glass of Coke and a glass of water for herself. They ate their food for a short while in perfect silence. Then Annie washed her food down and finally answered Toby's question with a question. 'Why'd you think you're here?'

'Well, 'cause you asked me too.'

'Tell me, what does it feel like to be an unsung hero?'

Toby shook his head. 'I'm no hero.'

'That's not what those girls believe. Tonight on a special programme on BBC Wales they will be speaking for the first time. They will, however, keep your name and identity hidden. They did as you asked – and did not said much, besides the fact that you are a hero to them and the nation.'

'You know it was me, don't you?'

Annie nodded, smiling. 'I do.'

'Then you also know that I killed a man,' Toby said with a stone-cold expression.

Annie looked away and felt the trouble of Toby's burdened heart. 'Yes... I am aware, my dear,' she said, her voice thick with emotion.

'I'm a murderer.'

Annie sighed and her shoulders slumped. 'Try not to think so negatively.'

'I am,' Toby replied. 'But it's hard. I went for a walk to clear my head. The visions and the voices were scaring the crap outta me. I don't want this... Shine. I wanna be left alone so I can live out the rest of my life in peace and enjoy some good memories. I'm young. As you know everything, then you know I lost a potential girlfriend and I just want to be normal again. It's great that I've solved a few crimes, but the other day I went into town in the market and saw an etching of me on the front of the newspapers. The owner saw it was me, 'cause I had my coat done up. He started raising his voice and pointing at me. I had to flee and get the hell outta there. You don't know what it's like. It's horrible.'

Annie was lost for words for a moment. Instead of becoming frustrated –like most people would – she studied Toby like a peculiar art exhibition.

'I am sorry,' Annie said after a long period of silence. 'Maybe you should go and get on with your life. But whether you want to admit it or not, you are psychic. You helped the police and the dead young woman's family finally find Danielle's body and the murderer to be brought to justice. Not to mention the three young women. Perhaps I shouldn't say that you ought to be proud. But you shouldn't ignore the voices. You have this incredible gift. And you're still so young. You have so much potential.'

'What am I supposed to do? Sit in my bedroom all day waiting to hear voices so I can don my Superman outfit and go and rescue a cat from a tree? I got feelings too, ya know.' He paused for a moment. 'I don't mean to get ratty about all of this but I got a life of my own. This isn't my idea of living. I want to be a Sports Education teacher and help kids find doing exercise to be beneficial. I'm not what you and the people I've saved say I am.'

Annie put her utensils down.

'I'm sorry,' Toby said, placing a supportive hand to his forehead. 'I appreciate the food and company, but this ain't what I call living. It's more like living with an illness like Motor Neurone Disease. I'm not God or Superman. I need to get a life of my own. Otherwise I'll go crazy.'

'Please leave,' Annie said in a soft tone of voice.

Toby closed the front door behind him, a burden on his shoulders, aware that neither he nor Annie had said or done anything wrong, per se. However, he knew what he had said came from the heart. He believed that there was no way he could handle being a psychic and spending the whole of his life being a "hero". He admired Annie Combs' supernatural gift and the fact that he had saved lives in the past, but it was just too much to take in. He wanted to do P.E. and do lots of sports locally. His mind was fertile in some ways, but it also made him feel vulnerable, what with all the voices and visions that scared the living daylights out of him.

What Annie was proposing was way over his head, he decided. No, he was going to go to college and study Sport Science and work in the local gymnasium and sport centre a half mile away from his high school. Doing sports always made him feel good. He loved all types of sports, like basketball, football, rugby and was thinking of getting stuck into bodybuilding. He had a good, wiry physique anyway, although he wasn't very strong and wanted to be able to lift weights and get some defined muscles. Doing so would make an impressive mark when he began his course and wouldn't do any harm when he applied for a job as a sports instructor.

He took a stroll on the main road of his village and stopped at a convenience store to purchase a bottle of Diet Pepsi. With the drink in his grasp, Toby ambled up the road, sipping his drink, clearing his mind from the conversation he'd just had with the nice lady who apparently took offence at what he had to say. Yet he was quite glad that she had told him to leave because the conversation was uncomfortable and close to the bone. It was prudent that she asked him to leave when she did. It gave him a chance to break free and think about his prospects.

*

Annie cleared the plates and glasses and placed them in the sink and proceeded to wash them. She sighed in disappointment at how the conversation had transpired. She had dearly hoped that Toby would be more open-minded and submissive. Yet the more she dwelled on the matter at hand, the more she began to realise and understand that the young man hated his gift. She had wanted above all else to show him how to use his gift, but he hadn't let her into his mind, face-to-face. Instead he had put up a defensive barrier and refused to let anything she said or was going to say get into his thought process. And, in all fairness, the boy was entitled to a life of his own. Perhaps Toby had been right. Yet in the deepest roots of her mind, Annie knew that no matter what Toby did from here on in, he'd still have the "Shine" and that if it did abate then it wasn't his destiny after all.

13.

TWO YEARS LATER

TOBY JONES had just finished his basketball game which he refereed for the two local high schools. He busied himself collecting all the basket balls and put them in a net bag. Then he collected all the empty water bottles discarded on the sidelines and put them in the recycling bin. It had been a good, hard-fought game with only five points in it. The home team won and their coach had escorted them out off the court and down the hallway to the dressing rooms to begin the celebrations.

Toby slung the ball-bag over his shoulder and walked to the two EXIT doors. His next destination was the equipment room. From there, Toby would get changed and head home for a much-required shower.

As he was doing all this, he felt a buzzing sensation at the nape of his neck. He reached his right hand over his shoulder, curious as to what was happening in that moment and released a small breath when the sensation subsided.

The day was overcast but dry. A gusty wind threatened to topple him off his feet as he crossed the football fields toward the entrance gate that was wide open.

Toby had quite a physique on him. He'd been training hard with dumbbells and barbells and also did dips and chins. He was a lot stronger and now possessed visible muscles all over his anatomy. His confidence had also soared immensely, and he felt much better in himself, mind and body.

When he arrived home, he went straight to the kitchen where his mother was reading *The Sun* newspaper and nursing a hot cup of tea. He announced his arrival. Abigail looked up from the article she'd been reading and was overjoyed that her son was home again. She couldn't put her finger on it exactly what Toby did, besides his aura uplifting her and the room she was in just by being present. Furthermore, she also noticed that he was looking a lot like Sylvester Stallone in his prime with all his rippling muscles.

'How was your day?' Abigail asked.

Toby told her that the day had been very productive and he was now ready to relax in his bedroom before supper. He had trained two elderly, retired men in the gym in the morning and assisted the basketball league game. The youngsters admired him for his well-developed physique and constantly asked if he would flex his biceps so they could take a picture of him on their mobile phones. At first Toby felt somewhat embarrassed flexing his muscles in front of folks, but the kids got so much pleasure and happiness out of it he began to do so merely to please them. He supposed it was a bit like being a celebrity, being stopped during the day to answer questions and so forth. He did remind himself to remain humble and calm during the process. He could now see why certain famous folks lost touch with reality and became arrogant and believed they were superior to everyone else.

He lay on top of the duvet and closed his eyes, waiting patiently for the sound of the sparrows chirruping outside his bedroom window. The dulcet, high-pitched singing never failed to put his thoughts to rest and made him hum along with them.

As he got out of his gym clothes and placed them in the hamper in the bathroom where he had a quick shower, Toby's thoughts were uncontrollably set on the psychic, Annie Combs. He wondered as the shower head soaked him and the hair and body wash ran down his torso and was swallowed up in the drain hole why Annie at this moment came to the forefront of his active brain.

He got changed into his pyjama bottoms and Daffy Duck T-shirt and headed downstairs in time for a microwave beef dinner. He devoured his food and drained a can of Diet Coke. Afterwards, he sauntered around the living room and dining room before retiring to his bedroom to watch a film on his DVD player.

Please don't get angry, Toby.

Toby stopped dead still at the last step on the staircase. A cold shiver ran down his spine that made him quiver. He gripped the balustrade in case he fell backwards into gravity's grip, steadying himself.

A moment's silence passed. Toby eventually stepped up onto the landing and disappeared into his bedroom and got into bed, using the remote control to turn the TV on.

Is that you, Annie?

Yes, I'm afraid it is. Please don't get mad at me. Please.

What's the problem?

I'm picking up some precognitive visions, but I can't do anything about them as I am old and frail.

So? Whatcha want me to do? You shouldn't be contacting me like this. This is an invasion of my privacy.

Please come to see me. I have much to tell you and to guide you to stop certain bad things taking place. I know you're getting on with life and prospering as a gym instructor, but this is very important. You have a gift and you can't just let it pass you by. I'll leave you to it. But my intuition tells me that you might start to see and hear things that are not part of your physical or mental make-up. Don't ignore them. Act upon them, and I will guide you along the way. There might be a lot of lives at risk. You must do this first and foremost or else it'll be on our consciences till the day we die.

The voice shrank into absence.

Toby lay supine under the covers, deeply disturbed by Annie Combs' message, and couldn't decide whether he hated her or not. She had no right whatsoever to intrude in his life… and that was undeniable. However, he knew that he was far more receptive to this "Shine" than almost anyone else.

If he did start to get more visions he'd go mad. For the first time in his life things were all good. He was enjoying his busy days and relaxing nights and had started contributing to paying his mother's bills and for a bed and a roof over his head. Now, all of a sudden, this cracker-jacker woman wanted him to give it all up to aid her in a nutter's quest to save the world.

He sighed deeply.

In his heart and mind Toby was well aware that he did have an extraordinary gift, and if he could help some innocent person from danger or death then he would do so. It just pissed him off that he had to have his new, pleasant life put on hold to do some of the dirty work with Annie.

He had thought about telling her to F-off. But that wasn't true to his whole being. He was a genial person who genuinely cared for folks who were weaker and less fortunate than him. Trouble was – what was he supposed to do now?

'Aw, this is so unfair, it's unbelievable.' And with that Toby punched the pillow.

*

A faint scratching noise at the bottom of his bed caused Toby to stir awake and swim to the top of his deep and peaceful slumber. He writhed about restlessly until he opened his eyes and could see nothing save the enveloping darkness.

Scratch, scratch, scratch.

Through sleep-deprived eyes, Toby focused on the end of the bed and jolted upright at the sight of a young boy with a bleeding scalp, blood matting his thick blond hair. There were rivulets of crimson streaks staining his mouth and neck.

He cussed under his breath and the boy simply stood still, staring at him with sunken blue eyes, prominent cheekbones making quick progress of his facial flesh.

Toby collected his frayed nerves together in a bundle and waited for them to reform to some kind of reality in this surreal happening.

'W-Who are you?' he cried out.

'I'm Jacob,' the boy said in a voice full of grit and liquid.

Toby threw the duvet off himself and swung his legs out of bed, not taking his eyes off the boy whose name, apparently, was Jacob.

'Where did you come from?' Toby asked, controlling his trembling. His newfound strength and stability from two years of strict training and eating well, without the influence of sports' enhancement drugs, alcohol and fatty foods had made him much stronger than he used to be.

If Jacob had arrived here in his room at this late hour a couple of years ago, Toby was certain he'd be running through the house or running full pelt out the front door for his life.

Jacob smiled. As he did this a mouthful of blood oozed out between his lips and ran down his chin and neck.

'My name is Jacob,' he said again in a juvenile matter-of-fact voice.

'Yeah... I know that,' Toby said, getting to a vertical base.

'I'm from the grave....'

Jacob's words hung in the air like blowflies.

Toby cussed again and slapped the palms of his hands onto his face and whimpered, 'What're you doing here, Jacob?'

'There was a bad man who came to my house and killed me and my mummy...'

'I don't believe this,' Toby said, shaking his head to and fro.

Jacob still hadn't moved from the foot of the bed.

'What do ya want me to do 'bout it?' Toby asked, half angry, half sympathetic.

'Come see,' Jacob said. 'I will show you where he put us. You must come with me now. The old lady can't handle much more. But you can help me and my mummy.'

Toby looked down at himself and placed his hands on his legs that shook right the way through him. He knew he couldn't allow himself to slip back into a fragile state as when he was younger and less sure of himself. Right now he had to be a pillar of strength for Jacob and bring him justice. Otherwise their murders would go on without ever discovering what happened and where the innocent victims could be found.

'Annie's right,' he whispered to himself.

And for a few seconds red hot burning hatred for Annie Combs and her insistence assailed the good in him. Then he exhaled. Jacob seemed to take all this in. The young boy, who couldn't have been much older than seven, walked out of his bedroom silently... and Toby Jones followed, albeit reluctantly.

14.

THE IRIDESCENCE of myriad colours of the night sky amazed Annie Combs and took her mind off the graphic visions she prayed to be released from.

Toby was a godsend in her humble opinion. If it had been anyone else they would have reported her to the police or got aggressive and might hurt her in order to stop her from her "shine". However, Annie could tell by intuition that Toby was very tolerant and patient. He had a clear conscience and that meant a lot to her and the boy. They were the type of persons that lie awake at night if they had done or said something immorally. It was an awful way to be in a lot of respects, although Annie knew all it meant was that she cared a great deal about herself and other, unfortunate people in the world. And times were getting tough with all this knife crime and the Brexit issue. It was very easy to fall into the group of folks who shut themselves off from the news and purely focused on their happiness and nothing else, which was quite understandable in the grand scheme of things.

She lay in her bed on her side and gazed out the window, wishing she had no worries or cares in the world and she could sleep peacefully and awake with a renewed vigour and zeal for life. Annie didn't have a great childhood. Her parents had never got married. They had a relationship with the result ending in her birth. Her father had another girlfriend, who was younger and comelier than her mother. It didn't help with her constantly asking the whereabouts of her father time and time again, Annie supposed in hindsight.

Her mother raised Annie until the age of nineteen when she began her job as a receptionist for a local law firm. She excelled at that job due to her prompt arrival at the start of the day and working on past her clocking out time.

In her spare time she discovered that she could sense things that had taken place during the time it was happening and sometimes being able to know things precognitive. She started experimenting with her friends from school. They marvelled at how accurate her readings were and suggested she charge folks to have their futures and past told. Word of mouth got around the small town, and soon enough Annie began making some profit financially in this endeavour. Then one day after her second and last reading Annie started feeling light-headed and woozy while on her feet. Everything started spinning. The floor moved in waves and she became unsteady and unnerved by this sudden physical breakdown.

She retired to bed and fell asleep as soon as her head touched the pillow and did not stir awake until twelve the following afternoon.

Exhausted and troubled, Annie quit reading palms and doing psychic readings. She continued to work at the law firm and turned down folks who wanted her to use her clairvoyant abilities.

She had had quite a scare that she was prudent enough not to repeat. Her health and wellbeing came first and foremost. She wasn't much good to anyone if she was feeling unwell, and she deduced that all those readings had had an effect on her busy mind until it reached the point of no return. Annie couldn't continue living in someone else's past, present or future. Not when she couldn't even read her own destiny. It would be like a child telling their parents how to do their roles as mother and father.

She brought to mind the previous evening when she had just finished her noodles and watched some TV; she had gone to the bathroom to begin her going-to-bed ritual when over her shoulder something moved at the speed of sound. She whirled around, shaken but not stirred, eyes bulging, attempting to discover where the sudden movement had come from and where it was now.

Annie insisted she didn't imagine it.

When she first started giving readings and amazing her clients by reciting their pasts to prove she wasn't a liar or a hoax but the real deal, folks, (her mother included) decided that she was crazy. Of course, no one said anything to her face but whenever she stepped outside to go across the road to the shops, she could sense the ambience and pressure on her consciousness all the same.

Being psychic wasn't fun, Annie reminded herself.

She recalled many a night when she asked God to make her ignorant of other people's opinions and what they had told her. It was all rather upsetting and unnerving. She could relate to Toby's emotions too. He hated her in some ways for bestowing this on him and disrupting his peace. Yet she was getting older and frail. She needed a protégé to take over and carry the mantle. She felt bad but on the other side of the coin – what else could she do? She couldn't very well let all those souls down.

Annie slapped her head in vexation.

'Stupid bloody conscience!'

She rose from her bed, stomped into the bathroom and slammed the door...

*

The night air was cool and calm. Toby had followed Jacob outside and felt no concern for himself, leaving his home the way he did at this ungodly hour when everyone else in the small town slept. The urge to blend in with the mass crowd was growing by the day. He hated this gift of clairvoyance and yet had no cure to break free from it. Instead, destiny demanded that this was his calling. Toby never really paid much thought about death as a child until he'd bumped into Danielle's murderer. He wondered aimlessly if he'd not bumped into that man if he would have continued living in complete obscurity. The detective at the scene of the crime seemed to believe he was a godsend and rescuing those young women who were to be sold as sex slaves made Toby realise that regardless or not this was bestowed upon him for a reason. Perhaps instead of seeking the reasoning behind certain things he had no control of, he should learn to adapt and get on with it.

Jacob led Toby to the hillside suburbs.

The streets were dead quiet. Up ahead, Toby saw a tabby cat cross the street to the children's playground. The sight of a pet veiled him with a sensation of love and adoration.

Then Jacob stopped walking when he reached the street sign, The Highlands Close.

'What's the matter?' Toby asked.

'I can't go any further,' Jacob said. 'I'm dead. What you'll see is where my mummy and my bodies are. This could've been you and your mum, remember. The others said I could come to you for justice. Is that true?'

'Others? Who are the others?'

Jacob simply stared at Toby... and his eyes shadowed the rest of his face with profound melancholy. 'The dead...' he said.

Toby allowed for that to sink in. Then: 'What number house do you live in... *lived* in, I should say?'

'Number five,' Jacob said.

'I'm sorry you died,' Toby said, feeling the boy's sadness. 'I will bring you justice.'

'He was my mum's new boyfriend,' Jacob said, breaking the silence. 'He drank a lot and suffered mental problems. But even that wasn't enough to excuse him for what he did to us.'

Toby nodded... concurring. 'May I ask...'

'He carried a large kitchen knife and used it to self harm. Mum made an innocuous joke and before we knew it, he slashed the knife through my mum's pretty face. I was upstairs listening to music on my iPad when he came in, grabbed me from behind, smashed me on the top of my head and then slit my throat.'

'Bloody hell.'

Jacob averted his gaze, his face draining of colour and the solidity wearing down until his whole being became transparent. 'I didn't want to die, Toby. I had a nice life. I liked playing with other boys and playing on my PS4, and helping Mum doing the chores... like you and your mum.'

Toby became choked with emotion at this boy's loss.

'What was the man's name?'

'Mark...'

'Surname?'

'Jenkins.'

'Mark Jenkins?'

Jacob nodded as he began to dissipate.

'What does he look like?' Toby had to be quick now with the information as Jacob was slipping away into the afterlife right in front of him.

'He's in his late twenties. Black hair. Black beard. And strongly built.' And with that Jacob's head dematerialised into fresh air.

Toby turned and walked up the street until he arrived at the bungalow with 5 on its front door. He tried the handle and it clicked on its latch, permitting Toby to enter the interior.

Immediately Toby saw stains the arterial blood that had sprayed across the beige-painted living room wall. This was where Jacob's mother was attacked and ultimately killed by the knife-wielding maniac. A trail of crimson liquid continued down the short hallway that led to the two bedrooms and bathroom and the kitchen on the right.

When the bodies came into clear sight, Toby swayed on his feet. At the wooden kitchenette table was a big, muscular man with a beard wiping away the copious blood with a wet rag, cussing under his breath at the mess he had made… and was in the process of cleaning up.

Jacob's mother's mobile phone sat on the worktop. Mark Jenkins had retrieved it and searched for any messages that would link him to her death. She hadn't told a soul. She didn't particularly have many friends to confide in, save the other mums from Jacob's school. Her husband – Jacob's father – had filed for a divorce. He couldn't handle the responsibility of being a good husband and father even though other men would have given their weekly wages for both his wife and son. She had seen a flyer for the local gym and met Mark, who was a gym instructor, which rang a bell in Toby's head, and was helping her getting back into her physical prime.

'What a bastard!'

Mark finished cleaning the tiled floor of any traces of blood.

Toby saw the back door wide open and stepped outside.

The lawn had been dug up in two separate places. One grave for Jacob, the other for his mother.

Toby was shocked and amazed at the absurdity of the gym instructor Mark Jenkins. Not only had he brutally murdered a mother but her only child too. Then he'd gone further to dig them both graves in their own back yard and cleaning the blood all over the bungalow. It didn't make sense. Why didn't he just leave and let someone else discover the two bodies lying on the kitchen floor to be discovered.

Guilt?

Yeah, that made sense to Toby then. It answered everything. Mark had been drinking and had a short temper. Jacob's mother had laughed and mentioned Mark's crooked nose and he'd literally lashed out, slaying her and watching the bulging eyes that signalled the finality of his actions.

Killing Jacob was easy. The boy had been in his bedroom, in a world of his own, relaxing when Mark ended his life maniacally.

Toby watched Mark get up off his knees, having cleaned the tiled flooring of any sign of blood.

'That oughta do it,' Mark said, nodding in satisfaction at his endeavour.

Mark actually thought that he deserved approval for what he had done. Toby crossed the kitchen to him and whispered into his ear. 'You are a murderer, Mark Jenkins. Don't you forget it!'

Mark jolted involuntarily, his eyes wide and alarm creased his features.

'Who said that?'

Toby took a minute of pleasure seeing the look of horror on the gym instructor's face, fully aware that Mark's thundering heartbeat was just the start of his problems. Toby swore to himself he would bring Jacob and his mother justice in this world by aiding police capturing this sack of shit once and for all.

And what he noticed palpably was how much easier it was to do this and possess this kind of power than turning away from it.

Jacob had come to him seeking help.

Toby watched as Mark Jenkins raced out of the kitchen, down the hallway, out the front door and into his Porsche, frightened by his voice. He that is so big and strong cannot overpower things beyond nature. Mark Jenkins would be brought to justice once and for all. And Toby now discovered in himself that if it meant no longer living in obscurity, then that was a small price to pay.

15.

THE SUN was a golden yellow disk, shining its resplendent magic over the town below. Toby had walked into the town centre and informed his local constabulary of the crime at Number 5 Highland Close. Two police constables got into their patrol car with Toby in the back seat and drove away to the alleged crime scene. They questioned Toby right the way up the hill and pulled up alongside the kerb of Jacob's house.

'This is it,' Toby said, seeing the house bathed in the sunshine that he saw the night before.

The constables got out of the car and ambled down the tarmac driveway to the side entrance. The door was closed but unlocked. Toby had been told firmly to stay in the car and wait for them. He watched them try the handle and successfully open the door to the bungalow and disappearing inside.

It felt like an hour had passed until the officers emerged with pallid and shocked faces. That was all Toby needed to confirm that his visions from the night before were true and accurate. A part of him always wanted there to be no crime whatsoever so he could go to a therapist and get mental help from a therapist. However, his heart deflated and his shoulders slumped in disappointment.

The officer who had been riding shotgun was talking into his radio while the other constable got in and closed the door.

'You've got one helluva gift, kid,' he said, half in shock, half in awe of Toby's psychic powers.

'I only wish I could be ignorant and live my life in bliss,' Toby replied in earnest. 'Was it bad?'

'You prepared us for a shock, but until you see it for yourself, with your naked eyes, then it really does make the whole thing more real than any dream. No offence.'

Toby shook his head. 'None taken.'

'Mark Jenkins... that's who the murderer is, you said... right?'

Toby nodded. 'That's correct. He has short black hair and a beard. He has anger management issues and obviously can't take a half-hearted joke. He's worse than the shit you step in. He's the kind of animal who'll do the same thing again. He's not the type of person who learns from their mistakes. He'll deny it till he's blue in the face, but mark my words, someone like that desperately needs to be taken off our streets... sooner rather than later I might add...' The constable glanced at Toby in the rear-view mirror. 'Run it by me again. I'm totally amazed at what you're capable of doing. You said the deceased boy's spirit visited you and told you all this while you slept... in a dream... or hallucination?'

'Had I been wrong or confused,' Toby said, shifting uncomfortably in the back seat, 'Jacob and his mother would still be alive and I'd be taken to a mental hospital. I kinda wish I was crazy. But then if that was the case my own mother would be the one suffering being on her own. She needs me.'

'Have you told her about this? Have you told her about Second Sight?'

Toby shook his head. 'No. And she doesn't need to know either.'

The constable coughed into his balled-up hand. Then he said: 'You have to tell her, kid. She needs to know. She must have some idea anyway. After all, you've done this before a couple of times. My partner is asking for DI Sark to come and investigate this murder. He'll need to speak with you personally.'

Toby said that that was fine by him.

'You're a great kid, Toby,' the constable went on. 'You've brought justice to that woman – Danielle? – and those young women in the warehouse out of harm's way. You've single-handedly got murderers and kidnappers to be incarcerated. You're nothing short of a hero.'

Toby sighed and averted his gaze. 'I'm no hero. If I had it my way, I'd not want graphic visions in my head. I'm a gym instructor. That's my job. I love my job. It's fun. It's easy. And it makes youngsters turn away from drinking and drugs and gets them doing sports and going to the gym, getting fit and healthy. I didn't ask for nor want this psychic ability. But if it brings the perpetrators to justice and saves lives then I'm only too happy to help.'

*

Toby met with DI Sark and reiterated in specific detail what he had seen and was shown by the boy, Jacob, the night before. DI Sark went inside while the forensics were preserving crime scene work before coming back outside and talking with Toby some more. The detective dug a hand into his winter coat pocket and brought out a small business card. He handed it over to Toby, who was now standing on the kerb, his face turned to the sun and handed him the card.

*

'This isn't the first time you've helped us,' DI Sark said. 'I spoke with the police constable. He told me what you said in the car with him and I'm fully aware that your peace of mind is greatly disturbed by all of this. I sympathize with you. I don't imagine for one second this can be pleasant for you. If anything, am I right in saying it gets in the way of whatever plans you make in life?'
Toby said that indeed it did.
'Here's my card,' DI Sark said, proffering the card to Toby. 'It's got my desk phone number on it and my mobile. We're chasing down this Mark Jenkins chap. Do you want me to keep you updated with what's going on in the case? We may have to have you identify a line-up of men.'
'I don't want to know what happens from here on in,' Toby said, as he reluctantly pocketed the card. 'I gotta tell my mum about this. The day is disappearing from me. It's Saturday. I can walk home from here. I have to tell my mum about this. And then I'm gonna get some rest. I feel exhausted already… and I haven't even done anything today yet.'
'Yes, you have,' DI Sark said in a firm and undeniable voice. 'You have identified two victims and the name and description of this awful homicide. I can't thank you enough.'
'And you'll never have to…'

*

The fresh breeze cooled Toby's cheeks from the heat within, never mind the sunshine. As he strolled back down the hill and went under the mouldy viaduct, he made up his mind that he was going to speak to his mother about the events that caused him to disappear from the house without much explanation. She had a right to know. Also, Toby reminded himself that Annie Combs deserved an apology. It wasn't her fault he had this supernatural gift. He had the power of knowing long before she came on the scene. She had only been trying to help.

He reached the house and saw Abigail sweeping up the front yard of leaves and litter pedestrians had thrown away carelessly without much thought. Toby knew that this chore of picking up plastic bottles of Pepsi and empty beer cans irritated her immensely.

'Hey Mum!' Toby called out as he pushed up the brown gate.

Abigail looked up from her chore and took a couple of seconds to realise that it was her son seeking her undivided attention.

'Where did you go this morning?' she asked, upset and a tad angry.

'I had to go somewhere...' Toby began, quieting his mind for being vague. 'I need to tell you something in private. So finish up here and come and sit with me in the living room.'

Abigail raised an eyebrow. 'You haven't impregnated a girl, have you?'

Toby laughed aloud. 'No Mum. It's not that bad.'

'You're not gay, are you?'

'Eww. No Mum. Nothing as extreme as that, but it's still something you need to know. It'll explain my behaviour sometimes.'

Abigail finished sweeping up and retired to the shade the living room offered and sat down on the sofa next to the one Toby occupied.

'What is it? Are you ill?'

Toby shook his head. 'No.' He paused and considered his words instead of blurting something out inarticulately. 'Mum... I'm psychic.'

Abigail showed no expression. Her cold stare focused, unblinkingly on her son. Toby could see as bright as the day that Abigail was looking vacant – her mind drawing a blank. 'Last night I had visions of a murder scene. This morning I went to where the murder scene had taken place and reported to the police what I'd seen while in bed last night. Unfortunately for the boy and his mother they were both found dead. Murdered by a stranger in their home. Before that the newspaper you'd been impressed by of the hooded figure who saved the sex slaves a few blocks behind the rubbish dump and recycling depot, was also me. I got spotted in town and kept my identity concealed for as long as I possibly could before coming open to you and the local police force. CID are all over the scene and the name and identification of the murderer is to be investigated.... I'm sorry I didn't tell you sooner. I just didn't want you to worry about me, that's all.'

Abigail exhaled and finally blinked.

'I know this is kinda out of the blue info, but I just wanted to let you know. Nothing has changed though. I'm still plain old me. I don't understand how this can be, but there is someone like me who has this gift also. I gotta talk to her sometimes for advice and to get things off my chest.'

Abigail pulled the hem of her rose patterned blue dress down over her knees and cleared her throat. Toby could tell she was nervous and a bit overwhelmed by this announcement as anyone else would have been in the same circumstances.

'When you were born and the midwife gave you to me, wrapped in a woolly blanket, I knew you were going to be special...'

'Mum...' Toby complained. 'I'm not special. I'm just the same as anyone else. No different.'

'Let me finish,' Abigail snapped.

Toby raised his hands in surrender and leaned back, permitting his mum to speak without interruption.

'I knew you were gonna be special, not 'cause you were my child, my only child, and not 'cause the gynaecologist had informed me a year before that I couldn't have children, but 'cause I saw the clock on the wall telling me it was midnight. That's when you were born. It was also meaningful 'cause at the exact same time my father passed away, without me knowing at the time. And I remember gazing upon you and you opening your eyes which made me think of my father. The unity in that one special moment where my two favourite men in my life entered and exited the world.'

Toby sat in perfect silence, stunned beyond belief.

Abigail looked at him with tears brimming in her eyes. 'I always knew you were special. But I don't want to lose you too. My heart couldn't take it. You being here today is what keeps my hope alive that I'll see my father again some day, somewhere, somehow when the world finishes bleeding and the do-gooders like you bring peace to the innocent.'

Had Toby known the conversation would have been so magnificent and awe-inspiring he would have told his mother sooner.

'I got you something for a day like this,' Abigail said and told Toby to stay seated. She left the room and came back five minutes later with a brown paper bag and handed it to Toby who gratefully accepted it. He ripped the wrapping paper off and saw a Batman graphic novel. His mother knew he adored Batman and loved reading. This was the perfect gift. Something he instantly cherished and would value for the rest of his life.

'Batman is a hero, sweetheart,' Abigail said, resting her hand on top of his. 'You are a hero…'

16.

THE MORNING heavy downpour abated to a drizzle and eventually ceased as Tom and Kelly came out of the ten-storey glass and brick building that was the HQ of the *Evening Post* and got into the Ford Mondeo parked at the rear in the staff car park.

Kelly got behind the wheel and waited for Tom to climb in and checked he had batteries for his Dictaphone before fastening the safety harness across him.

'Sure now we got everything?' Kelly asked.

Tom patted himself down, reached over his shoulder for the A4 notepad, checked he had at least two pens prior to him giving his fellow journalist the "Thumbs Up" signal.

With that, Kelly released the handbrake, pulled out of the parking space and drove out onto the main road headed for their destination. Excitement filled the interior with a warmness neither one could have articulated. Once they broke free of the long line of vehicles waiting for the red light to turn to green and on their way out of the city, Kelly finally relaxed her grip on the steering wheel and leaned back.

'I bet if he's really psychic then he'll probably know we're on our way to his house,' Tom said.

Kelly laughed at that. 'Shit. I mean how the hell does he do it? He solved a crime and knew exactly which house Danielle's murderer lived in, doing months or years of police work in a matter of minutes. I mean, that's just awesome!'

Tom shrugged. 'Makes the police look like amateurs a bit though, wouldn't you say?'

Kelly could see where her colleague was coming from and concurred with him to a certain extent. 'Just think about all he could achieve if he has this his whole life? He'll be like a god or somethin'.'

The city was now behind them and the overgrown cedars and foliage bent over, creating a tunnel of nature. Kelly wound down the window and inhaled the sweet fragrance, savouring the fresh air blowing her hair back out of her face. She remained on the main road as she wasn't too familiar with the roads the further away from the city and into this new, small town. The SAT NAV helped her reach her destination and as she turned off the main road onto a 10mph road, Kelly lowered her gears to reduce her speed and gently ride the speed humps. According to the device she had to take a right turn and then the next right before she was on the correct street. From there it would be easy, and as the street came into view Kelly kept her speed low, indicating she was about to pull over and park alongside the kerb right outside a semi-detached house with the front door open and where a young, fit, smiling eighteen-year-old stood with his hand raised to greet them.

'That's him!' Kelly blurted out.

Tom detected the zeal of her exclamation and was fully aware that his blond-haired colleague had instantly been taken aback by Toby's smooth, unblemished face and muscular build. The young man stepped down and opened the gate for them.

The journalists got out of the Ford and ambled up to the gate where Toby was standing.

'Hi!' Kelly called out.

Toby reciprocated the greeting.

Tom proffered his hand and Toby shook it firmly, full of genuine confidence. 'It's nice to meet you, Toby,' Tom said, unable to conceal his awe.

'Same here,' Toby replied.

'Can we come in?' Kelly asked, wondering why Toby was standing at the garden path blocking their way to the front door.

Toby closed the gate behind him, glanced over his shoulder and said in a quiet but delightful voice, 'My mum is busy doing the cleaning. Would it be any trouble if we go to the lake and talk there?'

Kelly and Tom glanced at each other.

'No problem,' Tom said.

'Thank you.'

Kelly handed him a bundle of cash notes kept together by an elastic band. 'Here you go. There's twenty grand up front, like we promised.'

Toby offered Kelly and Tom a nod. 'That's awfully kind. I'll just go and put this somewhere safe before we get going. I'll sit in the back. The lake is not far from here but if you don't know the area it can be quite tricky. Plus, hardly anyone goes there so we'll have lots of privacy to discuss the crimes and what I can do.'

Kelly and Tom nodded. They were fully aware that Toby was giving them an exclusive story and could hardly wait. The story was already known across the nation. However, the *Post* was the first and only newspaper to secure a deal with Toby to tell his story. It was imperative to Tom and Kelly who had been searching for a big break ever since they had joined the *Post* seven years ago straight from college. This was front-page material that would give an insight into the workings of the mind of a local and national hero.

They got back in the car and waited for Toby to return.

He closed the front door behind him and the gate prior to taking a seat in the back of the car. 'Okay, let's go!'

*

They arrived at the lake at the foot of a mountain not far from the Fish & Chip Shop. Toby bought them all some lunch before they sat down at one of the picnic tables.

Once they had finished their food and wiped their greasy hands on the serviettes Tom pressed PLAY on the Dictaphone and waited for Toby to give his name, address and age, to confirm he was who he claimed to be for the record.

Kelly had not long wiped her mouth and put all the rubbish in the bin provided, her back to the calm, rippling lake, before beginning to speak. 'So, Toby,' she began. 'Can you please tell us first of all when and where you had your first psychic experience?'

Toby told them both how the first incident took place in the Men's Room at the local cinema. He explained how from there he began having very graphic and detailed visions that induced the flashbacks and subsequent seizure on that day. Initially the doctors had suspected that the seizure was due to him being under a lot of stress and pressure or that he might have early symptoms of epilepsy. He had taken prescription drugs to help him with anxiety and depression. However, Toby did state that he truly believed he had not suffered with anxiety or depression. The only hiccup in his peaceful life was the fact that his dad went out the front door one afternoon and never came back. But due to that befalling him, his mother, Abigail and himself had grown closer and weren't just mother and son but also best friends. Furthermore, the visions – or hallucinations – were proven to be precisely accurate in accordance with the first murder and discovering the body of the young and beautiful woman.

Kelly glanced at her colleague, both wearing impassive expressions, totally intrigued all of a sudden, beyond uttering exclamations of surprise, finding themselves lost in the grip of this boy's yarn.

'How did you feel when the body of the first victim was found?' Kelly asked.

'All I remember is what the lead detective that I assisted in solving this heinous murder crime told me. I wasn't elated or proud. I was left dumbfounded. I remember going back to school the following Monday and I didn't say a word until one of the teachers had leaked the story to my fellow students and all of a sudden I was this great celebrity being carried on the shoulders down the hallway. At first it was kinda fun, but then came the endless questions and comments. It drove me into a cycle of repetition. That's all folks talked about to me. Instead of a "well done" and letting me crack on with my schoolwork, as soon as I stepped over the threshold of every classroom where my education was held, I was treated like royalty. I mean, yes I solved a crime, brought a family the body of a dead loved one home for them to give a proper burial and sent a murderer to jail, but months had passed since that day. In the end I fainted outside a Maths classroom. They took me to the school nurse who got me checked out there and then before calling my mum. I had an MRI scan. Nothing untoward or malignant was found, which I was more than grateful for. But I told my mum, "The world is too big for me." I didn't know precisely what I meant by that remark besides the fact that I couldn't cope anymore. That was when my mum decided she would obtain all the coursework of the curriculum and let me study at home until I felt better to return.'

'That's how bad it was?' Kelly probed.

Toby nodded. 'It seemed as though the walls in the corridors were fluctuating and vibrating all around and beneath my feet. I could hear the whispers from downstairs that was going on upstairs between the girls. I know that sounds kinda cool, but it ain't. Due to graphic novels and animated films and action heroes with big muscles, it sounds like being me is awesome. A lot of the other boys who played sports started staring daggers at me 'cause girls they fancied were taken in by my super powers. But it's not the slightest bit funny: I could hear *everything* that was said about me!'

'Bloody hell!' Kelly couldn't help herself blurting out.

Toby stared at her fixedly. 'Yeah. It's not cool. It was as if I was no longer part of the human race, and that I had become some kinda demigod.'

Silence descended and Tom rubbed his face.

'How do you know who, what, where and when certain events take place, Toby?' Kelly asked.

Toby shrugged. 'It's not straightforward to explain. But it's just like you know your way home after work. You don't need a map or anyone giving you directions, you just *know* intuitively. But I get visions sometimes and certain voices from real people.'

'Does it hurt?'

Toby considered this question seriously. 'Uh, I don't think it's got anything to do with pain, as such. It's more like a distraction that just comes to me as though I'm a radio transceiver. It's not nice, as I've already said. It is very annoying and intrusive. It has an echo effect that if I don't listen to it or pay it any heed it gets even more deliberate. I suppose it might be similar to being God. I struggled with things like reading and doing my schoolwork. It also means that I'm always a victim to the 'calling card' of lost and depraved souls.'

Kelly glanced at Tom, then they both gave Toby a genuine sorrowful expression, slowly realising that not only did this young spiritualist experience awful sights and sounds through no fault of his own, but he was also deprived of a good, fresh life. And that he would always be looking over his shoulder in case he was called upon, hoping and praying that that would cease and give him his life back so he could enjoy it while he still had a life.

'Does it feel great though? You know, like when you saved those young women from being sex slaves and bringing the traffickers to justice? It is one helluva achievement.' She asked this for two reasons. One: she wanted to keep this interview going for as long as possible. And two: the only way to do this was to change the tempo and introduce a positive impetus to Toby's story.

'It does,' Toby said, exhaling deeply. 'But I don't want this for ever. I don't look at it like an achievement. It's more like me just being there at the right time and right place and doing what any other good human being would do.'

'Well, that's incredibly humble of you, Toby,' Tom said, looking him directly into his eyes.

'People will be indebted to you,' Kelly added.

'People don't owe me anything,' Toby said. 'I'm just doing the right thing, but don't consider myself a hero. I love my job and want to immerse myself with that entirely, if I have the choice.'

'What do you do?'

'I'm a gym instructor,' Toby replied with a thin smile. 'I work with kids and elderly people in doing weights, cardiovascular and other sports, like netball, basketball, rugby and of course, football. I like to see youngsters running around, playing, having fun and exercising. It does them the world of good. I enjoy the whole process of watching them improve and feel better over the course of months and being happy and more confident in themselves. It's rewarding, plus I do get paid. So it's all good, if ya ask me.'

Kelly could see that merely talking about his profession, Toby felt the pressure lifting off his shoulders, allowing him to become more alert and upbeat.

'What about the recent discovery of the young boy and his mother being slain by Mark Jenkins? Can you tell us a little bit about that?'

Toby reminded himself that although instinctively he wanted to end the interview with him feeling a tad better these journalists had paid him a hefty amount of cash. He had to play their game. And the sooner he did this without hesitation the better for everyone.

'Yeah, of course,' Toby said after deliberating the incidents that led him to the discovery of the two victims of murder and the name of the killer. He told Kelly and Tom about how he had been in bed, asleep, but awake at the same time.

He went on to explain how the dead boy, Jacob, had come to him and beckoned for him to come outside and follow him to the crime scene. Toby explained how he was unsure whether it had been a dream, hallucination, or for real. That's how his senses responded to Jacob and how he entered the bungalow and so the macabre scene that Mark Jenkins had done, decorating the walls with arterial spray before leaving and heading back home, truly believing that he had got away with his crimes and would go unpunished.

Kelly and Tom could not hide their shock.

'What happened when you found out it was for real?'

Toby shifted uncomfortably on the timber bench and regarded Kelly once more. 'It's not a nice feeling at all,' he said. 'All of a sudden the world around you, above you and beneath you starts to undulate like your whole being is being swept away into the tidal wave that is invisible.

'I keep thinking that all this knowledge I have now, in my head, causes me to feel faint or like I'm gonna have a seizure. The sensation is horrible. I keep thinking that every time it happens I'm gonna die. I feel tired and groggy and require much rest in my bed. It's as if being in bed after one of those incidents makes me feel warm and comforted; that if I do die then it'll be all right. I know that sounds extreme, but if nothing else you take away from this interview, you must realise that there is nothing awesome about having all this knowledge. Hence why I love my occupation. When I'm not getting voices or visions and I'm in the gym, life for me is brilliant. I'm not on lots of money, but I contribute to the mortgage and other bills. And together, me and my mother get by. She brought me up single-handedly and needs me around the house to help do the chores and run errands. That's one of the reasons why I couldn't allow you into my home today. My mother gets scared very quickly. God knows what she'd be like on her own. She needs me. This whole thing scares her. The most important thing is she loves me no matter what. She doesn't rebuke me for little things like not wiping my feet. She's not overbearing. She just enjoys my company. And that goes both ways.'

Kelly asked a few more questions. Toby did his best to give clear and concise answers and was glad when Tom turned the Dictaphone off. Kelly asked if she could take a portrait photograph for the paper, to which Toby was reluctant to acquiesce, but finally surrendered to.

Tom thanked him for their lunch and then they all shook hands.

When they arrived back at Toby's house, he got out of the back seat, wished them farewell and then went inside where Abigail was waiting for him in the living room.

17.

THE GLORIOUS SUNSHINE spread its splendour on the small town of Skewen, and Abigail finished wiping the kitchen worktop before making herself a cup of tea. When the front door opened and the familiar size and shape of her only child entered, her heart leapt with comfort and excitement.

'I'm in the kitchen, sweetheart,' Abigail called out.

Toby entered the living room and ambled through the doorway into the kitchen looking bright and fresh from the cool air and natural warmth.

'How'd it go?'

Toby pulled a chair out and sat down. 'It went well,' he said after a couple of deep breaths. 'I guess I can go without obscurity for awhile. Tomorrow Detective Inspector Sark wants to meet me briefly to discuss something; I'm not sure what, though.'

'Oh.' That was all Abigail said and concern masked her features.

'It's nothing to worry about, Mum,' Toby said, fully aware that his mother was becoming very sensitive while he was getting stronger and more comfortable within himself. He had a job that he enjoyed immensely and now had a supernatural ability to receive visions and dead people coming to him, knowing that he alone could aid them in bringing justice. It did scare him, but he supposed that he must be quite strong himself for not freaking out and yelling and screaming at the top of his lungs. Instead he went through a calming procedure. He always remembered to breathe slowly and surely and to use mindfulness, (which consisted of living in the moment) to get his mind back to a safe place where he was at peace.

'You're growing into a strong man very quickly,' Abigail said, with a sense of disappointment in her tone. For Abigail loved to be in charge and look after Toby and not the other way around. She was very protective of him and had to admit that at times like these she became frightened for his overall wellbeing. In her mind, it was incomprehensible how her son managed to cope.

The gift/curse that had been bestowed onto Toby was not from her or Toby's wayward father. It didn't come from her mum and dad either. It pained her that Toby had to stop everything in order to help a complete and utter stranger from being hurt or killed. Abigail supposed she was being selfish and over the top motherly. But what else could she be? She couldn't be something she wasn't. She was made this way, and she had decided that when Erik had done the disappearing act that she had no choice but to take the reins and work long hours in the sewing factory to provide for herself and her only child.

Now that Toby had finally secured a job every week to help pay the bills, it seemed as though fate was now dragging him away from her affection and motherly instincts. She didn't like to dwell on this subject for too long, although it seemed awfully strange that now that she and Toby could start enjoying things in their life this psychic thing should turn up unannounced like a stranger in a party, a stranger to the host and all the guests.

'You all right, Mum?' Toby asked.

Abigail nodded.

'You don't want me to be psychic, do you?' Toby asked, watching his mother's tired eyes brimming with tears.

'I just want some kinda normality, that's all, my love.'

Toby nodded. 'Yeah, I know. But we got some extra money now and we can pay the bills for the next couple of months. And this "Shine" isn't going to be all the time, anyway. We can still have fun... and do stuff together. I know things have been hard for you, but it is my belief that things will get better for us both.'

Abigail took a long sip of her steaming tea and then waved her hand in a dismissive manner. 'Don't listen to me,' she said. 'You're growing up into the man you're going to be for the rest of your life. I'm just being silly.'

'You're not being silly, Mum,' Toby said, reaching out for Abigail's hands. 'It'll be front page news in the papers tomorrow. I'll get you a copy. But don't go worrying about me too much. I got things under control. Remember, people die every day. Even now, somewhere in the world, someone is dying. It's sad. Of course it is, but if you stopped to think about that fact and felt sorry for souls you've never known then you're gonna be a nervous wreck. I can't be sensitive like you. I gotta just go out through that front door every morning and go to work and do the best job I can. And that's all you can do. I do appreciate you as a person and as a great mother. But you gotta put yourself first. If you can do that then everything else will fall into place. And then you'll be able to enjoy life again and have some fun... How's that?'

Neither of them said anything.

However, what Toby had just said rang true in Abigail's mind. She looked at her only child with a resurgence of love and admiration at how he'd just broken down the basics and then effortlessly brought them back up again in a lucid and positive way that left her speechless.

'What does it feel like when you solve a crime by just knowing?'

'There's a profound sadness and a rush of adrenaline that courses through my veins. I have to come to terms with the fact that a death has occurred and realise that that aspect has nothing to do with me and therefore I am free from guilt. Once the initial horror is out of the way I listen to the voices in my head giving me the information required to bring justice to the recently deceased.'

You're a receiver?'

Toby nodded. 'I have a brain just like yours, Mum,' Toby said. 'But my mind has developed this "Shine" which enables me to pick up on things that I have no business knowing. It is scary, but I'm learning as I go.'

Abigail shook her head. 'I don't know what to say.'

'Don't say anything,' Toby said and gave his mum a big smile that lit up his eyes.

'I worry about you too much, do you know?'

Toby nodded. 'I pick up on it. So please, try not to. I'm okay. All I need is a roof over my head and something to eat when I get home from work. I like routine. I never used to. I used to get bored, but what with this "Shine" I wish I could go back to living like a normal human being again. But there are horrors out there in the world we live in that can't be ignored.

And if I can, I'll assist in doing everything I can to help the police find the criminals and put them away for a long time.'

This time Abigail smiled broadly. 'I was right about you being a hero,' she said.

Toby rolled his eyes in mock frustration. 'If you say so...'

*

DI Sark sat at the far table of the café reading the front-page article of *The South Wales Evening Post*. He was engrossed in the article and when he finished reading it, he folded the paper in half and whistled in amazement. The CID could definitely benefit from this young, bright and very handsome spiritualist who had already solved crimes and convicted the bad guys from a young, tender age.

The waitress crossed the tiled floor and placed his English breakfast in front of him. He thanked her, took a long drag of his coffee and then chopped up his sausages. The food was hot so he let it cool down before devouring it.

He consulted his wristwatch. 8:12AM.

DI Sark was waiting for Toby to arrive at the café at twenty minutes past eight before he went to work at the gym at 9:00AM.

Toby arrived at precisely 8:20AM and ambled over to the table where the detective was seated.

'Hey! How're you doing?'

'Not too bad, kid. Not too bad. Take a seat.'

Toby sat opposite the detective. They made weather chat for a couple of minutes. Then Toby grew weary of the preamble. 'What did you want to see me about?'

DI Sark washed down his breakfast and leaned back, knitting his fingers together on both hands and smiled broadly. 'I got an offer for you.'

'What kind of offer?' Toby wanted to know.

DI Sark licked his lips. The waitress arrived at the table and picked up the plate. She asked if Toby wanted anything. The young man asked if he could get a can of Diet Pepsi. DI Sark told the waitress that he'd get the kid his drink out of the ten-pound note he handed to her, which she pocketed. He waited until she walked away behind the counter before he turned his attention back to Toby.

'How'd you like a job assisting the CID Homicide Department?'

Toby's eyebrows went up as his eyes grew large and round in sincere surprise.

'Interested?' DI Sark said, hoping he would nod and say yes.

Toby shook his head, his wide-eyed expression still plastered on his face. Then he leaned forward on his forearms. 'That sounds really great 'n all,' he said.

'But you're not interested?'

'It's not that,' Toby said. 'As you already know, I can solve crimes and bring wrongdoers to justice without the aid of any police training, which of course is to my and your advantage, but it doesn't work like that. I mean, how many crimes are being committed as we sit here and talk? A lot. I don't sit in my room gathering information and then acting righteously upon it. You're getting me confused with God.

'The last case frightened the shit outta me,' Toby went on. 'I know my supernatural power sounds really cool, but believe me it's not. I already have a job. And I'm relatively happy.'

'What's your job?'

Toby explained briefly that he was a gym instructor and coach at the local academy.

DI Sark nodded approval, seeing now how broad and muscular his young friend was. 'The force could really use your powers to help crack down on crime. If you have these precognitive powers you can help us clean up this town and the city in next to no time. Imagine that? No crime. You'll be able to walk the streets day or night and not be afraid of some young punk stabbing you in the back.'

Sighing, Toby nodded. He knew where DI Sark was coming from, but he also knew that pigs couldn't fly even if they'd drunk a can of Red Bull. Thinking of cans, the petite waitress placed the can on the table in front of Toby and offered him a thin-lipped smile.

'I don't always get the info before it happens,' Toby continued. 'Sometimes I get flashes of eclectic visions and voices. Sometimes I go into seizures after seeing God-awful things. That's not to say I refuse to help you, but I have to make sure that what I'm seeing and hearing is real before I can act upon it. I'm afraid I can be of no service to you or the force, but if I pick up anything tangible again, I'll tell you.'

'Do that,' DI Sark said.

'I will. I promise.'

'Can I ask though… What is it like to be psychic?'

'Don't envy me,' Toby said in a firm, unwavering tone. 'When it comes it's like Satan himself has opened the gates of hell for you to enter. Definitely not recommended.'

DI Sark wiped his mouth with the napkin and shuffled back into his long raincoat.

'I'm not the only one,' Toby said out-of-the-blue.

'Oh?'

'Yeah. There's this psychic called Annie Combs. She gets visions the same as me, but she's getting too old to be able to do anything about crimes committed. At least I got my job. Otherwise I'd go insane and wind up in Cefn Coed.'

'That bad, is it?' DI Sark said, fully aware that this young man with the whole world waiting for him to live out his life suffered so much.

'Ignorance is bliss,' Toby said.

Ignorance is bliss, DI Sark repeated in his mind and took his leave…

PART TWO

18.

DARKNESS had cloaked the sky. The moon illuminated the town below. A taxi cab pulled up alongside the kerb and a short, petite woman with shoulder-length brown hair climbed out onto the tarmac footpath after paying the driver her fare. The taxi pulled away and Susan Cawthorne turned and ambled down the quiet street before turning left, entering the town centre.

The gentle breeze gusted and orange and brown autumn leaves skittered around her feet. Susan let out a small titter at this, always immersed with nature, especially when it came to the four different seasons and wildlife.

All day she worked as a receptionist for a local law firm and by night she studied Literature with her close friends who had met in Neath Library opposite Victoria Gardens.

Susan reached the terrace-house street and let herself into her home, sighing in relief as she removed her shoes and winter coat. Then she proceeded into the living room area and wondered where her only son, Matthew, was and what he was doing. She called out to him and Matthew materialised at the top of the narrow staircase.

'Oh, hi, my lovely,' Susan chimed, gazing up at her reason to have so much zest for life. 'Mum's sorry she's late. Have you had something to eat already? Or would you like me to do you something?'

Matthew descended two steps and the yellow light from the hallway revealed the boy's thick, blond hair and unblemished features of the ten-year old. 'I did myself one of those microwave beef dinners.'

'Are you sure that's enough? Are you still hungry?'

Matthew shook his head firmly. 'No. I'm fine. Thank you.'

'How was school?'

'Same as always,' Matthew said, evidently not interested in this discussion or any other with his mother or anyone else for that matter.

'Friday tomorrow, precious,' Susan said with a smile.
Matthew offered a thin smile.
'I was wondering if you'd like to do something on the weekend? Or have you made plans?'
Susan seriously doubted that her son had made any plans. However, he always appeared to love being in his bedroom alone, reading or doing push-ups and sit-ups. He was very taut around the chest, back and abdomen than was natural for anyone else his age group.
'Aren't the soaps on soon for you?' Matthew asked his mother, changing the subject entirely on purpose.
Susan nodded in agreement.
'Well, as long as you're all right,' she said, a little sadness in her voice. 'I'm gonna do myself a curry and watch the soaps. Fancy some Naan bread for supper?'
Matthew shook his head once and that was enough. 'No. I'm all right. You chill out. That's what I'm doing. Maybe go to the park Saturday and play Miniature Golf.'
Susan's eyebrows rose simultaneously. 'Really?'
'Why so surprised?' Matthew asked, knowing full well why, which was why he decided to throw an ace into the hole and take his unsuspecting mother onto another avenue, throwing her off course. 'You think I'm embarrassed being seen with you in public?'
Susan blushed but not in a good natural way. She suddenly realised that her son had had to say that because he thought that that was her way of thinking. She silently chastised herself, and then decided to pounce on this rare opportunity to bond with her son. 'How about we go to HMV in Swansea on Sunday and I give you a tenner to buy a DVD?'
'You got yourself a deal,' Matthew said, wearing a crooked smile. This time it was his turn to be surprised.
Susan walked into the kitchen and Matthew returned to his bedroom and sat down at the Oakwood desk his mother bought him as he had an interest in writing. Then he picked up the pen and began writing in his A4 notepad anything and everything that came into his young mind.

I dream of killing pets first and taking a bone as a souvenir. Those damn cats next door climb our fence and strut around the back yard as if they own the territory. That old bitch lets them out to do whatever mischief they want to without consequences. Well, that's soon gonna change, you mark my words. I killed a rat in school. Dirty fucking rodents, spreading disease wherever they go. Sidney saw me do it with my new pellet gun that belonged to her old man. It felt really good killing that dirty rat and ending the disease-spreading furball. But now I have a taste for it not to mention good reason, I want to do some more hurting. The pellet gun is good for not getting your hands dirty but it ain't good enough to kill those two damn cats. No. I gotta be nice to those cats, lure them in with treats, sweet-talking, plenty of friendly smooths until they relax. Then I'll put 'em outta their misery and restore some stability and peace. God how I hate those cats and rats. At least with a dog, it's still got the brain capacity to listen and obey your commands. I wanna kill again. The world is overpopulated and run down by lazy bastards and dirty fucking rats the lot of 'em. The world needs people like me. They'll hate me for the things I do, but in time they'll come to love me and understand why I gotta do what I gotta do.

  Jean would have kittens (which I'd kill) if she knew this or if I told her. But all I'm doing is keeping heaven and hell stocked with fresh souls to do whatever the angels and demons want.

  Mum's gonna be shocked if she reads my notepad, but I'm only writing down my biggest, deepest desires to contain my excitement and to hide it from those who'll think I outta be locked up in an asylum for kids. I can't let that happen. No sir. I gotta get to reading my books from the library and watching those documentaries of serial killers. One has gotta learn his craft before reaching the summit of his/her ecstasy.

Matthew finished writing. Then he closed the notepad and put it under his bed where he believed it would be safe and out of sight and reach for any intruder to stumble upon. His mother would be treated like an intruder also.

He went downstairs and sat with his mother talking and having a good time. It was in those moments when he was in the company of his mother and school friends that Matthew's soul shone. Perhaps if someone did happen to come across his notepad or talk to Sidney Knight then one might easily have mistaken the notes to have been written by someone else. For one thing, the prose was very mature and couldn't have been more eloquent than the writings of an educated madman.

The following day Matthew and his mother, Susan, played Miniature Golf in the public park then headed to Burger King. And Matthew wasn't, even for one second, intrigued or thought about his notepad. He was too busy being a ten-year-old boy with his birthday coming up in five weeks' time.

Five years ago his father died from lung cancer which left him and Susan all alone. He reminded himself during the night before knocking the light off that he must savour these precious moments now and for ever. Because as harsh as it might sound, the world was full of nasty surprises in itself. For Matthew Cawthorne to have the desires to add to that would be catastrophic and uncharacteristic. Furthermore, the strain he'd put under his own dear mother would break her whole. She would never recover from her husband departing so early and unexpectedly. God knew what state her mind would be in if Matthew did grow up and live out his very dark fantasies.

He killed the bedroom light and lay in the pitch-dark awaiting sleep, remembering the day's events and how much fun he'd had with his mum before finally drifting off.

Matthew Cawthorne had been born to a married couple who always wanted a child of their own. To Susan, Matthew was the last survivor. The cancer may have killed her soul mate but she was insistent that his spirit lived on inside his only child. Mercifully, Susan knew nothing of Matthew's troubled thoughts or plans for the future. As far as she was concerned, her son was her whole world, and nothing was going to separate him from her. The love she experienced today magnified her true, inner emotions.

As soon as her head touched the pillow, Susan fell into a deep, relaxing slumber…

*

Matthew ambled down the footpath in a world of his own, pondering the weather and his new piece of weapon. He had bought a Stanley knife from Sidney Knight's father for two quid and had it in his possession as he stared at the ground, looking for possible prey. He fancied a squirrel and pleaded inwardly for one to appear within sight so he could hunt it down and do what he loved doing since he was a ten-year-old boy.

The damn cats that his neighbour owned had been trespassing in his back yard and as he emerged from the back door, Matthew saw one of them in his peripheral sight. He did not hesitate. He sprinted across the grass and dived dramatically across the lawn just as the Tabby was bending itself to make its way through the undergrowth back to its own territory. His fingers dug into the cat's side and Matthew felt the cat's ribs and squeezed causing it to cry aloud. Then he lunged further still until he had a better, firmer grasp of the feline. By the creature's neck, Matthew dragged it, kicking and crying towards himself.

The cat's claws were visible and it took a swipe at Matthew's face, slitting open his flesh and drawing a line of blood. Matthew touched his face where he felt liquid trailing and became instantly incensed by the sight of his own blood. This took the set of circumstances to a whole different level. Matthew now seized the furry creature by the throat and tightened his vice-like grip and saw the creature's eyes bulge in agony and terror.

'There ya go, ya little fucker,' Matthew drawled, sneering at the innocent thing before mercifully snapping its neck with a god-awful crunch.

The cat deflated. All energy sapped out of its confines. It hung limp in his grasp... and Matthew smiled from ear-to-ear.

Then he looked up as he let the dead pet collapse in a heap on the ground and caught sight of his mother standing by the rear entrance, her yawning mouth in a shape of an O. Pure disbelief and horror etched across her features.

That was the day Matthew Cawthorne's childhood ended.

In later years he would call it the day the and his mother no longer loved each other...

19.

HEIDI JOHNSTON marvelled at the glorious rainbow as she slowed the Fiat into a lower gear and entered the gravel-stricken car park outside Cefn Coed Mental Institution. She removed a two-litre bottle of Diet Coke and crossed the spacious lot around to the front of the edifice, climbed the stone steps and pushed open the door at the reception desk.

Millie White, fresh from college, was seated at her desk going through and updating her files, seeing how many patients on her system matched the number of names on a sheet of A4 paper giving this week's tally. She looked up, removed her trendy spectacles and offered Heidi a gorgeous smile that magnificently lit up her eyes.

'Yes? How may help you?'

Heidi smiled but lacked the vigour and effort Millie had before speaking. 'I'm the psychosis therapist looking for Matthew Cawthorne. I believe he's staying in the East Wing. Is that right?'

'I'll just check for you now,' Millie said. Then she killed her page and opened the East Wing files of all patients to confirm or deny the patient's name for clarification procedures.

Heidi waited patiently, admiring the old train clock and glanced at the posters regarding health and wellbeing for anyone, mostly with mental health or drink and drug addicts. She turned back towards the lovely receptionist who met her gaze.

'Yes,' Millie said. 'He is here in the East Wing. May I take your name so I can contact the day doctor, please?'

'Heidi Johnston,' Heidi declared with a hint of pride. 'I'm the therapist from Tonna Hospital assigned to the case subject whose name I've given you. We have an appointment at 2:00PM. But I need to see the councillor Rahaeesh Komma. I have his number on me.'

Millie waved her off and picked up the phone, dialled the councillor's number and waited for the ringing to cease and for the doctor's voice to break through.

'Oh hi, Mr Komma,' Millie began. 'I have Heidi Johnston here. She says she has an appointment with Matthew Cawthorne. Would you like me to send her to you so she can formally introduce herself with Matthew Cawthorne, case number 005?'

Millie nodded and then placed the receiver back on its cradle. 'Do you need directions to the East Wing?'

Heidi shook her head. 'No. That's fine. Thank you. It's around the back where there were construction workers finishing off some fancy brickwork. Thank you, anyway.'

'You're welcome,' Millie said and watched Heidi leave, noticing the therapist's broad calves and long winter coat.

*

Rahaeesh Komma sat behind his varnished mahogany desk; hands knitted together with interlaced fingers, listening to Heidi discuss her credentials and queries in regard to the patient for an update. Rahaeesh Komma had explained in detail about how the staff found Matthew Cawthorne's presence to be deeply disturbing and frightening.

'Why is that?' Heidi asked, perplexed.

Rahaeesh shrugged. Then he tried to elaborate and suggested that times were hard in the world itself and often the quiet and calm of sedated patients brought relief to them. All the patients were deeply disturbed or had mental health issues. Some were so out of it they could barely stand let alone answer questions or have the capacity to engage in conversation with anyone.

'Initially the staff members believed that it was the high dose of medication that induced this eerie silence and abandonment from Matthew. I recall the day he came here and his mother and I had a formal chat. She told me of the day her son died by breaking the neck of their neighbour's cat. After that she and Matthew stared at each other, one in utter shock and devastation, the other calm and silent.

'Susan Cawthorne told me she didn't remember breaking the paralysis she was in, but recalled later how she found herself out in the front yard, trembling uncontrollably. Her neighbour, a fifty-nine-year-old heavy-set woman, burst outside and ran to her rescue and comforted her.

'She doesn't know what happened next or what she'd said, but before she knew it the ambulance arrived and came to her aid. She was in a state of shock and couldn't speak. Outside and beyond the window she felt the earth move. Of course it didn't; she was feeling faint or may have demonstrated side effects that would suggest epilepsy. She said she could see glittering stars pass by her vision and truly believed that she'd pass out and never be resuscitated ever again.

'High on medication, Susan was transferred to Ward F and lay in bed all day half in, half out of this comatose state of mind. A police officer in uniform arrived and asked one of the Sisters if he could ask her some questions. The nurse only permitted it if she could be there in case Susan started to react negatively.

'Susan told me she didn't recall telling the PCSO what had caused her sudden breakdown. She did however say that her son had died that day, and when the police went to the house there was no one at home. Then they contacted the grandparents and they also said that they had not seen Matthew for a couple of months. They were shocked by the circumstances that had caused such trauma and grief and made their way to Neath/Port Talbot Hospital to be with their daughter and to try and get to the bottom of the story. If Matthew was indeed dead then there was no wonder that Susan had gone into shock and was in hospital.

'She did tell them what she'd seen and reiterated that her son was dead. When her father asked who or what had killed Matthew, Susan explained she meant spiritually.'

Heidi listened attentively, intrigued by the facts of this story.

'When was he found? And where?'

Rahaeesh took a sip of water before resuming. 'Approximately a month later, Matthew was discovered in a McDonald's restaurant eating a large quarter pound meal when two uniforms identified him and entered the restaurant. Matthew sat there calmly and didn't flinch or glance at them with fear or concern. Instead he washed his food down with a large Diet Coke. The officers sat opposite them in the same booth and told him his mother was in hospital and had reported that he was "dead". Matthew fought the urge to laugh. Then he said he was sorry to hear his mum had thought that; then the uniforms told him that she meant in a religious sense, because he'd killed his neighbour's cat.

'He neither confirmed or denied that fact. The police asked him to come quietly with them to the police station and got in touch with DI Sark who would interview him and tell him he had the right to have an attorney. Matthew didn't contact a solicitor. Instead he waited in an interview room for the plain-clothed officer to arrive and begin the investigation.

'Matthew never said a word to DI Sark or anyone else for that matter. He was put in jail for the night and then brought out for questioning, thinking that one night alone in a dingy cell would be uncomfortable enough for him to snap out of his trancelike state and start answering questions and assisting the local authorities with their investigation.

'DI Sark asked if he understood what was happening and that it was in his best interest to cooperate otherwise there would be a police record on his name for life.

'Matthew didn't flinch or speak. He simply stared at the detective for a whole hour. DI Sark said it was quite an incredible feat and decided to have Matthew transferred here indefinitely where he'd receive medication, a cell and three square meals a day.'

Heidi absorbed every single detail and then made some notes on her writing pad. 'Has he spoken since?'

Rahaeesh shook his head. 'He's like a zombie. He doesn't talk or even react.'

'Is he managing functionally?'

'Oh, mark my words, Matthew is fully aware of his surroundings. He eats, sleeps and walks methodically. It's as if his mother saying that he is spiritually dead is accurate. Perhaps her diagnosis was the final breaking point of her son and the start of an entity taking over his mind, body and soul altogether.'

Heidi contemplated what she would say next and how she believed she could be an asset and not a hindrance in this delicate case. 'I think I'd like to see him today and assess him to see if there is any point for me to take on this case. The reason I ask is out of concern for the other patients. He clearly depicts a young man having lost his identity. I would like to speak with him and then maybe arrange a meeting with his mother who will have another perception of the patient. How does that sound?'

Rahaeesh nodded. 'That sounds like a sensible option. I shall give you Mrs Cawthorne's contact details after you have introduced yourself to Matthew and see if there is a possibility for further assessment.'

'Marvellous,' Heidi said and rose, admiring the framed canvas painting of Death Valley and briefly wondering if Matthew liked art, as that was another helpful option for one's mental state.

*

The muscle-bound male nurse unlocked the cell door and asked for Dr Komma and Heidi to wait in the corridor while he went in and put Matthew in handcuffs and chained his ankles to the chair to stop any movements or lashing out at the therapist. Matthew complied and sat at the desk. The barred window permitted four streaming slants of sunshine into the otherwise dark cell.

The nurse informed Heidi that he would wait outside and his colleague would be monitoring the interview from the security room down the hall on the left from the reception area. She thanked him immensely and pulled out a chair and sat down and faced the patient who gave her the schizophrenic stare that made the tiny hairs on the nape of her neck bristle.

'Hello,' Heidi began. 'My name is Heidi Johnston. I'm a therapist and I'm here today to see if we can make some progress with your current situation. I'm fascinated with your case and wondered and hoped I could be of some assistance in dealing with your situation and getting all the best preparation to aid you into making a full recovery. 'Cause, let's face it, you don't want to live out your life inside a padded cell because of one mistake, do you?'

Matthew Cawthorne showed no signs of emotion and instead sat back in his chair looking right through her. Not vacant, but dead to this conversation and this kind lady who only wanted to help him get back to normal and have a healthy life.

Heidi silently acknowledged that Dr Rahaeesh Komma's file and diagnosis regarding this young, troubled patient was accurate right down to the final detail.

'I appreciate that you have chosen not to talk, but really the main reason I am here is to see if I can get through to you, in spite of all the sedative medication you are on and help express yourself and find a solution. You can trust me. There is no confidentiality at this time. Today is more of a formal introduction. I shall attend every day between 10:00am and 11:00am and every session will last approximately an hour or more if I can gain your trust enough that you will finally break your silence, which isn't good for you. I hope you don't mind me saying so, but if you do show no signs or engage in the slightest way beneficial and you are stubborn enough to be spiteful to your own wellbeing then being incarcerated will become all that you see in life. And you're still very young and life will last a long time.'

Matthew focused his eyes on Heidi, breaking his impassive stare to a present silence but recognition towards her.

Heidi smiled. 'Hi! How are you today?'

An ever so small quiver of the lips very nearly hinted at a half smile, but vanished in the next moment.

'It's okay,' Heidi said, trying to be reassuring. 'It's okay to be a bit nervous or scared. You don't have to speak if you don't want to. Listening and being present, here in the moment with me, is a big step forward. You are a child who made a mistake. That's all. Everyone makes mistakes. I make about a dozen every day. Probably make more mistakes than you. But because I tune myself into the world around me, I am able to function in what is considered by today's standards as "normal".

'It's nice to meet you, Matthew,' Heidi said and gave him an enamel-white smile that reached her eyes. She didn't offer her hand in case he reacted. As of yet, she still didn't know how he would react to any physical gesture no matter how instinctive.

'Over the next three months I shall have a daily file on your case in regards to your progress. We will need to trust one another. And if you do begin to talk fluently with me during these sessions then I might ask if you can have a session outside in the summer without handcuffs. Today is just a precaution. I know that's easy for me to say. After all, I'm not the one who is incarcerated for having a troubled mind. However, if your behaviour improves and you do open up then I shall reward you.'

'I hated those cats...' Matthew said in a croaky voice that grilled his throat.

Heidi heard him and couldn't help being stunned into her own silence momentarily. 'Yes, I know. Your doctor and I have read your diary and you did kill your neighbour's pet. That was bad. But you are young and you made a big mistake. My job is to help you rectify that type of behaviour and help you turn away from thinking and doing things like that; after all, if repeated, such behaviour could see you behind bars for the rest of your days and you surely don't want that. The only way out those doors, out of this psychiatric hospital, is to change the way you think, having thoughts that ultimately become your actions, which is why you are here today.'

'I understand,' Matthew said.

Heidi nodded. 'Well, it's great that you've already started talking. That's more than I expected. So, we're headed in the right direction; that's a start.'

Matthew averted his gaze and Heidi watched him as he studied the linoleum.

'What's the matter?' Heidi asked, quite concerned and encouraged at the same time.

'My mother will never forgive me...' he said.

Heidi bit down on her tongue as she very nearly said that his mother would forgive him because she loved him more than anything else in the world. However, she had read the file and was fully aware that Susan Cawthorne had gone into shock at witnessing her son breaking the cat's neck for no apparent reason.

'Would you like to see your mother again?'

Matthew heard the question but did not give an answer.

'My mother disowns me.'

'I'm sure that isn't the case, Matthew,' Heidi said. 'She just needs a little time to get over the incident, that's all.'

'She thought of me as her little angel,' Matthew said in a faraway voice. 'But when she saw me kill that thing, trespassing in our garden, I instantly became the devil himself. I did her a favour. At least now there ain't no cat shit in the soil bed.'

20.

DR KOMMA was seated on his swivel desk chair going through some data on the computer when a knock rapped on the sturdy oak door.

'Come in!' he said loud enough for the person on the other side to hear him.

The door opened slowly and Heidi poked her head around the frame. 'Can I come in?'

'Of course,' the doctor said, surprised to see her, assuming she would have gone straight home after being ignored by the patient.

Heidi sat down opposite him and cleared her throat before speaking. 'May I ask for a copy of the file of Matthew Cawthorne, please?'

Dr Komma stopped typing, hit the SAVE button and then reclined. 'Yes, of course. What happened?'

'I got him to talk,' Heidi said, quite proud of herself for achieving such a feat and the doctor raised his perfect black eyebrows.

'I'm impressed, Ms Johnston,' he said, nodding and smiling approvingly. 'What did he say?'

'He openly admitted to killing the neighbour's cat and said he hated them playing in his backyard. I know it isn't much, but I think he demonstrated proper human emotions.'

Dr Komma listened attentively, yet remained in control both professionally and psychologically. 'That's an excellent start, Ms Johnston. However, we must keep in mind that Matthew may not have murdered anyone but he did kill a rat at school and the cat. In his diary he also wrote of his other innermost desires to escalate a death rate to human beings also. I have gone through the footage of his cell in the monitoring surveillance room. He often sits still for hours on end without any emotion, day or night. He sleeps... and then after breakfast he sits in his chair in his cell and doesn't move. He doesn't even flinch. It is quite surreal and eerie. One would be quite unnerved by his robotic lifestyle. He does sometimes get up off the chair and stands at the barred window.

'Tomorrow, I would like you to return and speak to him. Try to get him to talk about the diary and what thoughts go through his mind. I might trust him enough to give him a pen and a notepad and ask him to write whatever comes into his head. We've made a breakthrough. But of course, you understand that he is not well mentally. If he does this and cooperates with you, I can permit you to have sessions with him outside when the weather is nice.'

Heidi nodded with encouragement, taking on board what the specialist doctor was saying and how they could implement this into a daily routine.

'Does he exercise?' she asked out of interest.

Dr Komma shook his head. 'No. We did offer him the opportunity, but he showed no interest. However, I am certain that our patient is very strong. The first night he arrived here the security guards said it was nigh on impossible to move him by push or pull physics... and yet he wasn't exactly resisting or thrashing about.

'All these details of this patient are very disturbing. And yet he shows no signs of emotion, but at least now he has started talking. He must like you but please don't get too comfortable around him. The Risperidol we give him to make him lethargic and prevent the voices in his head seem to have no effect.'

When Heidi took her leave from the mental hospital that afternoon, she was feeling excited that she had managed a breakthrough and her job now presented her with a big case. Tomorrow she would visit and she decided she'd devote herself entirely to Matthew Cawthorne. The more she learned about him the more important the case seemed to be. She understood now why the patient was under strict observation. If he did become angry and manic the security guards had been ordered to Taser him or beat him with a truncheon. Furthermore, Heidi turned her thoughts to Susan Cawthorne and Sydney and her father who allowed him to use his pellet gun. Heidi could see why the patient was deemed very dangerous. It wasn't the mere fact that he'd broken a cat's neck. No. This is how serial killers started off. They killed small, helpless animals before moving on to people who irritated them.

And yet when Heidi managed to get him to talk and stop giving her the schizophrenic stare, he almost looked human.

The drive home blurred by automatically.

Once she pulled alongside the kerb outside her detached house and killed the motor, she undid her seatbelt and picked up the file on the passenger seat.

'I hope I can help you help yourself, Matthew,' she said to no one.

Then she got out of the car and into her home to prepare for the next day...

*

The security guard dutifully removed the handcuffs and his assistant kept the Taser pointed directly at the patient in case he dared make a move. Matthew sat stone still, upright in the chair staring impassively at the white wall.

'Heard that you've started speaking to the nice lady,' the security guard said, finally standing back, permitting Matthew to move now he was two meters apart. Matthew continued to stare unblinkingly as though he was a statue.

'Hey, Matthew,' he said, studying the boy's perfect features. 'How come you've gone back to your trance-like state? I only asked you a simple question.'

Still no answer. The boy showed no signs of life.

'The sooner you start talking and behaving like a normal human being the quicker you can get out of this joint and go back to civilization.'

The guards waited patiently for an answer, then shook their heads.

'C'mon, let's go,' one of the guards said, and the two of them exited the room and locked the door on the outside.

Matthew heard the keys turn in the hole and lock being applied. He had been sitting ramrod straight all day without even flinching after his appointment with Heidi Johnston. He had heard the two security guards quite clearly and only now registered what they had advised him to do. They were right.

And this thought challenged his mind thoroughly. He began to realise that although he was fuming about being a patient in a mental institution all for one petty crime and his notepad, he had to stop the "dead man" act and learn to speak and act more like a human. Otherwise they might keep him under strict observation and care. Matthew didn't want that. However, his mother had been distraught with his actions and even called the police on that fateful day. He hadn't seen her since. Even if he did manage to get out of this rotten place his mum wouldn't allow him accommodation in her home. From there he had no idea where to turn.

He didn't like the specialist Doctor Komma. The man always nodded and said he "understood" his patients' cases and believed he knew what their diagnosis was all because he studied at university. Matthew had the desire to shove a sharp object into his oesophagus for labelling him as "schizophrenic" and "murderous".

Heidi was nice. She spoke to him one-to-one regarding him as a patient and not as a criminal. She appeared to be delighted when he spoke and encouraging rather than patronizing.

But all that progress would be all for nothing if he didn't speak to anyone else, save Heidi. And Matthew mentally found it hard to do so. The mere thought of having a conversation with the two security guards and Dr Komma sent a shiver down his spine. And anyway, what was he going to talk to them about. The therapist had said that their sessions were confidential. And already the guards were well aware of the session. Dr Komma must have opened his mouth and told them, breaking the law. Maybe he could talk about that in the morning? That would be nice: to take them down a peg or two. It wasn't as satisfying as ramming a broken bottle into their faces and stabbing them over and over until they eventually passed out for the final time, but it was a start.

Matthew Cawthorne smiled broadly. Then he stood up and got on top of the single bed mattress and stared at the ceiling.

The last thing he thought about before sleep engulfed him was how nice it would be outside in the summer, killing people and bathing in the sunshine.

Yes, that would be very good indeed.

21.

THE SUN shone down on the village sporadically on account of the drifting clouds. Susan Cawthorne had just finished her breakfast of jam on toast and was now washing the dishes. She had visibly lost weight since seeing her only child breaking their neighbour's cat's neck in the back yard and it had taken a week for that image to erase itself from her mind's eye. She had no control over it. She tried to keep busy with household chores and run errands. However, no matter what she did the memory kept popping back up, cruelly replaying the scene all over again.

Today was the first day she truly felt she had put the incident in the past at the back of her mind. She dried her hands after washing and drying the dishes and placed them back in their correct drawers and cupboards. That was one chore done, at least. Next, she would apply some perfume before heading to Tesco supermarket to do her weekly shopping.

Once that was all completed and the items were put away in their places in the kitchen, Susan removed her brown leather boots and sat down on the sofa to read the *Radio Times*. As she was doing this the doorbell chimed, breaking her peace. Heaving herself up and out of the sofa that had almost swallowed her completely, Susan went to answer the call. She opened the door and didn't expect to not find anyone standing there. But as she looked down on the doorstep there was a small fire in a black heap of mess. Instinctively, Susan killed the flames with her feet and then the acrid scent of dog shit assailed her nostrils.

'Aww, bloody hell!' she cursed so the street could hear her.

As she was closing the door and removing her socks she could distinctly hear someone elderly giggling. Susan knew right away who it was and cussed inwardly at her neighbour and at her son Matthew.

'Cat killing bitch!'

Susan slammed the door shut, removed both socks and put them in the black bin out back.

Ever since Matthew had done that horrible and sickening thing, Pat, her next-door neighbour whose cat had been killed had taken it upon herself to get revenge. Apparently the whole street knew the story of Matthew Cawthorne breaking Pat's adorable feline pet's neck and had plans to murder more. All of a sudden home no longer felt like a safe haven where Susan loved to dwell, either indoors or out the back doing the weeding and nurturing her plants. Now home became a hostile place, and although her mind overreacted tremendously, mentally she empathized with families living in Syria and Yemen. Yes, she had a comfortable bed, a roof over her head and food in the fridge, so obviously being able to identify with them was a long shot away. However, her inner peace and relaxation had been robbed from her very soul, and lately she began wondering why she had bothered marrying her husband and conceiving Matthew.

All she felt now was pain and remorse, and yet she was no psychic. How would she have ever known that things would turn out this way? Susan had worked hard and committed herself to being a faithful and loving wife and doting and consistent in love and support as a mother. Now the two men she'd had in her life had deserted her, as if her wholehearted attempts to adapt to her new roles was not only not good enough but couldn't have been a worse outcome had she been an adulterer and a drink and drug addict.

She took the phone off its hook and returned to the living room, deciding to see what was on the haunted fish tank. She channel-surfed until she got to the local news and caught a glimpse of a boy the same age as Matthew seated behind a small round glass table talking enthusiastically to the reporter sitting opposite.

'The local constabulary and members of the public in your area are very pleased, proud and grateful for all that you've done in bringing criminals to justice, solving crimes that might have gone unsolved and saving lives. But what makes Toby Jones tick?'

'Well,' Toby said, musing. 'It's like a higher power is feeding me a line of trajectory in my mind's eye or in my dreams that are too graphic and detailed to be considered normal. I wouldn't wish the visions on anyone. They can get quite scary as I'm unable to stop receiving them. At first, I didn't want to say anything in case I caused my dear Mum to be frightened. But then someone began talking to me, mind to mind, and at first I really did think I was going insane. I thought I had what some might call schizophrenia, but how could that be? I thought. I speak coherently. I eat well. I keep fit and healthy. I work with other people and they never once said or thought that I had some kinda mental illness or was acting crazy; so when I sat down one day in my bedroom I went online and looked up schizophrenia and came to the knowledge that it wasn't just mentally unwell folks who hear voices. I tried to stop the voices by wearing headphones for a while, but as soon as I stopped listening the voices came back. Then Annie Combs spoke to me in my mind and said I should meet her. Which I did, and she told me that I had a psychic gift she called "The Shine".

Susan watched the rest of the local news programme and then killed the TV. She made herself some supper before retiring to bed and lay there staring up at the ceiling awaiting sleep to engulf her and sweep her away from this terrible world into the abyss or a pleasant dream where all her dreams came true and there was no memory of the events which had occurred.

*

Heidi had to go around the car park twice before she could find herself a vacant space. She slotted the Vauxhall into a space and straightened the vehicle allowing room to open doors on either side. Grabbing her file, she got out of the car and hurried to the entrance as rain started to lash down. This time though, she didn't need to go to the reception. Dr Komma was in the corridor talking to the security guards when she climbed the steps and walked on the glossy linoleum.

'Ah, Ms Johnston,' Dr Komma said as he glanced over his shoulder and saw Heidi approaching.

'What's happened?' she asked, fearing the worst.

'Matthew is up and has been compliant this morning. He's been asking when you'll be here. He desperately wants to talk with you. He has spoken to the guards and me, but informs me that he can't breach the confidentiality trust you have with him. He was quite adamant.'

Heidi stopped about three feet away from the big, broad-shouldered security guards and Dr Komma himself. She shook her hair to rid it of any droplets of rain and removed her coat. 'May I hang this up somewhere? I don't want to catch a chill while I'm talking to my patient.'

'Certainly,' Dr Komma said and took her folded raincoat off her and hung it up in his office.

Heidi followed him down the white-walled and glossy-floor hallway, heading towards Matthew Cawthorne's room.

'You must have made quite an impression,' Dr Komma said, talking over the echoing footfalls.

'Well, thank you,' Heidi said, understanding why Matthew didn't like talking to Dr Komma. The aura he gave was one of intelligence to the point of "Been there done that, bought the T-shirt and sent it back" attitude. If Matthew had spoken to him as openly as he had done to her the specialist would have come across as condescending. That would have only triggered off the anger switch and the foreboding silent treatment. Heidi was anxious yesterday and did not possess any of Dr Komma's attributes. Instead, she had talked to Matthew as a human being but kept everything based on the facts while being professional and interested in what Matthew had to say. This sudden alteration in character had been because of her. Matthew Cawthorne was not obtuse; on the contrary if anything. He had listened attentively, considered what he was going to say before opening his mouth. He clearly had no trust in anyone, and yet his crime although murderous could be brought to the light, understood and then treated with the right straightforward touch and eagerness that would help the patient leave the premises in time and have a future once the incident and the diary had been put to bed.

'Once again,' Dr Komma said, interrupting her reverie, 'there will be security guards and staff close by and your interview monitored. Please report back to me for an update so I may write it down on my online file. And good luck.'

Heidi gave the specialist her full attention. 'Thank you, Dr Komma. I appreciate all your help and assistance.'

Then she turned and rapped her knuckles on the door to Matthew's cell, held open by a shorter, fatter security guard.

'Come in,' Matthew said and smiled broadly.

Heidi very nearly let out a loud gasp.

Matthew was handcuffed to his chair, seated at the Formica top table, looking so much different to yesterday. His eyes were full of life. His cheeks in full colour. The enamel white teeth he showed as he smiled were clean and bright enough for this to be an advert for Colgate.

Heidi entered, somewhat struck with invisible lightening and couldn't quite grasp the turnaround in the boy, who now looked quite handsome as most boys his age.

'Well, hello… again.'

Matthew smiled again at Heidi's comment as she lowered herself to the seat opposite him.

'Dr Komma said that you'd been keen to see me today. By the looks of you I take that's true, right?'

'It certainly is,' Matthew said in a lively voice, as though this was a different patient sitting in the same room as the nasty boy with the schizophrenic stare had once been.

'Excuse my bluntness, but you're like a whole other person. What's changed?'

'Well, yesterday, after you left, I had a long hot shower and a good meal in me. I stopped resisting the security guards and had a great night's sleep. I woke quite early but kept my eyes closed and thought about the consequences of my actions. What I did and what I wrote down in my diary were only ever going to lead me to this place or someplace with a strict confinement, like prison, if I wasn't careful. So I went back – in memory – and tried to pinpoint where I'd gone wrong in life. And what I found was I had a lot of anger issues in my mind. My father was absent. My mother helpless. I should've seen it a long way off, but there we go. What can I do? Had I seen it coming a lot sooner, then I wouldn't be here today. But then I thought everything happens for a reason. After doing that awful thing that will hang around my neck for the rest of my life, I decided I had two choices: I could go on being silent and resistant and stay here until I died, or I could swim to the surface and admit my wrongdoings. There is a life out there for me if I want it. I am truly sorry for what I did to that cat and her owner. I'm also very sorry for hurting my mum too. But what's done is done. It has been brought to the light and now I have to face my demons and say, enough is enough and there's time for a change. So here I am, refreshed, physically and mentally and only too happy to help you do your job and to try and win back my freedom and return to society.'

Heidi sat still, stunned by this outpouring. She placed the file on the table and shook her head, smiling and in some kind of disbelief at what was transpiring in this present moment.

'And what brought you to this far more rational – *normal* – way of thinking?'

'You coming to visit me yesterday,' Matthew said… unable to stop smiling now.

'How?'

Matthew could see the cogs in Heidi's brain working, yet still confused by his sudden transformation.

'You came to see me yesterday,' he began. 'You went out of your way to see if you could help me get better. Isn't that the truth?'

Heidi nodded. 'It certainly is.'

'Then I thought if you're doing that all for me… and that you are excited and interested in this case, why don't I meet you halfway?'

Again Heidi nodded.

'They say talking helps with people who've got mental health issues, right?'

'Yes, that's true,' Heidi said.

'Then here I am making a big effort to turn my life around.'

'But how do I know you're going to continue to be this way and have you released?'

Matthew frowned and shook his head. 'Aw, don't do that, Ms Johnston. Don't do that. That's what those idiot guards and Dr Komma do. Don't you become like that. I've trusted you. Hence why I've made this turnaround and have asked for you all morning and now you're gonna judge me on one minor incident. Please don't do that.'

Heidi could feel the heat in her face rising as though she had a high temperature. She had judged Matthew, in spite of his transformation and good attitude.

'I'm sorry, Matthew,' she said, looking away, feeling guilty.

'Hey c'mon,' Matthew said, his face expressing sorrow and sympathy. 'That's all right. We all make mistakes. That's one of the reasons why I don't like the guards or Dr Komma. They think they can put a label on you just so they can get their weekly finances paid. They're dickheads, Heidi. You don't have to become part of the chain to get your weekly pay. You can stand out and be an individual. You should see them. They really do lick the shit out of their own arses. They assume I'm this bad guy and they are saving the world from people like me. As if they've never done anything wrong in their lives. You'd be surprised at what things people say and do in their own privacy, Heidi. They're far from perfect. Yes I made a mistake, but for Christ sake, I'm a bloody teenager. I'm not out there going out binge drinking on Friday nights, taking illegal drugs and starting fights and riots like some of the "*normal*" people my age.'

Shit! He's right.

'I see where you're coming from,' Heidi said, not looking at him for a few moments.

Matthew sighed. 'You have a conscience, Heidi. They don't. That's why I like you and asked to speak to you. Beavis and Butthead don't… and Dr Komma's breath smells like shit 'cause he talks a lotta shit. You get me?'

'I can't comment on anyone else,' Heidi said. 'But I do have a conscience. But I have to ask certain questions to cover my own diagnosis. Please keep being this person you are today. Just comply with the rules and regulations, and soon you'll be able to gain their trust and in the near future leave here like you are now.'

'This is the real me,' Matthew said. 'I just went off the rails there for awhile. Happens to the best of us. Could you ask Dr Komma if we have our session outside tomorrow, please? They've forecasted a hot spring day. I haven't seen the sun in nearly two weeks.'

'I will ask,' Heidi said... and she believed that being out in the sun and fresh air would help Matthew a great deal.

*

Dr Komma had been watching the small TV screen of the so-called "confidential" meeting and contemplated the complete turnaround of Matthew Cawthorne. He gritted his teeth, jealous of this young, inexperienced therapist. He had studied this patient assiduously since the day he'd been taken in and had asked and probed the teenager to speak... only to be completely ignored as though they had never even met. Now this same patient was sitting on his chair, lively, excited and content. This perplexed the specialist. Furthermore, the patient had informed the therapist that Dr Komma was an "arsehole" who had just put a label on him so they could give him the precise treatment and medicine.

He met Heidi at the door to his office and offered her a seat before closing the door shut.

'He's made enormous progress overnight,' Heidi announced, actually sounding quite proud of the fact.

Dr Komma lowered himself into his comfy chair on the other side of the mahogany desk. He removed his glasses and rubbed the bridge of his nose where the glasses had left deep indentations.

'He wanted me to ask you if the weather was what it has been forecasted, could he have his session outside? I think. I trust that this would be very good and therapeutic if we allowed him his request,' Heidi said.

Dr Komma nodded and made a short *hmm*, listening and thinking simultaneously. 'Have you ever heard of transformation, Ms Johnston?'

'How could I not?' Heidi smiled. 'I was just a witness to it.'

'Do you now think that Matthew Cawthorne is ready to be released back into society?'

Heidi knitted her eyebrows together, not liking or understanding what the specialist was getting at. However, she had nothing to hide. Her professional opinion and having listened to her patient had sculpted a fresh new piece of art and character in the shape and size of the disturbing schizophrenic she'd met yesterday.

'Why'd you ask that, Dr Komma?'

The doctor put his glasses back on, took a sip of his water and ran his tongue over his lips. 'The reason I ask is because Matthew's silence and resistance in the eleven days he's been with us, not answering my questions or showing any signs of life until today, are somewhat drastic. Now had he talked a little to me or shown signs that he was still part of the human race prior to your arrival, why now the sudden change?'

'He's seen the errors of his ways,' Heidi began, unable to understand why Dr Komma appeared to be not only reluctant but dismissive of Matthew's emergence from his shell.

'I already told him that when I spoke to him.'

'He doesn't think much of you,' Heidi said, a little tentatively. 'He thinks you are condescending. He prefers to talk to me because I have a more... relaxed approach. And this is my forte. Also, he has been kept confined to his room for nearly two weeks, so there's no wonder he slipped out of the normal, crazy world. That's exactly what society has done to him. It has taken him from his home and incarcerated him. From there he has been giving high dosages of medicine that have kept him severely sedated... with no one "normal" to see, to speak to, to help guide him to the Light and back into life. He's sincerely sorry for killing the cat and says he was under a lot of pressure and going through a lot of physical and mental changes that were unfamiliar to him. That's quite understandable, if you ask me. He's nearly eighteen years old. As Matthew said, he doesn't go out drinking, taking drugs, fighting, and breaking the law. He killed a cat. He has a weak mother who feels betrayed by what he did. He has no father. His life has been nothing but tough. He needs now for society to accept him. To love him. And welcome him back into the world. I can't let that be taken away from him. I wouldn't be doing my job if he's not even allowed to sit on a bench outside and talk in the fresh air and sunshine.'

Dr Komma nodded. 'Okay,' he said, seemingly satisfied. 'If that's what he wants and you feel able to trust him, then that's what we shall do.'

Heidi rose from her seat, proffered her hand and shook Dr Komma's right hand before taking her leave.

22.

THE SUN shone its refreshing splendour on this part of the world as Matthew had predicted. He seemed full of positive energy and contentment now that there were no guards about or cameras monitoring his every move.

'Tell me, Matthew, what are your plans for the future? You seem to have worked everything else out to this point.'

Matthew offered a radiant smile before saying, 'I'd like to go to college and get a trade. Pack some tools in a bag and do odd jobs for people, especially old folks in the community. Or something where I can offer my services to a good cause, like an NHS nurse... or something like that anyway.'

Heidi nodded and pinched her lips together, showing that not only was she impressed but couldn't fault him for trying. 'Dr Komma seems reluctant to believe that you have made this sudden U-turn in your life. However, I feel quite optimistic and I'd like to wager that you have found some foresight and intelligence that'll help you move on from that mistake, enabling you to have a prosperous life. What I would request, though, if you are released and you are sent home, that you attend more one-to-one sessions with me and then in the near future have some group therapy. It really does help to know that there are other young offenders out there with mental health issues and so on. I think that would benefit you and hopefully bring you some peace that you don't have to go through life with a burden on your shoulders. Does that sound reasonable to you?'

Matthew glanced at the sparrows chasing each other from one tree to the next, chirping cheerfully. 'I don't mind having the one-to-one sessions. I feel like I can trust you. After all, I made a request and you got me outside in the fresh air without those arsehole guards standing sentinel, watching every move I make.'

'What about the group therapy?' Heidi pressed.

Matthew sighed. 'I don't think sitting in a classroom with a bunch of strangers is gonna help me. I feel a little uncomfortable being around a lot of boys my age and men who've committed crimes explaining why they did what they did. I think being with people like yourself – a relaxed, calm and open-minded individual – is far more beneficial for me at this stage.'

'Fair enough,' Heidi said, understanding Matthew's opinion and emotions. 'I mean we are jumping ahead of ourselves a bit. How are you today? On a scale to one to ten, one being the lowest, ten being the highest, how do you feel?'

Matthew chuckled and that made Heidi smile.

'I think probably... a nine.'

'Really?'

Matthew nodded. 'I have everything at his moment. Good company. Fresh air. Glorious sunshine. Birds singing. Everything... well, almost.'

'What's missing?' Heidi said, jumping on the absence of perfection.

'Well, I'm still incarcerated for one thing, which is a major drag. And two, all my plans depend on one thing: and if that doesn't come about, I can kiss my dreams goodbye. And the big old nasty world we live in will suck the blood right outta me like Dracula.'

Heidi closed the file and leaned close so only Matthew could hear her and not the nurses walking by in their blue scrubs. 'What's the one thing that everything hinges on?'

Matthew looked her directly in the eye and said, 'My mother.'

There was a long pause as Heidi mulled that over in her busy mind.

'How'd you mean?' Heidi asked, trying to force Matthew into explaining what he meant exactly.

'The day I broke that annoying cat's neck, ending its miserable life, when I turned and my eyes met my mother's I knew right then that she'd never love me the same, if not at all, ever again. I don't think she could ever forgive me no matter what I'd say to regain her trust. A part of her died that day in those few moments. It caused a lot of guilt and pain towards me, even though I was the one in the wrong.'

Heidi averted her gaze and straightened her back. She had to admire the boy's intelligence. He was far from crazy as Dr Komma had first thought. Matthew was tuned in at a high frequency. He knew full well what he'd done was an act of pure malice. But now with his shiny white teeth smile and cherubic features and dimples he came across as a young Hollywood prospect.

'See what I mean?' Matthew said.

Heidi didn't nod this time. Instead she let her mind solve the problem and when she came to an idea she spoke. 'Would you like me to go and speak to your mother? Tell her how you feel. And that you'd like to see her to tell her how sorry you are and that you were a very sick boy in need of treatment?'

Matthew opened his arms out wide as if the holiest of the holiest had answered his prayers along with a special bonus. 'If you did that I'd shine your shoes and praise you till the end of my days.'

Heidi laughed at that, aware that he was mildly joking, but incredibly grateful for her perfect suggestion.

'That doesn't automatically mean I can convince her,' Heidi said, wanting to keep her patient's feet on terra firma and not get too far ahead of himself.

'No, I know that,' Matthew said. 'But the gesture is incredibly generous. That's what I meant about being here in the moment with you talking things out. I tell you my problem and you come up with a possible solution. Dr Komma would just nod and smile condescendingly at me... and then ignore me as if he had better things to do. But if you could do that, I'd be in your debt for my whole life. I don't have any money to stay at a Bed & Breakfast. And I could do with some company to keep myself on the right track to achieving my goals in the future.'

'It would be my pleasure, Matthew,' Heidi said, speaking truthfully, amazed at how ordinary and prudent her patient behaved and spoke so eloquently that if you didn't know his life story you wouldn't guess in a hundred years he was in a mental hospital.

*

The following day was hotter and no clouds had formed in the sky. Matthew nursed the bottle of Pepsi Max Heidi had got for him and a Mars Bar from the local convenience store. They had mostly talked about the lovely weather and the fact that Matthew was now sleeping a lot better in the nights, which he believed was induced because he'd got a lot off his chest and put the past into the past for good.

However, Heidi had to be sure to cover all ground if the road to recovery for her patient was to be a successful one.

'Okay. Let me ask you this, Matthew,' she began, somewhat tentatively. 'Do you still have runaway or intentional thoughts about harming anyone, anything or even yourself?'

He didn't show it outwardly but a spark ignited in Matthew's head, and all of a sudden an insatiable urge to seize Heidi by her ponytail and ram her head through the wooden picnic table filled his consciousness. 'I think I've passed that, as I've already said.' And it was the fact that he'd already told his therapist that he'd changed and had buried the past that angered him when she asked the asinine question, in his mind.

Heidi paused, trying to read his face for any hint of emotion. Nevertheless, Matthew stared at her until she blinked and took a sip of her Coke.

'You made any mistakes you regretted?'

Heidi sighed. 'Did that question offend you?'

'Don't dodge my question,' Matthew said and smiled.

'I'm not dodging your question, Matthew,' Heidi said as kindly as she could. 'These sessions are about you, not me.'

Matthew made a face and shook his head in utter perplexity. 'I gathered that, but now that you've given yourself enough time to think of a plausible answer why don't you answer my question?'

'Because it's not relevant, that's why,' Heidi said, suddenly feeling vexed by her patient showing her little respect.

'I can see by the look on your face that you're annoyed with me,' Matthew said, still smiling. 'Now doesn't that give you an insight into what it's like to be me? I have to take medication, which I do every morning and every night before bed. I get hauled here and there by two fat, smelly guards. I am put in a cage all day with nothing to do except stare through the barred window at the yard below and just 'cause I don't start pacing around the room, getting nasty, punching the walls or my pillow; just 'cause I killed a cat during a period in my young life where I was trying my best to make sense of my father's disappearance and my emotions, trying to make sense of it all so I could learn and grow into a better person. And when you ask me a question I've already covered I don't show any anger. Instead I ask a much simpler question and you get your back up. I bet that if you took a Lie-Detector Test right now and I was the questioner you'd fail to say that you weren't the slightest bit offended and disliked me for asking you a question about your life when all it would've taken is a simple Yes or No answer. Am I right?'

Heidi knew she had been caught out in a certain way. However, she hadn't been the one writing evil things in her diary or committing a felony. She said this to Matthew and he smiled and shook his head before taking a good gulp of his drink.

'So, you've never made a mistake?' Matthew said. 'That's amazing. You're the first person to be like Jesus in two thousand years to be able to say that. And yet the sad thing is Heidi, had you said yes and dropped the subject and moved on to other areas that haven't been covered you wouldn't have the need to bullshit me.'

'Just answer the question, please,' she said, matching his stare.

'I think it's amazing how I've managed to go from Z to A in one day when a lotta boys my age would be screaming their heads off being incarcerated for killing a pet that had been trespassing in the first place. I've changed for the millionth time. Why is that so hard to believe? I mean you just said you hadn't made any mistakes and I haven't questioned that when other boys my age who do all sorts of wrongdoings that are felonies would never admit.'

'I never said I haven't made mistakes, Matthew,' Heidi said.

'So, like I said, a question that took a second to answer honestly has now cost five minutes out of my therapy session. Maybe you should spend a night or two being incarcerated and manhandled and watched. I'm sure you wouldn't be able to cope half as well as me.'

Heidi lowered her head and gritted her teeth.

Don't let him see you like this. Control yourself. It's the job. He's the one who's wrong, not you. Just remember that.

'I'll speak to your mother tomorrow. I have your contact details and she is your next of kin. I'll call her and see if she can be persuaded to come and visit you or talk on the phone,' Heidi said, now pondering what life would be like if she had been incarcerated at a young age for nearly two weeks for some evil thoughts and the killing of a neighbour's cat.

'Look,' she said, gaining her composure. 'There are two ways of looking at this: one, you stay angry and bitter and stay silent and you live that way until the evil inside you contaminates your soul. Or two: you talk to me. You don't question me though, Matthew. I'm your lifeline. I can write down what I want in my file about you. Don't think I am as helpless as that cat you murdered. Don't think I'm afraid of you. If you want life outside this hospital then you comply. You answer every question I ask. Do you hear me? I have the power to make your days here short and easy or long and hard. Don't test me.'

Matthew didn't grin this time, but he leaned forward and whispered to her. 'There's a little fight in you… or anger. I like that. You know why?'

'Why?'

'I'll save it for now…' Matthew said and leaned back. He finished his Diet Pepsi and walked back inside to be taken to the canteen for lunch.

Heidi got in her car, slammed the door and started whacking her balled-up fists against the door, cussing.

Evidently, Matthew Cawthorne had got through to her and when she started to feel uncomfortable, which caused her verbal retaliation, he just sat there and took it with no hint of human emotion and then whispered to her as though he not only didn't care about her threat but embellished her expressiveness to the point that she almost felt helpless. And it was that thought that scared her. Matthew didn't have any of that, she now knew. He could cross the line of the intolerable and be just as confident and content as he was talking amicably in the sunshine about the weather, nursing his drink in his lap. Either way he was at ease. He had somehow found a place of calmness that no one could break through. And God help them if they did.

Then she realised her mistake.

She had let her emotions take offence at his throwaway question, breaking up the casual conversation. Matthew had apparently made a huge turn-around in one session, seeing the error of his ways. He did say how he felt like a new person. The question had already been answered in full. Yet it was one of those questions all therapists had to ask to be able to conduct therapy on a patient that aggravated him. She had to ask it because schizophrenics were often accused of crimes in society. Mass shootings caused by the deranged often claimed they heard voices telling them to kill or to do harm, so in that sense she hadn't done anything wrong.

Heidi sat back behind the wheel and exhaled in exhaustion. She decided to grab a pack of sandwiches from Tesco and take it home with her to write about the session in her file before retiring for the day out in her back yard, sunbathing in the glorious sunshine, and miles away from Matthew both physically and mentally.

Now that felt like bliss…

23.

HEIDI finished writing about the session that had turned into a heated conversation between her and Matthew and read through the whole file from start to the present. Overall, the week had been a successful one indeed. However, in her heart she still believed that Matthew might be hiding or holding back something he didn't want her to gain knowledge of.

Was he a danger to her?

No, she didn't think so, anyway.

Was he a manipulator?

She didn't think so. Yet he had got into her head and sparked off emotions when she should have just ignored his questions. Or had she fallen into the trap of talking casually to him that made her patient believe he could now talk to her any way he wanted?

Heidi couldn't tell. She had raised her hackles at him, although she did consider what it would be like if the roles were reversed. She did kind of insinuate that she had never done anything wrong, like what he did, but then again she had a duty of care to be professional at all times. Perhaps she was over thinking this and she couldn't stop it. It wasn't like her. She had dismissed the question Matthew had asked but he insisted on elaborating on it. And that's how he had got into her head.

She sat there at her Formica top desk with pen in hand, thinking how easy he had managed to rattle her. He could very well be manipulative. What she had to do was to be prepared for it. She also sincerely hoped that Matthew wasn't aware that he did have the power to do that. If he did when he was released, he could very well use that asset to his advantage.

Heidi wrote another paragraph and ended the update she had written in his file that Dr Komma would read and analyse at a later date.

According to the antique clock on the living room wall, Heidi saw that it was almost three o'clock. She riffled through the contact details before picking up the phone and dialling Matthew's next of kin contact details.

The phone rang four times before someone picked up at the other end.

'Hello?'

'Oh, hi,' Heidi said. 'Is this Susan Cawthorne I'm speaking to?'

'Uh, yes it is,' Susan said in a timid, polite tone of voice.

'Who may you be?'

'I'm Matthew Cawthorne's therapist. I was wondering if we could talk a little, if you wouldn't mind? I have some good news.'

'Uh, Okay,' Susan said, and Heidi hated herself hearing how timid and tentative the woman on the other end was and how easy she would be for her son to manipulate.

'Matthew has made some progress in his treatment,' Heidi said, listening to the unsteady breathing of Susan. 'He has been talking to me. I'm glad to report to you that Matthew has admitted and wants to apologise for the crime he committed and the stress he has caused you. He's now complying with the staff and his doctor. He understands that his actions have caused you a great deal of unpleasantness and his own incarceration. The reason I'm calling you today is because Matthew has asked if he could see you. Now, I know you're still upset and coping with the incident that befell your neighbour's cat, but he has been doing so well, talking about maybe going to college and getting a trade and getting a job to fund his own independence... and so on. I think it would do him the world of good if you attended one of our sessions and spoke to him. How would you feel about that?'

There was a long pause on the other end.

'Are you okay, Mrs Cawthorne?'

'He's m-made p-progress, you s-say?'

'Indeed, he has,' Heidi said, automatically loving Susan. 'He's been talking and complying with taking his medication, which he says makes him drowsy. Dr Komma even said that as long as Matthew keeps improving and complying he might reduce the meds because Matthew wants to have more energy to do stuff, like anyone else his own age.

'Listen, I know what he did was bad... and what he wrote in his diary was bad too. But I really think seeing you again for so long might make a world of difference. I know you're hurting, Mrs. Cawthorne. You don't mind if I call you Susan, do you?'

'No. Susan is just fine. What's your name?'

'Heidi Johnston.'

'Matthew wants to go to college?'

Heidi chuckled, hearing the pleasant surprise in Susan's voice. 'Yeah. Like I said, he hit a hump in the road and crashed. But he needs to be forgiven. Otherwise this incident will haunt him for the rest of his life. And that's not good. He's still young and fresh. As long as he complies with our team and doesn't do anything like this ever again then I think we ought to draw a line in the sand and put it behind us. What do you think about that, Susan?'

'My neighbour hates my guts because of what he did,' Susan said.

Heidi sighed, realising that this poor woman had probably suffered more than Matthew because of his actions.

'I'm really sorry to hear that,' Heidi said. 'But you still love Matthew, don't you?'

There was no answer for a good few moments and Heidi didn't know what else she could possibly do to make the situation any better.

'He's my son,' Susan said, breaking the silence.

'Please say yes,' Heidi said, understanding the imperative complications. 'If you don't the implications to Matthew's recovery could well cause further problems down the line.'

'My neighbour loved that cat as though it were her baby,' Susan said, her timid voice palpably shaking with emotion and fear. 'She put shit on fire right outside my house and laughed at me when I put the fire out – not realising it was shit – with my feet. Lord only knows what she'll do if she sees Matthew back home again.'

Oh shit! I don't believe this!

'That's bad.' Heidi didn't know what else to say. Her whole body slumped, and yet she couldn't make anyone do something they didn't want to. If Susan refused to come and see him and refused him returning home the council housing estate would have to try and find him accommodation. A council flat no doubt. Where he would be alone. Unloved. Which wouldn't do his mental health any favours.

'His session is tomorrow at 11:00am,' Heidi said. 'Would you like me to drive by and pick you up?'

Another long pause for approximately a minute. Heidi was about to end the call.

'I saw evil in his eyes...' Susan Cawthorne said. 'That day I saw something else take over my son's whole physical being. He wasn't the boy I'd loved, cared for and raised. He was a monster. A monster that took great joy in picking that lovely cat up by the scruff of its neck and breaking it, killing the cat an instant later. Then it turned to me and saw me... and then I knew.'

'What did you know?' Heidi asked.

'That my son was already dead...'

*

Heidi walked down the spotless corridor, her high heels click-clacking on the polished linoleum towards Dr Komma's office. She rapped lightly on the door and heard the faint voice from inside calling out, 'Come in.'

She entered and sat down in the comfy chair opposite the specialist who was finishing his sentence on the computer before turning his attention fully to the therapist.

'It is my understanding that you have spoken to Mrs Cawthorne. Is that so?'

Heidi nodded.

'How did that go?'

'She refused any persuasion to come and visit Matthew or offer any accommodation to the family residence,' Heidi explained, feeling a tremor of fear for Matthew and his mental state when he found out this unfortunate news.

'Did she explain the reasons why?'

'She said the day she saw Matthew kill the neighbour's cat was the day Matthew – her son – died and a monster was born.'

Dr Komma frowned. 'Hmm. That's going to be a setback for him.'

'I know,' Heidi said. 'His mother's lack of forgiveness has put a dent in the road Matthew wanted to be travelling. He has made some excellent progress thus far and had made positive plans to help himself get back on the right track. Now this is gonna hurt him and cause him to stumble. I did try to persuade her, but she was adamant and steadfast in her beliefs and decision.'

'He's in the TV room at the moment,' Dr Komma said. 'Let me call the nurses' station and you can break the news to him in his room.'

Heidi nodded in agreement and inwardly cussed Matthew's mother for making this situation even more arduous than it already was.

Matthew had a police record now and had been incarcerated for the best part of two weeks in isolation. God only knew what this was going to do to his mental state.

*

Susan Cawthorne replaced the receiver in its cradle and rested her left hand on the kitchen wall. Her breathing in shallow gasps increased with pressure and volume. She was sucking air in and doing her utmost to stop the trembling from head to toe. Her hands were clammy and her knees buckled. She crossed the tiled flooring to the dinette table and sat down heavily on one of the wooden chairs. The unexpected call from Matthew's therapist had caught her off-guard. She had been living in Matthew's shadow for the last couple of weeks. Being on her own for the first week had taken its toll on her. However, not having that monster, which she had given birth to and raised, was a huge relief.

She was doing her utmost to get on with life in complete solitude, dividing her time with work, housework and learning to relax that consisted of watching TV soap operas and doing her word searches. Apart from some stares from her neighbours, and the stunt pulled on her on her doorstep, Susan was living a life of pleasantness. The phone call brought it all back to the forefront of her mind. She buried her head in her shaking hands and exhaled with a long, strained gasp.

They were releasing Matthew in the foreseeable future and were now looking for accommodation on his behalf. And although these were positive signs, Susan didn't want to see her son ever again. She had no love in her for him. The expression on his face on that fateful day was enough to curdle her blood and send her fragile mind into the confines of hell itself. In Susan's opinion that's where that monster had come from and was going to after he died if there was such a thing as heaven and hell.

After another ten minutes lost in her physical and mental state of fear and misery, Susan stood up, crossed the kitchen and put the kettle on.

As she carried her steaming mug of coffee and made her way into the living room, she decided that no matter what, she never ever wanted to see the monster called Matthew Cawthorne again...

Could buy a gun for protection, she thought, instinctively feeling safer by the mere thought of owning a weapon.

*

Heidi Johnston had just broken the bad news to Matthew. Then she flicked a switch in her mind to a positive reflection.

'This will be going into your file,' Heidi told Matthew. 'We will find you accommodation. You will have your own flat and you'll be qualified to PIP and other benefits while you study at college. This isn't a setback. Yes, it would've made things a lot easier had your mother been forgiving and permitted you to stay with her until you got a qualification and then got a stable job, but that's life I'm afraid. It ain't easy. Indeed, I was expecting and hoping that your mother would be a bit more supportive. However, if that's her wish then going to live under the same roof as her would've only caused more problems for yourself and hindered your progress. The more you comply and conduct yourself in an appropriate manner, the more I can do for you,' Heidi gave a tentative smile. 'Be respectful of people who are willing to help.'

Matthew stared impassively at the wall behind Heidi, a look of loss and despair. 'I made a mistake...' he said and his words swallowed the silence. 'Everyone makes mistakes.'

'Yeah, I know,' Heidi said, gazing at the boy's lost expression after being informed that his mother wanted nothing to do with him any longer.

'Thanks for your help, Ms Johnston,' Matthew said in a faraway voice.

'That's all right,' Heidi said, feeling compassion for him in this moment, seeing the devastation and rejection on his face. 'You still have a future. And although you won't be able to afford a place of your own with your own income you will have your own flat where you won't be under your mother's feet.'

Matthew gave a faint nod.

'This will work out better for you in the long run. You'll have your own space; your own independence and... hopefully a certificate of qualification in your chosen trade. A trade will permit you to doing all kinds of jobs and projects. You're gonna be all right. Okay? Trust me.'

Heidi tried to read Matthew's lost expression.

She didn't know what else to say. Instead she simply sat there and waited.

'My mother doesn't love me anymore...'

Heidi didn't know how to counteract that comment. Unfortunately, what Matthew had just said was in fact true. And Heidi knew from speaking with Mrs Cawthorne how fragile her voice was and couldn't imagine the detrimental effect it would have on her sharing the same property together.

He's a monster.

No he's not. He's a mixed-up teenager.

He planned to kill his neighbour's cat, just like he planned to kill people whom he didn't like one day, according to his diary.

24.

THE DAY was as beautiful as you could get. Azure sky. Blazing hot sun and the chirpy birdsong enveloping the back yard where Susan sat filing her nails and sipping lemonade. She felt heavy hearted which came from the phone call with Heidi the day before, but now, as she finished her drink, she decided to pay her neighbour a visit. She ambled through the cool house and stepped outside via the front door. She pulled it closed but took the latch off so she wouldn't require a key to unlock it again. Then she walked down the paving stone path and up onto the porch.

Her neighbour Irene heard the doorbell chime going off.

'Gimme a minute!' she called out.

Then two minutes later the door opened and Irene gasped at the sight of Susan in her white sleeveless top and denim shorts standing on her porch, looking fit and healthy but forlorn.

'What the hell you want, bitch?'

Susan ignored the insult. 'I know you don't like me any more,' Susan said, shifting her weight from one leg to the other. 'I just wanted to let you know that my son won't be coming back here to live with me after what he did to your pet. I could've said yes, but I refused him for both our sakes. Please stop doing dirty tricks to me. My life is hard enough as it is. I lost my husband to another woman and now my murdering son. All I ask is for a bit of respect and to leave me be. I am ashamed of them both. If you do continue to treat me this way, I'll have to call the police. And I don't really want to do that.'

Before she could turn around and head back onto her property, Irene opened the door a little farther and spat in Susan's face.

'Take that for your bastard son!'

Susan wiped the spray from her face and eyes.

'Boy like that should've been aborted the moment you got yerself pregnant, I reckon. If ya want peace make sure he never comes back! You got me?'

Susan wilfully nodded.

The door slammed shut ending the heated conversation. And as Susan got back onto her own property, she nodded slightly to herself, realising for the first time that she had indeed made the right decision after all.

*

Matthew sat in his cell waiting for Heidi to enter. He sat upright in his chair, feeling in good spirits after being in the TV room. It had been a glorious spring day until the clouds had floated by, blocking the source of light and heat. Otherwise his session would have taken place outside. Matthew craved the outside. However, the wind had picked up and wailed around the grounds, like a monstrous beast.

The security guard on watch unlocked the cell door and permitted Heidi to enter. She carried her file and sat down opposite her client. She offered no smile or benign greeting. Instead she sat down and exhaled.

'What's wrong?' Matthew asked.

'Nothing, just tired, is all.'

Silence descended but unlike before there was no tension in the ambience.

'Have you ever self-harmed, Matthew?' Heidi asked.

Matthew shook his head.

'Do you have any hobbies that keep you entertained?'

'I used to go cycling a lot. I was hoping to do some more once I got out of this joint and went back home. I really have noticed some big changes from inside me and I feel like a better and kinder human being since my arrest and incarceration. Mostly because of you. Unlike everyone else you came here with an open mind and did not automatically judge me or label me like Dr Komma.'

Inwardly Heidi battled the truth that she would have to unveil. Which would hit him like an arctic lorry at full speed.

'How is my mum anyhow?'

'We'll get to that,' Heidi said, trying to avoid that part of their conversation for as long as she could.

Matthew leaned back in his hardwood chair, waiting for Heidi to take the reins of the session.

'If you were verbally abused, how would you react? Honest answer.'

'I'd do my best to ignore it,' Matthew said, without hesitation. 'What I have learned is that violence isn't the answer. And now that I've been incarcerated, I know what it feels like if I did stray again in the unlawful sense.'

Heidi nodded. 'Good. That's good, Matthew.'

He was pleased his answer was approved by his therapist.

'You don't have any violent thoughts, do you?'

Matthew shook his head.

'I have seen a big change with you as has Dr Komma,' Heidi said. 'They told me you've been allowed to watch TV and talked with other patients during meal times, is that true?'

'It is,' Matthew said, hardly able to conceal his smile. He was fully aware now that his demeanour and his verbal answers were that of what society claimed as "normal". For the first time in weeks, Matthew could see the light at the end of the tunnel and ran towards it as fast as he could.

'What else do you like apart from cycling?'

Matthew mused thoughtfully. 'I like a good film... and in school I used to do football and basketball, which my coaches said I was good at.'

Heidi couldn't fault her client. However, she had yet to deliver the bad news. She braced herself for that moment, and sincerely hoped that her announcement didn't have a detrimental effect.

'I contacted your mum,' Heidi said, silently praying for the best possible outcome and that the blow wouldn't knock Matthew off his perch of self-forgiveness and new life. 'She hasn't forgiven you, I'm afraid.'

Matthew's brows knitted together. 'Whad'ya mean?'

'She refuses you to go back home. You've been declared homeless... I'm sorry. I did try.'

The teenager scanned the room with disbelieving and baffled eyes, searching for the hole in the ground to come into sight and swallow him whole.

'Homeless?' Matthew said as though it was a foreign word.

'I have informed Dr Komma,' Heidi said, wanting desperately to move forward with the conversation all of a sudden now that she could read the confused and devastated facial expressions on this boy who had a good, concise plan to move forward and into a new, prosperous life. 'We've contacted Tai Tarian (the council), and they are looking for accommodation in a flat. One came up in Neath town centre. It's a one-bedroom flat with a cosy living room, kitchen and bathroom, ideal for someone who is single and with no income. You will be entitled to PIP due to your illness. That's all I know for sure. I'm sorry this isn't anything like what you'd hoped for but at short notice it was the best thing we could do. At least you won't feel a burden or get under your mother's feet. You'll have your own independence and your social worker will look at finding you a job part-time to help with the bills.'

Heidi left shortly after with the weight of her own burden on her frail shoulders. The click-clacking of her heels on linoleum reverberated down the corridor in the otherwise quiet mental institution. She exhaled as she stepped outside and ambled across the parking bay to her car.

*

The news of Susan Cawthorne's decision to deny her only child any accommodation or forgiveness was a left field blow. Matthew came out of his room and collected three biscuits and a hot chocolate before retiring for the night. Once he finished the late snack, he climbed onto the hard, single mattress. He rolled onto his side and visualised his mother's face from an old memory.

Together they were out in the back yard doing some gardening. Matthew had just mown the grass and Susan was scooping up the remains and shuffling them into her green bag for recycling. The weather had been scorching hot in the middle of June. He remembered quite vividly that they had sat just outside of the sliding glass doors, eating ice-cream and enjoying and savouring the precious moment.

Now all of that was gone…

Now the memory, like a scene in a film, evaporated.

Now Matthew saw red. And with that came the rage. The satisfying dreams of bitterness and revenge engulfed his consciousness and drowned out everything else.

Now the monster slept deeply…

25.

FIVE MONTHS LATER

MATTHEW CAWTHORNE sat on a second-hand brown sofa in his living room. He sat in solace having just finished his microwave beef dinner. He had lots of time to himself. He had no TV, computer, or Hi-Fi system to listen to music. All he had was what he managed to get from the council – the bare essentials.

It was summertime and the weather outside was hot and muggy. The clouds drifted languidly in front of the sun, blocking the splendid radiance and gorgeous, natural heat, perfect for sunbathing on the beach.

Yesterday Matthew had bought a pack of biro pens and an A4 notepad. He kept it safe under his bed so no one could see. He mostly wrote his thoughts and feelings regarding the events that had befallen him since the beginning of the year. Furthermore, Matthew still had his fortnight injection at Tonna Hospital and had attended a Mindfulness class that lasted six weeks. All in all, the boy on the brink of early manhood had prospered since killing Irene's adored cat. In fact, the more he thought about it, he couldn't help but smile. He now had a place that was all his… and he could do what he wanted.

The specialist Dr Komma still had referrals to see him every six months to keep a record on his file, and was pleasantly surprised when Matthew had seen him the week before. Matthew's colour had come back. He was saving enough money to take driving lessons which would hopefully lead to buying and owing a car to further his independence.

He worked six hours every day for the council, painting and decorating. He took his job seriously, although there were three other colleagues who he worked with telling him on a regular basis that there wasn't enough allocation for a fourth member of the team. Matthew had spoken with his supervisor who informed him that if he were to lose his position then he could do litter picking instead. This satisfied Matthew, and cancelled any worries or concerns he might have had.

It wasn't essential to have a job. After all, Matthew was declared a schizophrenic. Dr Komma and Heidi Johnston were encouraged and impressed by Matthew coping with this mental illness on his own and having to go to work during the week.

On the outside, Matthew was considered by his doctors and nurses as an example that following the guidelines they set, (taking medication, listening to advice, talking openly about their problem unlike some who chose to live in denial, etc) had worked wonderfully, and that their way of treating a patient was the proper and correct way to do.

Nevertheless, Matthew spent hours by himself. Things could have been a lot easier. He could have been staying with his mum, going to college and then getting a qualification, which would lead to a job that he was not only trained for but enjoyed doing. The painting and decorating was indeed a good job. However, he had all the crappy jobs, like holding the ladder or getting lunch for his colleagues and that sort of thing. He was only allowed to paint when it was absolutely necessary and easy enough so a physically unwell person could do it.

Matthew put the plastic tray in the recycling bag, washed his hands, dried them and then headed for his bedroom. Once he was there, he got down on all fours and scrambled for the notepad. In his grasp, he got onto the mattress and opened it while grabbing a pen from the bedside cabinet. Then he began to write…

The world slipped away.

Matthew was writing his deepest thoughts and desires.

The monster from within took over…

*

Tesco had been crammed with people and it was getting to the point of being out of control. She packed away her items into her big bag and a couple of plastic carrier bags and exited the store, pushing the trolley to where she had parked the car. After loading the boot, she got in behind the wheel and breathed. She had taken a bottle of Pepsi Max and a John Grisham book to look at while she drank her drink and caught her breath.

Susan was only now starting to enjoy life. The incident that had befallen her only child had been no fault of her own. It had taken a while to accept that as fact in her mind, but now she had buried the incident and her son. Life had been cruel to Susan, but now there were sunshine and blue skies. Living on her own had its perks, she reminded herself. She could watch TV, any channel she wanted. Go on the internet. Read a book. Or whatever other desires she had that had been shared in her adult life. There was less washing and ironing too.

She had paid her bills that had been reduced due to the fact that her son no longer lived with her. She would grab a Chinese takeaway later and read her book or watch TV. The world was her oyster. Had it not been for all the stress that was a result of what had happened the year before, Susan would be living in complete paradise.

She no longer had any guilt. She had to learn not to blame herself for her son's actions. She had paid the ultimate price by her neighbour and now she simply wanted to enjoy life without having to concern herself with anyone else.

Yes, life was indeed good for Susan.

But that was about to change… and soon she would be confronted with someone familiar and something so harrowing that it would paralyse her into shock.

Susan started the motor, released the handbrake and pulled out of the car park, back onto the busy road and headed home…

*

Birds chirped and flew from tree to tree in the suburban street as Susan slowed her car and rolled it onto the concrete driveway in front of the garage. After killing the motor, she unlocked the front door and carried the shopping inside (her exercise for the day). She put the items away in their correct places, grabbed the TV *Radio Times* magazine and collapsed on the sofa to see if there was anything good on.

An hour later, Susan's takeaway arrived at her doorstep. She paid the delivery guy and carried the pizza into the spacious living room. She finished it all in half an hour and poured herself a glass of Strongbow to wash it down. She had put the empty cardboard box down by her feet and savoured her time, relaxing and feeling good about herself. This had been a long time coming, she thought, what with her husband and now her murderous son out of the way. But they were in the back of her mind now, deleted from her consciousness for the time being at least. It really did feel as though a heavy burden had been removed from her back permitting her to get on with and enjoy her life.

*

Matthew closed the door to his one-bedroom flat behind him, turned on his heel and headed down the dirty street. All the grey-walled two-storey buildings were identical if you weren't familiar with the place. There was a garage depot at the end of the cul-de-sac. Litter populated the streets and front lawns that were in desperate need of cutting. He couldn't believe what a shithole he'd managed to wind up in. His temper boiled beneath the surface. Matthew headed up the road to the convenience store to buy some soda and microwave meals with the last of his weekly pay.

While he was working, Matthew played the role of an affable, down-on-his-luck teenager doing his best to clear the litter from the streets and maintain some integrity and dignity on the public roads and footpaths, which some took advantage of.

The job itself was nothing to be ashamed of. However, now that he'd been transferred to litter picking from the painting and decorating role, he was back on his own again. His thoughts turned to something not resembling humane. Rather, Matthew had the urge to hurt someone or some pet again. He believed that being ostracised by his mother, shown no love or forgiveness, triggered these emotions and setting them off like a firecracker.

Furthermore, the medication they gave him made him feel lethargic. After a five-hour shift all he wanted to do was get in bed and fall asleep.

He entered the shop and welcomed the cool breeze from the AC. He bought a handful of Yorkie Bars, two beef dinners and an eight-pack of Pepsi Max soda cans. He carried them home after paying and pocketing the meagre change. As he was crossing the road, Matthew noticed the BT payphone. When he got to the other side a good thought came to mind. He turned his attention to where he was going and carried his shopping back to the flat. He had a microwave meal, a couple of cans of Pepsi Max and two Yorkie Bars. Then Matthew made a decision to do something that could either give him a new lease on life or carry the last straw that broke the camel's back. He had an imperative decision to make... and the only way to reach a decision was to wait and see if the idea drifted off or insisted remained in the forefront of his troubled mind.

An hour later, Matthew locked the door of his flat, checked he had enough change and headed back up onto the main road to make a phone call...

He entered the booth, took the receiver off its hook and inserted the right amount of change. Then he dialled a number that he would forever remember and waited for the ringing on the other end.

On the fourth ring, the call was answered and a sweet, gentle voice said timidly, 'Hello. Who may I say is calling?'

The dulcet tones of his mother's voice soothed Matthew momentarily. Then he brought to mind the absence of forgiveness. The blood rushing through his veins from the jackhammer beat of his heart enraged him. This was the stupid bitch that had cost him his dreams and desires. How could he ever forget the absence of love on his mother's heart? She refused to come and visit him while he was in Cefn Coed Mental Institution and wouldn't allow him to start over, fresh. Her timid voice and her frail, skinny appearance were pathetic. A high wind could blow her over, she was so weak. No wonder his dad left when he did. According to his mother, his dad was an alcoholic and only came home for food and sleep. She erased the other reason – which was sex, as he'd been too young to know about any of that reproduction stuff.

Matthew couldn't even imagine this stupid bitch ever having sexual intercourse with anyone. He decided that she had just lain there with his father on top of her in the missionary position so he could do the deed for his own benefit.

He hung up and exited the glass box. Then he sauntered back the way he came with a new idea forming in his fervent mind.

When he entered his modest flat, Matthew went straight to the kitchen and dipped his hand into a ceramic dish and fished out a set of keys that were in his possession when he was arrested and taken into custody earlier in the year. He dropped them into his jeans' pocket and headed into the living room and contrived a scheme that would change everything and anything thereafter. His decision would shock the community and the nation itself. Matthew envisioned a crime magazine with the true story of Susan Cawthorne's gruesome death.

He would wait for daylight to surrender to darkness and move like a shadow towards a place he had once called home to avenge his justice once and for all.

Matthew didn't yet know how he would accomplish this feat, but one thing was for certain – tonight the monster would be allowed out of its cage for one night only…

*

Darkness slowly but surely swallowed the ebbing sun slinking beneath the horizon and offered an amazing sight of a thousand stars, twinkling like diamonds in light.

Susan hauled herself out of her seat and carried her glass to the kitchen and placed it in the sink, ready to be washed in the morning. The pizza had gone down well, and the movie she'd just watched, *Interstellar,* had captivated her and filled her with a sense of awe by the story itself. She climbed the stairs and went straight into the bathroom to brush her teeth and wash her face.

Today had been the first full day she had enjoyed and felt no guilt or remorse or sadness. Today had been the start of a life worth living and enjoying, Susan decided. She killed the lights and slid into the bedroom and got undressed before lying down and pulling the duvet over her. It was nice and warm and comfy. She smiled. Content. And excited about her future now that there were no concerns to become anxious about. Yes, Susan had to admit, the planet she inhabited was a good place. The horrors of the world were erased and only something she witnessed on TV and gossip magazines in the Tesco superstore, which she prudently avoided.

Sleep came quickly and she had no dreams.

*

Outside her window the only sound came from the oak and birch trees lining the street, and the distant drone of fast-moving vehicles travelling on the motorway.

A man ambled down the pavement wearing a black hooded jumper and black runner bottoms. He slowed to a halt outside Susan's home and glanced around, looking for anyone who might be peeking out their windows and seeing him standing there like a statue.

The coast was clear. The man walked down the footpath and up onto the porch. All the lights were off in the house and the figure dug a hand into his bottoms and extracted two keys on a ring. He selected the one he wanted and slid it into the keyhole in the front door. He had to move quickly and quietly if he was going to pull this stunt off without being detected and taken into custody.

The police sometimes drove down the streets of the suburbs, where good, hard-working folks enjoyed their simple and pleasant lives, on good terms with the local constabulary. Most of them were what you might call "Perfect People" as they watched the football and other sports on Saturday and went to church on Sunday.

This was something the intruder knew only too well. The suburbs were like paradise. Neighbours chatted amicably and often helped each other. The front lawns were mown on a weekly basis. The assailant craved for this type of life once more, but was only fully aware that he had blown his chances of an easy life with his mother when he committed his first crime.

This would be his second crime.

Murder.

The front door latch clicked loudly in the silence and the figure gently and slowly pushed open the door, closed it behind him and on tiptoes climbed the staircase in the pitch dark, ears wired into any sound or movement on the first floor.

As he reached the landing the figure stopped and breathed into the crook of his arm.

Something tangible, yet invisible disturbed his mind and contorted his pale face.

This was the house he had been raised in, played, eaten, studied and relaxed in. And all that was because of the woman lying in bed at the far end of the landing fast asleep, oblivious of the fact that there was someone in her home with an imperative and life-changing decision to make.

The monster took over.

The figure pulled out a large kitchen knife from the pouch in the front of the hooded jumper. He moved without sound towards the main bedroom and eased the door open ever so gently and poked his head around the side. His eyes had slowly adjusted to the night's darkness, and he saw the head of a familiar face visible above the duvet, eyes closed, unaware of what would probably befall her if she didn't climb out of the deep unconsciousness that made her vulnerable for attack.

The figure crossed the room to the side where the woman was lying and stretched out his hand and pressed it down on her mouth. The sudden intrusion and lack of oxygen caused the woman's eyes to snap open and bulge in alarm, still trying to swim to the surface as the assailant raised the bread knife overhead and brought it down into the woman's abdomen…

PART THREE

26.

DENMARK

THE DAY was overcast. However, it was Friday and the bespectacled man gazing out the window at the acres of land and the fringe of the forest would have the weekend to relax and enjoy.

The phone shrilled to life and the man in the navy-blue suit and matching tie picked up the receiver. A woman speaking Danish informed him that his three clients had arrived promptly and were waiting for the meeting in the boardroom to commence.

He answered the receptionist, placed the phone back in the cradle, rose from his leather upholstery chair and crossed the spacious room where all four walls sported varnished shelves from floor to ceiling crammed with books.

Out in the lobby, Enrik removed his spectacles and greeted the three clients who all wore their best suit attires specifically for this meeting. Once the introductions were out of the way, Enrik told them to follow him down the red carpeted hallway where black and white framed photographs of eclectic artwork covered the walls.

Enrik opened the big oak door and stepped to the side and motioned the three men into the boardroom where a long mahogany table took up most of the space. The men sat down and watched Enrik close and lock the door behind him. Then he sat down at the head of the table and opened a drawer and removed a remote control for the TV and another one for the DVD player, which he would use later.

'Would anyone like something to drink before we start? Or are you fine with the water? Please help yourselves.'

As English was now the universal language and the three men were able to speak it eloquently and understood the language, English would be the preferred and ideal language to use.

Two of the men poured themselves a glass full of water and then waited for Enrik to continue.

'First of all,' he said, loud enough so they could all hear him clearly, 'I'd like to thank you all for attending this formal meeting. As you are aware there has been a glitch in our plans regarding your benefits for such long-term service with the company. Evidently all three of you should have partners by now to sustain you when you're not at work. Man on his own with only his job is not good. I myself have a wife and a girlfriend. You have all worked hard at the law firm in protecting our shared interests and keeping the authorities and press away from snooping into our business affairs, if you'll pardon the pun. However, as I already said, there has been a glitch. And your three partners were unable to arrive in London to be at your service and pleasure.

'Evidently, things did not go to plan and one of our workers got himself killed by an assailant and set the young, beautiful women free where they contacted the authorities.

'What I have brought you here for today is to show you some of the footage of the assailant and the three young women who should right now be with you and not in the United Kingdom where they reside.'

On the opposite end of the room from where Enrik was seated there was a 40-inch flat screen TV and a Samson DVD player.

Enrik pressed the button for the TV to come to life and then followed the same procedure with the DVD player.

After a minute the screen came to life and a news reporter sat behind her desk and looked into the camera and began talking.

'Local police have been contacted by three missing women who had been kidnapped from their homes and lives and were reportedly being prepped for being sex slaves in a human trafficking organisation. And had it not been for a local hero who put his own life at risk and set them free the women claim they wouldn't be here today to be able to tell the story of a heroic man who is so humble that he kindly requested that they not give his name to the press.'

A gorgeous tall, blonde woman with no blemishes and beautiful full lips spoke at a conference table to the press and the authorities about their escape. 'If it wasn't for that boy, we wouldn't have been here today able to tell this incredible story of how there are such people who are real heroes, who put their lives at risk without wanting any reward or notoriety. I am so glad... and so are the other girls that we managed to get through this ordeal unscathed. If I ever see that boy again, I'd marry him; that's how much I love him, and am so grateful to be here today with my family. If he's watching this,' she said, and blew a kiss at the camera. 'Thank you so much, with all my heart.'

Enrik hit the PAUSE button and took a sip of water himself.

One of the clients who had thick auburn hair and freckles scattering over his face said, 'Was that one of our partners?'

'She would have been,' Enrik said and put his glass back down on the coaster.

'Is there any more for us to see?' the clerk with a heavily furrowed brow asked.

'There is,' Enrik said, not appreciating the lack of patience his clients had directed towards him.

He started the DVD again.

The screen dissolved and then came back to life.

The footage was jumpy and at first all three associates thought there was something wrong with the quality of the picture but then quickly realised that the cameraman and a reporter, carrying a microphone, were chasing after a teenager who had beautiful features and stunning eyes. He was jogging until he finally slowed to a halt and faced the reporter who was short of breath.

'Would you be willing to sit down with us and do an exclusive interview?'

The teenager sighed. 'If I carry on walking or running, are you still gonna be following me?' he asked.

The reporter shrugged. 'We just want an exclusive with you, that's all.'

'Whatever happened to my peace?'

'You'll have your peace once we've had our exclusive,' the reporter said.

'This is harassment,' the teenager said, shaking his head ruefully at the cameraman and the ITV reporter.

'Please,' the reporter said. 'There won't be no cheap shots, I promise. Just one good, honest interview. People are interested in you. Plus, we'll pay you three grand. How does that sound?'

'What about my anonymity?'

'Being an enigma generates more interest than telling everyone everything they want to know,' the reporter said, and Toby was fully aware that what the reporter said was undeniably true.

'Three grand?' Toby said, not looking too happy, but relenting.

'Three thousand pounds,' the reporter assured him. As soon as its news, given time and there'll be another story and you'll get your anonymity back.

'Okay…'

The screen jumped to the next scene, and the first thing the businessmen saw was Toby up close looking straight ahead, past the camera and at the reporter who was out of shot.

'So, how did you become a psychic?' the reporter asked, curious and intrigued at the same time.

'I don't know…' Toby began and expressed a subdued and troubled mind. 'I guess it all started when I came into direct contact with a murderer in the restrooms while at the cinema with my mum. An unnatural, yet brilliant, flash stunned me, I caught a glimpse of what that man had done and knew that he needed to be stopped and arrested. I was left on the floor, suffering from a nasty seizure, sweat pouring out of me to the point that I went into shock. Then, all of a sudden, as quick and unexpected as the seizure assailed me, I recovered fully, got up, washed my pale face, wiped the sweat beads away and left the restroom and joined my mum and never said a word about it.'

'What is it like to be able to know things that not even the authorities know about?'

Toby cleared his throat before replying. 'I suppose some would say it is a gift. But I say it is no gift to have your whole life disturbed by the evil in this world. I get visions during the night that I cannot explain. It's almost impossible to have a long conversation with someone. And the worst thing is, is that I feel guilty now if something bad has transpired in the country and I couldn't do anything to stop it. Guilt over something that I couldn't possibly do anything for. It's horrible, if I'm being honest. But I have brought a killer to justice, helped authorities find a body so her family can give her a burial. I have saved three young women from sex trafficking, and so on. My mum and my friend are trying to convince me that I'm a hero, but I don't see it that way at all. I'm just a young guy who walks the streets, trying to plan for his future.

'Why do you prefer to be anonymous in spite of all your achievements?'

'Well, let's put it this way, shall we? If I don't get stopped on the street I could help even more folks who need saving. I don't wanna be the guy who gets stopped on the street to shake hands, answer questions and pose for photos. If I chose that route then I have neglected those who are suffering that I might have saved.

'What else is this ability for if not to help good people from the evils of this world?'

Enrik killed the TV now that the interview was over and addressed his clients who were still fuming… even more so now that they had seen the teenager who had thwarted their plans to acquire trophy wives and luxurious lifestyles.

'So what're we gonna do about this piece of shit?' asked the man wearing thick glasses and a navy tie.

Enrik took a sip of his water and placed the glass back down on the coaster. 'We are sending one of our men to get rid of this young man, after all the trouble he has caused. Mark my words, we have our hands in a lot of avenues. Folks who are from his country are going crazy for him. They love his character and the fact that he portrays an innocent, humble, kind young man who only wants to help those who want help.'

'Like he's some twenty-first century Superman?' said the businessman with slicked back hair and a fine grey suit.

Enrik didn't answer. Yet now that he thought about it his client was right. Toby Jones had made a name for himself by bringing criminals to justice.

'If you've sent a Hitman to get rid of this look-at-me-I'm-so-perfect piece of shit and he's psychic, won't he already know by the time your guy enters the United Kingdom?'

Enrik cussed inwardly. His client had a valid point. However, he could not let it show. The three businessmen were CEO's of three powerful companies. One worked in Hollywood. The other was a proprietor of a law firm. And the third a businessman who owned two football clubs in Europe.

'Can he dodge a bullet though?' Enrik asked the three clients.

They all laughed at that and seemed content with the knowledge that Toby was marked for assassination in the near future.

'Those women were young and beautiful,' Enrik said when the laughing subsided. 'I know you all liked them. But there's plenty more young, fresh talent out there. But first we take care of this boy then we can celebrate before making plans for you men. After all you've invested £2.5 million in this firm and we don't want to lose you over some kid who's got a bit lucky with some criminals. There's no way on this Earth that we're gonna let someone like Toby beat us or intervene with our affairs in the future and the way we know that is by taking him out and finding you gentlemen trophy wives to come home to.'

The three businessmen voiced their approval and agreement with Enrik and raised their glasses. They were excited that this young man would get his comeuppance sooner rather than later. And just like that all was right in the world again for them.

27.

ANNIE COMBS' youth had passed her by in what seemed like a flash a long time ago. As she stared out the back window at the rising sun, she brought to mind a memory she assumed had been deleted by her brain.

Annie's mother died of leukaemia when she was six years old. Her father had taken early retirement from British Rail and worked part-time as a labourer and made money on the side fixing TVs. Together they lived a modest life; able to afford a flat, a TV, food and a car. Her father buried himself in his work endeavours. Annie knew as she reached the age of seven that her father provided her with the essentials required to live a fairly comfortable life. She had gained both wisdom and strength at a tender age and made acute practical adjustments that would aid her to keep living a steady, straightforward life. She studied her father, only too aware that there were things she would have to deal with that her father couldn't help with let alone offer advice. After all, as girls got to a certain age their bodies began responding differently to how they were throughout their childhood. This in itself had proven to be quite troubling. However, Annie had gone to her guidance counsellor for girls' advice.

As she grew into a teenager, Annie knuckled down and immersed herself in her classes and thrived on achieving good grades doing homework on time and passing her exams which would enable her to provide for herself.

At the age of eighteen, Annie lost interest in boys and opted not to attend their high school disco. Her long grey hair had once been a healthy black hue swept over her shoulder. She had dimples, and although she didn't require them, she wore thick lensed glasses. She wasn't the most attractive of girls. Beauty lay in the eye of the beholder, she taught herself and she didn't want to be fancied by boys for her looks or figure. After all, it was just flesh. As she got older her flesh would be worn and torn into a sagging appearance, hanging off the skeletal frame for dear life, her youth gone.

Her virginity had been maintained. No boys asked her out. She didn't possess a curvy figure like some girls who had fully grown gravity-defining boobs and desirable bums which the boys loved to grope.

To her father's relief and delight in equal measure, Annie had passed her exams with flying colours. She found a job as an accountant at Dawnus building firm.

However, the day that would shatter Annie's straightforward life transpired when she had not long turned twenty years of age. Annie had finished work at 5:00pm and crossed the car park to her moped. She hopped on and then as though a strong gust of wind hit her with intention, Annie rocked, bucked and finally fell off her moped and hit the unforgiving concrete.

A rapid sensation hit her and assailed her with an invisible yet powerful force. In an instant she became fully aware that something bad had happened to her father and he was thinking about her while he fought for breath and life, not wanting his daughter to see him as he was in the here and now.

To this day Annie truly and sincerely believed a higher power had sent her that immense gust to prevent her from the biggest shock of her life.

Her forearms and elbows were scraped and bloodied. She had got off the ground and to a vertical base, got back on the moped, started the motor and exited the car park and took the scenic route home, skin feeling like static. Her heart pumped hard against her small breasts and Annie was on autopilot. Her whole mind had been frazzled. All she thought about in a maintained anxiety was what had befallen her father to cause her to think of him and fall off her bike.

In the near distance Annie heard the piercing emergency sirens and squeezed the throttle.

Were the sirens for her father?

Yes, they were, she knew unequivocally without even the trace of evidence. She tried to convince herself that she was merely having pessimistic thoughts and that her father was indeed fine, yet the insistence of her mind insisted that this was no mistake or pessimistic deliberation which she'd developed after growing up without her mother.

The street she lived on was cordoned off by police squad cars, blurring blue beacons dancing in the evergreens. She killed the motor as a PCSO raised his hands in a STOP gesture. She explained to the officer that her home residence was here and that her house was the one with a big white door with a brass number 4 on it. The officer got on his radio and informed the Detective Inspector and then escorted her down the street where another two squad cars were parked horizontally across the street; and then Annie could hardly believe the sight of uniform-clad coroners donning baggy white overalls pushing a stretcher with a body zipped up in a black plastic bag towards the waiting ambulance.

Frightened and distressed, Annie turned around and came face-to-face with a detective who had the unpleasant responsibility of informing her that an armed Muslim had found the front door unlocked, let himself inside and was then confronted by her father. He shot her father in the abdomen and then without mercy one fatal shot into his head at close range.

Annie remembered the street and home spinning, slowly at first and then rotating around her, picking up speed and going faster and faster until she tottered unsteadily and the detective seized her and half-walked and half-carried her to the nearest squad car for her to sit down and try to overcome the shock and horrible reality of the situation.

Now Annie was older, wiser and the past remained buried in the past. Upstairs, in her bedroom drawer, were photos of her loving parents. The only proof, apart from their graves, that they even existed was survived by her life and the photo album Annie kissed before turning into bed every single night.

Her invigorated purpose of life now was the young man, Toby Jones, who had become like a son or nephew who she wanted to protect from the nasty world they lived in. She had the urge to simply wrap her arms around Toby and hug him close. He had the "shine", the same as she did. And although to the casual observer having psychic powers was considered awesome and cool, it was anything but. For one thing: it interrupted you and sent flashes and glimpses of people in desperate need of help.

Annie considered Toby a hero.

And the nation was beginning to see that too.

However, the pressure that came with such a gift or curse threatened to overtake you in an instant.

Annie had fallen off her moped.

Toby had a brain seizure.

The "Shine" had no emotions or consideration for those like her and Toby.

And at the first sign of threat, Annie would inform her protégé and guide him and protect him with every last bit of life she still had left in her... at all costs.

*

Toby completed his twelve reps of squatting and exhaled deeply, feeling the burn and heat in his quads. He did this for another three sets before crossing the gym floor to the leg extension and hamstring curl apparatus. Once he finished his session half an hour later, he popped open a protein milk sport drink and gulped it down before draining the rest of his water. Today had been a good day, which found him in good health, mentally and physically. It had also been a while since he'd heard voices which enabled him to strive to being the best at what he did work-wise and in the gym.

It had been Mother's Day yesterday. Toby had bought Abigail a bunch of pink tulips, a card and box of assorted chocolates made in Belgium.

Now once he got home and had a shower and a change of clothes, he planned on taking his mother out for a meal.

And that's what he did.

They sat opposite each other in the Harvester and enjoyed each other's company. Before they could only afford one day out to spend leisurely. However, since Toby had been on TV and on the front page of the local newspapers, along with his job, he was now able to afford some of the nicer things life had to offer. This was one of them.

'I've decided to start learning to drive,' Toby announced.

Abigail's eyebrows rose, pleasantly surprised by this sudden news. 'That's a good idea,' she said. 'Now that people know you around here it'll be a lot safer. Plus, you'll no longer have to rely on a bus when it's bucketing down on your way to work. It's also something to have that allows you a bit more independence. You must be fed up seeing me all day and all night every day.'

Although he knew his mother was joking, there was a trace of honesty underlining the comment.

'Mum. C'mon, I love spending time with you,' he said. 'We work well together. And with a bit of luck this "Knowing" gift I have will subside and permit me a new life with peace as the nucleus.'

Abigail looked sad all of a sudden as she chewed her lips.

'What's wrong, Mum?'

Abigail shook her head, evidently not wanting to say what she was feeling. 'Nothing, love.'

'Hey, c'mon. Tell me. It's not good to keep things to yourself – it only makes things worse for bottling it up.'

'It's just that neither I nor your father have what you got. There's no history of that in both of our family's history. I worry about you. It's a mother thing. I can't turn it ON or OFF. I'm just being a nagging, overprotective mother, that's all.'

Toby shook his head. 'No, you're not,' he said. 'You've had a tough time in this world, and you don't ask much of life. Peace of mind is all you seek and a few laughs. That's not much to ask, is it?'

Abigail smiled at her son and shook her head. 'No. I guess you're right. I'm the luckiest mother in the world. I got the greatest son who is even more than I could have ever dreamed for.'

Toby rolled his eyes comically. 'Just eat your food.'

Abigail laughed quietly, realising that she was embarrassing him. 'Motherly love. God forbid if anything bad did befall you,' she said, still smiling but being honest and serious as well.

Toby reached out his hand and rested it on his mother's hand. He looked longingly at her and said in a quiet yet powerful way, 'Nothing bad is gonna happen to me, Mum. Have faith in that, please. I hated those times when I could hear the screaming in my head from another soul, crying out for a saviour. But I'm not Superman and I or no one else for that matter can save everyone from the pain that they're in. I'm no hero. I'm a conscientious person who hates to see other good people suffer through no fault of their own. But the other day when I was walking home from work, an ambulance flew by followed by a police squad car, and I suddenly realised that in spite of the interviews on TV and the newspapers, I'm just the same as everyone else. We're all doing our bit to keep all evil out of our lives and that's all we can do.'

He broke off then and finished his meal.

Both Toby and Abigail felt like a burden had been taken off their shoulders now that they'd had that discussion. They enjoyed their desserts and Toby left a £5 tip for the waiter.

They went home and relaxed for the remainder of the day.

28.

THE MAN sitting in his blue and white striped Mini rolled the car to a halt alongside the kerb and killed the motor. Settled where he was, the man removed his seat belt and reached across to the passenger seat and picked up the file he'd received that morning in the post from a European employer requiring his services.

The man's name was Michael or at least that was the name known in the underworld organizations he often worked for. Michael was an expert hit man who had served time in Iraq and Afghanistan some years back.

He opened the file provided for him by his employer Enrik Stansen from Denmark. It might have been easier to have faxed or emailed the information but Enrik was a little old-fashioned with modern technology. He preferred a "hands-on" approach. Along with the file there was a cheque for five hundred British pounds only. In the brief letter, Enrik had promised that Michael would get another cheque of one thousand five hundred British pounds but only once the target had been terminated.

This alone was enough incentive to do the task he'd been told to do. Now here he was on Tabernacle Street facing the main road in and out of the small town.

According to the file, the target's name was Toby Jones. There was a black and white photograph of Toby included with the paperwork. Michael thought that his target was very handsome and could easily get a role in a movie if they were in Hollywood. Then he read how Toby Jones was indeed a celebrity and had appeared on TV and in the newspapers after using his psychic abilities to bring men to justice for all sorts of crimes that the local police would never have detected, or would have taken several years of ongoing investigations. And Toby had done their job for them within a matter of hours.

The case involving Enrik Stansen had been one of these unsolved crimes. Human trafficking. Sexual slaves. Toby had fought, then killed the courier and set free the young, beautiful women who were virgins from being forced into marriage in Denmark.

Of course, Michael was fully aware that sex trafficking was against the law, although that didn't matter to him one iota. A job was a job at the end of the day. The less he knew about the ins and outs of the case the easier and better it was for him. He didn't possess a conscience so life itself was pretty much simple and straightforward enough.

When his services weren't required, Michael drove for a limousine firm that specialised in famous folks, especially when the award ceremonies were held.

His six years in the military had hardened his heart so much he didn't even recognise the man he saw when he looked into the mirror. He remembered one time they had been in Iraq and he had strolled alongside a tank and veered away from his comrades and ascended a rusty steel exterior staircase to the roof of one sandstone constructions and removed his sniper rifle. He was the most astute marksman in his platoon and had already nine kills under his belt. Clean, fatal shots that cleared the path of his fellow infantrymen as they cleared out all the oppositions fighters.

There had been one occasion when Michael found himself on the roof, staring down his sniper rifle scope at a Muslim woman who crouched over her little daughter. The little girl was crying and trembling, tears rolling down her cherubic face, desperately wanting to be anywhere but in the heart of the war zone. No child – or anyone innocent for that matter – deserved to be anywhere near a conflict between rival nations, fighting for control and searching for nuclear weapons that would cause catastrophic ramifications.

The Muslim woman was holding the little girl by her shoulders, pressing herself against her, hiding something. Either that or she was pregnant.

Yet when the little girl wriggled herself free from her mother or carer, the woman turned sharply, swept her right arm up and whipped out a long piece of weapon in an attempt to fire at the unsuspecting soldiers below.

Michael did not hesitate for a second. Once the woman was in his sights, he removed the safety and fired one shot that exploded the woman's face in a geyser of blood, torn flesh and bone.

She was dead before she hit the ground.

His comrade pumped his fist with joy and then patted Michael on the back. Michael spun around, still armed and dangerous and shot his brother in arms in a cold-blooded reflex that would rattle his grandfather's bones.

The boy had an amazing gift, Michael thought, purposely bringing himself back to the here and now. The house was located right next to the cream stone-walled church. And how fitting that would be if Michael could take Toby's life right here and now in the presence of the Lord.

He reached over to the back seat and picked up his Colt .45, checked it had ammunition, then put the piece into the top pocket of his plain, long-sleeve shirt and glanced around him.

The front door opened.

Michael sat bolt-upright, ready to emerge from the car and take out his intended target with one or two head shots. Then he'd get back behind the wheel and get the hell out of this small town and back on the motorway before anyone saw him at the scene and gave his description to the authorities.

That was what he had planned as he pulled the handle on the driver's door, got out, slammed the door shut and got onto the pavement.

Ready to get his gun out and shoot Toby in the back of the head, he was surprised by a police squad car that came down the street, shot past Michael and pulled into the kerb right outside the Crown Pub and attracted the attention of the target. Toby leaned down and the passenger window of the squad car rolled down. He talked to them briefly and then much to Michael's astonishment, got in the back seat and was taken to an unknown location with the police, leaving Michael looking like a spare prick at a wedding…

'Mark my words, Toby. You haven't seen the last of me yet. Your number is up and it's time to take out the trash…'

*

The fluffy white clouds dispersed and permitted sunshine to filter through, giving the day in Wales a boost of activity and a resplendent ambience.

Two days ago, Matthew Cawthorne had done something hardly any boy or man would ever dream of, never mind following through with his horrific plan. So far all was clear. However, sooner or later he expected the local constabulary to be at his front door asking to speak to him regarding his mother's death.

Matricide was one of – if not – the worse types of murder known to man. Not even God could forgive that sin, Matthew decided, not that he believed in any creator or higher power. When you died that was it. You slept and decomposed in the ground six feet under and never resurfaced into some form of afterlife.

What he had done had been done out of vengeance and spite, evidently directed at Susan for refusing to forgive him and permit him a roof over his head until he found a job and could afford a place of his own, if that indeed was possible in the high rise residences in the twenty-first century. Instead she had cut all ties and bonds, like blood. Matthew had been devastated when his mother, the giver of his life, denied him, even after he had apologised. She evidently held a powerful grudge against her own flesh and blood. To Matthew that was unforgivable. Surely, she still had motherly responsibilities to uphold. Yet that had all been forsaken in her stubbornness and neglect.

He felt no guilt or any other emotion. However, now a couple of days had passed and he slept comfortably, Matthew began to believe that what he'd done was in some uncivil way justified, although he would never tell anyone that. People didn't think the way he thought. That much he learned from being incarcerated in the mental asylum. He remembered his fellow patients, all crazy and violent, running up and down the corridors in the night, being tackled by security guards, given tranquilizers before returning to their cells and sleeping until late the following morning.

Furthermore, Matthew had a tidal surge of adrenaline while in a state of frenzy from the brutal slaying of Susan as she lay in her double-sized bed in the pitch darkness, suffering immensely from the actions he unleashed upon her until he was certain she was dead.

Or maybe he hadn't killed her. Maybe all he had achieved was hurting her to the point of desperation.

Now, in his mind's eye, he saw Susan in her nightgown crawling across the bed to the cabinet, taking the receiver in her trembling hands and dialling 999 and pleading with the operator to send an ambulance as fast as possible to her home because she was bleeding from the abdomen and arms.

Perhaps the ambulance had arrived in the nick of time and got her to A&E to be treated and have her wounds cleansed and bound before she lost too much blood.

Matthew stood in the kitchen, sipping a cold can of Pepsi Max, staring at the sharp kitchen knife he had wielded, now washed clean of any fingerprints. He had worn protective surgical gloves to perform the macabre act, after having watched a lot of CSI a few years ago. Furthermore, when the local constabulary came by Matthew would feign shock and distress and explain that he had been home all night, reading a book prior to turning in for the night.

He practised his rehearsed dialogue and facial expressions for when the cops did come round to pay a visit and break the news. And Matthew had to be honest, in another life he might have made a pretty darn good actor.

'Ain't going to go to prison for you, mamma,' he hissed. 'No way! You made me suffer. Now you can suffer no more. And if you survived and told the cops it was me, I'd feign surprise and anger and tell the cops that you didn't like me and was only blaming me 'cause you wanted me to be locked up again over a stupid bloody cat that ain't even yours, mamma.'

Anyone from an outsider's perspective would concur that Matthew's mother was crazier than her son.

Matthew had left the house key on the hook on the peg board in the kitchen. So if the cops did come sniffing around his place they wouldn't stumble on a hidden key. If they asked, Matthew would tell them that he didn't have a key and therefore it couldn't have been him. Perhaps mamma had left the door unlocked or she did it to herself in a crazy attempt to send her god-awful son back to the infirmary.

'Damn bitch got just what she deserved,' Matthew said through gritted teeth.

*

Toby occupied the back seat relishing the cool interior breeze. The two uniform officers were in the front.

The constable that couldn't have been much older than Toby himself turned in his seat and faced him. 'DI Sark has asked if we could take you to the station. A murder has been committed in the Highlands estate. Hopefully you can make his job easier and quicker to solve.'

Toby nodded. Then he wiped the sweat beads off his brow.

'Hey, are you all right, mate?' the officer riding shotgun asked, seeing how pale and sweaty the boy in the back seat looked, almost fighting to stay conscious and well.

'Feel sick,' Toby managed to get out in a hoarse whisper.

The constable turned to his partner and said, 'Pull over somewhere convenient. He don't look so good.'

The squad car pulled into a slot outside a convenience store.

Toby opened the door and dry retched, embracing the cool air, wondering why on earth he was feeling this way. Perhaps he was coming down with a virus or a nasty bout of flu, he thought. However, as he inhaled fresh air and rubbed his face, drying it from perspiration, he already started to feel a lot better.

'I'm okay,' he called out to the two officers. 'Just had a funny spell then.'

'Are you all right to come with us?' the constable in the passenger seat asked.

Toby nodded. 'Yeah. I haven't eaten or drank anything since yesterday afternoon. Bound to feel the shakes, is all. Thanks for pulling over though.'

'We'll get you something to eat and drink at the station,' the constable said, genuinely concerned for Toby. After all, he was called the "Wonder Kid" to the police.

They continued on their journey and Toby breathed a sigh of relief. The fresh air had done him a world of good, and when they did eventually arrive down at the station the constable bought him a Lucozade sport's drink and a Mars Bar. Once he finished his snack, the constable escorted him down the hallway to an empty interview room.

DI Sark rose as if the Queen had entered the room.

'Hello, my man!' he exclaimed, wearing a smile as broad as his shoulders. 'How're you doing?'

Toby said that he was all right and that he had to eat and drink something otherwise he would have passed out.

'Your health comes first every time, Toby. You of all people should know that. Please take a seat.'

Toby pulled the chair out and sat opposite the desk to the detective.

'Has there been another crime?' Toby asked.

DI Sark nodded. 'There's been a homicide up in the woods. I'd like it if you came with me and see if we can get any info right away. I know you're probably a bit frustrated with been pestered and disrupted but you have an incredible gift that really does make a difference to the community. I only wish I had your power, son. I really do. I'd been Chief Superintendent overnight. But we don't get many murders... and I'd like to keep it that way. And I know you do too. So, will you join me to the crime scene?'

Toby leaned forward. 'I will do my best. But you shouldn't expect me to aid you every time. The "gift" that I have as you call it is not something I can control. Don't expect me to be able to solve all your crimes and other cases. I know you pay me. But you must understand that doing this does take a lot out of me. It's not good for my brain or my mind. And please don't envy me. Sometimes this "gift" of knowing things I shouldn't be able to know causes me a lot of stress.'

DI Sark shifted uncomfortably in his seat. All of a sudden he began to realise how bad being a psychic really was. The boy didn't want it, and now the detective inspector could fully understand why. After all, the officers had picked him up off the street and brought him here to do police work, and although he practically solved the crimes in a mere few moments the damage done to his life no doubt would hurt him and leave him an existence of suffering rather than fun and pleasure, like most boys his age.

Toby could see the guilt on DI Sark's face and regretted saying anything. 'Come on then,' he said in a new and vibrant tone. 'Let's go catch us a killer!'

DI Sark chuckled at that and rose from his chair, Toby followed him outside to his BMW.

*

CSI and forensics had cordoned off the house and were now investigating the crime scene that had drawn a lot of unwanted attention by the public, who gathered around, wanting to see a dead body and have something to discuss with their friends later on. Of course, it would be in the papers and on the local news channel, but they were the type of folks who would be proud to say that they were there, as if it were some bizarre claim to fame.

Toby felt a lot better since his snack.

DI Sark blasted the horn for a group of boys to get off the street so he could slip into the space provided. Once parked, they got out of the car and walked ten meters to the residence.

DI Sark showed his badge to a uniform officer who stepped aside, permitting them onto the property. He strode down the concrete path towards the front door and was about to be let in by one of the forensic workers when he noticed that Toby had hung back outside gazing up at the first floor.

'What is it?' he asked, urgent, desperate.

'The murder took place upstairs, didn't it?'

DI Sark called out to one of the CSI team members. They crossed the patch of grass and shook hands with the detective.

'How can I help, detective?'

'How many murders are there?'

'One.'

'Where was the murder committed?'

'Upstairs,' the CSI man said and then pointed to the bedroom window where the curtains were closed, the window

Toby had been staring at before he received any formal information.

'Any sign of breaking and entering?' DI Sark asked the CSI guy.

'No,' Toby answered. 'The victim knew the perpetrator well.'

Both the CSI guy and DI Sark stared at Toby, both amazed at how Toby already knew this after only being on the property for ten seconds.

'Is this the boy who has supernatural powers?' the CSI guy asked DI Sark.

'He sure is,' DI Sark answered. 'Creepy, huh?'

'I am in awe of you,' the CSI guy told Toby, who stared impassively straight ahead.

'The victim was stabbed repeatedly in the abdomen,' Toby said. 'It was pitch dark and she had been asleep, awoken by the excruciating pain.'

The CSI guy cussed. 'Aw this guy is friggin' awesome!'

'How did the victim die?' DI Sark said, mostly for fun and clarification.

'Stabbed repeatedly, like he said.'

After a few moments, DI Sark broke the silence. 'Shall we go inside?' he asked Toby, who was still in a trancelike state.

Toby followed the two men into the house and saw flashes of a gleaming silver serrated knife. He flinched and stepped back. Then another flash... and another... and another... again... again. Only as this continued, raping his mind, did he see that the gleaming murder weapon was now drenched in scarlet liquid. He crouched down until his head faced his feet.

Something else is trying to get through too, he thought.

'Hey! Are you all right, pal?' the CSI guy asked, taking his foot off the bottom step of the staircase.

The nauseous sensation had returned. Toby could see twinkling dots in his vision. The circuits in his head started to crackle like a hot furnace. Volts of electricity coursed through the nerve endings in his buzzing brain. As he managed to right himself to a normal stance, the ground beneath him started to wobble and his legs buckled at the knees.

'What's wrong?' DI Sark said, deeply concerned about the boy.

'What's happening to him?' the CSI guy asked, looking frantic.

'He told me down at the station that his "gift" of knowing things he couldn't possibly know has a detrimental effect on him and that it's not something to envy. He's gonna keel over any second now.'

'He solved the crime... Well almost,' the CSI guy announced, disturbed that a boy so young and gifted should have to suffer in this way when it ought to be the perpetrator who suffered. In his experience, it was always the nice, kind and genuine folks who suffered or died young rather than the bad guys. Why was that? Then he chastised himself for even giving in to the possibility that Toby might die.

'Toby! Toby!' DI Sark shouted.

'I'm fine,' Toby croaked. 'Just a dizzy spell. Can you take me home?'

'Of course I can,' DI Sark said.

'I'm sorry I couldn't be of more help,' Toby said, after clearing his throat.

The CSI guy hunkered down on his haunches the way a mammal would do. 'Dude, seriously, you got nothing to be sorry about.'

Toby returned to his full height and exhaled. 'This isn't the work of a serial killer,' he announced. 'But, unless I'm mistaken, then this crime was contrived and executed by an enemy of the victim or someone who sought vengeance for a wrongdoing. That's the best I can do.'

'You've been awesome!' the CSI guy said.

DI Sark looked at Toby and said, 'Are you all right to make your way back to the car or do you need help?'

'I'm all right,' Toby said. 'I haven't eaten since yesterday afternoon... and I didn't get much sleep. I'm just tired. All I was gonna do today was go to the library and buy my mum some flowers.'

Both DI Sark and the CSI guy exchanged a look of mutual respect for each other and admiration for this boy who was yet to reach manhood.

29.

MICHAEL had made a call to Enrik on his mobile phone and brought him up-to-date on what was happening. Initially Enrik was annoyed and cussed. Then he calmed and ordered Michael to stay on the street, take photos of the house and do the act when Toby returned home. However, Michael almost forgot to add that Toby had been picked up by a police squad car. Perhaps, Michael suggested, Toby – who was psychic – already knew their plan and had gone with the police to report him. But if that was the case, would he leave his mother at home... alone?

He had taken photos of the house and emailed them to Enrik. Then he slumped down in the driver's seat and kept an eye open for the boy's return.

Twenty minutes later, the sound of a vehicle in motion reached his ears and as Michael shot a glance in his wing mirror, he could see a BMW ride the speed hump and slot in to a space two car lengths away from Michael.

'I don't believe this,' Michael muttered.

Then he cussed as Toby got out of the car, waved goodbye to the driver and turned and headed for the front door.

Michael leapt out of the car and onto the pavement. He ran towards the house and got to the entrance gate just as Toby closed the door. He used the F-word, spun on his heel and headed back to his parked vehicle, shaking his head furiously as another opportunity passed by without success. He fished out his mobile phone and dialled the familiar number of his employer to bring him up to date with what was going on, as promised.

'You bloody idiot!' Enrik shouted down the phone. 'Can't you do anything right? I said I wanted him dead by *today*. He's a goddamn nuisance. Can't you see how much trouble he has already caused with my associates? I need him in the morgue sooner rather than later.'

'What if he already knows?'

'Yeah. That little shit has got certain powers!' Enrik bellowed. 'He's killed one of our employees before. He doesn't carry a gun. You do. Psychics can't dodge bullets.'

'How shall I proceed?' Michael asked, starting to get annoyed himself, being yelled at after he'd done nothing wrong.

There was a long pause. The only sound down the line was the breathing of the two men.

'The street has a doctors' surgery at the top end of the street and a popular pub at the bottom, which leads onto New Road,' Michael said, doing his utmost to be helpful and not a hindrance.

'You can't risk shooting from the outside, but when it goes dark wear something to cover your face and a pair of gloves.'

'I can do that,' Michael said, trying to sound optimistic and hopeful.

'Go to his house and try the front door and ring the bell. But make sure there's no CCTV anywhere that can catch you. If his bitch of a mother answers the call shoot her as well.'

Michael was calm again. He told Enrik that his plan was very good and in his mind's eye he could see it being achieved with little effort.

'It's gonna be a while till sundown,' Michael said.

'What am I? Your babysitter?'

Michael shook his head but prudently kept his mouth shut. His employer was a complete dick. There was a wonder anything got achieved with his attitude. So what if the boy-psychic had saved three young women and killed the kidnapper, he couldn't dodge bullets, as Enrik had said.

'Make sure they don't have a viewing hole in the front door,' Enrik added.

'They don't, the door is made of white plastic and has four small frosted glass squares.'

'Excellent!' Enrik said in a raised voice. 'Tell me when you've blown their heads off and I'll send another cheque your way.'

'Will do,' Michael said, smiling broadly.

*

Abigail was in the kitchen, making Toby peanut butter sandwiches when the front door opened and then closed behind her son. He walked through the living room area and entered the kitchen where the small TV reported the national news.

'Hi Mum!' Toby said.

'Your lunch'll be served right now, my lovely little boy,' Abigail said.

'Aw Mum! You didn't have to do that. I can make my own sandwiches. Go and sit down in the living room and relax.'

'I'm almost done, love,' Abigail said, placing the four pieces of sandwich onto a china plate and a cold can of Diet Coke to wash it down with. Then she saw how pale he looked in the face.

Toby avoided eye contact, fully aware that his mother would only worry about him if he told her about being plagued with insomnia and the feeling that someone with evil intentions was watching him.

'You look so unwell, withdrawn and fatigued,' she said anxiously.

'I didn't sleep very well, that's all,' Toby replied, seeing no point in making up a white lie. Then he went on to tell her about how the police had picked him up and how he'd helped with a crime scene in one of the cul-de-sacs beneath the mountains.

Abigail shook her head in dismay. 'I knew this would happen,' she said, not in the slightest bit impressed with how her only child was treated. 'This is what happens when folks see that you're quiet, shy and easy-going. They take advantage of your good nature and the fact that you're always willing to help. Then you become unwell while everyone gets the same wage while you do all the work. Look at you! You look like a skeleton, you're so thin and emaciated.'

Toby sighed.

'No, Toby,' Abigail went on. 'Don't huff at me. I'm your best friend; always have been. I know better than you. Charity starts at home. You're no good to anyone if you are like you are now. You might well be psychic or whatever they're calling it these days, but you have to put yourself first.'

Toby didn't have any argument with his mother over this. She was right, he knew that. Because he was who he was, he did lots of favours without money or any other kind of reward in return. Yet now he indeed understood and concurred with what his mother had just told him.

'I'll eat my food upstairs and try to get an afternoon nap, if that's all right?'

Abigail nodded. Now her son was making sense. Mothers knew best, after all. It wasn't her son she was annoyed at but everyone else. Police, media, fans. She did curse God inwardly though for not releasing Toby from his burden. She remembered Toby when he was just a boy. A pathetic, polite, obedient little angel. Back then he depended on her. And still today with this new ability, he needed her now more than ever.

She watched him walk out of the kitchen, into the living room and upstairs to his bedroom.

'Damn those cops!' she snapped.

*

Toby turned his TV on and watched the Formula 1 procedures while he devoured his sandwiches and drained his Diet Coke. He started to feel woozy and lay on his side and watched the fast cars whizzing around the track with weary eyes and gradually drifted off to sleep.

He awoke two hours later, groggy and dizzy. He took his plate down and placed it in the kitchen sink.

Abigail was in the living room. She picked up the remote control and put the TV on mute. She waited until Toby emerged from the kitchen and then asked him how he was feeling.

'I slept for a couple of hours,' Toby said. 'But I'm gonna get changed into my pyjamas and watch TV. I'll probably drop back off and sleep well tonight.'

'Why didn't you sleep last night?' Abigail wanted to know.

Toby shrugged. 'Just couldn't drop off. I was just lying there waiting for sleep to come and instead dawn came, the sun rose and I was still wide awake.'

'Was there something troubling you?'

'I dunno Mum,' he said in full honesty. 'My mind is different to a normal person. Perhaps it was this homicide that kept me awake. Who knows? But if it continues I'm gonna have to go to the doctors and ask for medication that will sedate me and allow me to sleep.'

Abigail concurred. She was glad that her son had already come up with a plan. Toby was right. The whole thing seemed unfair. He was a sweet, innocent boy who was treated like he was Superman when in fact he was a human being, same as everyone else. Abigail believed that the local authorities were using him, his supernatural gift, to do their work for them. And although that sounded brusque and unfair, in her eyes, her son came first. He had already helped them several times. However, at this rate, if it continued, Toby could become very unwell, lose his job and become bedridden for the best years of his life. To her that was unacceptable. She had a good mind to go to the local police and make a formal complaint on the basis of harassment.

'Drink some milk,' she told Toby. 'It might help you get to sleep.'

'Okay, Mum. I'll try that.'

*

A couple of hours later, Toby watched TV and felt his eyes becoming weary. They were beginning to get heavy and knowing he was about to drop back off to sleep, he killed the TV and closed his eyes. Sleep invited itself into him and soon Toby was dead to the world.

He found himself outside the house, staring up at the dull grey clouds, leaden with water, about to spill onto the small town below. He wondered why he was standing outside, but it felt right in some peculiar way that he couldn't explain or make any sense of. All the cars normally parked up alongside the kerb were gone. He saw his mother's car and a BMW a few yards up the road right outside the chapel.

Toby stepped down and ambled to the gate until he came to a halt on the cracked pavement. He wondered where everyone had gone. He listened to the background drone of vehicles whizzing past each other on the main road leading to and from the small town.

As he looked closer, Toby could see a man sitting behind the wheel in the BMW. He looked mean and strong. Toby didn't want to look at him any more. However, the man with steely, grey eyes and a powerful looking jaw got out of the car, having had enough of Toby staring at him. He could feel the pounding of his heart and see the left-hand side of his T-shirt moving with every beat.

Without having someone tell him, Toby became fully aware that this stranger who slammed the driver's door behind him and strode directly towards him was intent on doing something nasty to him. And as he drew closer, Toby could see that the man was over six feet tall, broad shouldered and had a strong physical shape. The man could have been a rugby player and deliver strong, bone-crunching tackles on his opponents.

He didn't have time to feel nervous. Toby stood rooted to the spot, trembling with fear. Why wasn't he running away or going back to the house? he wondered.

Going back inside the house wasn't just a cowardly act, but it also put his mother in great danger too.

Then Toby saw a silver .45 Colt that the stranger had drawn from his belt on his denim jeans; he saw that the man had raised the weapon and aimed the business end of the gun at his head.

The young man was facing the gun that would end his life in a split second.

'What do you want?' he asked the powerful stranger.

'To watch you die,' the stranger said in a deep, meaningful voice.

'Why?' That was all Toby had time to ask.

The stranger didn't give a reason. Instead he pulled the trigger…

Toby bolted upright after feeling a whack in his forehead. He placed his trembling left hand on his sweaty brow to feel for a hole or something. Then he realised with tremendous relief that it had all been a dream. He consulted the alarm clock. 5:59AM.

The young man had been asleep since 8:56PM, not to mention the two hours' sleep he'd had in the day.

He cussed under his breath and tried to relax. Then a thought came to him that rattled his bones which his ancestors could feel. What if there *was* a man outside, sitting in his BMW? The dream had been so vivid that he couldn't tell the difference between another precognitive vision or a nasty dream. Of course, the only way to find out and put his mind at ease was to get up out of bed, go downstairs, step outside and scan the street.

Before any further hesitation or deeply rooted concern, Toby threw the sheets off him, stood up, exited his bedroom, descended the staircase and went outside. He did his best to remain as quiet as possible so as not to wake his mother.

Outside the first dull grey light of dawn settled in the morning mist like the birth of a fog. Toby arrived on the pavement outside his home and looked left to right.

He gasped in utter shock at the BMW.

Furthermore, there was a man with the exact same features from his vision slumped down in the drivers' seat, asleep. He headed back inside and climbed the staircase, heart pounding like a racehorse. In his bedroom, Toby picked up his mobile phone and dialled DI Sark's number and waited for an answer.

'Toby? Why are you calling me at this hour?' DI Sark asked in a calm voice.

Toby chastised himself inwardly for awakening the detective. 'I'm sorry to wake you, but I had a vision and I just had it confirmed as authentic. I'm in grave danger. There is a man sitting in his BMW outside my house, wanting to kill me for some reason, I'm not sure why. I had this vision that I stepped outside and he spotted me and shot me with a .45 Colt dead. So I've just been outside and there's a BMW and a man exactly the same as the vision. Could you please send a car to my street to arrest him? Or at least find out if he has got a weapon. In the meantime, I'm gonna go back outside and take the registration code for his car.'

'I'm on it,' DI Sark said, fully awake and grateful that the young psychic had broken his slumber and given him the information.

*

Michael stirred in his sleep. Then he shifted on to his side, uncomfortable but relaxed in the car. The sound of a gate opening brought him to awareness, but his eyes were tired. He had grown tired and slack being cooped up in the car for such a long time, but as the seagulls squawked overhead, he opened his eyes and thought he saw someone standing on the pavement a couple of yards away facing him.

All of a sudden, he snapped awake, remembering why he was here and what his mission was. His eyes flew open and what he saw and realised was that his target had just taken a photograph on his mobile phone and was heading back to his house. Michael threw the door open, clambered out, nearly falling over his own feet and raced down the street. He drew his .45 Colt from his belt, took the safety off and fired. An explosion erupted, spilling blood onto the concrete and the young psychic stumbled forward.

Michael dashed closer as Toby was stumbling across the paving stones to the front door. As he did this he glanced over his shoulder at the assassin and crashed through the front door as another explosion thundered down the street and the bullet ripped into the back of Toby's leg, severely injuring his hamstring muscles and spilling more blood. Toby crawled inside and slammed the door shut. Then there were two more shots that burst holes through the front door. Michael charged the front door, shoulder first, but it didn't yield. Then he shot the living room window open and found pleasure in seeing the glass shatter and splinter in a tingling tune. He could see inside now. He spotted his target crawling on the floor towards the staircase and shot him again. This bullet exploded into Toby's other shoulder. He cried out in fear and agony.

Blood spilled out of Toby's mouth. Everything in sight began spinning, faster and faster, causing him to lose consciousness at the most critical time in his whole life, when he needed to be tuned in and alert to the dangers around him.

Shit! I'm gonna die!

At the foot of the stairs, Toby knew full well that getting to the first floor would be near impossible. He was doomed. Then through a blurred and unsteady vision, he saw a shape appear at the top of the staircase.

His mother! Abigail screamed at the top of her lungs.

Toby was starting to feel nauseous and light headed, as though something was drawing the veil to close the play at an art theatre. Only this time it was his story. His life that was drawing to a close and now Death awaited him. But Toby didn't want that. Despite the pain and the blood pouring out from his wounds, the teenager didn't want to lose consciousness. Instead he focused on the near future. And the only way he would live to see tomorrow would be to get to a safe place, out of sight from further onslaught.

Footsteps thundered down the stairs and Abigail reached her dying son, wielding a knife she kept under her bed ever since Toby's father deserted them when he was young. Now the knife didn't possess much power in a gun attack. However, being in possession of such a tool out of the kitchen gave Abigail the courage to hurry down and help her son.

Her screaming burst one of Toby's eardrums and suddenly a high-pitched noise sang, blocking everything out. He turned then rolled over and could see his attacker swinging his leg over the window ledge, fall on his back into the living room, slowly get to his feet and take aim.

Oh shit! This is it!

The attacker showed Toby the widest and most sinister smile he ever saw. Death was certain. He blinked and as he did so something with blinding speed and ferocity whacked through the back and torso of the attacker's body, spurting a geyser of blood on the cream-coloured walls and dark blue carpet.

The attacker fell to the ground face first and moved no more.

Evidently, someone unseen had killed the attacker, saving Toby's life in an instant.

Abigail turned his head; his neck and jaw feeling all too rubbery and unattached to the rest of him. He blinked once, slowly and then his eyes closed and the psychic lost consciousness and surrendered to death...

30.

THE STAR-STUDDED night sky looked like nature's jewellery collection, offering an innumerable wonder of galaxies. However, Matthew Cawthorne wasn't the slightest bit interested in all of that. He was headed to the Hope & Anchor pub with a twenty-pound note he'd got from doing the lottery a week ago. He had never won anything his whole life. Now that he was free with a place of his own that he could call home and had cash in hand, he was going to enjoy himself. And why not? He said he was sorry for his mistake, and had served his time in the mental institution healing himself.

Mother was gone. Stupid cow deserved it for disowning him over some pest cat! He did the neighbourhood a favour as far as he was concerned. The police were busy with the looting in the city several miles west and as far as he knew there was no news yet on his mother's passing away. All was good in the world again, according to Matthew.

The world was his oyster. He could do whatever he pleased now. He was a youngster looking for some company and a chance to lay down plans for the next few years that would see him rise up the ranks of powerful men and conquer the nation in which he resided and have his name in lights. He longed for power and wealth. Then with those things clear in abundance he could enforce his beliefs upon the local civilization.

The strong smell of beer as he climbed the concrete steps into the pub welcomed him, and the temptation to have his first drink of alcohol was as important to him right then as finding an attractive young woman to fornicate with.

Matthew Cawthorne's life was about to begin, now that he had everything under control. For the time being he would need to keep on taking his medication and going for his weekly injection for his mental health. Yet he felt in better shape both physically and mentally than he had ever done. He did a hundred push-ups and a hundred sit-ups every morning and every evening. He had built a strong core and an inner confidence so that he could put his mind to anything and achieve it.

The bartender caught his eye as he took his place on the other side of the bar, ready to serve him. 'What shall it be?'

'Gimme your best pint of beer,' Matthew said, savouring the moment and committing it to memory. Then he handed the twenty-pound note over and waited for his first beverage.

The drink gave Matthew an amazing sensation. It was pure pleasure and tasted and smelt so good that he would never go back to drinking lemonade ever again. Soft drinks were for kids, Matthew thought to himself. Beer was for men. And boy, what a difference it made.

He drained the pint and slammed the empty glass down on its coaster. The barman noticed the eagerness with which his young customer had put down the empty glass and headed his way.

'You are eighteen, aren't you?' he asked.

Matthew nodded. Then decided he needed to give a verbal answer too. He told the barman that indeed he was old enough and that was his first drink.

'Okay,' the barman said. 'But lemme give you some advice – take your time, that's how drunk you'll get and sick the next day if you keep guzzling them down. Be smart. You hear me?'

At that moment, Matthew envisioned that he would certainly seize the barman from the back of his head and ram his head into the bar several times until he was dead. 'Thanks for the advice,' he said, a little too quickly in a voice dripping with menace.

The barman got him another and placed it in front of Matthew.

'Oh, and another thing, don't mix your drinks," the barman said. 'That'll make you ill. Trust me, I know. I've been in this business nearly fifteen years.'

This time Matthew simply nodded, wiped his lips dry and glanced around the pub. In the far corner of the room was a man occupying a leatherette booth all to himself. The stranger's eyes caught Matthew staring at him. Instead of averting his gaze he raised his Martini and beckoned him into the booth.

Matthew wasn't here to make friends. He was solely here to drink and then walk back to his flat and sleep until midday on Saturday. Nevertheless, he possessed the knowledge that if he didn't go over, the night at the pub would quickly become tedious and pointless. So he crossed the room and sat down in the booth next to the frosted glass window.

'Well, lookit you,' the stranger with receding black and grey hair said as Matthew faced him.

'You asked me over to be with you,' Matthew said in a serious tone. 'What did you want? You better not be gay or I'll smash your head in with this glass.'

'Now, now,' the stranger said, licking the droplets from his stubble. 'There's no need for you to get angry. I'm not gay, my friend.'

'Good – but I'm not your friend,' Matthew pointed out.

'Ah, but we will be, I hope.'

Matthew didn't know how to assess this stranger. He wasn't gay, which was good. But it was as if coming to the Hope & Anchor pub had been a destiny of fate. Had he not killed his neighbour's cat and been put in the mental institution and been rejected by his mother, he'd be at home taking his A-levels or studying to get a trade. Instead of that he'd committed matricide and now lived on his own in a council flat.

'Why did you call me over here?' Matthew wanted to know.

The stranger took the last gulp of his drink, put the glass down and leaned over the table, closer to Matthew so that no one else in the pub could hear them speaking.

'I saw your eyes when that barman was talking to you just now,' the stranger said in a husky, relaxed voice. 'You've got the eyes of a lion.'

Matthew frowned, allowing his eyebrows to meet at the top of his nose. The stranger spoke and stank of alcohol, but he wasn't drunk – or if he was then he concealed it very well.

'What do you mean by that?' Matthew asked.

'There's something about you that would put the shivers down a mercenary's spine. You don't have to listen to me, but I know powerful men. I served in Afghanistan and Iraq just over ten years ago. I've seen the look in a killer's eyes. And I see it in you too. Yes, you are untamed. You have the killer instinct whether you like it or not. You've killed before, haven't you?' the stranger asked.

'Maybe,' Matthew said, staring at the stranger with steely eyes. 'Maybe I haven't. Maybe you're drunk and talking nonsense. Maybe you're all alone in this world and have nowhere to turn to. Maybe you just wanted me to come over here so you could get some company? And if what you're saying is true, why would a piss-artist want to talk to a killer, knowing he wouldn't give a rat's arse if he died?'

The stranger ran a hand through his shaved head and sighed.

Matthew took a gulp of his drink.

'What's your name, friend?' the stranger asked.

'Matthew.'

The stranger nodded.

Matthew didn't like the stranger. Come to think of it, ever since his mother had rejected him he no longer liked anyone.

However, Matthew decided to stay with the stranger for the meantime, wondering where this would all end. Perhaps he could put this know-it-all stranger to sleep once and for all. And that wasn't such a bad idea, the more he thought about it. But first he was going to permit the stranger to carry on rambling about God knew what nonsense and he was going to enjoy his drink.

The stranger asked Matthew where he lived. The mother-killer didn't tell him where exactly in case this bum wasn't drunk and remembered it and then came to call on him at the flat.

'What about your parents?' the stranger asked.

'Both gone,' Matthew said in a clipped voice.

'Gone?'

'Dead.'

'Shit. That's bad luck, Matthew.'

Matthew nodded once in agreement.

'How'd they die?'

'My mother cut his balls off one night and then hung herself in the kitchen.'

The stranger cussed in shock. 'I bet that really messed up your head pretty good, huh?'

'Not really. They were both selfish and self-centred. If they were still alive I wouldn't cross the road to piss on them if they were on fire.'

'You a killer?'

'Wanna find out?' Matthew asked, slowly getting pissed off with this stranger and his inquiries.

The stranger shook his head. 'Just curious, is all.'

'You ask me one more personal question and I'll rip your goddamn throat out, you hear me?'

The stranger sat upright and leaned against the leather padded wall. He stared at Matthew, suddenly realising that although he had found out some things about the lad and he knew what he was talking about due to his time in the military, Matthew wasn't someone you messed with. The boy had no conscience, the stranger came to understand. He wasn't lying. And a unnatural power oozed out of him. This scared him worse than all the conflict he'd been involved in and witnessed.

'I'm done for the night here,' the stranger said, not knowing why he had to explain himself to Matthew. 'I got some cans in the fridge that home, fancy joining me for a night café?'

Matthew scanned the pub.

The big screen showed a football game between Manchester United playing against Liverpool on Sky Sports.

'Go outside,' Matthew said. 'I need to piss. I'll meet you out there.'

The stranger got to his feet, not waiting for any further instructions. Out of the two men it was the man who had seen death on a daily basis and killed men with an assault rifle and grenades that was the weakest. Matthew had something inside of him that sent icicles into your arteries. He thanked the barman and exited the pub.

Matthew headed to the Men's room, did his business, washed his hands and finished his drink before bidding a farewell to the barman.

*

The stranger stood to the right side of the Hope & Anchor, sucking on a cigarette. Matthew emerged from the pub and caught sight of him. He walked over to the man and asked, 'Are you a homo?'

The stranger spat his cigarette out into the street and almost choked on his exhale of smoke. 'Jesus H. God, no! What in the hell makes you ask that?'

'Cause I wanna know who I am gonna spend some time with. I don't like homo's okay? I'm a heterosexual. If you try anything funny with me then I'll cut your balls off and wear them as earrings, do you hear me?'

The stranger knew that Matthew wasn't lying. If it had been anyone else he would have told them to get lost. But Matthew wouldn't allow someone to get away with that. He didn't want to risk answering back in a nasty tone.

Matthew scared him, which made him wonder why he even invited him back to his house. He supposed it was better to have a friend like Matthew rather than an enemy. Furthermore, although Matthew had this deadly aura about him, the stranger admired and was in awe of this teenager's presence.

'I'm not a homo,' the stranger said in as strong as voice as he could let out.

'Good,' Matthew said.

'Ready to go?' the stranger asked.

'Where do you live?'

'Christopher Road.'

Matthew nodded, knowing where that was. 'What's your name?'

'John,' the stranger said, no longer a stranger in the pub. 'John Thomas.'

'Nice to meet you, John,' Matthew said after a long pause.

They shook hands and John could hardly believe how strong and vice-like Matthew's grip was. He could crush a windpipe with not much effort at all.

They walked up the main road to their destination.

John Thomas owned a moderate semi-detached house which he inherited when his grandparents died. He unlocked the front door and closed it behind them prior to flicking the lights on illuminating the hallway and the sitting room. 'Take a seat. I'll put the heating on and get the beers.'

'What've you got?'

'Carlsburg and Heineken.'

Matthew nodded, familiar with the labels and relaxed on the soft sofa, scanning the walls adorned with black and white frame photographs of elite boxers in action. Muhammad Ali, Joe Frazier, Rocky Marciano, Floyd Mayweather Jr. Matthew sat back, impressed. Then in his peripheral vision he caught sight of a samurai sword on the wall lying on its brass hooks, concealed in its scabbard.

John returned from the kitchen and handed Matthew a can of Carlsburg.

Matthew took a sip of the beer, liked it and then drank some more before nestling the can between his thighs. 'I like your photos.'

John smiled. 'Yeah. They're great. Me and my father used to spar when I was younger. He wrote a few newspaper articles on Hall of Fame boxers. *Boxing Monthly* published some of his writings too. He was a hard man and approved of me joining the military. Mum didn't want me to go off to the Middle East. She didn't believe there were any nuclear weapons. And when Saddam Hussain had been captured and was due to lose his life and his statue had been brought down, I should have returned home immediately. She lost her father in WWII. She was a Catholic and believed that all conflict would be the downfall of man.'

Matthew listened to John Thomas but he couldn't help his mind drifting towards the samurai sword and how it would make such a splendid weapon to possess.

'Where do you live?'

'Opposite the chemist and the library,' Matthew said, not missing a beat.

'Any hobbies?'

Matthew shook his head. 'Not really. I work Monday to Friday with the council as a painter and decorator.'

'Is that your dream job?'

'No. If I had my way, I'd like to keep my job and make a few thousand bucks on the side. But you were right, I *am* a killer.'

John Thomas' eyes protruded and looked like two small cue balls.

'I'd love to grab one of my nurse's or doctor's throats and rip their heads off. They put me in an institution for breaking my neighbour's cat's neck, then reward someone for murder in the Middle East. The whole world is messed up. And there are two ways to look at it: trust no one and put yourself first so no fucker can do anything to you or lie down and let the government take over and provide you with a team of "experts" who'll be watching over you, like you're some kinda criminal.'

John Thomas stared agape at the young man before him, frightened. Matthew didn't seem to have a conscience. He had just admitted killing a cat and from what little he knew that was how some serial killers started, by killing pets from a young age until they moved up the proverbial ladder to people.

'I had been taken to the mental institution after the cat episode and they'd lock you away in your cell, allowing you half an hour outside in the fresh air. They provided food and drink but almost every day they would check your vitals and then ask questions all day every day. I asked for my mother, but she had turned her back on me and was unforgiving. So as soon as I could I got out and the carers worked with council to provide a job and a flat for me to live in. From there I swore to myself never to trust anyone ever again… and I had a good right to follow those deadlines after everything that had befallen me.

'Then a couple of days ago, I stabbed my mother to death… Sweet revenge for turning her back on her only son when he needed her most.'

'I thought you said your mother hung herself?' John asked, bewildered and trembling with fear.

Matthew put the can on the round table and got to his feet. He crossed the sitting room to the wall where the samurai sword was kept and took it out of its brackets, slowly slid the scabbard off and held the lethal weapon in his grasp.

John Thomas sat perched on the edge of the sofa, breathing heavily, heart hitting his chest walls in protest. 'Oh... That's a c-c-collectable,' he stammered. 'Got that from an old Chinese g-guy in Hereford.'

Matthew sliced the air with a deadly swing and stroke of the weapon.

'P-Please d-don't d-d-do that,' John said, hating himself for being so afraid of his guest and what he may or may not do.

Matthew spun around and faced his host. He withdrew the sword, glinting in the light. Then as John went to take it off him, Matthew swung the sword in an upward arc, slicing flesh and causing a huge crimson line which gushed liquid out of the abdomin and torso.

John Thomas had no breath to scream or to gasp. Instead he staggered backwards, the back of his legs coming into contact with the armchair, causing him to slump down. The last thing he saw was blood spilling from his fatal wound and the smiling face of his murderer. Then darkness enveloped his whole being and he succumbed to the nothingness...

'Thanks for the drink,' Matthew said. Then he dropped the sword, picked up his can of Carlsburg and finished the contents with two gulps, savouring the taste, content that he had satisfied his evil desires and wiped the splotches of blood off his coat in the kitchen sink. Once it was clean, he stepped outside and nonchalantly walked home with a spring in his step...

31.

THE SUN shone radiantly in the azure sky. DI Sark had just emerged from a formal meeting with the chief superintendent, explaining, in detail, what had transpired on the day of the incident that had forced him to fire a fatal shot in order to save Toby and his mother Abigail from certain death.

The detective had told the whole truth and nothing but the truth to the man above him and now desperately wanted to step outside and get a bit of sun on him. He lit a cigarette and sucked on it for a while, his mind racing, going over the meeting intricately, trying to rationalise what he had done and satisfy himself that it had been the right move. Indeed, he did do the right thing and it had only been out of concern for Toby that he had rushed to his home after his call for help.

The boy had worked wonders at the crime scene and saved forensics valued time in order to solve the puzzle of the homicide. The unknown assassin had been climbing over the living room windowsill, armed and deadly when he turned up and reacted instinctively.

When he had found the teenager on the floor, three bullets in him and losing blood fast, DI Sark had made an emergency call and then called his Chief Superintendent to get some backup pronto.

The ambulance arrived in very quick time, thankfully, and Toby was laid out, drifting in and out of consciousness as the paramedics wheeled him into the back of the ambulance, Abigail following. DI Sark told her hastily that he would be there soon after he'd got the CSI team and his colleagues to cordon off the street and the crime scene itself.

It had been the busiest of days in his whole career, crime scene wise. As night descended as slow and methodical as a midnight lover, DI Sark left the crime scene and headed to the hospital before returning home. The moon glowed high above and followed him to his next destination.

When he arrived, the receptionist gave him directions after he had flashed his badge and he climbed the steps rather than take the lift. Then as he took a left turn off the main hallway, he saw Abigail sitting outside with a bottle of Evian water, stressed, distressed and exhausted.

'Hey!' DI Sark called out, noticing the ICU sign overhead. 'How is he doing?'

Abigail looked up and wiped the constant flow of tears away with the back of her hand, grieved and pallid. 'They've taken the bullets out of him and treated him. They gave him a high dose of sedative for the night. They told me he'd be fine. The wounds and the shock had knocked him into oblivion, but because he is young and strong, he should make a speedy recovery.'

DI Sark lowered himself onto the chair next to Abigail and put an arm around her and pulled her close. 'Well, that's good news. He'll pull through easy enough, you wait and see.'

Abigail folded herself into her lap and finished the rest of water. 'Why do you have to call my son in police matters? Can't you see that he's not gonna have a life unless you stop calling him every time something goes wrong?'

The detective didn't let Abigail's comment get under his skin. She had nearly lost her son after all. 'The last thing I ever wanted was to put Toby in danger. But we, the police force, do need him. And we don't force him to help us he comes willingly. I am truly sorry for what's happened. The murderer of the crime scene earlier today had stabbed a woman repeatedly, killing her in her bed. Toby came down and told us where the body was, how she was murdered and that the suspect either was invited in or had his own key. Then later in the day a would-be killer found where Toby lived and attempted to kill him… and you.

'I'm sorry what's happened,' the detective went on. 'But now we have a perp and evidence of the two separate crimes. And these happened, not over a period of time, but in less than twenty-four hours, thanks to Toby.'

Abigail didn't show any sign that she had been listening to the detective. She straightened up and leaned back, exhaling deeply. 'But what about your next crime? Will you be calling Toby again to let him do your job?'

That hurt DI Sark. However, he also understood a mother's love. 'Look, I am truly sorry. But Toby has done wonders.' He shifted in his seat and dug his left hand into his suit jacket and extracted an envelope and handed it to Abigail.

'What's this?'

'A hundred pound out of my own money that I want you and Toby to have,' DI Sark said, looking uncomfortable. 'It's not exactly legal, but I'm trusting you not to tell anyone. I've grown quite attached to him. He has done wonders for this part of the country, and has saved the police valuable money, time and effort.'

Abigail hesitantly took the white envelope and put it in her fleece. 'I won't tell anyone,' she said no louder than a whisper. 'But there is something you need to know.'

'What's that?'

'Toby is friends with someone else who is a psychic,' Abigail said. 'Why not ask her for help instead of relying on my sweet boy?' She paused and considered her next choice of words. 'He has a job, you know?'

DI Sark nodded. 'All right. I'll tell my colleagues and superior to lay off Toby. But he has worked miracles for us as a unit. He is your son though, and I respect that. I really do.'

DI Sark got up from his seat and looked down at Abigail. 'I'll grab you a coffee…'

Abigail met his eyes. 'Thank you,' she whispered.

*

At sunrise the following day, Toby stirred in his bed and blinked open his leaden eyes that offered a blurry sight of the ICU. He shifted to an upright position and groaned at the discomfort and pain coursing through him. In a sudden tidal wave that crashed down the clouds of forgetfulness, the events that had assailed him upon waking came back to him.

He had been shot, of course.

How the hell did he survive?

What happened to his dear mother?

These aimless thoughts were blown back into oblivion when a blonde nurse with a comely figure approached the foot of his bed, took the clipboard and jotted something down. 'You're awake,' she said. 'How'd you feel?'

'Sore,' Toby said in nothing much more than a grunt.

'Well, you're bound to be,' the young nurse informed him. 'Do you remember what happened?'

'Vaguely.'

'You were attacked at home by a murdering man who shot you. Three bullets were deep inside you. The doctors managed to extract them, but you lost a bit of blood and passed out before the ambulance arrived. Your mother has gone home and will be back later, but she can't stay long because of the strict rules we have to adhere to in ICU.

'May I have some water, please?' he asked and smiled.

The young nurse got him a cup of water.

He drank the small amount in one gulp. Then he leaned back. The nurse pulled the top half of the bed up so he could stay in an upright posture.

'You're gonna be fine,' she said, seeing the anguish on Toby's face. 'You had a close call.'

Toby nodded. 'I know. But what happened to the guy who nearly killed me and my mum?'

'Your detective friend had come to check on you and fate brought you a lifeline, because he came at the exact moment when you were in plain sight for killing when the attacker got shot right through the spine. It's all over the news. You're a famous psychic. Is that right?'

'Kind of,' Toby said, wincing in pain.

The young nurse came around and took his blood pressure. Then she glanced around, seeing that there was no one else watching and leaned over and kissed Toby on the cheek.

Toby looked at her with an awry grin across his face. 'What was that for?'

The young nurse was smiling and blushing now. Then she said: 'I always wanted to kiss a celebrity and they don't get any bigger or better than you.'

Toby was about to call her bluff, saying that indeed she was humouring him, but the redness in her cheeks told him that that wasn't the case. Far from it.

Later on Toby's mother came in and pulled up a seat beside him and kissed his hand.

'Detective Sark killed the assailant,' Toby said. 'Must've been the same guy that killed that woman. Probably followed me home from the crime scene and decided it'd be better for him if I died before I could find out where he was so he could be apprehended.'

Abigail held her son's hand and kissed the back of it again, not really caring about anyone else. Her little boy had very nearly lost his life, along with hers, and when it was all unfolding right then and there before her, she did think that she would witness the death of her son before facing the same fate.

'I want you to do something for me,' she said in a low, soothing voice.

'What is it?'

'Don't get involved with the local police anymore, my sweetheart,' Abigail said. 'It's great that we're all still alive and well considering what might have happened. But you're not trained to defend us against bad guys the way the police are. You've proven time and time again that you can see and know things most humans can't even think of or dream of, but you've got to put yourself first. Because if you're dead, from your perspective, it's blackout.'

Toby gazed into his mother's eyes. 'I know what you mean, Mum. But I can't say what the future holds for me. All I want to do is get better and get back to my job and to spend the weekends with you. Maybe we could get a cat or a dog as a new addition to the family.'

Abigail snorted laughter. 'Maybe, my love. Maybe.'

*

DI Sark arrived after lunch and faced his young wonder friend with a pained expression. He could remember all too vividly the events that had led to Toby being very nearly killed, all because he helped at a homicide crime scene. The killer had to have been a local, but at the moment the man was on a slab in the mortuary as a John Doe.

'Tell me something,' Toby said. 'How do I look?'

'Apart from the little nicks scarring your face, you're looking a lot perkier.'

Toby gave him the "thumbs-up" signal.

'Ya know, this is all my fault,' DI Sark said, glancing at the glossy linoleum, head down, evidently full of guilt and distress.

'Don't be hard on yourself,' Toby said, rebuking him. 'You saved me and my mother from being shot to death by that bastard! You're a bloody hero!'

DI Sark chuckled at that. 'Thanks pal.'

'No need to thank me,' Toby said in a softer, more normal tone. 'My mum just reacts sometimes in haste 'cause she frets over the slightest things. She doesn't want her little bubble to be broken. See, I'm all she's got in the world... and as you know the world is a big, mean, nasty old place that will beat you to your knees if you let it. She's been through a lot and just wants to live a normal, stress-free life. I mean, when it comes right down to it, isn't that what we all want? My mum is stressed 'cause there was a killer on the loose and came after me and her. I'm recovering slowly. You're carrying a bag of rocks, unwilling to let them go 'cause you think that feeling guilty right now is the normal thing to do. It isn't, let me tell you. You are a life saver. You're a terrific policeman and a good friend of mine.'

DI Sark thanked Toby again and had to admit getting an approval from the young spiritualist made him feel a lot better than he'd felt for a whole twenty-four hours now.

'Go home, get some sleep,' Toby advised.

'I'm not allowed to contact you again after this incident,' DI Sark said.

'That's my mum for you,' Toby said. 'Give it some time. Let me recover in peace and get back into my normal working routine. And if you need me or want to keep in touch, leave your mobile number and I'll call you every week.'

Just then DI Sark's mobile buzzed. 'I gotta take this,' he said, getting up, turning and walked out of the ICU.

The gorgeous blonde nurse looked healthy and fresh as she entered the room. She walked straight over to where Toby was, sitting upright, feeling more like himself after he'd first been when they took him in.

'Hello, my love,' she said.

Toby could feel the beautiful, tingling sensation coursing through his veins as he answered the nurse and couldn't help but notice her amazing figure in her tightly-fitting scrubs.

So far apart from the dull throbbing and aching in and around his back, Toby came to realise that this wasn't so bad after all. He was alive and well and he rather found himself fancying the nurse who had been taking care of him.

Might ask mum if she can shoot me next week just so I can be here again with this lovely young woman, he thought with a wry smile.

*

Annie Combs had been awake all night, her nerves tingling and scratching away inside her brain unmercifully. She had lain in her bed, under the duvet trying to sleep by closing her eyes, only for her "shine" to keep her awake and alert.

She knew without evidence that Toby had been in deep jeopardy and was now unable and unresponsive to her troubled mind. She had had bouts like this when she was in her twenties and early thirties and the sensation wasn't pleasant. On the contrary, if anything. She didn't have the ability to see it all for herself, but she knew the the gist of the crimes themselves had been committed by a young, merciless man – this had crept into her consciousness.

She often wondered why she had to have this "shine". Did God not love her? Had she done something in a previous life that might have warranted such unstoppable punishment? Older and much wiser now, Annie knew for certain that she was just complaining. Other people all around the world suffered from all kinds of things. At least with her gift/curse she could sometimes – not often – see beyond the mushroom clouds in her mind, preventing her from seeing the bigger picture paid off.

When through her "shine" she had been able to tell someone, who was unaware, a message from a dead loved one, or tell a person that they had to stop their bad habits or they would suffer greatly in the long run, it made it all worthwhile. But this attack did not relent even for a second.

As she saw a vision of a young teenager seated under an umbrella at a bench, opposite a mental health carer, she came to knowledge that the boy had done something nasty and had been incarcerated and treated to prevent him from doing such evil ever again.

A cat!

Wow!

Annie stayed very still, catatonic-like and waited for the knowledge to pass her by. She prayed for sleep and even wondered what was happening. This occurrence was totally unlike any other experience she'd ever endured before. Her parted lips were curled in upon themselves and with her sandpaper-dry tongue wet her lips and blinked purposefully, thinking maybe this wasn't her "shine" but old age and psychic powers succumbing to an illness such as schizophrenia.

She flung the duvet off her emaciated form, placed her feet in her slippers and descended the stairs to pour herself a glass of cold milk.

'Where are you when I need you, Toby?' she croaked, feeling bad for what she said, but urging his "shine" to come through and soothe her soul, a breath of fresh air to a nearly deceased person.

One thing she did know as she sat down with her drink was that the cat had been the first – an experiment. She wasn't sure if the young boy was still receiving treatment inside a mental institution or prison but she did know he would kill again.

The boy believed he was born to kill… again… and again… and again…

32.

THE DAY was overcast and the heavy gunship clouds spat droplets down from the darkening sky. Matthew Cawthorne had gone back to work on the Monday and worked hard down Baglan Bay, scraping the cracked fissures in the children's pool area and painting a thick, fresh coat of light blue and filling in the cracks and holes with putty. The job was quite a rewarding duty as it involved children. Not directly, obviously, but a task aimed at children's wellbeing, the pool ready to use for the approaching summer. Matthew worked with utmost concentration, briefly bringing to memory the death of John Thomas.

On Wednesday evening Matthew arrived home, had a quick shower, did himself a microwave meal and sat down in front of the small TV to watch the news. He was keenly attuned, leaning forward, watching, waiting for the headlines to come on and announce the murder of which he had committed... and when it did, he felt no fear or panic or even the slightest amount of guilt. That part of his psyche had died. Matthew assumed that all moral conscience had dissipated in his overturning mind.

Now the mentality was, 'Well, people die everyday. My father left me. My mother betrayed me. And anyone who wasn't a girl wanted to get close to him and provide him with an opportunity to live out his fantasises would wind up dead... it was that simple.'

The news reporter explained briefly how a samurai sword had been the weapon the murderer used, and been cleaned spotless thereafter. They showed a few seconds' footage of the semi-detached house where the victim had lived as the place where the savage crime had been committed.

Then the news reporter went on to talk about another crime in the same small town occurring just down the other end of the street where the local surgery was located. According to the news the boy wonder psychic had been within seconds of dying from gunshots if it wasn't for a popular detective inspector arriving in the nick of time to kill the unidentified assailant, literally saving Toby Jones' life.

And as Matthew ate his delicious beef dinner a broad smile spread across his face when the news reporter said that the two crimes might be linked and committed by the same man DI Sark had managed to kill.

Got away, Scot free, Matthew thought, shaking his head in disbelief and feeling blessed by the gods of violence.

He finished his meal, washed it down with a Diet Coke and then decided to watch an adult film before going to bed. In his sinister and distorted mind, the world was a great place to live in, filled to the brim with all kinds of different things going on. All he had to do was live out his fantasies in private, where no one would be any the wiser, and if he did that he could go on and on for quite some time yet. Matthew loved the adrenaline rushing through him as he relived the scene through his mind's eye, almost as if he was possessed by some demon or even the devil himself. It was the awesome power that he contained in his two hands, being able to decide there and then in a moment without hesitation the fate of whether a human being lived or died. Not even the queen could make those decisions or anyone else without concrete evidence… and that was the key factor all along. That was what kept his motor running. He could see the blood in a geyser bathing the cream-coloured bookcase as John crumpled into a heap.

'I got the power!'

With that thought and belief, Matthew fell asleep, dreaming of more scenarios and possible victims he could kill in many different ways.

'Who knows,' he said out loud to himself, 'maybe I can start a collection as souvenirs from now on.'

*

Thursday sunrise crept over the horizon from Toby's bedside window. Today would be the day he could leave the ward and go back home to his own bedroom. He still felt sore and aching, but nonetheless apart from that he was fine.

The young, blonde nurse popped her head around the corner and caught sight of Toby getting to his feet and hurried over to him, even though she wasn't supposed to be on the ward; she worked in the ICU department. However, she really fancied Toby and wanted to grasp her one and only chance of asking him out before he left today.

Toby raised his head at the sound of the nurse's footsteps, squeaking louder and louder until she stood right in front of him.

'Hey! What's up?' Toby smiled, glad to see her.

'I dunno how to do this…' she said, all of a sudden affected by a shower of nerves tingling through her system.

'Do what?' Toby asked.

'I was wondering – I dunno if you do or not – if you'd like to g-go out on a date with me one day?'

Toby did a double-take, amazed and pleasantly surprised at the question this beautiful young woman had asked him.

'Yeah… Sure,' Toby said, his cheeks filled with heat as he reached over to his bedside cabinet for a pen and a piece of paper.

The nurse opened her hand and handed him a piece of paper with her mobile number on it, saving Toby having to write down his own number.

He looked at the piece of paper and saw her name above the number – Anastasia. Toby raised his eyes and found his future girlfriend's eyes. 'Anastasia,' he said. 'That's a lovely name. How'd you do, Anastasia?'

'I'm very well, now that that's over with,' Anastasia laughed, looking more radiant and alluring than ever.

'What do you like to do?' Toby asked. 'Any interesting hobbies you like?'

'Perhaps we could go for food at TGI Friday's in Swansea?'

Toby nodded. 'I've never heard of it – but it sounds great. I'll not be coming out for a couple of days 'cause of my injuries, but once I'm feeling more able-bodied, I'll give you a call and we can go there. Look forward to it, Anastasia.'

Anastasia stepped closer and lifted her head so that Toby had no room to move and kissed him passionately on the lips for two seconds before breaking away. The sensation of their parted lips meeting and engaging one another sent their hormones into overdrive.

'I gotta go now,' Anastasia said, whirled around and headed out of the ward, not before looking over her shoulder at him one last time.

Toby stood motionless, scarcely believing his good fortune and the fact that Anastasia would be his first proper girlfriend.

*

As soon as Toby and Abigail arrived home, she ran him a hot bath to help with the throbbing aches and pains. Toby sat in the bath for forty-five minutes, simply relaxing and savouring the relaxation method, already feeling more like himself now that he was back home. After the bath Abigail made him peanut butter sandwiches served on a china plate along with a can of Coke.

He ate his lunch at the dinette table. He decided to tell his mother that he had met a girl while at the hospital whom he was going to go out with to see if they could have a boyfriend/girlfriend relationship. Abigail, who had been standing at the kitchen worktop with her back to him, whirled around like a ballet dancer. Her smile was full of pure radiance and joy.

'A girlfriend?'

'Maybe,' Toby said. 'Calm down.'

'What's her name?'

'Anastasia,' Toby replied. 'She's a nurse. She treated me when I was in the intensive care unit. She seems really nice.'

'What does she look like?' Abigail blurted out, unable to contain her excitement.

'She has long blonde hair, about the same age as me and is a really sweet girl. I gotta recover first before I do anything, like work or dates. So please don't get too excited. It might not work. We don't know anything about each other, so we might find we have nothing in common.'

Abigail calmed herself and decided to listen to her wise son. He, of course, was right. His recovery was paramount. He had a nice job as a P.E. Instructor and she also believed that after the incident at their home where the old living room window had been replaced by a double pane glass that there would be time for the nice, normal things in the future. Not now but in the foreseeable future.'

'You're right, my love,' Abigail said. 'How was your bath?'

'I needed it,' Toby said. 'I feel a bit numb all over, but at least I'm not in pain. It was a miracle that I didn't get shot in an artery or in one of my internal organs. Then I wouldn't have made it. And I'm sorry for putting you in that situation. After all you've done for me. I put you in danger where you had nothing to do with any crime and where you very nearly lost your own life... all because of me.'

'Now there'll be no talk of that,' Abigail said in a firm tone. 'But if you must know, I'd like it if you stopped or ignored this ability of yours of helping the police out. I do want that to stop. I even told your detective friend.'

Toby leaned back in his chair and sighed. 'I'm not sure I can do that, Mum. I have this *ability* for a reason. Annie calls it the "Shine". It means that my spirit glows. Not something which the human naked eye can see but supernaturally. I won't put you in danger ever again. I promise you that, if nothing else. But I've got to use my "shine". It's like a paradox. I put you in danger, but at the same time I got to pay attention to it more closely so I can save you from any further incidents.'

Abigail didn't answer. She was a bit annoyed with Toby's announcement, but tried her best to see it from his perspective to have a deeper understanding and knowledge. If he ignored it, when he could have done something to stop someone from a near fatality, like what had happened to him, then he was as bad as the murderers themselves for turning a blind eye.

Toby finished his lunch and then headed up to his room to watch *Friends* before drifting off to sleep. He stirred awake nearly three hours later, feeling a lot better. After going back downstairs, Toby found his mum in the living room watching one of the quiz games and sat with her talking idly about lots of unimportant things. He had a stir fry for dinner and then went back upstairs. He read a Bentley Little book before turning in for the night, still exhausted and slept till six the next morning, feeling fresh and full of vitality.

*

A week had passed since Matthew Cawthorne had slain his mother and John Thomas. The murders had been all over the local news and national newspapers, but as of yet there was no evidence linking to him, for which he was grateful.

Heidi Johnston would be arriving in less then twenty minutes and Matthew had busied himself all morning, washing and cleaning and using air fresheners. The flat was spotless, so when his therapist arrived it would give her the impression that life had been grasped by the young man at such a tender age. Furthermore, he felt a lot better in himself. His two slayings had definitely improved his overall mood and demeanour.

Killing his mother and John Thomas successfully, without leaving a trace of evidence, had satisfied his desires and given him a new lease of life and fulfilment. He told Heidi Johnston over the phone two days earlier that he'd seen on the news that his mother had been a victim of a heinous crime, and even sobbed quite convincingly. Then he asked if Heidi would call soon as he was struggling with the news and didn't know how to proceed.

The doorbell chimed.

Matthew opened the door and smiled at Heidi, then stepped to the side to permit her entry. They sat down in the living room and Matthew even poured her a glass of squash.

Indeed, Heidi did notice the tidiness and the condition of the flat and Matthew's appearance, and complimented him.

'Thanks,' Matthew said. 'I am trying my best. The painting and decorating job with the council is going well and I'm keeping up with the household chores too. I'm not one of these spongers who wants everything for nothing. But the news of my mum's brutal death has knocked me for six, if I'm being totally honest.'

'I can imagine!' Heidi said. 'Listen, your mother didn't get a chance to write a will. And as you're her next of kin you inherit her savings. I will assist you in paying the funeral and casket costs. Did your mother wish to be buried or cremated?'

'Buried,' Matthew said.

'The police are still trying to figure out how the crime was committed.'

'Someone broke entry, I suppose and killed her, I heard,' Matthew said in a heartbeat.

'That's what the news said, yes,' Heidi said. 'You will have to be interviewed by the local police, as is the norm, but if you'd like me to attend I can.'

'I'd prefer it if you did attend,' Matthew said. 'I don't think it has properly sunk in yet. I know my mother didn't want me back home after the incident with the neighbour's cat, but for someone to have killed her… it's all a bit too much.'

Heidi nodded. 'Because of your past the police will be a bit suspicious, I'll tell you now.'

Matthew nodded. 'I wouldn't break into my mum's house and kill her.'

'There was no break in,' Heidi pointed out.

'So she knew her attacker?'

'I'd think so, yes,' Heidi said.

'Shit. Oh, that's even worse. I can't cope with this right now.'

'Did you have a key to your own house?' Heidi asked.

Matthew shook his head. 'I didn't. Anything that was found on me was in my bedroom or on my possession when I was taken into Cefn Coed Mental Institution.'

Heidi nodded again, entirely satisfied with his answer.

'Were you still a bit bitter with your mum for not letting you stay at your own house after you were released?'

'Heartbroken is the word I would use,' Matthew said. 'Like I've already said, my mother didn't even want to see or hear from me ever again. I never went round to my mother's home at any time, let alone kill her. She wouldn't have let me in anyway. The news said she was stabbed. There was a detective here a day or so ago questioning me on the doorstep. I told him all that I've just told you. Then he went on to say that I'd have to give them a written statement. Apparently, the incident happened during the night. Well, I have no alibis but I was asleep. I had work the following morning.'

Heidi couldn't bring herself to even consider that the boy before her could do such a thing. He spoke well. He was a bit uptight and above all genuinely upset regarding the topic they were currently talking about. She finished her drink, gave him the fortnight injection and then departed.

Matthew waved her off and then returned inside, smiling like a Cheshire cat, impressed with his acting talent. He knew now that he had Heidi in his back pocket. The kill had been sensational but the aftermath of pretending to be innocent and upset was working in his favour. The police would be told the same story in the same fashion, but for now there was a funeral to prepare for and Matthew would stand as the only heir to his mother's savings. Nothing quite beat killing your own, neglectful mother, and then getting a lot of money out of it.

Now all he had to do was buy himself a black suit and pay for the funeral arrangements.

*

Annie Combs had slept well and made herself some breakfast at the dawn of a new spring day. She sat in the kitchen, bathed in the golden sunlight filtering in through the gaps in the shades. The vision last night had left her feeling empty inside without any further explanation besides what she'd seen.

As she slept, a pretty woman with long brown hair stood outside her home while a team of forensics wearing white overalls walked in and out of the open door. She stood on the short path and stared right at Annie, her mouth moving but the sound on mute. Then the woman pointed to a bedroom window and Annie realised without any further doubt that that was where the incident had occurred… and that this woman was dead.

The woman was wearing her nightdress, stained and shredded with crimson splotches and sprinkles.

She had been stabbed to death and was visibly upset and emotional that her life had been brutally cut short while she had slept. Annie talked back using her mind.

Who did this to you?
My son. He's a murderer.
Why?
Because he's not human. He's insane and a danger to society.
What's your name?
Susan Cawthorne...

Annie sipped her strong cup of coffee and then put the steaming mug down on the coaster and wondered what had happened to Toby. She couldn't get through to him and didn't know where he was. In a few hours she would try again to contact him through her psychic powers to tell him what she had been told the night before. The whole vision had upset her greatly and she needed her younger accomplice to aid her.

33.

THE DAY was heavily overcast with gunmetal grey billowing clouds ready to burst open. However, as a condolence offering the rain held off for the church service and the burial thereafter. Matthew had discovered that none of his relatives were aware of his incarceration due to the killing of a neighbour's cat… and for the time being, until he could conjure up a plausible story.

Matthew got into the black sedan with his grandparents and uncle. The driver was taking them back to the family home for the wake. A small spread of food and beverages had been put together by his uncle and his partner.

'I should never have left her alone,' Matthew blurted out, breaking the silence in the funeral car.

His grandfather looked up and stared at him closely.

'Whatcha mean by that?' he asked in an accusing tone.

'Exactly what I said,' Matthew replied. 'I had some mental health issues which are being dealt with and I decided it'd be better for me to move out and take the burden off my mum's shoulders. If I had managed myself better and stayed the killer would never have had a chance to do what he did if I'd been around.'

Uncle Paul wrapped an arm around him and pulled him into his warm embrace. 'No need to blame yourself, Matthew son; it's just one of those things that happens every once in a while. Don't blame yourself.'

Matthew glanced over at his grandfather who was still staring at him in an intimidating manner. 'Why are you lookin' at me like that?'

'I'll look at you whichever way I want to look at you,' Grandfather Tom answered, with a slight grimace of anger.

'There's no need of that, Dad,' Uncle Paul said. 'You have no right to blame Matthew. He feels bad as it is. He just lost his mother. Be kind. What the hell is wrong with you?'

Grandfather Tom broke away from Grandmother Jane and leaned closer and hissed under his breath: 'I heard that neighbour hated your guts and you couldn't cope with it so you went to a mental hospital. Isn't that so?'

Matthew gently pulled himself out of his uncle's embrace and leaned forward and matched his grandfather's stare and held it that way until he could see the anger ebb away into a cold fear. 'That neighbour never liked me; said that I was up to no good, even though I never saw her that much. If I played football in the rear garden and accidentally kicked the ball over the hedges, she wouldn't answer the front door to give me my ball back. My father leaving us and my mum having to work two jobs left me alone and frightened. So you could say that I couldn't deal with much more stress. You can stare daggers at me all you want, grandfather. But where were you when my mum and I needed you?'

'A phone call away.'

Mathew leaned back so that his back was straight again. 'So it was up to me and my mum to come crawling to you, begging for help, is that it? What would you have done? Nothing, that's what. You sit on your arse all day watching Sky Sports and reading the newspapers. Then get drunk in the evening. So before you start blaming me and anyone else for mum's awful death, take a long hard look in the mirror.'

Grandfather Tom leaned back, clasped Jane's hand and gazed out the window at the world passing by.

I'll rip his head off if he tries that again! He thinks he's hard, love him. Ooh, look at me, I used to be in the army. I'm so hard. I'd love to fight him.

The wake was just what Matthew needed. His relatives offered their support and gave him their contact details in case he needed anything. However, Matthew would be kind and polite to them. Afterwards, he'd be by himself with his mother's savings and relax in his flat. His Uncle Paul was a nice guy, he thought. He didn't judge anyone. He just wanted to get along with everyone and try to talk to as many people as possible to avoid the hard reality that his sister was no longer a resident in the world. Matthew hugged him at the door and watched him go.

Jane came over to him as she and Tom were getting ready to take their leave. 'Please forgive your grandfather, Matthew. He's just very upset and a bit emotional at the moment. I know you can understand that.'

'I do,' Matthew said. 'But I'm suffering too. But I forgive him.'

'Okay,' Jane said and took his hand into her grasp. 'Such an awful thing to happen. I lost my baby girl. I love you, Matthew. Please don't hesitate to call if you need anything, even if it's just a chat about things. You hear me?'

Matthew said that he indeed understood and would keep in touch. Then he watched them as they got in their car and drove off down the street out of sight.

The day matched the weather in mood. However, no one apparently noticed that Matthew was the only family member in the service and the burial who hadn't cried or felt profound sorrow. Nor would he, he told himself. His mother, Susan Cawthorne, had abandoned him, so he returned the favour.

He gathered up the small spread and the six-pack of Budweiser and headed back to the flat to eat, drink and watch videos on YouTube for the rest of the day. Then he turned in for the night and thought how nice it was that his mother's earnings would now be transferred into his bank account.

There were definitely good perks for being a serial killer, he thought with a wry smile as he lay in bed. And for the time being, Matthew would rest up and purchase some luxuries before he made any more plans. Now that he thought of it, Matthew decided that he would like to get a girlfriend so he could shag on a regular basis. With all that decided in his brain, he turned the gold-framed photograph of Susan Cawthorne when she was just twenty years old towards him and drifted off into a deep, dreamless slumber.

*

Toby's wounds and bruises ached as he rolled over in bed. He winced in discomfort, but was glad that the pain had reduced to a great degree. He had a long, hot shower. Then he went about his morning ritual. Clean, refreshed, he made his way downstairs for a bowl of Frosties. He finished his breakfast at the same time as his mother was about to wash the dishes. He helped dry the cutlery and dishes before placing them back in the cupboards and drawers.

'It's Saturday,' Abigail pointed out, as if he wasn't already aware. 'What are your plans for the day?'

'I'm gonna go to town to BodyTalk gym, come home and I might give Anastasia a call. It's been three days. I feel much better, and hopefully, if she's still interested, I might like to meet up with her this weekend and do something nice together. Unless you want me to give you a hand with something? Like the shopping?'

Abigail shook her head. She enjoyed the weekly shopping, and actually preferred to do it alone. She normally did her shopping either at Tesco or Asda, and once she got all the shopping into the boot of the car, she'd treat herself with a bag of chocolate and a gossip magazine. Furthermore, she was still excited about her son's first girlfriend, and wanted him to go to the gym and call the girl straight away afterwards. It was what any boy ought to be doing at his age; not getting visions and voices that helped the police solve crimes. He was her superhero, but that didn't mean it was up to him to save the world. That wasn't fair. Toby had every right to his freedom.

Abigail got dressed and then gave Toby a lift to the gym before turning around and heading to Neath Abbey. Toby waved her off and then entered the gym.

Today, he decided he would do his chest and back muscles. So, to start with he did some deadlights, one arm dumbbell rows and pull downs, three sets each. Then for his chest muscles, he did some incline dumbbell presses, incline flys and finished off with high-rep barbell presses. By the time he had completed his daily routine his trained muscles were engorged with blood and adrenaline. He sprayed some Lynx deodorant all over him, drank his pint of milk and then headed outside to begin the two-and-a-half-mile trek back home.

Toby took out his mobile phone and dialled Anastasia's number that she'd given him, and after only three rings got an answer.

'Hi, Toby!' Anastasia said in a cheerful tone.

'Hi, Anastasia!' Toby replied. 'I've just finished my workout today and wondered if you weren't too busy this afternoon, if you'd like to meet up and do something, seeing as though the weather is nice. I'm feeling much better now. I've still got some bruises where I was shot, but they're not stopping me from doing stuff anymore. Anyway, how are you?'

'Oh, I'm fine,' Anastasia said. 'I'm at work at the moment…'

'Oh, crap!' Toby said, cutting her off. 'I didn't realise. Sorry.'

'No. That's okay,' Anastasia said. 'I finish work at three. So it's only an hour or so away. Perhaps if we can meet up we can go for a McDonald's, if you fancy? I haven't eaten all day and am starving. How 'bout you?'

'That sounds great. Perhaps you can meet me at the entrance gates of Skewen Park. Do you know where that is?'

' I do,' Anastasia said. 'My dad goes there sometimes to play tennis with his work friend. So, I shall be there at about half past three, is that okay?'

'That's great!' Toby said, smiling. 'I shall see you then. Bye.'

'Bye. See you soon.'

Anastasia terminated the connection and Toby put his mobile phone back in his fleece pocket and had a spring in his step as he walked all the way home, deciding that he would have another quick shower, just so he smelled nice. He'd also brush his teeth again and apply some aftershave too. He wanted to look his best for Anastasia. First impressions went a long way, he decided.

*

Anastasia pulled up in the gravel car park and killed the motor of her Renault Clio. She had sprayed half a week's worth of perfume all over her body in the changing room at the hospital. She wore a tight white, sleeveless top and denim jeans. She saw Toby in the distance growing bigger as he climbed over the grassy knoll and approached her. She found him very attractive and first thought that from spending days with him in the ICU that he was one of those gentle souls who never asked for much in life. He had lovely big green-hazel eyes and thick, stylised hair, a slim waist and muscular body.

As he drew closer, Anastasia got a better look at him and liked what she saw. She felt a tingling sensation in her stomach stir again and relished the feeling. And she couldn't help herself wonder how it would feel to be beneath him during sexual intercourse. She was turned on and had to focus on trying to hide her thoughts more carefully. However, she did hope that the date would go well and that she could kiss him again.

Toby raised a hand in greeting as he crossed the deserted car park and opened the passenger door. He sat down and got comfortable. Anastasia leaned over before he even got chance to buckle himself in with a kiss on his cheek. He smiled broadly and was about to ask what that was for when Anastasia leaned in again and kissed him on the lips, her own lips parted, ready to kiss him passionately, which sure enough Toby reciprocated. Eventually Anastasia broke away and felt her loins damp with desire. Yet she had to focus and control herself.

'Well...' Toby began... then drifted off.

Anastasia laughed. Of course she was lost for words too.

She started the engine and turned to him. 'Are you hungry?'

Toby nodded. 'Yes. But gimme a chance to recover and reset my emotions to food again.'

Anastasia chuckled. She released the handbrake and drove out of the car park and back onto the main road. 'Which one would you like to go to?' she asked.

At first Toby didn't quite understand the question. Then he knew. 'I don't mind.'

'Shall we go to the one in Glynneath? It's a bit quieter with plenty of off-road places to park up.'

'Okay. Sure, Glynneath, here we come!'

Anastasia had never felt so good as she did right then, joining the Dual-Carriageway and putting her foot down.

Toby marvelled at the scenery, the golden sunshine highlighted, and asked his new girlfriend how work had been for her earlier today.

They spoke of a lot of subjects and thoroughly enjoyed each other's company. And in some ways it was the talking and eating and merely spending some time together that would later become a lovely memory they both cherished, even more so than the initial lustful desires… and that's what both Toby and Anastasia appreciated the most that glorious afternoon…

*

The following day was Sunday. Matthew Cawthorne had woken early, fresh and full of vitality. He locked his front door behind him and as the weather was glorious, he took a walk back to his family home to get rid of the personal belongings before contacting the housing estate agents who would then put the house up for sale. Had he more income and the mortgage been paid off, Matthew would have loved to have lived there on Tabernacle Street. Yet beggars couldn't be choosers, he thought. When he arrived at the residence, he unlocked the door and stepped inside.

The living room had already gathered clouds of dust. Matthew went directly to his mother's writing desk, made of Oak, and opened the drawers. Most of the paperwork was bills and different types of catalogues. However, Matthew came across an A4 notepad and opened it, expecting it to be empty. Yet nearly the whole pad was filled with his mother's easy handwriting.

Intrigued by this discovery, Matthew glimpsed the dates and numbered pages. This was something sacred to her as she hadn't told anyone. Without hesitation, Matthew placed the notepad, along with two others into a cardboard box he'd brought with him.

Then he went about the house with Mr Muscle and wet wipes. He vacuumed the carpets on both floors and then carried the cardboard box back to the flat. As he got closer to his own residence his arms began to ache. Nevertheless, the exercise would do him good. Once he got in and locked the door behind him, Matthew made himself a ham sandwich to enjoy with a can of Budweiser.

Afterwards, he washed the dishes, took the garbage bags out the front alongside the kerb for the rubbish men to collect the following morning and went back inside, sat down in his second-hand reclining armchair and began to read his mother's notepad.

Wednesday 1 April.

It has been five years to the day since Henry departed. He has not bothered to call or write or use any other form of contact. I went to the police and they put me in touch with a private investigator who got back to me six weeks later.
Henry is now living in Haverfordwest with a young model from Croatia. They live in a caravan and had been seen frolicking at the beach. The private investigator had taken photos, but I decided that I didn't need to see them. It was better and easier in the long run if I didn't look at photos of my cheating husband kissing and fondling with a young model. All I wanted was clarification that Henry was alive and well. I did ask the private investigator for his contact details and tracked his home phone number. I called him three times. The first and second time, he hung up when I told him it was me. Then on the third call, he answered. I told him that he had a son, as though he had surely forgotten Matthew. A few days later I received a cheque for £500, and when I tried to phone him again the number was unrecognised.
I guess the £500 cheque was admission of guilt. Now that the cheque has been cashed, in Henry's mind he had committed to his parental and husband business and no longer felt obligated to answer any more calls or accept responsibilities.
Henry and I married when we were both in our early twenties. For whatever reason being a husband and father with a job as a building constructor hadn't been enough for him. Lord knows why. Money hadn't been an issue. I worked hard as a receptionist with a prestigious law firm, and together we paid the bills and had money left over to spend on ourselves and each other lavishly.
In hindsight Henry hadn't done anything wrong, per se. When he did spend time with Matthew, nothing

interrupted him or got in his way. He treated me the same every night when we would talk through our mundane problems before turning in. We had an active sex life, which he enjoyed immensely. So, for him to just do the disappearing act on us without any forewarning or indication left me and Matthew shocked and bewildered to say the least. I just couldn't fathom it. He was never violent or argumentative. He helped with the weekly shopping. He went out cycling with Matthew for two hours on Saturday and Sunday and otherwise sat in front of the widescreen TV watching a film or sport.

Had we argued or had a fight then maybe I'd be better able to understand what had caused the collapse of our marriage. But I literally hadn't seen it coming.

As the weeks turned rapidly into months, my main focus was on Matthew. He kept asking, 'Where's Daddy? Where's Daddy?' to which I had no answer. I couldn't even bring myself to lie to him. He may have been very young but Matthew wasn't dull witted. He knew right away that something was awry.

Then he started asking, 'Is Daddy dead? Is Daddy dead, Mum?'

I couldn't handle it. But worse was yet to come. I hadn't told anyone as of yet and dreaded the reality that in the next few days the relatives and close friends would begin to ask the same questions.

My dad was the worst. He had a short temper. He used to box in the army when he was younger and was very strict. Matthew didn't like him. He even said that grandfather looked like he was trying to squeeze a shit out of his arse that wasn't willing to leave.

Of course, Henry and Matthew pissed themselves laughing at this analogy and when we were alone I too would laugh. My father lacked a sense of humour, which Henry said was as much fun as watching people on the racetrack asking a man with no legs to come and join them. And once again he and Matthew pissed themselves with raucous laughing.

So, to get back to the point in question – Henry leaving as sudden as a change in weather with no explanation whatsoever, baffled me. I did put two and two together and quickly realised that the reason Henry wasn't speaking to me was because he knew what he'd done was wrong. But instead of announcing to me in person that he no longer wanted to be married to me, he went behind my back and found himself a new lover.

Strangely, I didn't get angry with him. Or jealous, for that matter. In fact, in comparison to how most women would feel if they were dealt with the same circumstances, I was quite calm and collected. I just seemed to accept the fact that I had lost my husband and father to my only child to a younger, much prettier model.

With the help of our attorneys, we did manage to get an official divorce, and I was glad when Henry didn't even bother to fight for custody of Matthew or an agreement to see his son every weekend. I was hurt by that. That was brutal and offensive. I felt hard for my son. Neither of us had caused this sudden change of Henry Cawthorne. He had been the one who was guilty of the whole scenario. I kept thinking about the irrevocable damage it could do to stem the growth and happiness of Matthew. He didn't say much about it either. And I guess he just accepted the fact like the change of weather and got on with life. In fact, I distinctly remember how he inspired me to keep moving forward no matter what life threw at him.

Matthew finished reading the four pages and then riffled through the notepad, intrigued and keen to re-read the pad from the beginning to end. His mother's writing was more engaging than any bestseller currently available in WHSmith. After all, the diary included him. He was also spurred on to gain more knowledge of his absent father. Yet what he didn't let on was the fact that there was a burning sensation inside his gut induced by reading his dead mother's words, thoughts and feelings.

Matricide was very rare. It was only now on a subliminal level did Matthew seemed to consider how awful a crime that is. After all, Susan had kept him safe from the day he was conceived till the day she chose to abandon him when he needed her the most.

He wondered: would he have forgiven her had he known she kept a journal? That question didn't appear to come from him. It was more of an intrusive thought that had slipped through, confusing him and knocking him off track.

No, he realised all of a sudden.

Susan wouldn't even let him near the house, never mind permit him inside and sharing this notepad or the other one on the desktop.

As he ate his lunch in the small kitchen, Matthew gazed out the window and saw the heavy, thunderclouds looming over the town centre, gradually drifting up towards the hill toward his small town. And instead of being vexed by this fact, Matthew smiled, pleased that the nice, outdoor weather had changed just as quickly and defiantly as his father had abandoned them all those years ago.

Full, Matthew rinsed the plastic tray and put it in the plastics bag. Then he washed the utensils, grabbed the six pack off the worktop and ambled into the living room, ready to kick back and relax. He drank half a can before putting it down to the side of the armchair and taking the top notepad off the arm, opening it and found where he'd left off and began to read…

29 April.

The night before I had a phone call direct to the house number. I had no idea who on Earth would have dared call me at this later hour. Nevertheless, peeling myself off the couch where I sat watching a documentary, I answered the call.

To cut a long conversation short, to save my wrist from locking up again, Henry's dad, Patrick was on the other end of the line. He introduced himself and kindly offered me an apology on Henry's behalf for the way things had worked out between us. Clearly, he was in shock at how Henry had lost all love and respect for both his wife and son. He enquired as to our wellbeing before asking kindly if he could come by tomorrow in the morning to pick up Henry's belongings. Initially, I was reluctant. And it had nothing to do with the fact that I still loved Henry and wanted to see him again and try to talk him into changing his mind and staying with a family we had made. I hardly knew Patrick. He lived in Bristol, and we only briefly spoke over the phone or at the wedding and birth of Matthew. Nevertheless, it would save me a trip to the rubbish tip and so agreed that I would indeed be home at half past ten to eleven o'clock to permit him entry. Although I did ask why Henry couldn't come and get his belongings himself.

Patrick didn't answer my question. He seemed to hop around it until we bade each other good evening and retired for the night.

I woke twenty-five past eight and woke Matthew.

We had our breakfast in the living room. Then I went for a quick shower before getting dressed and Matthew got dressed and stayed in his bedroom, shooting hoops with his mini plastic basketball, pretending to be one of the NBA stars he'd seen on TV.

Patrick arrived promptly and I handed him bundled clothes I had sorted into black bags to make it easier to lumber back and forth in and out of the car. Then I informed Patrick that our bills when we were married had been fed through the paper shredder in the spare bedroom upstairs. I handed over a basket of Henry's toiletries and books and DVDs. I helped carry some of the stuff to hasten the time. Otherwise Patrick would be back and forth all morning long.

By that time, Matthew came downstairs and gazed upon his grandfather of Henry's side of the family.

Patrick hunkered down and opened his arms out wide.

Matthew went to him and they hugged. Patrick gave Matthew a five-pound note for pocket money. Then with a sad, forlorn look, Patrick took his leave, got into his hatchback and drove down the quiet street.

And so Henry was gone for good.

'I like Patrick,' Matthew said, and it was that comment that caught me off guard and almost reduced me to a sobbing fit.

I remember that day clearly. It was a Saturday and I decided that both of us needed not to sit around the house being miserable that Henry wasn't coming back ever again. So we put our trainers on, got in the Renault and took a trip down to Mumbles to have a nice long walk across the beach. The sun beat down on us and in the distance the waves crashed inexorably. Matthew started to make a sandcastle, but due to the ice-cold wind whipping us all over we decided to head back and grab a Joe's Ice Cream.

We took our time driving back, enjoying the sights, sounds and smells of clean fresh air and the exuberance of folks doing all sorts of fun activities.

'Can we both go cycling tomorrow?' Matthew asked.

Immediately I wanted to say yes, but was fully aware that I had to do all the washing and cleaning on Sundays which often left me weary and drained. I explained this to Matthew. He shook his head in disappointment, then turned and gazed out the window.

'I'm sorry, Champ,' I said. 'Why don't you go up to the park where the cycle track is? Go all the way around and then you'll be turning back on yourself back to the house?'

He did a funny little nod at this. And then approved of my suggestion. 'Did Dad leave 'cause of me, Mum?'

My heart wrenched and I was relieved when the traffic came to a halt at a red light. 'No sweetheart,' I said. 'Daddy didn't like me and found another woman. It's just us two now. Just the two of us against the world... and do you know something? They don't stand a chance.'

At this Matthew smiled and even chuckled.

To this day, just being with my son in that moment was pure nirvana.

3 May.

Work has been hectic and I'm glad that my next leave of absence is in a week. I've had a lot on my mind these past few months and am quietly content that I have managed to come through it without going crazy in the meantime. And as far as I'm aware Matthew seems to be coping really well in and out of school.

Nevertheless, in spite of all that's befallen us this year, last night I couldn't switch off, (which is unlike me) and go to sleep. Instead I simply lay in bed, feeling feeble and frail. I guess what I missed most was Henry's presence, sharing the same bed with him every night where we would sometimes just hold each other till we drifted off.

I remember one night – it hadn't been that long after we bought the house – we were both still awake, exhausted from having sex twice in quick succession. I leaned over to my husband and asked him what his biggest secret was. I was merely trying to be intimate on a much more personal level that superseded sex.

Henry seemed to be in deep deliberation over the question. I was still out of breath and fully and entirely in love with him and waited patiently for his response.

'If I tell you my biggest and darkest secret from my adolescence, do you promise not to tell anyone or leave me?'

I chuckled. 'That bad is it?'

Henry nodded. Then he said: 'It isn't good, but it's not the end of the world. I didn't go to jail or anything. I don't even know why I'd done it. It just kinda happened, and then as soon as it had been done, I felt like shit for days afterwards.'

I remember pulling away from him, now startled by his honest declaration. 'What did you do?' I asked him, wary and concerned.

> *Henry appeared to brace himself and I started to feel my cheeks burning from somewhere deep inside.*
> *'I broke a stray cat's neck...' he announced and then closed his eyes and sighed.*
> *As you can imagine, I was stunned into silence that may as well have been a big dark chasm prior to the Big Bang of creation.*
> *'Why?' I asked, incredulous.*
> *Henry shook his head, clearly ashamed as well he should.*
> *'That's awful, Henry,' I said, moving away from him.*
> *'Just a spur of the moment thing, that's all,' he said. 'I knew then that I couldn't play on my own any more. My childhood was over. I had become a man. A killer.'*

Startled, Matthew placed a receipt slip on the page he'd just read and closed the pad. He sat there in his armchair, stunned at how history had repeated itself to the next generation.

Although he would never admit it to himself, Matthew could now see why his dead mother had been so shocked and appalled at him for killing the neighbours' cat. However, in his mind that didn't excuse her for her later actions – refusing to come and see him and allow him back home so he could go to college and acquire a trade.

But none of that mattered anymore, he decided. You couldn't change the past, no matter how hard it was on the folks' who knew you. That's why folks kept secrets. And the more he contemplated on the topic, the more sense it made.

He had been punished for his unforgiven crime.

The only way Matthew could move forward from his own mistake was if he kept secrets. There was no other way for him. That's how folks managed to do it. And that's the way it had been since the dawn of mankind. You did what you did. The only difference was between himself and Henry was that as far as he was aware, his dad hadn't killed anyone.

Matthew had already killed two people. However, he began to use his experiences and knowledge to become safer with his plans for the future. Of course, the job with the local council painting and decorating was an honest way to make a living,

Matthew knew that for his plan to work he would have to think outside the box. He needed to prepare. First thing he'd do next weekend was take a look at his bank balance, which had grown significantly thanks to inheriting the semi-detached home he grew up in.

His mother had been very smart when it came to money. His parents had bought the property outright nearly twenty years ago. He was going to sell the house and stay in his flat. Some of the money had already been spent on funeral costs, but that aside, Matthew was starting to go up on the ladder of the world.

The other plan was to get a girlfriend.

If he could bring someone new into his life and she could be trusted then the plan to form an alliance would indeed become tangible and not just a mere imaginative pipe dream.

Lord knew there were a lot of unstable youngsters out there. The world had shafted these potential prospects, but under his leadership, they could hit back against society and the folks who had ruined them, denied them, and labelled them as no good. And if anyone got in their way, they would cause anarchy.

Matthew sat back and rocked gently, a broad smile creasing his face as he imagined the possibilities the world had to offer.

His parents had neglected him.

The world had neglected him.

Now was the dawn of an age that Matthew would create when all those folks who had written them off would have to take notice.

Money.

Yes, money.

Money in the world meant power.

Power meant prosperity.

Power and prosperity would not be ignored.

Then from just a thought, a dream… Matthew could build an empire…

34.

THREE WEEKS LATER

TOBY finished working out at the gym and was noticing how big and mighty his chest was looking in the walled mirrors. As he made his way out of the gym and walked home, he decided to give Annie Combs a call at her house, just to see how she was doing, and to tell her that he now had a normal life. A job. A hobby. And a stunning and loving girlfriend.

Half an hour later, he knocked on the door and beamed at the little old psychic as she answered his call.

'Hey, Annie! What's up?'

'Well, if it isn't the prodigal son,' Annie said aloud. Then she opened her arms wide and embraced him.

Toby could feel how bony and frail she had become and accepted her invitation to come inside. They sat down in the living room and Toby got down to telling her the three things that were making his life worthwhile and making him happy and content. Then he asked about Annie. He listened as she told him about what had been happening in her life and that in an hour's time she would be settling down to watch *Murder, she wrote* on one of the Sky channels.

'I wanted to tell you something,' Toby said, being serious all of a sudden, grasping Annie's full, undivided attention.

'Go on,' she said, eyeing him closely.

'I haven't had any visions or seizures for a while and I'd very much like to keep it that way, if I can. I have everything I could ever hope to wish for. And I don't want that to change. I function better without this "shine" as you call it. I don't want to "shine" any more. I love my girlfriend. I love my dear mother, and being a gym instructor for youngsters is a fulfilling job. And I also think that you should consider trying different things in life. Do you mind if I speak bluntly and honestly for a moment?'

Annie shook her head. 'No. Not at all. Fire away.'

'I think all this psychic business is doing you more harm than good. You're too old to be having to go through with all this. Maybe me and Anastasia can come by one day and take you out for a meal and a stroll along the beach. How about that? That'll do you the world of good, healthwise, and wellbeing-wise. Just don't use the "shine" to contact me if you do carry on with all this. Please. You are my friend. And I love you. But even the superheroes have to hang up their capes sooner or later. That's what I think – what I believe – we ought to do. Otherwise our lives will pass us by without us even knowing about it and before it's too late to enjoy the gift of life.'

Annie leaned forward and rested her emaciated and wrinkled, liver-spotted hand on top of Toby's left hand and looked deep into his caring eyes. 'You might be right, my good boy,' she said very sincerely. 'You might be right. And I'd love nothing more than to go out for food with you and your lovely girlfriend in the near future. Thank you.'

'Any time.'

With that, Toby grabbed his gym bag, hugged Annie again and took his leave in good spirits. He headed home with a skip in his step, his burden lifted and setting him free...

*

Annie Combs made her way out of her bathroom, still damp from the shower. She lumbered into the bedroom, relaxed and ready for a good night sleep. She slid under the duvet in her plaid pattern pyjamas and flicked the goose-neck lamp on after turning the bedroom light off. She picked up her Clive Barker book and read for just more than half an hour before her eyelids became heavy and she faded into a deep slumber.

She found herself at Cefn Coed mental institution and wondered how she had got there and what the purpose was for being present there. Nevertheless, she floated – not walked – across the asphalt car park towards the entrance. The entrance door to the male ward was unlocked. She pulled it open and winced at the high-pitched screeching of the hinges. Then she climbed the short staircase, pushed open the two glass-panelled doors that offered access to the main corridor. From there she floated to a small cubicle station where a nurse sat at a neat desk on her computer. She was hard at work and didn't look up as she was typing something from one of the files on paper to the monitor for a patient's records.

The door to the right opened automatically even though there was no one present in her vicinity. Yet Annie accepted the invitation and crossed the threshold onto the ward itself. The door hissed as it closed again behind her, like an angry snake.

Annie floated down this glossy corridor that went on for a while before the two nurses' and doctors' stations came into full sight. The doctors' station situated at the far end of the recreation room was locked and empty. The nurses' station had two female nurses and one male nurse stuffing his face with a cheeseburger and wiping the crumbs off his mouth and shirt.

The rooms were to her right. Annie knew instinctively that she was supposed to take a right even though she still had no idea what the purpose of all this was. It almost felt like she was having an out-of-body experience. Yet what she saw was so clear as crystal that she forgot what was real and what wasn't. Her brain didn't give any indication and neither did her other senses... at least not in that moment.

She checked that the coast was clear prior to making her way to the first cell door where there was a small square window offering a view into the room. And Annie was about to check door number 1 when her body, her whole being refused to move at her request. Instead she found herself floating down the wide corridor to a door on the left. She turned and faced door number 4 and moved towards the glass panel and saw a boy standing motionless in the cell staring right at her. She shivered and reflexively shook it off with trepidation. Then she refocused and matched the eerie, schizophrenic stare that had no emotion, soulless and black as a chasm. The fear enveloped her and it grew into a tangible, malignant thing that squirmed inside her, threatening to take over her whole being entirely.

'His name is Matthew,' she said, having no idea how or where she got this information and what the significance was. Of course, if she managed to rise out of this dream or vision, she'd dismiss it as too much paranoia and isolation.

'Hello, Matthew,' Annie said to the boy behind the cell door.

'He can't hear you,' she said in a darker tone, as though there was another entity occupying her earthly vessel.

'Who -?'

'Don't ask,' she said in another voice. 'Just listen.'

Annie remained silent.

'Matthew is a very evil young man,' the voice informed her. 'He is a cold-blooded murderer. He killed his own mother and a guy he met at a local pub. He is very intelligent and cunning. He deceives everyone who believed that his bad patch was a momentary lapse due to being raised by his mother, abandoned by his father at a young age. He is planning on bringing more evil into the country and will succeed for a short time. This message is given to you to do something to prevent this from happening any worse than it'll continue to be if nothing is done.'

Annie's stare at the boy and his stare at her left her trembling from head to foot. He didn't blink. Didn't even move, for God's sake! He wasn't human.

'He looks as if he's already been apprehended and taken care of,' the elderly lady croaked.

'This is just a vision,' the voice that moved Annie's lips said. 'Matthew isn't in the mental institution anymore. He has a girlfriend and is known as a good worker for the local council. My time here is running short. I must go soon. But you must act, Annie. There's no turning a blind eye to this situation. Matthew doesn't see the world the way you see it. His motto is "An eye for an eye and the world goes blind". That's what he wants. He wants notoriety, power and money. You've been warned…'

The voice was swallowed with a cough and a gasp.

*

The sun blazed in the azure sky. The youngsters had just departed from their game and were now heading back to the sports centre to get dressed and clean. Toby had watched the whole match and acted as a water-boy for the local team. He collected the rugby balls into a black carrier net along with the empty bottles of water and kicking tees. It had been a good match, both sides playing high class skills which finally ended 15-15. And considering the home team were the underdogs, a draw game was certainly an achievement.

He consulted his wristwatch and was pleased to see that it was only 12:00 noon. The rest of the day he planned to go for a drive up in the mountains with Anastasia. They hadn't seen each other all week due to their work patterns. Toby worked 9-3 in the day and Anastasia worked 4-11pm. It may have been a little unsociable but rather than whining Toby always looked forward to his weekends now.

In the week he played Scrabble with his mother, Abigail, who cherished her time with him as Toby did with her. He had spoken to her about what he'd said to Annie. Abigail informed him that she indeed thought the decision a prudent one on his part, one that demonstrated a maturity in his young age.

'Life is for enjoying,' she said one night.

And Toby was starting to believe her. He no longer looked back at his childhood with bitterness and regret. Instead he filled his mind with prosperity and thankfulness. He paid his mother a large sum towards rent and was thinking of taking driving lessons to further his independence. Furthermore, every Wednesday after work, Toby and Abigail went to either Tesco or Asda for the weekly shopping.

With all the equipment now and the rugby pitch clean of debris, Toby sauntered back towards the sports centre to return the belongings to the staff. Then he headed back to the school edifice four football fields away, grabbed his backpack, said farewell to the P.E. coach and then took his leave.

The day's duty had been done and now Toby ambled across the playing fields towards the gate that led to the public footpath alongside the busy road leading into the town centre. The din of traffic broke his peaceful reverie, and as he got closer to the entrance gate a high pitch electrical sound threatened to burst his eardrums. He stumbled forward as though he had been pushed by the Invisible Man. He righted himself and managed to keep himself from hitting the dirt. Then he ambled over to an oak tree and sat on the grass in the shade believing that because he hadn't eaten and been out in the scorching sunshine all morning, he had begun to feel light headed and didn't want to faint.

Then a voice spoke from within, above the din of the relentless line of traffic going to and fro.

'Toby? Toby? Can you hear me? I need you.'

Recognising the voice, Toby sighed in exasperation and didn't feel guilty about this thought. 'Annie? Is that you?'

'Yes,' Annie said.

'Christ!'

'I'm sorry, Toby,' Annie Combs said in a timid voice. 'But I need your help.'

'Yeah. What kinda help we talkin' about here?'

'There's a boy about the same age as you,' she started, her voice trembling. 'He's a murderer and an evil manipulator.'

Toby's head started to ache, dully at first then felt like static had exploded inside his brain. He held his head in both hands and closed his eyes, fearing the worse for himself.

'Toby? Toby? Are you still there?'

'Shut up! Shut up! Shut up!' he cried out.

'Please…' Annie's frightened voice trailed off.

Toby's head started to hurt like someone was sticking needles into his head and probing his entire being.

''Scuse me. Are you all right?'

Toby still squeezed his eyes shut and recoiled at the touch of a soft hand on his shoulder. He snapped back to reality with a jump. His eyes flew open and suddenly, there, standing close to him, a middle-aged woman with curly blonde hair and big round glasses looked down on him with the same compassion she would have if he was a kitten left at the side of a highway.

Annie had departed from his head that no longer pounded.

Toby got to his feet and was embarrassed by his actions and words, regardless that he was innocent. At that moment, he hated Annie Combs. He hated her voice. Her face. And he hated her presence, and mentally told himself that she was no longer welcome to go out for food with himself and Anastasia.

'I hear voices,' Toby told the kind lady. 'It's not serious but it does drive me mad from time to time. Thank you for your concern. It is greatly appreciated.'

The lady stepped back and noticed how he was sweating profusely and proffered him a half full bottle of water. 'Here take this. It might wake you up a bit. You look a little pale.'

Toby nodded, not knowing how else to act. 'Thank you... again. I have been up early and working without a single drink or any food. The sun and not being nourished was the catalyst for this episode.' Then he proffered a hand and the lady gave her his hand and they shook. 'I best be on my way now,' Toby said.

'Take it easy,' the lady said and then carried on walking.

Toby inwardly chastised Annie. Then he opened the bottle of Evian water and gulped down the contents. Once he had done that, Toby continued on his way towards home, his anger abating and his natural peace calming him, erasing the bad thoughts directed at the elderly woman.

Don't contact me again like this, Annie.

*

Matthew Cawthorne spent that Saturday afternoon fornicating with Gemma in all kinds of positions. Afterwards, Gemma rolled off him and sighed in pure satisfaction.

'Fantastic!' she gasped and stared impassively at the ceiling.

Matthew stretched out his limbs and yawned. Then he threw the covers off himself and walked into the bathroom naked as the day he was born. He urinated, washed his hands and then dried his face on the towel. When he emerged back into the bedroom he got dressed into his jeans and a red T-shirt.

Gemma Hayes had been his girlfriend for two whole weeks. She had left school with A and B grades and then went onto college where she studied the Performing Arts programme. She could sing in tune, but her real passion was for acting and modelling. And with her unblemished tawny tight skin and wavy brown hair that brushed her shoulders there was no denying that on stage or in front of a camera she would be able to turn heads and suck the energy out of a room with her presence and beauty alone.

'I'm gonna take a shower,' Matthew said. 'Do you need the bathroom before I go in?'

Gemma shook her head. Then she said: 'Could you get my handbag from the kitchen, please?'

'Sure.' Matthew turned on his heel and headed for the kitchen. As he did this, he grabbed the handbag by its handles and it toppled upside down, spilling the contents on the tiled floor. Matthew cussed under his breath at this clumsy error. Then one of the items caught his attention. It was a photograph of four men dressed immaculately in suits staring at the person taking the picture. They looked serious and powerful. This, Matthew deduced, was not the kind of photo one carried around with the rest of their belongings. The photo was unique in itself. He picked up the other items strewn across the floor but kept the photo in his other hand, rose from his haunches and headed back to the bedroom, frowning, perplexed.

Matthew handed Gemma her handbag then held out the photo so she could see it clearly. 'Who are these men?' he asked.

'Those men are just some guys I know, who helped me get onto the ladder to kickstart my career in the entertainment industry.'

'Agents?' Matthew asked.

'Kind of,' Gemma said.

'What do you mean "Kind of"?'

'They're friends of my father's,' Gemma said, fastening her bra.

Matthew considered her clipped response but still was unsatisfied with her answer.

'They work in the entertainment industry?' he wanted to know.

'They're men that make things happen if you join their elite organisation.'

'Like Freemasons?' Matthew asked, pushing her more and more for a definitive answer.

Gemma nodded. 'If you are a member of their organisation, sometimes they do favours for something in return.' She paused, looking unnerved now. Yet she continued with her explanation. 'My father joined their club after selling his club.

He used to own a club for people who like jazz and country music. For the first five years the club did well financially. Then there was the recession and suddenly the business folded. My father knew these guys and offered to pass it on to them where they would hold conferences to the other members for initiation and meetings.'

Matthew could see that Gemma didn't look too comfortable in her own skin right then. Evidently this topic of conversation made her nervous and anxious.

'They saw me in one of the plays I was in,' Gemma went on, gaining her natural posture and confidence, realising there was nothing to be afraid of. 'They were impressed and so agreed to find me an agent in London. My father did them a favour too, but he never said what it was... and never will.

'The agency booked me for two catalogue magazines selling women's fashion clothing. Then I got a part in a play, playing the part of Mary Magdalene. From there I had some extra work and one-liners in some soap operas and low budget British films.'

Matthew handed over the photo, nodding with approval, impressed by the power these men wielded. 'Do you still keep in touch with them?' he asked.

Gemma turned the photo over and pointed to the number on the top right. 'That's their number.'

'May I write that down?'

Gemma gave him a funny look. 'It might be better if I called them for you. Anyway, what do you want that they can provide?'

Matthew sat on the end of the bed and glanced at Gemma. 'I don't intend working for the council for the rest of my life, contrary to how I behave and act sometimes. I want to address a large number of folks and start my own cult.'

Gemma had no words to offer her boyfriend. However, she could see that he was deadly serious in what he had just said. 'Why do you need this club to help you?' she asked, perplexed and on edge.

'I need to attract folks... and the only way to do that is by getting a venue and promoting my preaching through the local media. But I know TV won't aid me. Neither will newspapers for that matter. I need workers to help spread the word that there is an evening free of charge for a speech to do with life and the world we live in today and how we must fight for our desires and human rights which the government clamps down on to keep us at the bottom end of the ladder into poor society amongst other things.'

Gemma studied his features and realised Matthew was very serious and honest about what he had just said.

'I could call them and request that they have an interview with you,' Gemma said, feeling nervous all of a sudden. 'But if I do this and they agree to help you, then you must understand first and foremost that you will then have to do something for them in return. That's how it works, you see. Before committing yourself, have a think about what you're proposing. Because if you are serious then there's no turning back; if folks don't turn up or ignore your preaching, then it has nothing to do with the gentlemen in this photo. They don't mess around, Matthew. Sleep on it and then if you're still interested and adamant about what you want then I'll call them on your behalf.'

Matthew nodded. 'Thank you, Gemma,' he said and then went to take a shower...

*

The day was glorious. The sun spread its vibrancy onto the small town in Wales. Matthew had slept well and got his eight hours of slumber in and had risen at the sound of the digital alarm clock at precisely 8:00am. Today was the day he would be meeting the four gentlemen in the club that did favours for each other.

Gemma had a modelling gig in Cardiff so Matthew was by himself. He had no fear of the meeting and had written down the address he must arrive at in the town centre at 11:00am sharp.

He went about his usual morning ritual, and then got dressed into his pin-striped grey suit prior to heading out the door and catching a bus. Matthew wanted to be in the town centre Carnegie Hall with time to spare. From the bus stop he ambled down the bricked streets, seeing the owners opening their shops at 9:00am to accommodate their first and eager customers of the day.

Matthew headed for Morrison's superstore and purchased a bottle of water and a newspaper. Then he went outside and lowered himself onto one of the many benches and read the stories while sipping his drink.

After an hour, Matthew got up, scrunched the newspaper up into a ball and fed it to the bin prior to taking a stroll towards the WHSmith store. The interior had air-conditioning and refreshed Matthew palpably. He stood in the aisle admiring the bestseller releases and then moved up to the array of paperbacks he hadn't read since he was a kid. Then school made it obligatory to read certain prescribed books. Matthew resented books thereafter. However, if he had endured Shakespeare and left school with a healthy habit for literature, he'd adopt this store as his second home.

He browsed for more than twenty minutes and then took his leave, not purchasing anything, which left the desk clerk confused and irritated. He smiled at that and then headed to the public gardens and closed his eyes, tilted his head back and let the warmth and shine of the sun refresh him with its goodness.

At 10:45am Matthew made his way to the Carnegie Hall. Ascending the steps between two carved pillars, painted white by his and his co-worker's own hands, Matthew stood on the platform, faced the broad hardwood door, and grabbed the brass knocker that had a demon's face and rapped three times.

From the interior he could distinctly hear the sound of footfalls click-clacking their way to the door. The brass letterbox four feet from the bottom of the door slid open and a man's voice asked, 'Who is it?'

'Matthew Cawthorne,' Matthew said. Then he added: 'I have a meeting here today at 11:00am.'

The letterbox snapped shut, bolts were retracted and another lock was released prior to the large door opening and permitting Matthew to enter the stone-walled interior, which appeared to be from the bygone age of a monastery.

There was a black metal door to his left and a tight, stone-crafted spiral staircase offering access upwards to the bell tower and downwards to a subterranean level.

The gentleman, who Matthew recognised from the photo, pointed towards a long marble bench and said that at 11:00am the door would open and he'd be permitted to enter. This would take place in approximately three minutes' time, as Matthew was a tad early.

Three minutes later the black metallic door opened and the same gentleman who had fast thinning hair peered around the side of the door and said, 'Enter.'

Matthew rose and crossed the short hallway into a room where a long varnished conference table took up almost all the space. At the far end three men Matthew instantly recognised were seated, smiling at him and tidying up the piles of letters scattered on the table in front of them where they each had a tall glass of water on coasters.

The man at the head invited Matthew to take a seat on the chair he was standing by and not any closer. Matthew obliged and shifted in his seat so he was directly facing the suits, all eyeing him with what could only be curiosity.

'I'd just like to take this opportunity to thank you for holding this meeting with me at my request,' Matthew said in the most professional voice he could summon.

The four men gave a curt nod and said that was all right. And immediately, Matthew came to be fully aware that this meeting would not have even the slightest hint of humour or any suggestion of a laid-back approach. This was what average folk called a "formal meeting".

The man at the head of the table with short black, thick hair and a goatee to match clasped his hands together and leaned forward. He stared at Matthew without expression and said, 'I believe you are Gemma Hayes' boyfriend. Is that correct?'

'Indeed it is,' Matthew replied.

However, Matthew decided in his own mind that all four of the associates knew this to be true and were simply testing whether or not he was a liar.

'And so it is my and my clients' curiosity to ask you first why you wanted this board meeting, and what you would be willing to do for us in return? It is my understanding that you have had a distressing past. Isn't that so?'

Caught way off guard, Matthew did well not to gape in astonishment at the four businessmen at how they knew about his past. He couldn't understand it. He hadn't even told Gemma about being locked away at a mental institution.

'Before you ask us how we know,' the head told him, 'understand that we have unlimited resources in many aspects. That is why people come to us and join our club. We believe that there is only one life for humans. We refuse to let our clients feel worthless. If they have the tools for a certain job or way of life that we believe it should be then they receive it after doing us a deed in return. That's how all businesses should operate. There are many scams from businesses out there all over the world. Promising to take all your troubles and burdens and make your bills go away and your dreams come true. What we hope to offer is a lifelong partnership for a better, more rewarding life. All you need to do is look out your proverbial window, read the news and understand that we don't tolerate suffering within our club. We believe "if you scratch my back, I'll scratch yours" is the type of mentality that enables people to get things done; to achieve their goals, and live a life full of wonderful memories.'

Matthew nodded. 'That's how it ought to be.'

The head nodded once. 'Now, what is it that you seek? And please, consider what you say, for if you do us a turn and we agree to return the favour, make sure it isn't something you will forget. Is that understood, Mr. Cawthorne?'

Matthew nodded and verbally said that he understood, at the same time hiding his shock at how these men had already done their homework on his background prior to this first face-to-face meeting.

'Good,' the head said. 'Now please, tell us what you so dearly desire?'

The young serial killer met the head's eyes and knew that from now on his life would take off in accordance with his wishes, and that there would be no other concerns thereafter.

Now was the time to take a stand…

35.

ANNIE COMBS sat out at the back on the paving slabs, enjoying the summer sunshine and the cool breeze that tousled her hair. The night before, she had slept well and had awoken early, feeling much better. She knew that there was a teenager out there in the nation whose future curdled her blood and caused the fine hairs on her arms to bristle. However, she had gone through her old photograph book from when she was a teenager herself. She had her gift from a young age. Her first job after school was sewing clothes for the army. After that she went and worked in a warehouse as a courier.

A day as warm as this present day had altered her life forevermore. She had been minding her own business, walking down the street when a flicker of electric blue light flashed before her eyes and caused her to wince and shield her face instantly. All of a sudden, she felt herself trying to stagger like a drunk on the pavement. Tentatively, she opened her eyes and saw people in their vehicles going to and fro, staring out their windows at her. She hated people for that singular reason. Then she righted herself, calmed herself with words of promise prior to leaving the spot she had nearly fainted on and moved forward gingerly.

Another brilliant white flash blinded her and sent a shiver of panic through her veins. She had to sit down on the nearest bench and get a grip, as though an entity had taken over the controls without her consent. As she closed her eyes she saw the street behind her lids of a man in his early thirties with long black hair, kissing his girlfriend and then stepping out onto the main road without looking properly and being struck with a sickening slap of flesh and crunch of bones by a heavy goods vehicle.

Terrified, Annie's eyes shot open and narrowed against the sun. Shaken by what she'd just witnessed, Annie got to a vertical position and took her time walking on her way.

What she saw next was so surreal and yet normal it could have quite easily have blown her mind. In the near distance she saw a red Ford with a young woman with a gorgeous tan wearing a black top that had straps over her shoulders keeping it in place. She sat behind the wheel talking with her boyfriend. They kissed each other on the lips, then the young man got out of the car, slammed the door and was about to cross the road without looking.

'Wait!' Annie had called out, loud enough for the young man to stop and turn in the direction of her voice.

A heavy goods vehicle roared down the street inches from the young man who stepped back, looking to and fro from the vehicle and Annie.

'Didn't your mother tell you to look both ways before you cross the road?' Annie shouted coming towards him, close enough to see his handsome features.

The young woman who was evidently the man's girlfriend shook her head at him for nearly getting himself killed for not paying heed to the traffic.

As the elderly woman sat enjoying the summer day, she started to feel at ease with herself. An invisible hand rested on her bony shoulder and took all the pressure away, leaving her with a warm reassurance that no matter what bad things happened, she had done more than enough. Over the years as a psychic, she had aided innumerable folks with revelations, good advice, and forgiveness as they grew to become better people.

If this young murderer was permitted to act out his evil desires then so be it. After speaking with Toby, Annie made a profound decision not to contact him again through the "Shine" and began to relax for the first time in her life, properly. She was sixty years of age and was now officially at retirement age. What it came down to was this simple fact of life on Earth as we know it: before she'd been born folks committed all kinds of evil. During her youth and younger years, she had been unable to help lots of people in their distress. And yet every time she watched the news on TV she kind of felt that when there was a story about someone dying in tragic circumstances she could have done something to prevent this. But that wasn't the case at all. Ultimately, Annie Combs could only do so much for folks.

That fateful day when she had saved that young man's life had taken her down an arduous road. She had felt obligated towards that way of life... and to all intents and purposes, that's precisely what it was. However, Toby had found a life worth protecting and cherishing until his dying day.

Now Annie began to see that although Toby had demonstrated the same "Shine" as she'd possessed, that didn't mean he was her protégé. After all, he had a job as a gym instructor. He had helped the local and national police and other emergency services in difficult cases that would have gone unsolved. But now he had a girlfriend whom he loved and a mother who deserved good things after all her work as a single parent left to pick up the pieces when her husband had left.

All of this Annie had gone through mentally until she came to the decision: she couldn't care less any more, either.

If Toby didn't want to know, then why should she?

Sixty years on Earth and more than forty years of service was more than enough contribution to mankind in her neck of the woods. Now she deserved her peace and tranquillity. Nothing or no one would change that fact.

Annie lifted the tall glass and sipped the lemonade, fanning herself.

Another aspect of being a spiritualist was the fact that from a young age, Annie had lost her friends and found herself alone in a lonely life. Nevertheless, nowadays she was spoilt rotten. She had TV, radio, a library card and she enjoyed going for walks around town and down by the sea.

This was the life that had forsaken her youth.

Now in the autumn of her existence she would learn to switch off and take it easy...

*

Matthew finished explaining what he desperately desired from the four wise men. Then he sat up ramrod straight and stretched his back. The Head and his associates stared at him closely, and Matthew had no idea or clue what they were thinking about him. The silence was deafening and the electric ambience had turned up a few notches in intensity.

The Head took a sip of water before returning the tall glass to its coaster. 'Why do you want a crowd of people listening to you preach? I don't understand. Even if we advertise you as some kind of preacher do you really think people will listen to you?'

Matthew demonstrated not a trace of trepidation. Instead he spoke confidently, better than an experienced actor who had memorised and believed his lines effortlessly. 'I don't just want any people,' he said. 'I want to talk to the downtrodden. The homeless. The people who already know the harshness of this world in which we live. They will listen to me, you mark my words.'

'But then what?' the Head asked, evidently still not coming to terms with what Matthew's intentions were.

'They will listen to me and act accordingly,' Matthew went on, growing in confidence, not at all perturbed by the men's expressions directed at him.

The Head stared impassively at the table in front of him, totally bewildered by the young man and his words. When he looked up again Matthew was leaning forward waiting for a response.

'What do you want me to do for you in return of my request and membership to this exclusive club?'

The Head had many business errands to be done and was in the process of analysing this Matthew Cawthorne, trying to figure out how his request and their request of him could be executed.

'I want a pasture and a large open tent filled with chairs and a small stage at the front with a microphone and speakers,' Matthew continued. 'I want my people to come to me and listen and be rejuvenated by my words and philosophies. That's what I want.'

'We could advertise you as a therapist, one who preaches powerful sermons that make you a confidence-booster for those who don't have jobs and are looking for something to join to make them feel important in society again. How does that work for you?' the man with a bald head and a thick goatee said.

Matthew nodded in agreement. 'Just get those poor folks on the seats and I'll do the rest. And you still haven't answered my question.'

The Head raised his hand to call for silence, allowing him to take over again. 'We have your address. We shall provide you with a folder of a job we would like you to do for us prior to you getting what you want. But please, everything we have discussed today in this meeting is in strict confidence.' The Head handed his associate two sheets of paper. The associate then rose from his chair, unclipped a pen from his jacket pocket and walked towards Matthew, informing him that his initials and signature was required on both sheets on dotted lines in agreement with the terms and conditions.

Without hesitation, Matthew signed the two sheets of paper and handed back the pen to the man smelling of strong cologne.

'What happens now?'

'You will receive your mission tomorrow. If you refuse to go ahead with the case then both you and the contract will be terminated without trace. Is that understood?'

Matthew nodded. 'Indeed, I do.'

Then he hauled himself out of the chair and stood up, gave a curt bow and then exited the conference room.

As he descended the stone steps, Matthew embraced the fresh air blowing his hair on the beautiful day, feeling as though he had accomplished a great feat.

Sunday he would wait in the flat all day for the folder to see what his task was and to prepare his mind for anything so he wasn't shocked in the moment by what was expected of him.

You scratch our backs, we'll scratch yours.

He headed for Morrison's again and purchased a bottle of Pepsi and a Mars Bar, deciding to walk home as the weather was so nice.

One more errand and Matthew's biggest dream would come true. He would accomplish his goals and desires to the unsuspecting world. What no one knew was that Matthew's dream had a sinister plot to it. He hadn't elaborated this to the Freemasons. If he had done so he wouldn't be able to show his face in this town until he was so old no one would know his name. But there was one word that illuminated in his mind like a neon light.

Anarchy…

*

Rebecca Adonali had been quietly investigating the secret societies for more than a decade now and had learned many different things that she would eventually amass in a book at the end of this year. However, after learning some of the powers that are influenced and associated with the secret societies, Rebecca had a harrowing surprise over a year ago.

She had been working for the BBC as a journalist and returned home to find a letter on the doormat inside her residence.

In haste and curiosity, Rebecca had opened the letter and read the typed script. It said:

Ms Adonali,

We are well aware of your hidden research and investigations regarding legitimate groups of wealth and power of the present societies. It has come to our attention that your investigations over the past few years have tainted us with immorality and unlawful suits. I regret to inform you that your investigations are not accurate, and that you're meddling with people in powerful positions that control this country and its people. We advise that you no longer probe into the unknown for your own safety and wellbeing. Please don't write, speak or suggest that our organisation is dangerous and sinister. If you continue to proceed with your investigations, I can only regret to tell you that there will be dire consequences for you and your loved ones. Please take note: your foolish investigations are not only inaccurate but juvenile and insulting. Consider this letter a friendly warning and as long as you cease your investigations, no action against you will be taken. For your sake.

The blonde beauty with dimples and a refreshing sunshine smile had brooded over the letter for nearly four months. Terrified initially, Rebecca had folded the letter and slid it back into its envelope for safe keeping and placed it in her top drawer. However, as time passed, Rebecca came to the realisation that what prompted that formal warning regarding her investigations had to be close to the truth. Otherwise why would this organisation take the time and the effort to write to her in the first instance?

In late February, Rebecca went to her own filing cabinet and pulled out the file titled Secret Societies and rifled through it to see all that she had accumulated and if there was any need to address any of the issues she hadn't covered previously.

It was her dream to use all her research and write a book. In her heart and mind, Rebecca firmly believed that the public would be intrigued by this topic and would grab her book off the shelf to find out more about this topic with the same zeal and enthusiasm she had when she first began the project that had taken up a lot of her life.

'A friendly warning,' she said to herself, trying to get to grips with the letter. 'Jeez, girl. I mean, are they serious? All I have to do is go to the police with this letter and they'd make a much more thorough investigation. I mean, a warning is the same thing as a threat. Surely anyone I dare show this letter to would see that clearly as day.' She paced back and forth, contemplating how she ought to proceed and whether or not she could go ahead with this project undeterred.

The only aspect that did cause concern was how this organisation had managed to discover her investigations and gained access to her full address considering it wasn't listed on public records.

She sat down in her comfy chair and swallowed some beer, unable to switch her mind off in order to concentrate on the national news on TV.

After the news she decided to put her investigations in order and outline a book idea. Introduction page; first chapter and so on and so forth, until it all came together and made sense. Then she would have to come up with an eye-catching title that would make readers look twice.

Another aspect of the letter was that there was no postal address, phone number or email or name. For all Rebecca knew it could have been a prank. It could have been a work colleague winding her up, fully aware of her ambitions. Yet, off the top of her head, she couldn't think of anyone she knew or was associated with who would do such a thing to her, even for a joke.

Nevertheless, in spite of the letter, in spite of her fear, Rebecca sat down at her home desk and went through her notes systematically. And worked the whole night through.

At 12:38am Rebecca called it a day and retired to her night time ritual prior to turning off the bedside table lamp and snuggling down for some much required sleep. She slept deeply without the intrusion of dreams or nightmares and awoke at 8:11am.

Today was Saturday. No work. Which was great because she could focus all her attention on outlining her book. She also needed to go into the city and purchase a writer's handbook for a list of publishers and literary agents. As she got dressed and ate a bowl of Coco Puffs she started to feel pure excitement. After all, she was in the process of writing a book on a subject that had only been tapped into briefly. She also knew of a young actor who had openly spoken out against an establishment called "The Society" that had aided him getting good roles for film and TV on both sides of the Atlantic. He allegedly had to sell his home in California and pay an additional fee to "The Society" that had got him the best agent in the UK and the US. Hollywood had dropped him like a dirty rag with no use when he turned down a film role that involved him having sex directly in front of the cameras.

Rebecca had heard of him through a work colleague, but had not got in touch with him. She would love to do an interview with him to be included in her book.

And she had the young actor's home phone number from her work colleague. Initially she had doubted the claim and continued her research until she started becoming obsessed with the topic and uncovered a lot of truths that most folks were completely unaware of. A lot of it was quite harrowing.

She caught the bus that travelled to and from the city centre, purchased a copy of the *Writer's Handbook*, picked up some other assortments, including a key drive where she would keep all her data about "The Society" and nothing else. Then after lunch she went through her paperwork in her desk drawers and finally fished out the number of the actor who now went by a different name to the name used for his acting career.

Rebecca sat at her desk and dialled the number and waited for the shrill ringing on the other side to end and a voice to answer her call, which is what happened five rings later.

'Hello?'

'Oh, hi,' Rebecca said in an excited and pleasant voice. 'Is this Tad Little?'

'Speaking,' the man's voice said. 'Who may I say is calling?'

'Oh, my name is Rebecca Adolani. You don't know me but I'm an investigative reporter. I am writing a book on secret societies and was wondering if we could meet up for a conversation about any knowledge you have on the said topic. Would you be willing to do that? I'll pay you fifty pounds cash and your name and information in my book would remain anonymous, I promise.'

'What makes you think I have any knowledge about secret societies?' Tad asked, clearly frustrated.

'You used to be an actor,' Rebecca said matter-of-factly.

'Where did you get this number?'

'From a work colleague,' Rebecca said, crossing her middle and index finger, praying Tad didn't cut the transmission.

Silence...

'Are you still there?' Rebecca wanted to know.

'I'm still here,' Tad said in a much softer tone.

'Please say yes to a meeting,' Rebecca practically begged.

'Why?'

'People have the right to know how powerful this organisation is to avoid making the same mistake you did before it's too late. They've already convinced the public they don't exist and any rumours are nothing more than a myth.

Help me to unleash my book and reveal to the blind what they haven't seen and how we're all controlled by these powerful men?'

Another long pause ensued.

'And how do I know for certain you'll keep my identity anonymous?'

'I could draw up a legislature that would be signed by me and my lawyer that your name and identity will not be used. I'll use parts of your story and disguise you as a woman to maintain your obscurity. Even if someone did think of you, they have no proof. And if asked, all you can say is that your acting career dried up because you weren't getting any roles.'

Tad sighed heavily. 'Do you really realise how powerful the society is? I don't think you do.'

'Why don't you tell me face-to-face?' Rebecca asked. 'I won't even bring a Dictaphone or write it down word for word. I promise. But if I can't get one person to tell their story and what goes on behind closed doors that affects the world then we might as well let them control us and subject us to their way of thinking and living without freedom of speech and equality.'

'Meet me at Tesco car park,' Tad said. 'I drive a white Jaguar.'

'Okay,' Rebecca said.

And as she was about to thank Tad for agreeing to do the interview, he hung up…

*

Rebecca did finally call back to arrange a time and day.

Tad had said today at 4:00pm would work best for him so Rebecca sat on the wooden bench outside the superstore and waited anxiously, scanning the car park for a white Jaguar. When she spotted the car, her heart skipped a beat. She hurried to the vehicle that had pulled into a vacant spot. Its engine turned off as she neared.

She knocked on the passenger window and Tad, who had short, thick black hair and ice-blue eyes and full lips, unlocked the vehicle, permitting Rebecca to climb inside right next to him.

Safe in the confines of the Jaguar, Rebecca thanked Tad enthusiastically for doing this. He could see it clearly meant a lot to her and he flashed her a heart-warming smile.

'You're welcome,' Tad said. Then he added with much deliberation that she pulled out her pockets to prove she wasn't recording the conversation.

Rebecca did so without hesitating.

Satisfied when she'd done this, Tad nodded in approval.

'So what do you know?' Tad asked, undoing his seat belt and shifting in his seat to face her better.

Rebecca could feel the heat in her cheeks and was fully aware that she was nervous and blushing. She could now see why Tad, who was handsome, had initially done well in the movie industry.

'This establishment goes back to the seventeen hundreds,' Rebecca began. 'There are members of this organisation that call themselves Freemasons and live under a certain code exclusive to its members. On occasions they meet up to discuss worldly matters. The Society has top leaders who control and have influence on all sorts of things that govern the world in which we live. Not just in the entertainment industry but in all kinds of matters. It is my belief they also control the media, TV, newspapers, government secrets and anything that the unknowing public may like in order to make money and gain influence out of it.'

Tad's eyes widened and nodded. 'Impressive. Not just a pretty face after all,' he smiled.

'Tell me your story,' Rebecca said, leaning closer to Tad, instantly relaxed and comfortable in his company.

'Well, to cut a long story short, I guess ever since I was a young boy, I'd love to get involved in anything to do with being on stage. During my school and college years I starred in Biblical plays and other plays from Shakespeare and Charles Dickens. Of course I didn't make any money in those days. I did it for the pure joy inside me and it was my passion that spurred me on along with all my family, friends, teachers and members of the local public telling me that I had a wonderful gift and that I ought to share it.

'I graduated from college and found out quite quickly that, great actor or not, life didn't surrender to my hopes and desires. I went to acting classes during the evening and worked as a waiter in the Blue Moon bar for three years, landing small parts in West End plays. My teacher concurred with many others who had seen my plays that I was indeed very talented and had honed my craft.

'Then I joined a company from Chelsea who specialised in modelling and extra work, but I had to quit as it was too sporadic and my waiter job demanded more hours of me.

'I left work in the early hours of Sunday morning, exhausted and devastated that I had my dreams dashed and I was left like a street rat in the alleyway.

'I discovered The Society through a friend from college one night at a local pub on Christmas Eve. He introduced me to a group finely dressed and sober men on the top floor, enjoying their evening discussing all manner of things over brandy and smoking pipes. My friend went inside, leaving me standing in the hallway. Then he came out and told me that he had given the businessmen my full name and their office address for me to contact on January 5 the following year.'

'What happened then?' Rebecca said, unable to restrain herself.

'I went to Carnegie Hall and met a gentleman. I told him that I worked long hours for shit pay in the Blue Moon bar but did have great ambitions for acting. I told him about the high praise I'd received over the years in the dozens of plays in which I performed but had no such luck in maintaining it.

'He gave me a free of charge membership certificate to sign and some other sheets regarding the Terms of Conditions and promised he'd be in touch. From there I was taken on by an agent based in London and got my first film role in a small TV series produced by the BBC. "Catching Flies", it was called. It only aired two seasons and I was not the lead role. But I learned a lot and gained experience along with confidence. Anyway, from there I went from strength to strength. But the day came on the set of an American picture where I was to have unprotected intercourse with an actress. I couldn't go through with it. My stubbornness, my integrity wouldn't allow it. The scene would show the woman on top, riding me in writhing passion. The director said it would take no more than twelve takes.'

Rebecca gaped in astonishment, feeling Tad's the discomfort.

'I just couldn't go through with it…' Tad averted his gaze and looked out the window. Then he turned back as Rebecca laid a hand on his shoulder. 'It was a Warner Brother feature and yet it felt like pornography. The crew started chiding me and making fun of me. I left the set.

'A week later I had a letter through the door from "The Society" informing me that I had broken one of the contract terms and conditions and now owed them three quarters of my earnings. I called my agent six times but the line did not ring as before.

'I left the US and returned home to my UK residence to find it was for sale. All my belongings had been stripped, and the only money I had left was what was in my bank account. Barclays had called and sent me a letter to ask where all my money had gone. I had five thousand seven hundred pounds left to me.

'The organisation had taken everything else back without any formal warning. I returned home to my folks and had to somehow explain what had happened.'

Rebecca cussed under her breath. 'What did they say?'

Tad turned back to face her. 'They said they were proud.'

'Proud?' Rebecca said, missing the point entirely.

'Proud that I hadn't done that sex scene. Sad that I'd almost lost everything.'

Rebecca nodded. 'You did the right thing…'

36.

THE SUN ascended the horizon early on Sunday morning. The scuds of clouds broke and dissipated into thin air leaving only an ocean-blue sky. Matthew rolled out of bed and peered through the parted curtain. Today would be a very important day, he knew. Today "The Society" would be posting mail through the door that was highly confidential in regards to his duty towards his fellow associates.

Matthew should have been overjoyed about the fact that his dream would come true once this deed had been completed. However, it was the unknown that tinkered with his mind causing him to feel restless and agitated. This emotion was unfamiliar to him. He liked having total control of his actions and future plans. He had surrendered that with his signature to this firm.

Gemma hadn't slept over. She had gone out into the city with her friends eating and hitting the clubs. Matthew would have gone but he needed to stay off the alcohol to remain focused and clear minded about what this task entailed. Gemma had asked him how his meeting had gone and he told her that he believed everything went well, there were no problems and that he was now a client of their establishment.

What he hadn't told Gemma and "The Society" was how the roiling urge to wreak havoc and/or kill another human being was driving him to the point of despair.

After his meeting with the members of the firm, Matthew had gone to the town library and kindly asked if he could use one of the computers and obtain a library card. He had given his name, address and mobile number, and just like that the librarian made him a member and handed him his card with the number on it and the library's phone number on it.

Satisfied with the cordial endeavour, Matthew had gone onto the internet and used YouTube to watch a documentary of the renowned serial killer, Jeffery Dahmer. The documentary lasted almost an hour, and through all that time, everything else faded away into the back of Matthew's consciousness. Immersed and inspired, Matthew absorbed the content, returned to the screensaver, left the library and walked home, smiling broadly to himself.

Sex with Gemma was very good. Killing though, gave him such an overwhelming feeling of power and awesomeness he couldn't articulate to another human even in simple terms. To say it gave him an adrenaline rush was the understatement of the century.

Now he was wide awake, fully rested and ready to face the new day. He ambled out of the bedroom and enjoyed a bowl of cereal, then showered and got dressed. His demeanour and nonchalance would fool even the very best of psychologists. Matthew functioned not only ordinarily but with a spring in his step. No one would ever assume he had done anything wrong, let alone accuse him of being a murderer. Yet not only had this young man killed, he did it with such finesse and pride he actually had a knack for the process. Some people were born to do certain things, some experts would say.

Roger Federer was born to play tennis. Muhammad Ali was born to be a boxer. Al Pacino was born to be an actor, and so on…

And maybe if there was such a thing as the devil then maybe Matthew was a spawn of the evil one, and took to murdering someone as easy as a knife through warm butter. Of course, Matthew had thought of it just like that which, in his mind, excused him from all wrongdoing. It was as though because he had a lonesome upbringing and felt neglected that the world's cruelty had damaged his mind and thus absolving him for the crimes he had committed. To Matthew, it wasn't his doing; it was the world and its harshness towards innocent folks who never had the joy of having a loving family and a pleasant childhood. To Matthew, because he didn't have these attributes, he was a victim to his own desires. He would say he was a prisoner in his own body, like another entity had taken control of his thoughts, words and actions and he was merely a passenger, waiting in anticipation for the urge to abate so he could lead a normal life. For this this reason he felt free from guilt and had no remorse.

Yes, it was his own body, but it wasn't his mind.

Another dark force was in charge and dictated the way of life and the irrevocable and unforgivable things which he did.

As he sat in his comfy chair, Matthew heard something being pushed through the letterbox and then slap the floor before the flap snapped shut again.

Without hesitation Matthew hauled himself out of his chair and went to see what had been delivered.

He saw the manila envelope, bent down, picked it up and carried it back to the living room. He ripped it open and tipped the stapled paperwork out onto his lap, dropped the envelope and addressed the file. On it was a brief letter describing what was expected of him. Matthew read the typed writing with undivided concentration and knew then that joining "The Society" was the best move he had ever made. Now the world that had been so harsh and cruel to him was paying him back with interest. He sat there smiling to himself at the name and details of the intended target and the black and white portrait of a beautiful young woman.

'This is gonna be a lotta fun...'

*

Rebecca was just finishing her first chapter when she heard the postman ram her mail through the letterbox. She hit the SAVE button, got up and went to the front door to retrieve the two letters. One was from Barclays, another was a letter from a literary agent expressing interest in her project and would like to read the manuscript when it had been completed. This unexpected news sent a pleasant buzz of excitement and eagerness through her veins and spurred her on to do her best in writing this book.

She reread what she'd written and apart from two typos was pleased with her endeavour and experienced prose. She shut down the computer, removed her glasses and put her trainers on. She had to go to the shops to pick up some essentials. Then she decided that she'd stay home for the remainder of the day, relaxing, reading and watching the movie channels.

Locking the door behind her, Rebecca descended the concrete steps onto the pavement and walked at a brisk pace into the city centre where all the shops were situated. It took her twenty-five minutes to reach the High street and she already felt her best for getting out and exercising her body now that she had spent the entire morning exercising her mind.

Once she got her essentials, Rebecca headed home, going the same way she had come, staying on the back streets, away from the hustle and bustle and inexorable traffic.

For lunch she made herself some ham sandwiches with pickled onions. She ate the modest meal in front of the TV. She didn't feel up to reading after writing nearly three thousand words earlier on so put the latest Star Wars instalment on and stretched out on the sofa.

*

Matthew had found the destination using SAT NAV and now pulled up in a space between two cars alongside the elevated kerb, killed the motor, picked up the paperwork from the passenger seat and checked the numbers on the front doors of every house that his limited view offered.

He found the big white door with a black metallic knocker and smiled. He had successfully found the residence he'd been looking for and felt a huge weight lift from his shoulders, knowing that the difficult part of the job had been completed.

The young man was wearing navy blue overalls with a British Gas logo on the right breast. The idea was to knock on the front door and ask to read Rebecca's meter. As soon as the front door closed the fun would start. However, he had to be quick in doing the unlawful act because the neighbours would hear and report the crime to the police. The street consisted of affluent homes all terraced together. It was a close community. Matthew took in this fact and was well aware that he had to perform this act swiftly and precisely. If he didn't do so he could kiss goodbye his dreams and would find himself in prison for God knew how many years.

He had contained his rage that was boiling inside him. Taking a life gave him such a rush of adrenaline and power he couldn't articulate even to himself let alone anyone else. If he was caught, he'd be back in the mental institution for the rest of his days. And Matthew knew better than the other doped up prisoners that that wasn't a good place to be in for any length of time. The ironic thing about the mental institution was that you could enter the premises as a patient and be sane, but by the time the doctors, specialists and nurses were through with you, you were insane.

They asked the same questions every time you had a discussion with them. Then they would cart you off to the medicine room where they gave you Rispiredol injections and took your blood pressure and your heart rate. From there, if everything was working fine, they took you back to your cell and left you there until the next meal. If you were so intoxicated with drugs, they left you to sleep during the day. And sometimes that was preferable since at night a security guard came by every hour and flashed his torch beam through the glass panel onto your single bed to see if you were asleep or not. What it did was wake you and you felt like shit the following day until you eventually slept so deep that you might not ever surface.

'No way am I going back there,' he muttered to himself.

Matthew reached behind him and grabbed the lump hammer from the back seat, undid his safety harness and exited the Renault Clio, locked the vehicle and crossed the street to Rebecca's house.

There was a nice cool breeze that quenched the humid air in the car. Matthew ambled down the street, said hello to an elderly man who was carrying his shopping and then climbed the concrete steps, grasped the knocker and announced his arrival.

If Rebecca wasn't home there was no need to panic. The mission had no time limit. Matthew would wait all day if he had to for Rebecca to arrive. No big deal either way.

Then he heard footfalls approaching, getting louder.

The door opened and a young, attractive blonde woman peered around the side of the immense door. 'Yes? How can I help you?' she asked in a cordial and gentle voice.

'I'm here to read your meter,' Matthew said. 'Can I come in?'

'Of course,' Rebecca said and stepped back, opening the door all the way for easy access.

Matthew stepped over the threshold and into the hallway. He turned his head so he was facing the lovely woman and asked, 'Where is it located?'

'In the living room. Underneath the stairs.'

Then Rebecca motioned for him to follow her as she led the way. Her blonde hair was dark at the roots and mixed very nicely as though a professional hairdresser had done it. But he could tell it was her natural colour. She pointed to the box and Matthew sidled passed her and hunkered down on his haunches.

'You married?' Matthew asked with his back to her.

'Uh, no,' Rebecca said, slightly uncomfortable answering that personal question to this stranger.

'Nor me,' Matthew said. 'I don't mind. I get to watch whatever I want on TV. So it has its perks... being single.'

Rebecca smiled. It was true. Being single meant that there were no arguments over who was entitled to watch their favourite TV show and who wasn't.

Matthew waited until Rebecca turned away and gazed out the living room window. He rose to his feet, crept up behind his unsuspecting victim, gently pulled his right hand out from his overall pocket and held the lump hammer by its thick handle and...

'Surprise!'

*

Annie Combs was lying in bed, channel surfing. There wasn't much on to her fancy and after another five minutes she hit the Red button on the remote control. The TV and her own vision got swallowed by the darkness. She placed the remote on her bedside cabinet and got comfortable. When she was settled, Annie closed her heavy-laden eyes and invited sleep to take her away.

Some time later the ageing clairvoyant found herself on a busy street where vehicles were parked on both sides of the road which made it arduous to drive to and fro.

She was standing erect like she had done in her youth. Yet the panorama displayed before her was as real as being wide awake. Every miniscule detail was highlighted in her unblemished vision. However, as splendid as this might have been, Annie was fully aware that she didn't just happen to be on this busy street a mile away from the city centre of London. This wasn't going to be tea and biscuits with an old acquaintance Annie knew there was a purpose. Without the control of her legs she began to move forward up the pavement and came to a stop outside a white façade of a terraced house.

She heard the distinct sound of a scream, but that was soon drowned out by the din of the rubbish men emptying the bins left outside every residence.

Annie pushed open the black gate and climbed the four steep steps to the front door. She noticed the black brass knocker but knew instinctively there would be no need to use it. This was a vision. She was aware of that fact due solely to a lifelong experience. However, it didn't stop making her unnerved and the tiny hairs on her arms bristle.

The door opened as she stretched out her right hand and gently pushed to permit herself entrance to the crime scene. As she entered the sunshine disappeared and at the end of the narrow hallway was the flight of stairs. She turned to her left and found access through a doorway to the living room.

What she saw next would be engraved onto her very own soul.

There was a pretty blonde-haired woman lying sprawled out on the carpet with a massive colourful contusion swelling up and around the right-hand side of her face. Her eyes were slightly open, but not enough to permit light into her consciousness. She moaned and moved spasmodically. Then the man wearing working man's overalls bent down, wielding a large and heavy hammer and struck her severely until he heard the bone around the temple crack audibly.

'Oh shit!' Annie croaked.

She had just witnessed the woman's death and couldn't do anything to stop it. The young man rose to his full height, kicked the woman with all his power in the head again, knocking her head back so fast and hard that a bone in her neck made a crunching noise.

Annie began trembling and reached out for the doorframe to steady herself. Her colour drained from her angular features and her knees buckled. Satisfied, the murderer pivoted and headed to the hallway via the next doorway farther down the hall beyond where Annie was struggling to stand.

A trickle of crimson blood ran across the dead woman's face and Annie crumpled to her knees. She reached out and cradled the woman's swollen head and focused on her own erratic breathing.

Her eyes blinked open and for a minute Annie thought she was dead herself, the dark was so oppressive. Now she had to get up and control her respiration and dry the film of perspiration away.

She rolled off the mattress and slid her feet into her slippers. She got up gingerly and tried consciously to think of something else besides what she'd just witnessed. She made it to the bathroom, washed her face with cold water and then dried herself with the towel.

'That poor woman,' she muttered to herself, unable to fight off the anxiety and helplessness. Then she bunched her left hand up into a taut fist and banged the sink in anger at herself.

'People die all the time, you stupid woman,' she said to her reflection. 'I thought you said you weren't gonna care anymore; thought you'd given up the ghost. What you saw was most likely real, but it's got nothing to do with you. I'm not going down this road with you anymore. Now you're even talking to yourself. That's crazy. Stop being so bloody scared and nervous all the sodding time. Get a grip. This is life. That's just the way it is. No one else cares, besides that woman's friends and family. You're not a doctor or an officer of the law, so don't get involved.

'But I couldn't help it,' she said as though there were two people having a carry-on conversation.

'You're losing your mind.

'Okay. I'll stop caring, but I didn't choose this vision, something or someone chose me. In all fairness it's not my fault.'

'Just get back to bed and stop being such a wimp,' she told herself, irate that her whole life had been affected because of this supernatural gift/curse.

Annie envied "normal people". And now she could truly understand and acknowledge how Toby felt. He did his best to maintain their friendship but he refused to sacrifice his own life to do the authorities' work for them. Together, during the span of their lives, both she and Toby had saved lives, got justice and saved years of police work in a matter of minutes. They should be rewarded with a medal or something, not suffering every tragedy that occurred.

Rebecca Adonali.

Annie froze. Her eyes enlarged in their sockets.

She lives in Tottenham, North London.

Annie bolted out of the bathroom and into the spare bedroom where she kept a notepad and pen on a luminous green desk. She scrawled down what the voice in her head had said and then dashed out of the room and down the stairs, picked up the phone and dialled 999...

*

Toby stirred awake at sunrise, having retired to his bed early the night before. Work had taken its toll on him and he'd been helping his mother out the back. He had laid patio slabs and pumped iron in the gym. Abigail said it was a good job he did workout. Otherwise he might not have been strong enough to help the construction worker laying down cement.

Something damp was running out of his nose. He gently dabbed his index finger, expecting it to be snot and came away with blood. For whatever reason his nose had started bleeding. He hauled himself out of bed and crossed the landing to the bathroom to attend to his nosebleed. He washed his face and rolled some tissue paper up his nostril and five minutes later extracted it to find that he'd staunched the bloodflow and that there were no other adverse effects.

During the night he recalled a dream of a hand clenching the wooden handle of a very heavy object and it being driven downwards repeatedly.

Toby had no notion what it had meant and now that he'd woken and was out of bed the dream abated to a very faint memory. With that in mind the young man descended the stairs and got himself a bowl of Crunchy Nut Corn Flakes for breakfast.

Anastasia was working today. Toby planned on going to the gym, popping by to ask Annie if she wanted to go out for lunch with him and his mother. If she did that would be great. Then he would spend the evening watching a film on TV or DVD.

*

Annie felt that an enormous amount of pressure from origins unknown was weighing down her whole body and brain. She had just come off the phone after being put through to DI Sark, who had forwarded her message and was now on his way to her home to take a statement.

She was well known to the local authorities as much as Toby. The amount of help and generosity among the local constabulary was appreciated and her name highly praised and regarded by the officers for saving them so much time in cracking unsolved cases spanning four decades.

Now as she heaved herself out of her comfy armchair, Annie's eyes started joggling as though she was some kind of game mechanism. The floor moved beneath her feet in undulations and as the ageing woman spread her arms out to regain her balance, she felt her whole self being lifted up and out of her physicality. She moaned in fear and instability and did her utmost to reach the kitchen doorway. Instead her joggling eyes blurred her sight and her knees buckled cruelly beneath her and nothing stopped her from falling forward and hitting the carpet with a violent slam.

*

Phone calls were made to Tottenham police station with an address that a spiritualist had given to be investigated. DI Sark took the information very seriously. He gathered the information and then sprung to his full height and hurried out of the station towards his car. He didn't know why he felt the urgency to run but adrenaline pumped through his veins, igniting his heart. He unlocked the vehicle, threw himself behind the wheel, started the motor and drove out of the car park onto the main road.

The power of the psychic was beyond his own imagination or understanding. For the life of him, DI Sark couldn't begin to think what it must be like to be psychic and to have everything else in your life take a backward step into oblivion, memories substituted for all sorts of evil occurrences.

Annie was nowhere near Tottenham, (north London) to be able to feel the change in ambience where the crime was committed and that fact alone shook DI Sark's nerve endings. The more he thought of it as he drove past the dense traffic the more he felt deep sympathy and remorse for one to have such an existence serving the authorities and not getting a penny in return. Or peace of mind for that matter…

'Jesus! How in God's name do they cope?'

He flicked the turn signal to go right at the busy roundabout. When he saw an opportune gap, he floored the accelerator. The Ford shot forward and before Sark knew it he was exiting the town and heading to the suburbs two miles west.

After meandering through the cul-de-sac, DI Sark found a space outside the refurbished residence, locked the Ford and knocked on the front door. He waited patiently before rapping hard on the wood again. Two minutes ticked by and the detective was now frowning. He made certain that he had the correct address details. Then when he discovered that he had found the right house, he wandered around the side of the house and peered in one of the windows, hand over his eyes to block out the reflective daylight.

What he saw shocked him…

Annie Combs was lying on the floor, possibly dead.

'No way!' he said, breathing hard.

Then he dashed back to the front door and barged into it with full impact, shoulder first.

The door splintered and creaked at the heavy blow and after two more attempts it eventually snapped apart at the frame, permitting DI Sark access to the unconscious psychic and calling for back-up and an ambulance.

37.

ANNIE COMBS stirred back to consciousness, startled to find herself in unfamiliar surroundings. She was in a ward with other women, four beds either side. She tried to sit up but the leaden weight hampered her movements. She was stiff, rigid all over and her legs did not cooperate with her brain instructions.

Fortunately, only a few minutes passed before a male nurse in dark green scrubs entered the ward and noticed her wide awake, eyes bulging, scanning the enclosure, coming to terms with the events that led her into this set of circumstances.

The male nurse, who according to his name tag was Gary, approached her with a cheerful smile. 'Hey, you're awake,' he said. 'How're you doing?'

'What happened?' Annie asked, evidently unable to put everything in order that made sense, which meant she had been brought to a hospital.

Gary explained that she had passed out and had fallen in her home with a big thud that made her face swell. An ambulance had brought her here and she had been given treatment and a bed to recuperate.

'Do you remember now what happened before you lost consciousness?' Gary asked, in an affable tone of voice.

Now that she was told where she was and what had transpired, Annie recalled being on the phone and feeling very anxious and agitated. She thought back further to a murder that came to mind, but could no longer remember the dream/vision which had caused her to phone the police. She told Gary all of this information. His smile disappeared and a mask of concern spread over his chubby, boy-like features.

'There's a policeman – a detective – who wants to speak to you as soon as possible. I'll go and get you something to eat and drink, does that sound good?'

Annie nodded and thanked Gary. Then she added: 'Is the detective here?'

Gary nodded. 'Yes. He wants to talk with you, but if you're not feeling up to it, I'll tell him to wait until tomorrow.'

'No,' Annie said, shaking her head and then wincing at the throbbing sensation. 'I'd like to see him.'

Gary stood and said he would get her something to eat and drink and would also send the plain-clothed police officer in to speak with her promptly.

Once he disappeared out of the ward and Annie's sight, the elderly psychic leaned back and sighed. She was in a great deal of pain and wondered how bad the fall must have been to have caused her to be battered and bruised. She needed to talk with DI Sark about the incident in North London. As she closed her eyes, Annie recalled that she had briefly seen a murder and wanted to know if it was a vision or a dream that had no truth to it. Of course, deep in her heart, she hoped and prayed that it was her imagination playing a cruel trick in her mind's eye and could be instantly disregarded.

She controlled her respiration and told herself that she was in a good place. She was safe from the mayhem of the world. Now there was no need to feel scared or anxious or a combination of the two highly escalating emotions. Ever since she was young, Annie had always found herself playing by herself. Her mother took her to one side one day when she had been a little girl playing in the park with the other children. 'You can't play with them, Annie,' her mother had implored. 'You are too sensitive. You get upset very easily. You either need to be strong soon or you're not gonna have any friends.'

And the sad fact of the matter was this: her mother had been right. Annie had no friends. She mixed in school, but she was never invited to parties or dances. For a short while, she played rugby with the boys and had a talent for tackling, but she never got the same opportunities like other kids her age to socialise. Instead she'd obtained a library card. Her best friends were authors. Now they could really tell a good story.

Annie's father would start a campfire out in the back yard and tell stories of his childhood. She found it all fascinating. Her father had been to the Middle East and Egypt in the military (and died in action). Once her father had erected a big blue tent, and Annie would sleep there for as long as the summer lasted. She would eat a bag of marshmallows and read Edgar Allan Poe and the Holy Bible.

Sometimes when she was on her own, and had just finished reading a good book, Annie wished she could be someone else. In truth, she wasn't all that fussed on being herself. Which others found odd. After all, she was psychic and just by reading someone's palms or being in their presence, she could tell their futures and pasts.

Now most folks, Annie knew, would envy that supernatural gift. However, her special powers cost her a life. She went to church every Sunday and asked God personally if He would remove her supernatural powers and permit her a "normal life". A life where she'd have friends, a boyfriend, and do nice things, like going to the cinema and going on holiday. Instead she had been an advocate to people's knowledge and wisdom.

She sighed again, only this time it didn't emanate from her physical self but from her whole persona. She was tired... used and abused. She loved watching action films starring Sylvester Stallone and enjoyed Toby's company.

When she opened her eyes again, to her right she saw DI Sark heading directly towards her.

God I wish this day would end...

*

After talking with DI Sark about what had happened to induce her to be where she was in this moment of time, Annie felt exhausted. She struggled to keep her eyes open.

'What's the time now?' Annie asked.

DI Sark consulted his Rolex wristwatch and said, 'Ten to ten.'

'Did you get through to the police in North London by any chance?' Annie asked, to put her mind at rest and permit her to drift off into a deep slumber.

'I had a call sent directly to me and my Chief Superintendent,' DI Sark said, 'and there has been a crime reported in the district, but they are still investigating and getting details.'

He held Annie's small, bony hand in his grasp. 'You need rest,' DI Sark said, matter-of-factly. 'I'm gonna shoot off now and leave you to get some sleep. Is there anything else you'd like to ask or tell me in regards to this report?'

Annie opened her heavy-lidded eyes and said in a throaty tone of voice, 'The killer is from Wales, not England. He had to drive a long way to reach the intended victim.'

DI Sark was an experienced police officer. He had twenty-two years of service under his belt, but his mouth gaped and he released his hand from Annie's. 'How'd you know that?'

'I just do,' Annie said. 'It's my gift. My curse. The thing that'll set me free. The thing that'll kill me in the end. Good night, detective.' Then without any further words or expressions, the ageing spiritualist closed her eyes and turned on her side away from DI Sark.

He wrote down what Annie had just told him in his notebook, reread what he'd written today and left Annie. His chief would want this report first thing in the morning. He would spend the rest of the night typing out all the relevant information to put into action immediately before anyone else lost their life.

*

Two days passed. Toby and Anastasia spent the weekend camping out in the Brecon Beacons in the glorious sunshine. They had not yet had sexual intercourse. However, sleeping in the same tent meant that Toby and Anastasia had spent their evenings eating, talking, kissing and groping one another. They were both attracted to each other and enjoyed their privacy. They got a ride back to their local town by hitchhiking. Finally, a farmer had been driving past and slowed to a halt down the main, meandering road, seeing Toby's thumb up and dutifully gave them a ride to Seven Sisters. From there, Toby and Anastasia caught a bus that took them to the bus station in the town centre.

On the bus ride Anastasia had looked forlornly at Toby while he gazed out the window and the world rushing by, even though it was only the bus that was moving. A funny paradox when he thought about it.

'I love you,' Anastasia said in a low voice so only Toby could hear.

A tingling sensation purred in his heart and Toby averted his gaze from the world outside and gazed longingly at his girlfriend. He was amazed and taken aback by her natural beauty and personal statement.

'I love you too,' he said. His expression was full of concealed joy. The words were a cliché. And had this been a movie in the cinema Toby would have most likely rolled his eyes. However, this moment was special. Not a lot of people knew special moments in their lives in the present. They miss the purpose of what was said and done that would define their lives and their souls as people.

Anastasia looked stunning as usual. Her long blonde hair brushed the back of her shoulders and her black sleeveless top and red shorts revealed her smooth, tawny legs. Toby felt his loins burning with inexorable desire.

'You're the best thing to ever come into my life,' Toby whispered.

Anastasia smiled.

'When we get off this bus and go our separate ways, I want you to know that I'm not interested in any other women. I don't even look upon them with lust anymore. I am happiest when I'm with you. I don't just mean the physical stuff, I mean sharing my life with you. I hope you don't find this too corny – but you're my soul-mate.'

Anastasia smiled, revealing her perfect white enamel teeth.

Then Toby put his arm around her and pulled her close. That was how they stayed until the bus slowed into one of the vacant spaces at the local bus station.

They got off the bus and walked past passengers also getting off buses and the queues of folks waiting for their ride. They crossed the road and stood outside the large church.

They kissed and held each other close.

Then they pulled apart and for some unknown reason Toby felt like they were saying goodbye for ever. Anastasia looked sad too. She forced a smile, turned and then walked away, heading for home. Tears welled up in Toby's eyes. One tear dripped off his eyelashes and trickled down his cheek. He too turned and headed for home.

Toby didn't mind the two and a half mile walk as he had a lot on his mind. Shortly he would be commencing driving lessons. He was looking forward to obtaining this new skill, although he was also a bit nervous and apprehensive. Evidently everything new and uncharted was a tad daunting for any living human being, so he reminded himself that this was normal and it was good that he had these emotions.

The resplendent sunshine scorched his back and by the time Toby was almost at the top of the hill he was drenched in sweat. First thing he was going to do when he got home was to take a shower and put clean clothes on. He was looking forward to spending some time with his mother, Abigail, and wondered what they would get up to for the rest of the weekend.

As he was mulling these things over in a cycle in his mind, his mobile started vibrating in his shorts' pocket. Startled initially, Toby then fished out the phone and answered the call.

'Hello.'

'Toby!' came the genial voice on the other end. 'It's me, Detective Sark. I've been trying to get hold of you.'

Toby dropped the hand holding the mobile down by his side in vexation. If this was a call regarding another crime then he was going to start raising his voice and being firm.

'Why?' he asked.

'Annie is in hospital,' DI Sark explained. 'She had a very nasty fall and is all battered and bruised.'

'Sorry to hear that,' Toby said, meaning it but still annoyed that the detective was passing this information on to him.

'Before she fell she had a vision of someone murdering a blonde-haired woman in North London. This morning I got a call from my Chief Superintendent telling me that there has been a homicide in North London. The victim is one Rebecca Adaloni who has lovely long blonde hair. Last night when I went to visit her at Morriston Hospital she told me that the murderer is not from North London or any other part of England. The perpetrator lives somewhere in South Wales…'

Toby couldn't hide his shock. However, he hastily regained his composure and continued walking faster now that he'd ascended the peak and was on flat ground once again. 'Why are you telling me this?'

Silence...

Then: 'I'm telling you 'cause I thought you and Annie were tight and had the same supernatural powers of the mind. What's up with you? You sound agitated.'

Although Toby didn't really have a temper he did wonder sometimes if he should do something to release some of his inner emotions to ease the pressure gently. 'I don't have visions or supernatural powers of the mind anymore,' he said. 'I've moved on from all of that. I have a job. A wonderful mother and a terrific girlfriend. That's all I ask for, along with peace of mind. I sleep better and my wellbeing has improved a great deal. I'm positive you don't need my help, even if I did still have the "Shine". You're a great detective. I'm sure you'll be able to track down this guy in no time. Believe in your own abilities. Your greatest gift is your independence and qualified skills.'

There came more silence.

'Why are you being like this?' DI Sark asked.

'I don't have the "Shine" anymore,' Toby said, shaking his head in disbelief. 'By the sounds of it, Annie has already narrowed it down for the entire police force.'

'What if he kills again before we get him?' DI Sark asked, not liking Toby's attitude, but also realising that maybe the lad had a point.

'You can't dump that on me,' Toby said. 'That's not nice. Maybe when Annie is feeling better she'll be able to aid you.'

'She's old, Toby,' DI Sark said, matter-of-factly. 'I'm calling you because you gave all your contact details to the police force in this jurisdiction in case we required your services. Don't have a go at me, lad. This is imperative.'

Toby sighed. 'I'll visit Annie in hospital later on, see what she's got to say about this,' he said. 'But I can't help you anymore. I know what I did in the past, but I don't live in the past. I chose life abundantly. You are right though, Annie is too old for this kinda crap. We've both done more than our fair share for the local police. It's now time for me to move on.'

'Yeah... whatever,' DI Sark said and then killed the connection.

38.

MATTHEW CAWTHORNE was sitting outside on a deck chair enjoying the glorious sunshine when his neighbour emerged from his flat to his left. They both chatted for a while about the weather amicably. Then the neighbour who was obese and had long, thinning hair opened his gate and sauntered to his grey van, climbed in with some difficulty, slammed the door and got the engine running. He drove away down the street raising his hand in farewell to Matthew, who reciprocated the gesture.

Earlier that day Matthew had visited his GP and brought him up-to-date about his medication and how he was feeling. His GP – an Indian male doctor – admitted with false charm that indeed Matthew was looking and sounding like an entirely different person than when he'd been admitted to Cefn Coed Mental Institution.

'Well, I always said that give me half a chance to prove myself and I can do great things. I mean there was a slight setback when I heard of my mother's brutal passing away and I did self-isolate myself for two whole days while I grieved. But I knew that if I let the situation come over me for too long then I would lose control and wind up a wreck. The medication does slow me down quite a bit, but I haven't let it affect my performance in work.'

'What do you do in your spare time, if you don't mind my asking?' the GP said, encouraged by his patient's totally effervescent mannerisms.

'Well, I have a girlfriend,' Matthew began. 'I just bought some dumbbells which I do exercise with to help tone my physique. I like to read. And soon, my friends and I are going to set up a camp on their private farmland where folks from all over are invited to listen to public speakers in regard to modern life and the world we live in today and have music and barbeque food and beer, of course.'

The GP couldn't help but grin, impressed with his patient's motives and good vibes. 'This will take place in the summer?'

Matthew nodded. 'Yes, it's supposed to be educational, fun and bringing a community together. I'm really looking forward to it and have booked three weeks off work to commit myself fully.'

The GP leaned forward and proffered his hand which Matthew shook vigorously. 'Keep up with the medication for the time being, as it seems that it's had an excellent effect on you, and good luck with your job and your summer camp. I sincerely wish you all the best. And I'll see you again to see how things are in early December. You'll have a letter through the door telling you what date and time.'

Matthew stood and gave his GP his best smile, bade him goodbye, turned and walked out of the office.

Now with all that dealt with, Matthew could sit back and relax. Gemma would be over to see him after work and together they were going to go to KFC for food. All was well in Matthew's world and nothing or anyone was going to stop him executing his plan no matter what.

*

Abigail was busying herself washing the dishes when the front door opened and Toby walked in, closing the door behind him. He kicked off his trainers and entered the living room and en suite kitchen.

'Mum! I'm home. Do you need a hand with anything?'

Abigail smiled benignly at him. 'No, thank you, my love,' she replied. 'How was your run?'

'Good. I did three miles with no break. It's different from weight training but it'll burn any excess fat and highlight my muscle groups.' He came into the kitchen and stood by her side. 'Why don't I dry these?' he said, referring to the dishes and glasses on the drainer.

'Okay,' Abigail said, pleased that her only child still helped out around the house.

'Mum, yesterday I got a call from the detective,' Toby said while drying the plates with the towel.

'What did he want now?'

'Annie collapsed in her home after seeing a vision of a homicide.'

Abigail turned her head so that Toby could see he had her undivided attention. 'That's awful. Is she all right?'

'She's in hospital,' Toby said, facing his mother. 'The thing is, DI Sark wanted me to go visit her. Her vision was an actual homicide crime and the suspect lives somewhere in Wales.'

He could see his mother's bottom lip tremble with renewed anxiety. She snapped her head back so she was staring only at the utensils at the bottom of the sink. 'So why does he want you to go see her?'

'Well, she is a dear friend,' Toby said and exhaled at his mother's stoic dislike for what was about to come next.

'So you go see her. She tells you exactly – in her own words – what she saw, and then they involve you and expect you to work miracles again and all that you've worked for is placed to one side for however long it takes to track down the suspect. This police officer clearly doesn't give a toss about you as a person. He's using you to do his work for him. So what if Annie brought it to the police's attention and knows what country in Britain he lives in. Can't they just take over themselves from there? Are they that lazy and indolent?

'What about me? What about your own well-being? What about Anastasia? If you lose her because of this crime you'll never find anyone that suits you better, as a person, ever again. That girlfriend of yours is beautiful and with a flawless personality. You'll be heartbroken. Do you understand what I'm saying? Don't let this go through one ear and out the other. You'll be sorry you ever helped the police in any crimes.'

Toby's throat worked convulsively. His mum was right. However, his damned conscience insisted that the least he could do was visit Annie in hospital. He told Abigail this, finished drying the utensils and got into the shower. When he came back downstairs he was fully dressed in clean clothes and smelled of deodorant and cologne.

'Where are you going?' Abigail demanded.

With some hesitation, Toby wet his lips so he could speak clearly. 'I'm going to the hospital. I said I would. It's the least I can do.'

Abigail shook her head at him. Serious. 'Don't blame me when this ruins everything you've worked for. If you do get involved, you'll have to live with the consequences till your dying day. Can you honestly do that?'

'Annie's my friend, Mum,' Toby said. 'Friends stay together and support each other during troubled times. I'll see you later.'

'How are you gonna get there?'

'Bus. It's due in ten minutes. I gotta dash.'

And with that Toby stepped out of the house and closed the door behind him.

Abigail stood rigid in the living room, angry and anxious at what would pass between the two psychics and what it would ultimately cost her kind, caring son. She dearly hoped that her opinion was inaccurate, although it didn't seem likely. In that moment, with the deafening silence and static in her cheeks, Abigail hated DI Sark and Annie Combs...

*

Heavy, grey mushroom clouds hung ominously overhead. Toby watched from the window seat as the first drops of rain spat at the ground. He had listened to his mother. However, conscience advised him that visiting his oracle friend in hospital was his highest priority. He had no idea what Annie would say. Maybe she simply felt so hurt that they might talk about the accident and other mundane topics. After all, Toby recalled a couple of times when he had visited her at her home where she made him a snack. They talked for hours of their shared ability. Toby had been afraid of his "Shine" and although he had done great things with this gift, he felt abandoned and forlorn. Annie was his mentor. His buddy. She knew what to say and how to get it across so he could understand. They were both wise beyond their years and the wisdom isolated them from the rest of the public.

By the time the bus slowed to a halt alongside the kerb outside the hospital grounds, it had started raining inexorably. He pulled his hood over his head and hopped off after thanking the driver.

When there was a break in traffic, Toby sprinted across the main road and slowed when he arrived on the hospital grounds. He used the pelican crossing and entered through the sliding glass door and went straight to reception.

Once he was given the information and ward that Annie Combs was in, the young man took the stairs and got to the correct floor, heading down the glossy linoleum.

He found Annie at the far corner eating Jelly Babies and reading a newspaper. As he approached, the spiritualist glanced at him, recognised him and tossed the paper to one side and smiled benignly.

'Well, hello, Mr Handsome man,' she smiled and gestured him to take a seat alongside her bed.

'Hi, Annie!' Toby said, and lowered himself to the vacant chair. 'That's a nasty bruise you've got there.'

'I know, sweetheart,' she said. 'But it could have been much worse. Our detective friend saw me and got me medical assistance straight away. If it wasn't for him seeing me that day I'd still be there now.'

Toby shook his head, relieved.

'How are you anyway?'

'I'm all right,' Toby said. 'I've been doing great in work and I'm in love with my girlfriend, Anastasia. My mother sends her good wishes to you.'

Annie already knew that Abigail wasn't impressed by her son getting involved with her again due to the "Shine" they both had that worked wonders against lawbreakers.

'I'm happy to hear that,' she said.

'Thanks.'

'Why have you come to see me today, Toby?' Annie asked after a long pause.

Toby didn't fluster. Instead he leaned forward and fixed his stare on the oracle. 'Detective Sark told me about the crime you had a vision of in North London, of a killer here in Wales.'

Annie moved her head, almost to study her friend's features at a different angle, as though she could see him in a different light from a new angle and read his mind accurately.

'Tell me something, did you come here to see me with your own volition or did someone persuade you?'

'You already know the answer to that.'

Annie laughed out loud. Then said: 'I do. But your mother is awfully concerned about you mixing with me and using your gift. Do you fear losing your girlfriend because you want to help the police catch this madman?'

Toby closed his eyes and buried himself in contemplation. 'Anastasia is the love of my life. We have this kind of connection. It's really hard to explain, but whenever I am with her there's this kind of funny, but lovely, sensation in my whole being. Merely being in her company is soothing. I've never ever felt so much emotional love and affection towards anyone. Yes, I am afraid of losing her, but I also care about you. You got me through some of my most difficult times. But I'm not sure I can go through life at the police's beckoning call to every crime scene in the country.'

'Does this Anastasia girl feel the same way about you, Toby?'

Toby nodded. 'Yes, she told me. She wants to marry me and have children.'

Annie averted her gaze and was fully aware of Toby's dilemma. She wasn't joking when she said he was handsome. He was. He had film star looks, a lovely heart and actually cared for those who were in his life.

'What's the matter?'

Annie looked back at him. 'Maybe you should leave, good boy. This isn't your problem. I had this vision and now the police are doing all they can to track down this murderer. That's their job. Perhaps you're right, you can't live like this, always on tenterhooks just to solve crime. It would be easier if you were an officer yourself.'

Toby glanced at the double doorway entrance and exit of the ward and wondered why he didn't make a move. After all, Annie was offering him a way out. She was basically saying, "You're free. Go and enjoy life."

Instead he remained rooted to the chair, his full, undivided attention on his mentor. 'I've already heard from DI Sark, but tell me again – in your words – what you saw.'

Annie didn't hesitate. She recited the vision and the events that unfolded thereafter.

'Any description on our suspect?'

'He has thick blond hair and steel-blue eyes. That's all I know.'

Toby nodded, deep in thought. 'I don't think I have the "Shine" any more, but if I get a vision of this guy then I'll go straight to the police. You rest up and don't worry about anything. You need your beauty sleep. You've done more than enough. At your age – no offence – you need to start relaxing. Is that understood?'

Smiling and nodding, Annie thought of Toby as a son. 'Will do,' she said. Then she offered her emaciated hand and Toby took it.

A brilliant electric-blue flash went off in his sight and his eyes rolled back in his head, mouth gaping.

Annie shook as though she was being electrocuted in intertwined spasms with the young man on the chair.

A horrible, long gasp erupted from Toby's mouth before his head slumped down and his chin came to rest on the top of his chest.

Eventually, Annie broke away from the vice-like grip that came from a force of supernatural nature neither her nor Toby possessed.

When Toby's eyes rolled back down out of the roof of his head, he blinked tears that chased each other down his quivering cheeks. He pulled away from Annie and rose on unsteady legs.

'You need to go to a public place and see if you can find him,' Annie said in a tremulous voice.

'This guy is very dangerous,' Toby said in a faraway voice. 'He must be stopped.'

Annie nodded in agreement. 'You now have the "Shine".'

After that Toby couldn't remember exiting the ward and the hospital edifice itself. He made it to the bus shelter and slumped down on the bench, exhausted and heavy laden. The events that had unfolded minutes ago had left him in a state of shock. There was no denying his destiny now. There was a reason why he was born. He wasn't just a number in the masses. He had a specific duty to accomplish for the benefit of the masses of folks that were left unprotected by this madman.

When the bus finally dropped him off in his small town, Toby invited the drizzle to cool him down. He walked at a leisurely pace in the direction of home as though he'd been struck by lightening and lived to tell the tale.

The current that had exploded through his entire self still tingled in his veins. Toby went into the convenience store and purchased a bottle of sparkling water. He gulped it down outside the shop on the pavement and then arrived at his house, unlocked the door and disappeared inside.

39.

THE OVERCAST SKY sprinkled Wales with a light shower and humidity. The man driving a red Honda Civic slowed its pace as he drove through the open metal gates into the cemetery. He killed the engine and ambled down the pebble-dash path carrying a pink rose to a grave at the rear of the grounds and laid it down on the marble plinth.

The name on the headstone read "Susan Cawthorne". The man had to be at least six foot, possibly more. His raincoat bumped languidly off the bottom half of his trousers. He removed the fedora and stood motionless for a good five minutes, studying the grave with a hard expression.

When he was finished, he turned and headed back to his vehicle, and had the cemetery not been empty no one would have noticed him. Evidently, he had brought a bit of colour and life to the deceased's memorial of their time on Earth before heading back into the mad world that is the twentieth century.

*

Toby told his mother, Abigail, that Annie was looking a bit battered and bruised, but otherwise fine, and kept the rest of the events to himself for both their sakes.

They had Chicken Korma curry for dinner. Then Toby got in the shower, changed into his pyjamas and got into bed. He turned on his mobile phone and gave Anastasia a call. She answered after four rings and he told her the same thing he'd told his mother and that he might have to aid the local constabulary in a crime case.

'I thought you said you'd given all that up,' Anastasia said in a sweet, non-condescending voice.

'I know I did,' Toby said in a light-hearted tone. 'But I do have a duty of care for the public in certain cases which have lack of evidence. I'll tell them that I'll do this for them this one last time and then implore them to delete my contact details and declare my retirement, so I can spend more time with you.'

Anastasia couldn't help herself giggling. 'That's sweet,' she said. 'But you don't want to get too involved. I'd dread to think what would happen if you got hurt all because of volunteering and a good conscience.'

Toby smiled. Anastasia was his girlfriend. She was also a special soul too. One that he could never lose. But once he was willing to risk his life to help the innocent, he wondered if he still had the moral fibre to do so again now that he had such a good life.

Would he be able to chase down this madman with full velocity? Would he fight the bad guys in hand-to-hand combat if necessary? Could he basically put his life on the line and have no fear like he did before?

Only time would tell, Toby realised.

Now that he thought back to the murderer at the cinema restroom, it was almost as if his destiny had already been laid out before him. Did he have a choice? One thing he did know for certain was that his conscience was both his best friend and his mortal enemy. It came across as though there was this force roiling and rumbling inside him ready to explode with a fantastic ethereal light that he needed to let go of before it consumed him. And the only way to do that was to stop this madman before he killed again in cold blood.

You have the shine, Toby. Shine on.

That didn't come from his own mind. It was most likely from Annie Combs. After all, he did have the shine. The incident at the hospital had frazzled his brain, leaving him with no distinctive memories of saying goodbye and exiting the hospital. Instead his head had been in La-la Land while his body went through the basics. It was not amusing in the slightest. Now conjuring all that up sent a shiver down his spine.

'Toby? Toby? Are you still there?' Anastasia asked, slightly alarmed.

'Yes. God, yes. Sorry. I just kinda drifted off there. Listen, I'm gonna get some kip. I'll call you in the morning and maybe we can go for a breakfast at Cresci's, if ya like?'

'Yeah, sure,' Anastasia said. 'Are you gonna be all right?'

'Yes, of course,' Toby lied. 'I'll call you in the morning, okay?'

'Okay, my love. I'll speak to you then. Bye.'

Toby waited until she ended their conversation and turned his mobile off. He lay in bed awhile wondering what his life would be like in five years' time. Hopefully by then he still would be with Anastasia. Maybe they would get engaged and be closer than they were even now. He decided right then and there that she was the love of his life. He couldn't imagine being without her or being with another woman. However, as much as he attempted to make his dreams come true there was no telling what life would throw at you. After all, life, when it turned nasty, could be a real mean mother.

The world was full of unthinkable crime every single day. Murders, rape, sex trafficking, drug dealings, robbery, all sorts. And to Toby, who had grown wise due to his gift/curse, had seen the ugly side of life at a young age.

Life was a precious gift.

It only took a slash across a main artery to kill someone.

Toby thought about Anastasia and his mother, Abigail. He would do his damn best to make sure they were safe and out of harm's way. Tomorrow he would call DI Sark and tell him that under no terms or conditions this would be the last crime he'd be involved in, and if they didn't like it, tough shit.

His mind fully made up in stoic fashion, he closed his eyes and released his consciousness to weariness... and slept.

*

Toby found himself in endlessness green pastures and a dense forest circling him in the environs. His eyes widened, absorbing the amazing splendour of a fresh and unfamiliar countryside. Overhead the sun blazed in an azure sky. The grass was long and required cutting. However, for this moment there was nothing to criticize. Sparrows flew from one oak to the next, singing sweetly.

The teenager began walking at a leisurely pace, not wanting this moment to end. He wasn't aware of the basic, human questions that normally came to mind if someone was dreaming or daydreaming. Instead his whole being had been engulfed with the many different hues of flowers, bringing life and colour to this endless joining of fields. He continued in a mesmerised state and had to use a stile to clamber into the next field which was a darker shade of green and had been cut, releasing the sweet smell of freshly cut grass.

Toby drifted languidly and turned his head left and right to capture all the splendour, not once wanting to miss a single detail, he was so amazed.

In the distance he saw a pavilion but no people. Intrigued with this anomaly, Toby moved forward beneath the sun's glorious radiance. Soon he arrived at the field where a large white canvas tent was erected and ambled closer until his eyes began to see and his brain processed the scene. The closer he got the more tentative his gait became. For what he saw shocked him, and when he approached and saw the first lifeless corpse, the vista of the beautiful countryside was destroyed. His heart was filled with a profound foreboding.

Toby gazed up ahead of him and then saw the bodies of men, women and here and there, children, all sprawled out in different postures... dead...

He stood motionless and then felt his nerves cramping until he trembled from head to foot. His breathing became erratic and all of a sudden, the amazing sights of the beautiful rolling pastures vanished and all he now saw was the carnage of some kind of mass homicide or suicide which killed every last one of these people.

Toby lowered himself to his haunches, unable to process what he was seeing with his naked eyes. The static in his cheeks frizzled and a wave of ice cool air assailed his face until he staggered backwards and fell on his arse.

From that new, helpless position, Toby heard a swish, swishing noise and craned his neck to look behind him when a man in a long winter coat and fedora approached him. He had a thick brown beard and carried a shotgun.

Without being told to do so, Toby, in his weak state scrambled off his arse and got to his feet. Then he could run through the field towards the fringe of the environing forest.

However, he knew by doing this he would make himself an easy target and only tempt this mean son of a bitch to use his gun to put a hole through him.

The man came directly towards him, and Toby swallowed with immense difficulty. He breathed heavily and wished his jackhammer heartbeat would slow to a gentler pace, permitting him to try and stay calm through this whole crisis.

The man came to a halt two feet in front of him. Toby could now see sweat beads on the man's lined brow glistening in the shade of the fedora. He didn't need any more convincing that this man meant business and death had at last reached him.

The man raised the shotgun and pointed it at Toby who now threw his hands up in a surrender posture. He asked this crazy man to consider his actions and spare him his life. The man didn't answer. His eyes were steel-blue and his face and hands were all dirty. He must have been the proprietor of the land he'd been found walking on. Maybe all that this farmer wanted was for Toby to get off his property and not to trespass here or anywhere else, for that matter ever again. Maybe the shotgun was an object of defiance; to signify who was boss around here, and if that were the case, Toby realised he owed this stranger, this scary-looking man, an apology.

He opened his mouth, ready to verbally apologise when the dirty, mean man, flicked the safety switch off and said, 'There ain't nothin' for you to say that'll make your chances of survival any better. You're dead meat. You're supper.'

Toby was about to blurt out, pleading for his life when the armed man pulled the trigger and a huge blast broke the silence…

*

Toby shot up in bed and gasped. His right hand slapped the left side of his chest where he could feel the drumming of his heart. The left hand went straight to his forehead, checking that he was still in fact alive and that he'd had a very authentic dream and hadn't had his brains blown out.

'Shit,' he gasped.

Toby sat ramrod straight and controlled his breathing. His mind replayed the dream and the young man could hardly believe how vivid it had all been.

Not true, he told himself. *Just a nasty dream. Maybe if I could afford to go to Disney Land and watched cartoons my dreams would be much more pleasant.*

*

DI Sark rolled the Ford Mondeo into the gravel car park and slid into a vacant space. In the near distance he caught sight of Toby, who had been leaning against a concrete wall waiting for his arrival.

He killed the engine and got out of the car, then ambled towards his friend and colleague.

Toby met him halfway. He was wearing a white hooded sweater, denim jeans and Addidas trainers. The detective was wearing his wrinkled black suit and brown suede shoes. His usual attire for work. He smiled as the young man approached him and they shook hands.

'Welcome back aboard,' DI Sark said, not in the slightest way hiding his enthusiasm and even excitement that Toby was now committed to this investigation.

'Just this once,' Toby reminded him.

DI Sark raised his hands in a non-serious gesture of defence. 'Yeah, yeah. I know. But this is potentially a big one.'

Toby nodded. There were no jokes from henceforth. Now there was nothing but seriousness and studious behaviour for every single detail directed solely at this unsolved case.

'I have what Annie calls "The Shine",' Toby announced.

'What does that mean?' DI Sark was keen to find out.

'I'm a spiritualist, detective,' Toby said. 'I am having visions and dreams again. I've got nothing tangible with evidence at this moment. Nevertheless, I would like to ask you where in South Wales there are rolling pastures. Where there might be large white awnings being erected for large gatherings.'

DI Sark looked confused. However, he ran what the boy had told him through his brain and did his utmost not to sound obtuse. 'Christ! There are loads of fields belonging to farmers. Where shall I start?'

Toby shifted his weight from his right leg to his left, contemplating all the while, not missing a beat. Then: 'How about we go for a drive, see if that joggles my mind and helps me gather my bearings.'

'What's this got to do with finding our murderer?'

'Do you want my help or not?' Toby asked, no longer the introverted, polite kid he'd once been. He was easily irritated by the detective's asinine questions, wasting his time explaining everything when they needed to act, promptly. He explained all this, and before DI Sark asked any more questions, they both got in the car and drove out of the public park on the way to the Swansea Valley main road.

'I got killed on a farmland last night in my dream,' Toby said, as DI Sark stared ahead at the line of traffic waiting for the lights to turn to green.

'By whom?'

'It was a man, with a furrowed brow and steel-blue eyes. He was wielding a double barrel shotgun. He approached me and after watching me suffer and beg for my life, blew my head off.'

'Do you think you'd be able to recognise this man if you saw him in broad daylight?' DI Sark asked, hoping for an affirmative answer that could possibly be identified and taken in for questioning. The detective understood good and proper that Toby as a spiritualist had the edge on him, but he was quick and thinking ahead. He had to be on his toes and quick when he was around Toby. Most officers would be asking far too many questions that would hinder the investigation. DI Sark knew that when Toby was fully engaged in a homicide case there was no fart-arsing around. If an officer slowed him down, Toby would walk away and take the law into his own hands.

The puffy white clouds parted and the resplendent sunshine cascaded golden rays of light as they went straight on at a busy roundabout, under a motorway bridge and continued forward in the direction of Pontardawe. They arrived at an Asda superstore for a break. They discussed this situation some more.

'Hope you don't mind my asking, Toby,' DI Sark began, 'but what are you hoping to find or see when we pass more fields further ahead?'

'Recently cut grass and all kinds of different, beautiful flowers,' Toby answered, gazing out the passenger window. 'Could you get me a Pepsi while you're in there?' he asked in a faraway voice.

'Yeah, sure,' DI Sark said.

Silence...

Then: 'You still haven't told me everything, have you?'

Toby shook his head, deliberately not looking at the detective.

'What else did you see?'

'Just get us some drinks,' Toby said, as though he was talking to a friend and not an experienced man of the law.

Nevertheless, DI Sark unfastened his safety harness, opened the driver's door and headed for the entrance, leaving the young lad by himself.

Toby sighed.

He decided to tell the detective everything. However, that would put more strain on this affable police officer. Yet what troubled him more than anything else was the fact that the field in his dream could be anywhere in the country. They could be driving around looking for something that was suspicious and end up having to head back downtown with not a shred of evidence to hint at foul play.

DI Sark emerged from the superstore and ambled across the parking bay. He opened the car door, got in and handed Toby a bottle of Diet Pepsi. 'There you go, champ?'

'Thanks.'

They sat there for a few minutes, sipping their drinks and gazing up at the mountain towering over the main road beneath.

'Are you gonna tell me the rest?' DI Sark asked.

'If we're gonna be working together then I better had,' Toby said. 'But I guarantee you're not gonna like what I have to say one bit.'

DI Sark shrugged. 'How bad is it?'

'Very...'

DI Sark nodded, put the cap back on the top of the bottle and leaned back in the driver's seat and closed his eyes. 'Tell me.'

Reluctantly Toby told the detective how he'd stumbled across a mass group of carcases lying sprawled out on an overgrown field, flies buzzing around them obsessively.

'And the worst thing is that I'm not sure that the vision is a premonition or something that has already been done...'

DI Sark cussed and then threw himself forward.

'We better go take a look,' Toby said, beating the detective to it.

They left the parking bay and returned to the old main road on a mission that was still somewhat vague in the glorious sunshine...

*

Abigail answered the door and was pleasantly surprised to see Anastasia in front of her.

'Oh, hi! How are you, Anastasia?'

Anastasia looked stricken. 'Just call me Ann, okay?'

Abigail nodded.

'Would you like to come in? The kettle is about to boil.'

Anastasia said that she would like to join Abigail and then followed her down the short hallway after closing the front door shut.

They sat in the living room, waiting for their steaming mugs of tea to cool down before they were able to consume the drinks.

'I'm assuming you're here today to talk about Toby. Is that right?'

Anastasia nodded.

'He's not here right now,' Abigail began, hardly able to contain how stunning her son's girlfriend actually was close up. 'He's out with the detective trying to solve a homicide crime.'

'Toby spoke to me last night on the phone,' Anastasia said, filled with deep sorrow.'

Abigail hoped in her heart that Toby hadn't said something idiotic that would jeopardise their relationship. 'What did he say?'

'He told me that he'd have to cut all connections between us in order to concentrate on this crime and capture the suspect before anyone else loses their life just to sacrifice this madman's sick desires. I cried a lot last night. I do understand him, though. He can't be distracted under no circumstances; it's just I've never been away from him for so long after being together as a couple. I just want to cling onto him with dear life and refuse to let him go into something so incredibly dangerous. It almost feels like I'm saying goodbye to him before he heads off to war… and to all intents and purposes, I guess that I am.'

Abigail watched this poor young woman pour her heart out. She was fully aware that her son was doing this in Anastasia's best interest and told the girl that that was the case.

'What is this "Shine" thing?' she asked Abigail, evidently frustrated and feeling at odds with the peculiar name.

'He's psychic,' Abigail said in an unwavering voice. 'My boy has an incredible gift for seeing things that have either happened or will happen that involve death. The local authorities adore him. He has aided them for most of his life, preventing things getting worse for victims and solving murders where the perpetrator would otherwise get away with their crimes. He accepts no money or prize from anyone. He does all that free of charge due to his good, moral nature. But he has told this detective that this is the last time. He's found something worth living and dying for that he never thought would come his way.'

'And what's that?' Anastasia asked, perplexed.

'You, my love…'

40.

THE ORANGE DISC that was the sun bled, colouring the sky in pink and purple hues. The man who had visited Susan Cawthorne's grave and appeared in Toby's dream leaned back in his rocking chair on the porch and sucked hard on a cigarette, exhuming wafts of blue smoke out of his nostrils.

The man sitting on the porch of the timber and brick farmhouse gazed out to the main road approximately nine hundred yards in the distance, waiting with a high degree of patience and without a care in the world. That was one aspect of this fellow's character – he never worried or cared overtly for anything or anyone. He simply went with the flow of things, and whatever life happened to throw at him, he dealt with and then deleted it from his brain as though it were a minor problem or chore and nothing more.

In his peripheral vision something moved. He turned his attention to his right and narrowed his eyes, focusing on the black object that was a car moving at a steady pace closer on the only road to and from his residence. The black Mercedes was closely followed by a new grey Toyota pick-up truck. Both vehicles rolled to a halt directly in front of the farmhouse. In spite of this the man simply took another long drag on his cigarette and exhaled blue a puff of smoke above and away from himself.

As the vehicles came to a halt a swirl of dust enveloped them and obscured the man's vision momentarily. A door opened and slammed shut. With that the Mercedes and the Toyota pick-up truck took off again, kicking up more rooster trails of dirt in their wake.

A young man or boy by the looks of him walked down the narrow dirt path heading directly for the farmhouse carrying a rucksack on his back. He had short black hair and was sturdily built. Evidently the boy looked fit and healthy. This was his physical prime. After that was the inevitable decline. Nevertheless, the moment and time was now.

The man dabbed his cigarette out in the translucent glass ashtray and got to his feet, already fully aware who this teenager was.

'The prodigal son returns,' he said, loud enough for Matthew Cawthorne to hear.

The boy crossed the mown lawn and onto the first step that led onto the porch. When he caught sight of the man, Matthew stopped suddenly. The man knew then that Matthew hadn't been told who he was, although there was something in the boy's eyes that informed him that he somehow knew who he was.

'Welcome home, Matthew,' Michael Cawthorne said...

Crows cawed loudly in the distance and then flew away again, leaving the scene.

Man and boy eyed each other up.

'It's true,' Michael said, hoping he'd read his son's expression accurately.

'Dad?'

Michael nodded in the affirmative. 'It sure is...'

Matthew wriggled the backpack off and let it slump to the ground in a heap. 'It's really you?'

'Yeah.'

'Christ! Where've you been all this time?' The question had no anger in it, although had it done Michael Cawthorne wouldn't have been at all surprised.

'We'll get to that soon,' Michael Cawthorne answered.

'Do you know who dropped me off?'

Michael nodded.

'You want to borrow land for some kind of public speech experiment. Is that so?'

Matthew nodded this time.

'What's that gotta do with you?'

'I own five acres of land and will provide my land to you for the rest of summer. How cool is that?'

Matthew shook his head forcefully. 'This can't be. This is way too uncanny for it to be real...'

Michael laughed at that and understood exactly what his son meant.

'Come here and give ya old man a hug.'

Matthew climbed up onto the porch and was embraced with force into his father's mighty embrace, squeezing him hard like he'd never let go.

'You abandoned me,' Matthew said in his ear.

'That's not actually true,' Michael said. 'But I do know how it must look to you all the same. Please take a seat. I'll go get us a couple of cold beers.'

Matthew lowered himself to one of the two rocking chairs and gazed impassively, doing his utmost to make sense of the way things had suddenly turned when he was least expecting it.

He hadn't seen his father since he was four years old and even then they were vague memories.

'Shit... this is intense,' he muttered to himself.

When Michael Cawthorne returned to the porch with two bottles of Heineken, he handed one to his long-lost son before taking a seat in his chair. They sat on the porch drinking and enjoying the sights and sounds of nature.

'I was very saddened to hear of your mother's passing away,' Michael Cawthorne said, breaking the tranquillity.

'She got killed by a thief,' Matthew lied.

'I know. I read about it in the local newspaper. That must have been hard on you.'

Matthew gulped down the rest of his drink and then put the empty bottle down by his feet, careful not to kick it over. 'Did you know that I was in a mental hospital?'

Michael shifted in his chair to get a better look at his son. 'No. I didn't...'

Matthew considered his words carefully. 'I made a mistake when I was younger. Mum never forgave me.'

'What was your "mistake"?'

'I killed a neighbour's cat 'cause it always kept shitting in our garden.'

Michael laughed aloud, easing the tension and unease Matthew had felt having spilled a bad thing. 'That's not good. But, I mean, everyone lets their temper get the better of them now and again.'

Matthew smiled at that, automatically loving his father even more than in his dreams of him. 'Mum never forgave me,' he went on. 'She refused to come and see me at the mental hospital; she was so ashamed of me. She refused me from returning home. In the end I had to put my name down for a council flat as I had been made homeless when I left the institution. You see, she saw me strangling the cat and held onto it forever.'

Michael took a sip of his beer, his lips dry all of a sudden.

'I never saw her again…' Matthew finished.

'That must've been hard on you.'

Matthew nodded in agreement. 'Yeah. But you know now that I've gained my feet and have my own place; in the long run it has done me a world of good. Living with Mum was hard anyway. She was a bit neurotic at times and lived a boring life. She worked at the mill factory for years and spent Saturday afternoons doing the food shopping. Her idea of relaxing was reading while eating a slice of cheesecake. She never did anything different, never mind spontaneous. I always found it hard to break down the invisible barrier to talk with her, but she only ever talked about the weather, the world news or books.'

Michael drained his Heineken and asked his son if he'd like another one. Matthew said he would, as long as his dad was having one.

When he returned Matthew took a gulp of the cold, refreshing beer and then held it in his lap. 'So,' he said. 'What's your story?'

Michael Cawthorne knew it was coming and didn't particularly want to talk about his life after only now being reunited with his only child. Nevertheless, he was fully aware that his son deserved – and needed – an explanation. After all, he had just divulged his life and thoughts of his recently deceased mother.

'When I was young my father would punish me for all sorts of reasons, merely to justify his actions of caning me across the palms and fingers. I was definitely afraid of my father. He was very strict and if I didn't agree with his principles; if I did something that was of no interest to him, I'd be whipped. You see, my father had no intention of raising me as a child and letting me enjoy my childhood, no. He was cloning me… to be just like him. My mum said once that he had wanted to name me after him and call me junior.

'I had no friends. As I got older this became a tangible problem,' Michael continued. 'The boys my age liked to go exploring up in the mountains or go fishing or something which involved fun and innocence. Instead my father would sit me down on the high chair in the kitchen and watch me studiously as I did my homework. I remember one day when Mrs Davies gave me homework for Maths and English and I started crying in front of everyone. No one could understand why I wept and shed tears and trembled. Mrs Davies did ask me what was wrong, but not even for a split second did I consider telling her or my headmaster.

'I'd walk home, taking my time, fearing the homework that I had a whole week to complete would have to be done the moment I got home. If I didn't finish my homework that evening, I went without food and was sent to bed at ten sharp. I complained once that I was feeling light headed and needed something to eat and drink to help me with my concentration. He whacked me upside the head. I saw stars and felt dizzy.

'I tried to ask my mum to stop him from doing this to me, but she ignored me. I suppose the older I got the more I realised that she too was frightened of my father. I asked once. Then I never asked again, fearing that they might both turn on me.

'There was one time when I got a few equations wrong and I didn't achieve a perfect score. That night my father dragged me by the hair on my head into the living room, and put a serrated knife to my throat and sneered at me. I'd never seen such a look in all my life even now. But by that time, you see, I had got so used to being a victim of abuse, I really didn't give two shits about having my throat sliced open by this madman.

'Anyway, I passed my exams and became a model student.

'I met your mother while studying bricklaying and construction in college. She had long, wavy brown hair and was admired by a lot of the boys. A few asked her out, but she turned them down. One day in the college canteen her eyes met mine amidst the small crowd of students. She gave me this great smile, and I couldn't believe my luck. I saw her again as I was finishing my workout and went outside to rest in the sunshine. She was playing netball with her friends on the concrete court.

'She approached me on her way back to the college. And just like that I asked her if she'd like to go to town and get some ice-cream. Once we got talking it felt really easy. Your mother was very open-minded. She didn't judge me or was easily offended. And she genuinely seemed interested in me and what I had to say. I didn't have much of an education, like her, but she did later admit that me being kind, nervous and sturdily built was more than enough for her to be fond of me.

'From there on everything else fell into place. She met my parents. I met hers. The more time we spent together, sharing our daily problems, the more we enjoyed being in our little bubble.

'We got married at a registry office at a fairly young age and you were conceived two years later.'

'Why did you leave?' Matthew wanted to know.

'We were struggling financially. We had just bought the semi-detached house and the weather meant I was not working as much as I ought to have been. Your mother worked as a receptionist and an editor of a local teenager magazine, day and night. It all got to me until one day I went to the bank and drew out five hundred pounds and returned home and placed the cash on the worktop next to the stove. I grabbed my backpack, put as much clothes in it as I could and made sure you were fast asleep. Then I took to the streets. I used my trade to get myself some hobbles along my journey west.

'I arrived here on this farm doing odd jobs, free of charge of the old farmer who owned it. He had no family and his only true friends had already died. He very kindly bestowed this house to me and his five acres of land.'

Matthew shook his head in disdain. 'You could have written. We could have stayed in touch. You abandoned us.'

Michael Cawthorne nodded. However, the truth was he had forced the old timer to put him in his will before he died or he'd blow his head off with a double barrel shotgun. And he would have done. Instead the old man passed away in his sleep and he'd inherited the land. He often thought about his wife and son. Nevertheless, the more time passed the harder it was for him to feel the urge to go back and see them. Instead the single lifestyle was too much to want to give up. He only had to look after himself. His trade got him work in and around the countryside, and his reputation as an excellent bricklayer got around and before he knew it, Michael found himself inundated with work. Furthermore, he had won nearly one hundred thousand pounds on the National Lottery.

Michael opted not to tell this to his only child in case he turned around and headed back home and had nothing else to do with him.

'I'm sorry you feel that way,' he said and laid a hand on his son's shoulder. 'I messed up,' he added. 'I guess I wasn't cut out to be a good husband and father. Although I did leave five grand to your mother in the post. I didn't write to tell her saying it was from me, but your mother was very bright. She probably had an inkling that it was me.'

Matthew Cawthorne finished his drink. Then he placed the empty glass bottle on the small round metal table and sighed in exasperation, having absorbed everything his father had just told him and did his utmost not to let it affect him.

'So this is your house…' he said, gazing out at the beautiful panorama.

'This is *our* house,' Michael said.

41.

TWO WEEKS LATER

THE GLORIOUS SUNSHINE and light breeze made the small town a quiet haven for Abigail who was driving home from the leisure centre. Her hair was damp from her swim. However, once she'd gone through her mail and had something for lunch, she decided to go for a walk. Lately, she had been taking her physical health very seriously and improving all the time. She had lost half a stone and the love handles around her waist had all but gone.

Abigail rolled the car up the drive on the back street, killed the engine and fished out her house key. She walked down the short passageway and came to a halt by the round wooden table and coat hangers. On top of the round table there was a piece of lined A4 paper with the word MOTHER on it.

Without hesitation, Abigail got hold of the letter, turned it over and the right side up and read her son's clear handwriting...

Mum, in case you're wondering where I am, all I can tell you is that I'm safe. The crime I'm working on is far harder than I first thought. But please, for my sake, as well as yours, don't worry about me. I'm fine. I gotta live on my own in order to capture this criminal. The police don't have anything on this guy... and that's why they need me and my psychic abilities to help prevent anyone else from being a victim. In order to track down this criminal I must be seen as an outsider. A homeless person. I need to appear a ghost of myself in disguise so I can get close to this guy without raising eyebrows. Once the case is brought to justice I shall return, and have an official agreement that I'll be taken off the records in order to live a normal life with you and Anastasia.

Neither of you must tell anyone of this. Please let her read the letter too. I do love her, Mum. But I can't relax and be at peace with myself if I don't do everything I can to stop this madman, who is a threat to a lot of people.

Toby xx.

Abigail stood motionless, reading the letter a second time before taking her trainers off and placing them on the shoe rack. Then she picked up the phone and called Anastasia.

She got an answer straight away and read the letter out loud for the beautiful young lady. Anastasia asked politely if she could come over in the evening. Abigail told that she would love to have her company and decided to tell her son's girlfriend about her getting fit and healthy.

When she said goodbye and hung up, Abigail burst into tears. Her whole anatomy shook as tears the size of crystalline droplets ran down her quivering cheeks. The letter hadn't said that Toby was in danger. However, Abigail could read between the lines and intuition flashed a red light into her consciousness that her son would have to go to extreme measures to apprehend this criminal.

Then there was another side to her that demonstrated courage and faith in her son. All his life he had been given this gift/curse and had achieved many great things. Toby had always put himself into perilous situations right from the word go. She started to think very differently, and instead of her mother's love a presence or awakening came over her whole being and she fell into the comforting arms of love. She believed Toby had been blessed with this ability and had the utmost confidence in him reaching his goal.

My son is special...

The thought came out of her from nowhere. Maybe just a hint of this sudden realisation. Once she had reached a calm state of mind, Abigail went into the kitchen, feeling reassured about the current circumstances and made herself a cup of tea and a chicken pasty for lunch. She went and sat outside, permitting the warm rays of the glowing sun to bathe her face until she finally felt totally relaxed.

*

In the town centre shoppers ambled to and fro. The man sitting under the overhanging roof attached to the jewellery store and RSPCA charity shop had a thick beard and a dirty face. His overcoat was laid out in front of him. He chomped down on an apple and finished it. He wiped his lips dry with his shirt sleeve. Then he stood up, staggered, righted himself prior to picking up his coat from the dust-covered pavement and headed on his way to the missionary.

When he arrived there were two homeless women smoking and chatting. Their teeth were like mangy, sick yellow miniature tombstones. They smiled at him, their saggy flesh distorting into their deeply etched faces.

The café for the homeless and unemployed was humid and warm from the oven in the back room. The young man approached the counter where two middle-aged ladies welcomed him.

'What'll you have, my love?' one of them asked.

'Can I have some bread and soup?'

''Course you can, my love. You go sit over there.' She pointed to a vacant table to his right. 'I'll bring it over now.'

He took a seat and wondered why he had a vision of this Community Café on Orchard Street, fully aware that there had to be a reason for him being here and making himself homeless. This very duty was not easy, and the young man sympathised with the other folks, feeling sorrowful for them. It was only now that being here and living on the streets that he truly realised that he was beginning to take in the enormity of these other folks' problems and lifestyles.

He scratched his beard and glanced around at some of the other people who came to this place for food and shelter. He found it hard to imagine what they were all going through, mostly barely surviving from one day to the next. This was no life, he thought, and shook his head inwardly, like a drink and drug addict no older than thirty sipping soup through chapped lips and no teeth.

The lovely lady with her hair tied up in a bun approached him with a bowl of hot tomato soup and two loaves of bread. 'There you go my lovely,' she said and smoothed his upper back with the palm of her hand.

'Thank you very much,' the young man said. His eyes searched hers and looked forlorn.

The woman misunderstood his expression, thinking he looked alone and unwelcome in the world.

'What's your name, my love?' she asked.

'Billy Joe…' Toby said, hating himself for lying to this woman.

'You don't look like a "Billy Joe" to me. Listen, there are a couple of flyers on that desk over there.' She pointed to the table in the far corner of the room where the phone was on the cream wall. 'There's a man speaking publicly to homeless folks like you. They'll be sending a bus into town on Friday; I think it is to take you to the venue. It's in Pontardawe. Free of charge. You might want to go. They'll provide food as well. I think you should go.'

Toby nodded and said he'd pick one up once he'd finished his meal. Then he thanked the woman again and began his meal.

The story behind all this was that he had been having more visions again and finally decided that it was solely up to him to take annual leave from work, lose weight, not shave or wash in order to attend this café and one of the sermons to see what else unfolded that would lead him straight to this murderer. Yet it was all being unveiled to him little by little. This frightened him to a certain degree. However, Toby had sternly told himself that he must have faith and continue to pay attention to the details. Furthermore, he had decided to cut all connections with DI Sark to avoid getting bogged down with questions and suggestions with the local and national authorities.

DI Sark had spoken for him to his chief superintendent, about how they ought to do their job and be patient with this crime that had been brought to their attention in Wales and England.

Toby finished his meal and felt better for it. Then the teenager crossed the café and took one of the remaining flyers and read it...

> ATTENTION HOMELESS PEOPLE! THE TIME IS AT HAND TO RISE UP FROM THE BOTTOMLESS PIT AND FREE YOURSELF OF THIS BURDEN. YOUR INSPIRATION FOR A BETTER LIFE STARTS RIGHT HERE! COME AND SEE AND YOU SHALL BE ENLIGHTENED. FREE SUBMISSION. FREE FOOD.

Toby read the cover twice and studied the photo of a large white tent in a field. He studied the photo for a minute and then bent the flyer in half and slid it into his jeans pocket before taking his leave.

Shit! That's the reason why I had to come here. This is really real! Oh, I hope this will be the end soon.

With that thought fresh in his mind, Toby headed outside and walked towards the town public park. He did have some cash in his coat pocket and felt bad pretending to be a homeless person and getting himself a free meal from those lovely women. Nevertheless, he had gone there with blind faith and progressed with this case.

He supposed he should have felt elated – or at least satisfied – about this, but instead longed for Anastasia. Being in love with someone and being loved back wholly and completely was a very precious thing. He had found his soul mate for life and had his conscience not been so strict, Toby would have turned on his heel, run the two and half miles home, get out of his grubby clothes, shower, shave, and call her at her home.

*

The big day had arrived at last. The sun displayed its glorious magic on the town below in the azure sky. Toby stirred awake and fished out his mobile phone. 8:23AM, it read. The bus would arrive at the Community Café at 10:00am promptly. So he still had time on his hands (no pun intended).

At the bottom of his feet were a can of Diet Coke and a Yorkie chocolate bar someone had kindly left him while he had been alone and fast asleep on the bricked ground. Tears brimmed in his eyes. For now he truly knew the life of a homeless person and the kindness of some folks who provided for them as they slept rough, vulnerable to attack.

'Thank you,' he whispered in a choked, strained voice.

He consumed those items and eventually came fully awake just as a DPD van pulled up over yonder and dropped off two parcels for the WHSmith store.

Toby hauled himself into a sitting position and stretched his arms and legs out, releasing a big wide yawn. He rubbed his face and then got to his feet.

He wandered around town for an hour before turning back and headed to Orchard Street where the bus would arrive and take him to the green farmland pastures in Ystalyfera. He had no idea really what to expect, besides what the flyer had said.

The vision of standing in a field with corn and overgrown grass, surrounded by dead bodies prior to having his head blown off by a rough looking man armed with a shotgun never left his mind. He wondered ponderously if that was to be his fate. Maybe there would be no happy ending, after all. Maybe by committing himself to this mission on his own was suicidal. If all of that came true then the mission was pointless. He might as well turn around and head back home and wash his hands of this mass-death and destruction.

At 9:31am Toby made his way to Orchard Street and saw that the Community Café was now open. He went inside and was surprised to see that there were eighteen homeless and downtrodden men and women waiting patiently for the bus to arrive.

Toby had to sign his name (fake name) on a sheet of paper held firm by a clipboard. Then he went and sat down and listened to the bustling conversations and the feelings of wonder and excitement. The homeless clearly needed something like this event to stir them awake from their hardship in life. Maybe the flyer that introduced this event would be a very good thing and that his visions had been distorted due to his overactive imagination. For the first time in his young life,

Toby began to doubt his abilities as a spiritualist. Maybe instead of being psychic from a young age his "gift" had developed into a mild form of schizophrenia.

Whatever the case, soon all would be revealed to him, and from that point on, Toby would have to make a choice, not just for himself but for all these folks' sake.

Of course, what kept him sitting in the Community Café was the fact that his hunches had always had some element of truth. But why would something so uplifting for these folks that society had ignored put them in peril?

There's more to this than meets the eye.

With that last deliberating thought, Toby leaned back in his chair and waited just like everyone else.

When the bus arrived it slowed its speed considerably, past the Community Café, and went farther on so it could turn around and face the One Way street.

Twenty minutes later all eighteen homeless folks were seated on the private cream coloured private bus with ocean blue stripes on either side. Toby was the last to get on. He found a seat next to the window and slumped down and peered outside and prayed sincerely that everyone would be in good hands from now on...

*

Matthew Cawthorne had kept his mental health concerns private. The members of this secret society were aware of this secret and agreed not to leak this information to anyone. Knowing that removed any concerns the nineteen-year-old might have had.

Downstairs, his father was making him a full English breakfast. Matthew threw the sheets off himself and dashed into the bathroom. He brushed his teeth, washed his face, shaved, took a shit, washed his hands and had a shower. Once he was back in his bedroom, he combed his hair back, slick and off his brow. He sprayed about three days' worth of deodorant all over him and then got dressed in his new Levi denim jeans and a white Mickey Mouse T-shirt.

After breakfast he stepped out onto the porch and gazed across to his right and saw the large white marquee and smiled broadly. Cobblestones were laid from the fringes of the cut grass, creating a path leading directly to the marquee. From what he could see, Matthew believed that the first sight the homeless people got when the bus arrived would make them feel this was the same kind of setting you'd expect for a wedding.

He chuckled to himself at that thought. Then he went back inside and read through his notes, regarding the speech he would give to them today. It had to be inspirational. Matthew knew that above everything else. However, what he hadn't told anyone was his intentions of building an army or a following to commit heinous acts throughout society.

The six security guards arrived early, dressed in black suits and cleanly pressed white shirts. They were all bodybuilders with big, strong muscular physiques. They were armed. However, Matthew thought it highly unlikely they would be called to any kind of action. It was merely a precaution.

He checked his watch – 9:37am.

Now was the time to commence and fulfil his destiny…

42.

THE SHORT JOURNEY on the bus had been kind to Toby. The half hour it took to reach their destination he spent gazing out the window as the world went by. It reminded him of when he was younger and his mother and he used to go shopping or to the cinema together. Those were the good old days, before he had this supernatural ability that had imprisoned him to the life of crime and robbed him of his childhood and adolescence.

However, there had been some good memories, even if they were overshadowed by the bleakness his shine had on him. He thought back to his long conversations with the oracle, Annie Combs. She bestowed her wisdom onto him and, very quickly, Toby had matured and experienced the highs and lows early on in the crazy world we live in.

Now there was another assignment. Now he had to use his wits and supernatural powers and visions in an attempt to stop fate from claiming the lives of many folks... all innocent in their different walks of life. He hated his conscience sometimes. It was because of his values that he was unable to turn away from the pleas and cries of those desperate and in need of a saviour.

The bus rolled to a halt alongside the A4068. The driver left the rumbling motor running as the tour guide rose from her seat and faced the passengers. 'Okay folks,' she said loud enough for everyone to hear, 'we're here. Please follow me two at a time down the gravel path towards the white tent. There will be drinks and refreshments provided free of charge and the event won't start for another twenty minutes or so. Enough time to get to our seats and await further instructions. Is that understood?'

The homeless and downtrodden called out in unison that they all agreed and understood her instructions.

'There are guards here for health and safety reasons. Any misbehaviour will be dealt with hastily and strictly. So I'd advise you all to be compliant and on your best behaviour at all times.'

Then without further delay the automatic doors folded inwards and a warm breeze drifted into the humid interior. The guide stepped out of the bus and soon the folks got out of their seats and made their way down the aisle and onto the gravel path.

Toby brought up the rear watching the folks as they exited the bus and headed down the trail. He thanked the driver for his duty and then he too followed his homeless chums to the marquee.

The sun warmed him delightfully. This was the kind of day he and Anastasia would love to go out and do something exciting. Anastasia had mentioned that the summer was here and that they could go for a bike ride all the way up to Glyn Neath. Deep down that's what Toby craved for. He loved Anastasia with all his heart and mind. A tingling sensation could be felt in his abdomen and he associated that with the pure feeling of love.

They made their way into the large white tent and the guide was assisted by another guide who helped pour soft drinks for everyone and provide chocolate biscuits. Once that had been accomplished, they all took their seats, murmuring to each other in hushed excited voices about how nice and cool it was and how they appreciated the hospitality, the environment and the way they were being treated.

Toby found a chair towards the rear and sipped his orange squash. He ate his chocolate biscuit and then waited along with the others for the event to commence. He almost forgot that he wasn't like the other folks. He had a home. He had his own cosy bedroom, for God's sake! What the hell was he doing here? He could have had a lie in and then gone out with his beautiful girlfriend.

All of this spiritualism or "shine", as Annie Combs called it, had to come to an end sooner rather than later. Abigail was right, if he wasn't careful Anastasia would eventually get fed up and she wasn't the sort of girl who would wait for ever as time passed for him to be done with being a spiritualist. There were lots of boys his age who fancied the pants off her. Toby had seen their glances as she walked into a room with her tanned and sinuous curves.

Please Annie! Help me with this!

At the front of the tent was a varnished wooden stage with a microphone at its centre, awaiting the arrival of their speaker and host. Only God knew what would commence. Why would anyone who has money and power want to speak to the homeless and the downtrodden? The folks lastly thought of by society. The folks who slept on the streets in their blankets and sleeping bags, begging for food and drink throughout the day and ignored by the affluent who passed by without even so much as a glance, never mind anything else.

There was an opening at the front of the marquee and two heavily built bodybuilder men stepped to one side, permitting a young man to enter the tent and head straight for the stage and the centre of it. He had long, thick black hair and had a similar physique to Toby. Evidently, he used barbells and dumbbells at a gym, but unlike the security guards the young man didn't use steroids or Growth Hormones to make himself massive.

A sharp stab at his heart made Toby wince unexpectedly.

He wondered where it had come from. Then he ignored it and realised without a shred of proof that this young man who was still a teenager in years was indeed the culprit of the murder that had occurred in London.

Shit! It's him! It's really him!

Toby puffed the air that had inflated his reddening cheeks and waited with a slight trepidation for his nemesis to proceed...

*

This was the moment he had been waiting for since being with Gemma Hayes (who couldn't make it because of employment duties) ever since he'd begun his murdering spree. Now he would have devoted followers. Here he was in this awning addressing a hundred folks, ready to bring his aspirations into something very tangible and not to be ignored by the nation and possibly the whole world.

'Greetings everyone!' he called out and instantly the whispering of the crowd ceased. All with undivided attention turned to him. 'I would like to thank you on behalf of myself and my team for joining me today. There will be a spread of food later on, all free of charge after my speech. Some of you might be interested to know that although I myself might not get around to talking with you one-to-one, I shall be present for some time afterwards.' He deliberately paused and scanned the many faces of his crowd and was pleased with what he saw.

They were surely the dregs of society in the whole world. Hungry, thirsty, dirty and pleading to their fellow humans for something they could use or consume while day turned to night. Now that they were all here, Matthew's dream wasn't that of a madman, he believed. All of a sudden the next step would be crucial if this was ever going to be anything more than a sermon. Above all else, Matthew wanted to change their hearts and minds and to permit them to take control of their own lives and realise their destiny. And if that meant bending or breaking the rules, then so be it. After all, every single successful person had done the same before.

'For the next hour or so you shall be invited as my brethren,' Matthew went on, not missing a beat. 'The reason I have managed to bring you all here and to talk with you and make you understand my beliefs is because the world we live in is obscure and fucked up.'

There came a tittering from the crowd and smiles.

Matthew ignored it but offered a broad smile to demonstrate his casual demeanour.

'How many of you who live on the streets think that more could be done from the local council?'

The crowd glanced around the gathering, looking for someone to raise their hand first.

'Go on,' Matthew said. 'Be honest. This is not a trial. There are no bad answers.'

Once he said that a couple of hands were raised and quickly followed by others. The majority of the crowd confirmed Matthew's suspicions.

'That's what I thought.' Matthew motioned for them to put their hands down again. 'How many people give you something useful to help your situation?'

Half a dozen hands were raised followed by a few more.

'Most common folks who have their debit cards and loose change and notes in their wallets and coat pockets walk straight past you every single day, not even seeing you or acknowledging you sitting there on the cold concrete, shivering, stomachs empty, with only your blanket or a grubby sleeping bag to keep you from freezing to death.'

The crowd nodded in unison.

Matthew nodded too. 'Not nice when you think about it, is it?'

The crowd chorused, 'No.'

'Look at what I've done for you for one day,' Matthew said. 'Does being nice hurt? No. There are many people, especially living in the suburbs and in the cities that only think about themselves. It makes me sick, to see a fat bastard eating a doughnut and drinking a Coke, who gives nothing to the poor.

'The rich folks are the worst. They buy themselves fast cars and mansions and work behind a desk, never getting their hands dirty. They are overpaid and live luxurious lives in their heated saunas and have all the expensive channels on TV. Not to mention that they are famous and are treated like gods whenever they step outside. The Paparazzi are there to make their money taking photos of them. A football player gets paid a hundred thousand a week if they are really good. A hundred thousand pounds! I mean, what the hell is going on?'

The crowd were stone silent, faces frozen in a state of seriousness. This young man was speaking bluntly but truthfully. These weren't wild opinions of a madman. These were the facts of life in the United Kingdom.

'How is that fair?'

The crowd cheered, totally agreeing with him.

Matthew had to suppress a smile, seeing how effortlessly it had been to get these unfortunate folks to gaze upon him as their saviour and leader.

'A long time ago when I was incarcerated in a local mental institution, I met a patient who had everything stripped from him from a young age. He was out walking one day when youth was his ally and was seized by the throat by a gang of vicious bullies. They punched him, head and abdomen, until he could barely stand. They half-dragged, half-carried him down to the lake and threw him in. The boy cried out and swallowed some water and began coughing and choking fitfully. The bullies laughed and prodded him with a stick from the bank where he was trying to haul himself out of the freezing water. In the end someone spotted them, called out to them, and they fled the scene in fear of being apprehended.

'When he was older the boy grew into manhood and still hadn't forgotten that day. He had suffered with pneumonia as a result of being thrown into the lake and broke a rib from the countless punches. His head had ballooned and shone purple, red and yellow. The boys nicknamed him "Pumpkin Head". He remembered that too. But instead of telling his parents or the school principal, this man waited with inhuman patience and tracked down the three bullies.

'The first one that had seized him by the throat had moved out of his house and shared a house with one of the three boys and their girlfriends. The other boy had to do his A-Levels because he had failed all his exams in high school.

'One day, after college, this boy decided to walk home and unbeknown to him was being closely followed by this patient. The boy took a short cut through the woods, as it was easier than using the pelican crossing on his way home.

'The victim of the bullying was wielding a lump hammer and took to hiding behind an old fir tree and as the boy came within touching distance, he swung the hammer as hard as he could and smashed it into the bully's head. There was a large *crunch* as the boy's nose was shattered across his angelic face. He covered his horrific wound with trembling hands, trying his utmost to stop the flow of crimson blood.

'The boy walked away, leaving the boy writhing on the overgrown grass, holding his face together before his whole skull cracked open.'

Matthew took a sip of water before continuing the tale.

'The two boys' and their girlfriends' house was situated in the same village of Skewen.

'The man sat in his car and watched the two young men and their girlfriends arrive home after spending the night at the local tavern getting drunk and waited until they got inside and turned all the lights out before falling into a drunken slumber. Then the man used the same lump hammer he'd used to break the other teenager's face a couple of months earlier and broke the living room windows before hurling Molotov cocktails into the interior. There was an explosion. The fire caught the rug and carpet and quickly lashed onto the furniture. When he stepped back to admire his handiwork the lights upstairs flicked ON and the young man headed back to his parked car and watched them all rush around, panicking.

'When one of the young men emerged and scanned the street he couldn't see anyone in the vicinity. He went back inside and that was when the man who had done this got out of the car and strode back to the burning house and knocked on the glass panel of the front door. The door was thrown open. The man carried a serrated kitchen knife and slashed the air with it. A very thin crimson line had opened the neck of the bully who had seized him. "Now we are even," he said and got back in his car and drove off.

'The point of the story is simple: don't let other people take you for granted. You may not be rich. You may not be famous. You may not be good looking enough for Hollywood, but you are unique. But I say take control of your life. Don't lay around all day and night, your dreams withering away like a brittle leaf in the Autumn. If you want to do something and fight back against the harshness of life, then go for it! Who shall stop you? There are those who live the First-Class lifestyles. But there are those who say, "All men are equal". So take what's yours and do unto your brother as he hath done to you.'

Toby listened attentively, quietly marvelling at Matthew's speech. After some more stories in the context of righteousness, the boy who was the same age as Toby thanked the crowd, gave a short bow and then stepped off the stage and out of the tent into the fresh morning sunlight.

People stood and applauded raucously and were guided out of the awning's openings into the bright daylight. Once out from beneath the large canvas tent, Toby and the crowd turned and saw six tables full of buffet food and another, much larger table with drink refreshments.

This act of kindness went down very well with the crowd, as might be expected. Toby had to admit that he was actually impressed. This young man, Matthew, did not come across in his prudent opinion as someone who had evil intentions or a sinister demeanour. In fact, if he disregarded the vision he had suffered a couple of nights before, Matthew was indeed a kind and generous man. His speech was ruthless. Nevertheless, it was all in favour of these folks and in recognition of the cruelty of life.

Toby might not have been officially homeless, although he had lived as one for a fortnight now, and was very hungry and thirsty. He got in line and helped himself to a glass of orange squash and some party food before sitting in the freshly mown grass with his homeless and downtrodden friends.

Half an hour had passed and the glorious weather encouraged the folks to devour all the food and drain the drinks and enjoy the light conversations about the sermon Matthew Cawthorne had bestowed upon them without any binding obligations.

The young man appeared to the crowd in the green pasture with a security guard standing either side of him. He sat down on a wooden armchair and called out so everyone could hear him. 'I hope you have enjoyed the speech and the hospitality I have extended to you. Now those who choose to do so may come closer and introduce themselves to me.'

The crowd turned on themselves, searching for someone to stand up and take the lead. A man whose brown hair was in dreadlocks rose and then walked across the field to Matthew and proffered his hand. Matthew shook his hand and said something Toby couldn't hear. Then the man was escorted down the gravel path to an auburn-haired lady seated at a writing desk, ready to take his details for some unknown reason.

Toby finished his food and watched as one by one the folks got to their feet and followed. He supposed that sooner or later he too would have to rise and make his way towards this spokesman. He decided to simply give his thanks and appreciation for the speech and the food before heading towards the highway where the bus awaited their return.

He got in line and a wave of anxiety came over him as he neared the boy. Matthew's aura was one of great self-confidence and certainty. As the line diminished, Toby stood behind an older man with ash-grey sideburns and a patchy head of hair, who when his turn came shook Matthew's hand. Toby blocked everything else out and tried to hear clearly what was being said so he could prepare himself for what answer he could give the young leader.

'Will you be my servant?'

'Yes...' said the man.

'Go and fill out a form for me.'

'I will,' said the man. Then he headed towards the freckle-faced woman at the writing desk.

This is it! No turning back now!

Toby braced himself... then stepped forward and came face to face with his adversary.

'Take my hand,' Matthew said and smiled at Toby.

Toby joined his hand into Matthew's right hand and an electrical blue flash of light blinded him and rendered him unconscious. Matthew's hand was withdrawn sharply and he sat bolt upright, watching in horror as Toby collapsed into a heap on the freshly cut grass and went into a violent seizure...

43.

THE BUS purred along the highway, half full of homeless folks. The sun still shone radiantly but now there were big white puffy clouds in the sky. Toby stirred awake and needed a few moments to catch his bearings. His forehead was resting on the window and hummed in unison with the engine. He peeled himself away from the outside world and opened his eyes as large as they would go, searching for a familiar face. He spotted one of the guides and realised he was sitting directly behind the driver. Something had happened, for there was a long gap in his memory.

In a groggy voice he caught the guide's attention and asked, 'What happened?'

'You fainted,' he said and then turned to face the front again, evidently not wanting to talk any further.

Had he pissed the guide off? he wondered.

How?

If you fainted – you fainted. It happens sometimes, Toby rationalised. Then he too returned his gaze to the window and the world beyond. After some time he remembered he had been standing in line and eventually got to meet Matthew Cawthorne face-to-face and shook his hand. Then there had been an instant power cut.

Did Matthew Cawthorne possess supernatural powers?

If he did, Toby didn't want any further part in this undercover investigation. If Matthew did... and he could make someone collapse at a mere handshake then someone in authority would have to end this murderer with a weapon. It would be far too risky to try to apprehend him without force, if he was capable of doing what he had done to Toby in a blink of an eye.

Then Toby remembered the first time he'd come into contact with a murderer. It was the same kind of thing. Only he had had a seizure in the men's bathroom in the cinema. It proved that Matthew had done something so bad that the power of connection was too much for Toby's senses to cope with in one single moment.

He leaned forward and asked the guide, 'Where're the others?'

The guide sighed, clearly irritated at him and then faced him once again. 'Some stayed behind,' he said.

'Why?'

'Matthew is going to help them, which is more than the council can do. Just go back to sleep will ya.'

Toby frowned at the guide, shook his head in disdain and then averted his gaze.

I've embarrassed him.

For the rest of the journey, Toby remained silent and closed his eyes to relax himself. All of a sudden he felt bone weary tired and wanted to get back to the small-town streets, get into his sleeping bag and drift off. Today had brought him nothing that was worth going over and over in his ever-busy mind.

They arrived back at the Community Café.

Toby collected his backpack and sleeping bag and departed without so much as a word.

As he headed to his favourite spot, he thought back to what Matthew had said earlier in the day. He talked about the rich and healthy and the poor and downtrodden, like he knew all too well from personal experience. But what Toby failed to understand was what Matthew's motive was. No one went to all that trouble to feed, shelter and give advice to the nobodies in the world without wanting or needing something in return.

He arrived at his spot and rolled into his sleeping bag and did the zip up. 'Christ! I'm no good to anyone if I keep going into seizures every time I meet someone who has done something really bad. I got a name anyway. Maybe I could give Sark the place and the name of the speaker and sit back and watch the police do the rest.' However, as good and prudent as that all seemed, what evidence did he have? Matthew had now put himself into a Samaritan position and had got himself some followers who now lived for a purpose far greater than merely surviving.

Perhaps Toby was in over his head here. This was the first time he doubted himself and his abilities. Before there had always been a reason. Now, coming out of retirement where he was happy with his occupation and lifestyle, not to mention his beautiful girlfriend, made him wonder what the hell he was doing. If someone had approached him here in town and told this yarn, would he have thought that person insane?

Maybe.

And his inner voice frightened him to the core.

Perhaps he was delusional. Perhaps there were a few screws loose and his mind had gone and taken a vacation.

A guy in working overalls strode pass and dropped a pound coin on the floor in front of Toby. The spiritualist thanked him and went and got himself a bottle of water. When he returned and had drained half of the bottle's contents, he sat back down and realised there was something awry going on behind the scenes.

Nearly half the homeless folks stayed behind in the green pastures of the farmland to be with Matthew Cawthorne. The free sermon and buffet and drinks all free of charge were an enticement to them doing something for Matthew. Yet whatever it was it remained a secret to him. Perhaps Toby would have to use some psychology at this moment in order to make him think and act like a murderer. The trouble was the speech itself was full of facts. And Toby, living as a homeless person, understood and even agreed with a lot of points that Matthew had spoken of.

Could there be any salvation?

Toby didn't think so.

However, there was some underlying factor that he hadn't cracked, and he desperately needed to know before it was too late.

He finished the rest of his drink and wanted another one.

No money.

No drinks.

No food.

No TV.

No bed.

No life even.

Toby could now understand why so many of the others stayed behind. They loved Matthew Cawthorne. He spoke up for them. There was no admission fee. Nothing. Just one awesome speech that would rattle the cages of the affluent and greedy.

Toby lay down and propped his head up from the bricked pathway with his backpack and closed his eyes, wanting and needing a good night's sleep.

*

Matthew, Michael, two security guards and a group of four homeless folks stood in the living room of the farmhouse around a rectangular-shaped wooden table where a map of the capital city was laid out. Matthew had made marks with his red felt-tipped pen and explained to the group where their intended target resided along with places he frequently visited.

The target was that of a very successful actor, well known and respected both in the United Kingdom and the United States for his movies and innumerable interviews.

'How much is he worth?' one of the homeless men asked Matthew.

Matthew checked his laptop which had internet access and came up with an answer two minutes later. 'He is worth $39 million and is only twenty-seven years of age. He's divorced and lives on the outskirts of the city a mile from the nearest house. He is a bachelor and what he earns he keeps and spends lavishly on himself and women he dates and sleeps with. Two weeks ago he returned home after promoting his new action thriller which will be opening this week after his appearance on the Graham Norton show.'

'How are we to pull this off as we are?' a heavy rotund woman with black teeth asked.

'You'll drive the car,' Matthew said. 'The others will be dressed as officers of the law. You shall be provided with uniforms, tazers and a battering ram to break down the front and back doors. You'll have helmets and bullet proof vests. Only kill if he is home and tries to resist. You will drive back here and nowhere else, is that understood?'

The four homeless folks glanced at each other and then nodded acquiescence. They realised that this was a big opportunity for them to change their horrible lives and make some serious money under their new leader. They listened attentively to every single detail.

'The car will be equipped with Sat Nav. One of my men will put in the two addresses. Here and the mansion. Is there anything else you'd like to ask?'

'What if something goes wrong and the police get involved?' one of the grubby men asked with owl-shaped eyes.

'If there is a fuck up,' Matthew said in an even tone, 'do not mention my name. If you do and I become a target I shall get my guards to torture you for however long it takes for you to die. Mark my words – do as I say for your own sakes. I am above the law.'

A couple of hours later a black sedan pulled up alongside the highway. A man wearing a black and white Armani suit emerged from the vehicle and left the door open for the four homeless folks to get dressed into their uniforms and take off towards the male actor's luxurious mansion.

Matthew smiled seeing them in their uniforms. They had washed and cleaned themselves up, and from a distance, unless you knew who they were, you wouldn't question them being genuine officers of the law. The car pulled onto the highway and its red taillights looked like devil eyes growing smaller in the distance before the darkness of night swallowed them completely...

*

Thomas Edwards was sitting on his leather sofa in his capacious living room holding a glass of beer that he had just poured from the can. Whenever he went out for a meal or for film premiers or award ceremonies he normally drank straight from the can, but tonight he'd uncharacteristically decided to get a stein and drink from it. He felt quite posh doing this, but there was no one apart from him in his Cardiff residence. He sipped from the glass instead of gulping down the contents and placed the glass onto the Formica table. Then he picked up the heavy manila envelope packet and extracted a film script which he'd collected earlier from his agent, who had rung and told him that this was an action feature with two top producers and a well-respected director already on board.

Intrigued, Thomas sat upright and read the synopsis first. Then he got stuck into the script and killed the TV in the process. Now this script sounded very interesting; something his career could do with to put him back in the game in America, after his reputable gangster thriller last year that had won two Golden Globe awards.

Thomas was a young, handsome bachelor, not out of choice but of circumstances. He had had two relationships. One with a film producer who got him a role in a classic horror film sequel that had got his name around the executive producers' offices. That didn't work out because Thomas lived in the United Kingdom and she lived in sunny California. His most recent relationship was with the actress, Shirley Jackson, who was now being recognised for her lead role in a BBC drama where she had fornicated with her on-screen lover in two scenes. Thomas had kindly asked her not to go through with it for their relationship's sake, but Shirley verbally accused him of "trying to sabotage her career". Nothing was further from the truth, so she took the role and fornicated on film.

Thomas ended the relationship immediately and was now focusing on his own career and life for the first time since he'd got a debut role in that low budget but profitable horror flick.

This action thriller was well written and as he read it with undivided concentration, the living room seemed to disappear, and he now visualized himself running across the rooftops being chased and shot at by his adversary that he'd caught in the act of rape and murder.

After an hour, Thomas finished his drink and carried the script upstairs to bed where he read for another forty minutes. He planned on calling his agent in the morning, after breakfast, to inform them that he was very interested and keen to get this part and arrange a meeting with the executive producers and the director.

All was good in the world, from Thomas Edwards' point of view. He switched the bedside cabinet light off and surrendered himself to the black veil of sleep for the next eight hours or so.

*

The Oracle slipped into his consciousness like a heavenly angel. It was still dark. The night was at its zenith. The world spun languidly on its axis, but none of those details mattered. Toby forgot where he was and didn't care right then what happened to him. All he craved for was peace and unawareness. Fighting crime had taken its toll on him. Retirement beckoned him forward into the loving arms of his doting mother and his beloved girlfriend (if he still had one that is).

'It's okay, Toby,' a soft, melodic voice told him.

Toby murmured and then rolled onto his side and breathed labouredly.

'Remember me when I am no longer with you. For your days on earth are many and mine have passed.'

Toby recognised the voice but couldn't quite place it, not through lack of endeavour though. He tried to speak, but his lips were chapped and dry as sand.

'You are chosen for this gift and everything in your power to stop things getting worse, which they will do,' the female voice said. 'The world is a crazy place, Toby. You of all should know that. You have no guilt, so don't burden yourself with things that you cannot control. You have this "Shine" which has been bestowed to you. A rare gift... and soon you shall see what anarchy will be spread if you don't do something about it. If you fail, you fail. But you can't live in fear anymore. Living in fear will make you weak and as scared as a nervous cat. You must stand up against all this evil before it gets out of control. You'll suffer horrific visions that are accurate. The dead want you to bring him to justice. Here's the flash of lightening you suffered. Here find your strength to see into the eyes of a madman.

'Don't be afraid...'

*

Matthew Cawthorne and his father Michael Cawthorne were rudely, but expectedly awoken by the sound of a motor engine drawing close to the farmhouse. Matthew threw the covers off him and hurried downstairs. He threw the door open and flicked the porch light on, staring wildly into the darkness. He could see small oval-shaped lights bobbing up and down, closing in as they approached and dark shapes became the bodies of three men and one woman...

'This is it,' Matthew said under his breath, stepping down while Michael pulled back the screen door onto the porch and watched with excited anticipation.

The four homeless folks were gasping, and one of the men's faces was dotted with the victim's blood.

'Well, how did it go?'

It took the group a short while to catch their breath properly.

'He's dead!' the shortest of men cried out.

'We got his bank card and forced him to give us the ID number and emptied one of his accounts by using a cash point. Then we killed him. It was safer. Otherwise he would've identified us.'

Matthew shook his head and smiled. 'Amazing!' He stepped down off the porch steps and told them they had done brilliantly. Then he advised them to go and get out of their clothes and take a shower.

'Where's the money?' Michael Cawthorne asked.

The tallest and most muscular follower dug into two of his jacket pockets and handed Matthew two thick wads of notes.

'This is a great deed that you have all done in keeping with my speech earlier on. You shall be rewarded for this...'

The four homeless people who had committed the crimes of robbery and murder smiled, proud that they had made their leader happy.

44.

THE DAY was young and yet the roads to and from town were jammed. Toby was heading towards the Community Café for a small English breakfast and some orange squash. He had slept well and suffered no bad dreams or visions, which he thanked God for.

He arrived at his destination and ate his food while a dirty, broken woman, who was as thin as a rake, pulled her pack of Marlboro cigarettes out of her jeans pocket and then headed outside to smoke. Toby was grateful that he'd been left on his own to finish his meal prior to heading back out on the streets, hoping that the black clouds that formed together, huge and threatening, would hold off until he found a place to shelter.

As he ambled down the street he came to a stop outside a TV, Radio and DVD shop which caught his attention. There was a small TV in the front window. A female news reporter was speaking but Toby couldn't hear her as the glass blocked all sound. However, as the report of the presenter was replaced by a live recording, the name on the screen came up and announced "THOMAS EDWARDS FOUND DEAD AT HOME!"

'Remember,' the dulcet female voice inside his head said, *'you can't stop everything bad from happening. The harshness of life shows no compassion to anyone no matter their gender, age or success or failure. Remove the burden from your shoulders and relax.'*

Toby listened, and deep down he knew that the faraway voice was telling him the whole truth and nothing but. However, he couldn't help realising how rough the world was, (not just in the UK but the world over) and how one had to apply oneself with vigilance and intellect in order to avoid attacks from the hunters in this world. The world itself couldn't give a flying monkey's if you were a nice person or a bad person. It didn't give a shit if you had already suffered something awful and then suffered with another heap of it without a break. It would beat and batter you to the very ground you were standing on if you let it. No man was tougher than life, no matter how hard he fought against his fellow man.

It was these thoughts that eventually got through into Toby's consciousness and he realised that he did have a rare gift and that he wasn't merely battling with all matters that life could throw at him. Maybe that was why he struggled so much – because he was battling against the forces of nature in all wicked men and now found himself standing in the street, unclean, stinking and with a beard growing thickly.

He peeled himself away from the shop window and ambled down the street wondering if he was on a fool's run and ought to head back home with his tail between his legs. His mother was the kindest person he ever knew. She would be delighted and relieved from stress if he returned home now. However, it would mean that he would have to turn his back on the victims of these kinds of atrocities.

'Thomas Edwards' death is linked to the evil boy,' he said aloud without his confirmation in mind. It was as though someone else spoke the words for him.

He drifted back off to sleep an hour later down an alley between the town library and a block of council flats.

*

Thomas Edwards' death shook the nation and Matthew watched the news report the following day with keen intrigue, proud of his followers for doing this deed and making themselves £70 each. The rest of the stolen money was in the safe box in his father's farmhouse. Furthermore, Heidi Johnston had met him at his council flat for his injection and noticed that there seemed to be colour in his cheeks and a whole different demeanour about him.

'You're looking well,' she said, smiling, proud of her patient.

Matthew nodded and returned the smile. 'I've found my father and have been bonding with him the last week or so. My mother's untimely death made me realise that holding grudges and not forgiving someone is bad for your own health and wellbeing. I'll be heading back tomorrow. He lives on a farm in Goedre 'g graig. I love the smell in the morning and helping him plant seeds and so on and so forth.'

Heidi couldn't take her eyes off him, realising that he was a whole different person. She voiced this to him, still marvelling.

'Had I not been incarcerated and abandoned by my mother you would have seen this almost right away. Mental institutions make you crazy because that's how you are treated by the authorities. That's what I was trying to tell you and Dr Komma. You listened to me but that doctor was a know-it-all son of a bitch. He just marks off my record with a medicine that he thinks is categorised after his inaccurate diagnosis.'

Heidi shrugged. 'Yeah, he is a bit proud of himself, I suppose. Anyway, it's been great seeing you. Your next depot injection is in three weeks. You've got my number and free phone numbers of all the mental health organisations if you feel you need a bit of support. But I guess you'll be too busy being with your dad, working on his farm to need much further assistance – but it is always there if you need to talk.'

Matthew watched her take her leave and then went back in the living room, picked up his pen and notepad and jotted down all that was required for his next plan of action.

He was in his element... and nothing or no one could stop him.

*

He was standing in an open field facing a recently painted farmhouse. He wasn't quite sure how he got there, but for this moment in time it didn't really matter one way or the other. Instead what did matter was that here were approximately ten to fifteen people hanging around the property all clean and fresh.

Matthew Cawthorne emerged from the interior out onto the porch and gazed out at the panorama before him. Toby wondered what he was thinking right then, realising that the death of the talented actor, Thomas Edwards, was his undoing. Yet what really disturbed him was the fact that Matthew was now fast becoming a prominent figure out here in the Welsh countryside. He wasn't famous or rich, but the poor and the downtrodden were fervent followers of his movement and were rewarded with purpose. The homeless were now clean and had duties to enforce. They all reigned supreme out here in the green pastures.

Toby felt himself move forward as though he were a ghost and not a human. Nevertheless, he floated across the overgrown grass onto the pathway.

Matthew stepped down off the porch and addressed a tall, skinny young man wearing a black leather jacket, wielding an AK-47 assault rifle.

Shit! This is serious...

This wasn't merely some young man promoting himself as a preacher to the dregs of society. This was a faction outlawed by society for not being able to support themselves or contribute to the economy. Instead they were employed to serve their new master and defend the property of the two men, father and son, who took them in, cleaned them up and made them feel loved and cared for, unlike the world beyond that had kicked them into the dirt and then left them there to rot and perish.

Toby backed away, not so much frightened but realising that there was a part of his mind that insisted that Matthew Cawthorne had done a good job here. He had taken folks off the streets, fed them, clothed them and made them feel worthy... something they'd never thought they would feel.

He's not good. He is corrupt. He's only using them for his own purposes. But what does Matthew really want from them. It can't last for ever. His army would now expect him to look after them all for now until their lives begin to expire. Then what? What is his master plan? How can I stop this before someone else suffers? Or is this an internal warning that I have no chance in hell of bringing this man and his army to justice. Why don't the police investigate?

He came to and realised that there was only one thing he could do right there and then – and that was to face his fears and go to the farmhouse and see for himself what the hell was going on?

'Hey punk!' a man's voice called out, startling him.

Toby glanced over his shoulder and saw a big, broad shouldered man approach him, a can of Carling in his right hand. He put down his can and kicked Toby who was still inside his sleeping bag in the ribs. The blow was more of a shock than the impact itself, but Toby rolled away and used the wall to pull himself up and face this adversary.

The guy watched him with beer goggles and watched as Toby unzipped and stepped out of his sleeping bag. 'Not today, my friend,' he said, serious and firm.

He rolled the sleeping bag up and tucked it into his backpack. The man didn't avert his stare even for a second. And Toby didn't wait to find out what would befall him if he stayed there. He walked back down the alleyway and made it certain in his mind that the destination he was heading might be his last… and to his surprise he felt no fear.

45.

ABIGAIL was sitting in her favourite spot on the couch reading the *Sun* newspaper, intrigued and appalled with the story of a famous female singer who had been murdered in cold blood in the suburbs of Cardiff city. Her home had been ransacked and all her expensive belongings (jewellery, purse and food) stolen. She had been an Emmy Award winner and her latest song had been made platinum both in the UK and the US. She often stayed in Wales as it was less hectic than London or New York, where she could write her own songs of a classy, retro edge to them.

Her tour across America next year had sold out and she had already made four albums before she had reached her thirties. She had dated lots of high-profile men but the relationships didn't last because she was so determined and dedicated to her career.

All of that had gone in a matter of minutes.

Abigail couldn't help but shake her head, clearly disturbed by the kind of folks that resided in the country she was so proud of.

The front page had the story in a small title next to an intentional explosion by arsonists in a computer factory, killing twenty-two people.

'Jesus Christ, what's wrong with people?' she muttered.

It was news stories like these two that had made the frontline news that induced anxiety for her one and only child. Nevertheless, Abigail knew this feeling applied to all mothers whose children's occupations required them to risk all to get the job completed before anyone else got hurt.

My son is a hero...

What Abigail didn't realise was how true her words were on this day, when her only child was now walking to his adversary's destiny intent on facing the future with the real possibility that he might lose his life.

*

The night sky was hazy and humid. Nevertheless, Toby was tucked in a niche in an alleyway in his sleeping bag, stirring in his sleep.

He found himself back at home in his bedroom. The TV was on and illuminated the bedroom with flashing lights. He didn't know what he was doing being back at home, but the feeling was nice and he craved for it all the more. It was only until recently that the young man realised and fully appreciated how fortunate he was. He had his own bed and a TV and a bookshelf in the corner with all his books waiting to be read and waiting to be read again. He even had a copy of the Holy Bible.

Was the mission over?

He didn't understand what had happened and why he was back at home with his mother without knowing one way or another if he'd brought the murderer to justice or if he had gone missing. Then as he rolled off the comfy mattress, Toby stood by the window and stared out impassively.

'It's all right, my darling,' a soothing female voice informed him.

'What happened?' Toby asked, suddenly realising that he might well be suffering with psychosis or schizophrenia due to the fact that he was having a conversation with a voice in his head.

'You were born for this reason,' the familiar female voice said. 'But now you have a very important decision to make. The young man has started a movement and has very powerful friends. Your life is at risk if you continue with this mission. You have to decide whether or not you're willing to give up everything in order to confront this evil or head home and continue life with a job you enjoy and a girlfriend you love and want to spend the rest of your life with.'

Toby didn't answer immediately. However, the importance of the words unfolding in his brain was triggering his subconscious thoughts. Did he truly want to go all the way with this? I mean, what was the purpose? And not only that – what good would one young man – psychic or not – be able to achieve on his own?

'I have a conscience,' he said, only then fully realising that it was his conscientious that had led him down this life path ever since he was a young kid going to the cinema and bringing a murderer to justice. Did he really have a choice? he wondered. He didn't really think so, if he was being totally honest with himself. But what did trouble him was how he was going to manage if he did confront Matthew Cawthorne. He had no evidence to prove Matthew's guilt. And if he had powerful friends who were above the law... or had enough influence to bend the law to their advantage, what chance did he have?

This is a suicide mission!

'Everything worthwhile is high risk, my darling,' the female voice told him.

'Who *are* you?' Toby asked.

'I am the Oracle,' she said. 'I will protect you.'

Regardless of the fact that he might most likely be losing his mind, the voice announcing that it was an Oracle comforted him a great deal.

'Your greatest fear is dying, am I right?'

Toby said that indeed it was and added that death for him was a fear of his due to the unknown. And nothing in his life he found more frightening was the fear of the unknown and the inevitability of it.

'Tomorrow you must journey to the farmhouse and confront the evil doers. But you'll never be alone. I am with you in spirit. All you have to do is trust me. I know more than you, my little pup. Whatever befalls you tomorrow, know that this is your destiny... and that you are doing the right thing. Otherwise if you quit, this will continue and your conscience will be plagued with overwhelming guilt. You can't live thereafter with that burden on your shoulders unless you change your mind and become a different person...'

Toby didn't say a word. He listened attentively and was patient.

'I like who you are,' the female voice said matter-of-factly.

'I shall go to the farmhouse tomorrow, but I don't know how I'm supposed to bring them all to justice on my own.'

'You are the lamb,' the Oracle said.

'That I am,' Toby said before a deep sleep enveloped his dream.

*

The full moon shone radiantly. Michael Cawthorne and his son had just received news that some of Matthew's followers had murdered a football player and broke into his safe at his residence. Now there was thousands and thousands of pounds worth of cash to be shared equally with the homeless folks, who now held Matthew as their own Messiah. Everything he'd said about the affluent folks was true to them. They lived luxurious lifestyles, earning millions annually while they fought for spare change and a roof over their heads.

Matthew stood before them with his back to the farmhouse and addressed them with open arms. 'Now you're beginning to see for yourselves what I have preached, don't you?'

The ten followers nodded in unison.

'The whole world is full of corruption,' Matthew went on, everyone's attention focused on his words. 'We're not corrupt. We're restoring the balance. If some of them fight to their deaths to keep their worldly possessions, then so be it. No sweat off our backs, right?'

Again, the followers' concurred.

'The poor aren't as poor as before. Isn't that fair?'

The small gathering said aloud that it was indeed.

'Then take your earnings and be free. Those who want to stay around go and set a place for yourselves in these green pastures and tomorrow I'll give you all some squash. Until then, go and take your rest and I shall do the same. We haven't committed any crime. We've balanced the scales in the name of justice.'

Matthew dropped his arms, pivoted and then ascended the porch steps where his father now stood, gazing out and beyond as the followers either took their leave from his property or lay down in the field.

Matthew and Michael stayed out on the porch; clinking Budweiser beer bottles… a toast to their hard endeavour finally paying off (no pun intended) and discussed the rioters in Cardiff and Swansea.

'This is the perfect life,' Matthew said. 'This is what I dreamed of. I'm in control. And look what I've achieved so far.'

'What have you achieved exactly?' Michael wanted to know, as he didn't understand his son's decisions or motive.

'Anarchy.'

Silence dropped like a stone.

'What pleasure do you get from that?'

Matthew glanced at his father and leaned back in the rocking chair. 'While I was incarcerated in the mental institution, I felt much anger; but I managed to play a role of the silent schizophrenic. I didn't talk. I didn't listen. I just lay in my bed, staring up at the alabaster ceiling and padded walls with no thoughts. I killed a neighbour's cat and the next thing I know I'm being monitored daily by this Pakistani doctor. I mean this guy was a fucking expert. He'd diagnose me almost immediately and if I didn't respond like an obedient child, he'd change my meds. It was this that poisoned my brain and rotted my guts. I'd have to take oral medication and be injected every day. Then this therapist came along and I decided that I'd have to change my role to a nice, genial sick patient who had learned his lesson and simply wanted to return home to be with his momma.

'I took my meds willingly... I ate properly. I'd be polite and talk to the doctors and guards and fellow inmates until it became apparent to them that this was no ill boy but a much happier boy who wanted to get out of that hellhole and start a future doing something he was passionate about.

'Now all I needed was to be forgiven and given a bit of help...

'But Mummy refused to forgive or help. Instead she totally abandoned me when I needed her most. It was a *cat*, for Christ's sake! I said I was sorry and wouldn't do something like that ever again. But mummy wasn't having none of it. So all my future plans got ruined. I ended up having to live with folks who are too lazy to get up off their arses and go to work. The council came and cut the lawns – but I was now filled with rage. Here I was, eighteen years of age, living in this squalor, meeting my therapist who gave me my injection and seemed very pleased with my progress.

'I'd always feel that way unless I did something about the one person who had given me life and had now taken it away... even after my apologies and pleading. Now I would return home. At night. Mummy was sleeping and I kept her that way until I stabbed her five times in the stomach. Now, do you think that makes me mad? 'Cause I gotta whole lot more rage in me when people who think they're better than me piss me off.

'Now you come back out of the blue from nowhere in my life and take a share of my money and I don't question you or get into a dispute with you... and if some of those doctors and nurses saw me now, they would think I'm evil...'

Michael was still reeling from hearing that his only child had murdered his first love in cold blood. Ice cold blood froze in his veins and he very nearly let the beer bottle slip out of his grasp.

'You killed your mother?!'

Matthew faced his father, face contorted in a mask of evil. 'You're damn right I did. She abandoned me. I desperately tried to reach out to her to help me be a better person and she refused. In my eyes the day she refused to even come and see me face-to-face was the day my mother died. All that was left was a middle-aged woman whose life contained soap operas and Dean Koontz paperbacks. I did the world a favour.'

Michael finally pushed himself out of his chair and steadied himself, feeling faint all of a sudden and turned to face the screen door. 'I can't believe you killed your m-mother...' he muttered under his breath.

'She left me for dead,' Matthew said to no one in particular. 'All I did was return the favour.'

*

Before midnight, Matthew had gone into the kitchen and poured beakers of lemonade for his remaining followers who had stayed close. However, what no one saw was Matthew taking out a sealed jar with a skull and crossbones label indicating the contents were full of poison. He poured plenty of the translucent liquid into the beakers and stirred the content with a fork before adding the fruit juice to conceal the lethal substance.

Once that was accomplished, he placed the beakers on the table outside and encouraged the followers to drink their drinks and leave nothing behind.

Satisfied with his daily endeavours, Matthew took another bottle from the fridge and sat outside on the porch gazing up at the full moon. His father had retired to bed for the evening, and when Matthew could no longer keep his heavy-lidded eyes open any longer, he entered the farmhouse and lay down on the sofa and fell into a deep, dreamless sleep.

*

Michael Cawthorne found himself standing at the front of the church, dressed immaculately in a grey suit, white shirt and navy tie, awaiting the arrival of his bride. The familiar wedding music started when mother and daughter entered the church (Susan's father had died late the previous year of bowel cancer). As she got closer and the guests 'ooh'd and aah'd' in delight and wonder, he told himself that he was the luckiest man on the planet. He really did feel emotional and knew that the best thing he had ever done was to propose to her.

Susan Cawthorne was delighted as they left the church ceremony and held his hand tight as they stepped outside into the glorious sunshine and posed for photos prior to getting into the back of the light blue Rolls Royce on their way to the hotel where they'd all dine and party into the late hours.

His soul mate had been a perfect wife. Michael had lived modestly working in a Ford engine factory on the outskirts of Bridgend and was later made redundant when the recession took its toll on the British citizens. Thereafter, the pressure of his wife bearing him a son and being low on money produced a lot of stress and anxiety through no fault of his own. He got jobs bartending and providing a car cleaning service, but couldn't hold down a steady income for his family. Furthermore, when it came to holding baby Matthew, Michael just didn't have the knack to do anything right. It got to the point that he dreaded being left alone with him in case something went wrong. Susan hid her vexation well. However, Michael knew that as time passed by and more and more people were being paid off, the chance for a proper job became less likely.

Michael would lie awake at night, staring at the ceiling, unable to turn his mind off. He worried that he would attend every job interview that the Job Centre set up for him, giving him hope, only for that same hope to be flattened outright when he was informed he was unsuccessful, or worse, had no response from the managers at all.

Susan worked as a receptionist at the local surgery, and then got Michael a job working as a cook at a local café. That job lasted seven months before they were forced to let him go due to cut backs. All his hopes and dreams had been dashed.

There would be no new home suitable for a family. No money in the bank for a summer holiday and a trip to Disney Land. Instead he decided to take his leave, and wondered if he had done so sooner it might have stabilized Susan and Matthew's future. He had sent cash in an envelope on two separate occasions, but could no longer afford it. He did lots of painting and decorating and bricklaying. It was a miracle that the previous owner of this farmland had no next of kin or family or friends to leave his property to.

And in spite of this all Michael wanted to do was to return home (to their first house) with money in abundance. However, it took many years to get himself into the position where the mortgage had already been paid off.

When the news of Susan Cawthorne's death arrived at his front door, Michael just felt numb all over. He supposed you could call it some kind of shock, but he was catatonic. He wasn't certain she was dead. For years death had been a distant chapter in his life and everyone he knew. He never sat there dwelling on the subject of death. To do so was insanity. He encouraged himself and everyone he knew to enjoy life. To grasp the wonderful gift with a fervent eagerness to do something that would make you happy.

Then he went to the burial site and saw the granite headstone itself… and all too suddenly with full impact did death arrive and grasp his pounding heart with an arctic hand.

She *can't* die, he remembered thinking. She's beautiful, inside and out. She's a perfect human being. She loves me. The only reason I didn't return home sooner was because I was ashamed that I had let her and Matthew down by always being laid off, regardless of the fact that it was all to do with the recession.

Matthew was going on nineteen. He wouldn't be interested in going to Disney Land.

Where had his life gone? he wondered.

Susan didn't just die, like his father. She was murdered in cold blood! And not by some thief or serial killer. Neither did she die of some gruesome accident or mistake. She had been knifed.

She had been murdered by their only child.

His son!

Michael Cawthorne stirred in his sleep and rolled over. His eyes snapped open. He threw the duvet off and got out of bed. At the far wall he had propped his twelve-bore shotgun and quietly opened his bedroom door before stepping studiously onto the landing. He made his way down the stairs, cringing at the sound of the creaking wood, exhaling deeply as he reached the ground floor and caught site of his son, sprawled out on the sofa in the living room.

He cornered the room and then came to a halt, aiming the double-barrelled weapon at the young man who was fast asleep. He took the safety off and clicked back the hammer.

'You're not my son,' Michael said as hot tears brimmed before finally streaming down his face.

Matthew awoke and all of a sudden his wild eyes found the double-barrels pointed fixedly at him and the man he knew as his estranged father standing over him.

'Dad?'

'You killed your mother!' he cried out.

Matthew was about to say something, to protest, but he never got the chance.

The blast of the shotgun caused the crows to scatter into the night, cawing in disdain at the flicker of light illuminating the farmhouse interior and the deafening bang that shook the foundations.

46.

THE NIGHT BEFORE, Anastasia wanted to forget for she was ashamed at her behaviour. She had attended a college graduation party with an old friend, Ellie. She hadn't intended to stay long as she had tallied long in her bedroom in the evenings to watch the national and local news reports for any trace of where her absent boyfriend might be. She was still in love with Toby. However, time had passed with the crime rate soaring due to these random attacks on the rich and famous. She knew Toby was out there amidst the whole thing, but she couldn't decide if she could endure this kind of lifestyle of being an anxious recluse.

Her father had come up to her bedroom one evening with a steaming mug of hot chocolate and perched himself on her bed and talked amicably about her future.

Anastasia listened...

'This is the prime of your life,' he said to her in a soft, caring voice. 'You've passed your exams. This boy... what's his name?'

'Toby.'

'Toby. Right. This Toby guy. You really like him, is that so?'

'Dad!' she whined.

Her father shook his head and dismissed her whining with the back of his hand, not interested in embarrassing her.

'Where is he?' he asked. 'You haven't seen or heard from him in weeks. He helps the police fight crime with these special, supernatural powers, apparently. Is that so?'

Anastasia nodded. Her hands were set on her hips and she gave her father a deliberate frown that showed she wasn't pleased about this topic of conversation.

'Yes,' she said, her mouth starting to go dry.

Her father stared at her with serious intent. 'Then where is he? Crime rate in this country is at an all-time high. Surely, if this "Toby" guy was good at what he does, shouldn't it be the other way around?'

Anastasia bit down on her lip, realising as her face flushed red that what her father had just pointed out was in fact a relevant point.

'These thugs on our streets, robbing folks of their purses and wallets and setting fires to rich folks' houses are getting away with these crimes. The police can't keep up. The recession has forced the local authorities to make cutbacks... and this is what happens when there is a suppression of money. And where's Toby? He should be there, ready to stop these attacks or being able to help the police with legitimate suspects.'

Anastasia could see where her father was coming from, but felt the obligated excuses to defend the love of her life. 'That's what he is doing, Dad! But it doesn't just happen overnight. He puts himself in the firing line of these cases. He promised me this would be the last time. He said he'd do this for the police this one and last time, then he wants to return to his job and maybe go on holiday with me to celebrate the end of all of this. I love him. He loves me. That's all there is to it. Don't you get it?'

The silence was oppressive. The argument had favoured her father more than it did Anastasia.

'You only love him 'cause you've gone into hibernation, cutting yourself off from society. If you go out with your friend, Ellie, and live like a normal girl your age, who knows, you might have some fun even if by accident. Toby isn't the only boy in town. There are lots of nice young men who would kick their own mothers out their house to be able to spend time with you. This Toby chap has some nerve to make you wait. And why should you? You love him, you say, but don't know what love is. And if he loves you the same as you love him, he would've called you by now in spite of this duty, don't ya think?'

The more she listened the more Anastasia started to see that her father was thinking of her best interests.

Why should she stay cooped up indoors, hoping and praying that Toby would call and ask if he could meet her?

'It's a party,' her father reiterated. 'Go and enjoy your life while you're young enough. Toby chose a different route... and if he is out there putting his life at risk, then good on him. But it doesn't mean you have to suffer. If he loves you, he'd tell you the same. You're my daughter. I just want to see you happy again. Be sensible. I trust you on that score. But that doesn't mean your youth should be sacrificed for one guy. Know what I'm saying?'

'I do, Dad,' Anastasia said and smiled. 'I'll give Ellie a call before dinner.'

At the party Anastasia had passionately kissed a young bodybuilder who was training for the Mr Wales competition. He had groped her, and she had reciprocated. Then she found out later on from one of Ellie's college buddies that he'd taken growth hormone to get so big and ripped.

She lied to her parents when she got home and told them she had a good time, but was feeling tired and wanted to hit the sack. Instead she spent the next hour crying into her pillow...

*

DI Sark slept fitfully, and got dressed before six in the morning, watching the darkness drift farther and farther away and the first dim grey light ascend over the distant mountains.

An armed policeman had used brutal force on a protestor yesterday afternoon at a film premier in Central London. The young Caucasian male had later died of a crushed larynx on his way to hospital. Now there were crowds gathering outside police precincts in London being stoned. Squad cars were being destroyed by hooligans and vandals. Something wild and crazy had overtaken society in the last couple of months.

There were gatherings in Cardiff and Swansea too. A Vue cinema had been graphitised by youngsters who couldn't get into university due to government financial issues and overpopulation. They supported the attacks of the rich and famous, claiming they were being unfairly treated and had to find a temporary job while waiting a whole year for enrolment.

Some of the claims were induced by genuine cases. However, the current recession was the worst in the last century or more and lots of companies were cutting employment due to technology being upgraded to do jobs more quickly and efficiently than a human being.

He grabbed his mobile phone from the dresser and turned it ON. He noticed that he'd received a text message and opened the file and almost staggered when he saw Toby's name.

GO 2 COMMUNITY CAFÉ
ASK 4 LOCATION DETAILS
GODRE 'G GRAIG FARMLAND!
I HAD A VISION!

TOBY...

Sark reread the message, closed the phone and dashed into the bathroom. All of a sudden at the crack of dawn he found a purpose for the day. His great friend was working his arse off in the field, getting visions and doing his damn best to bring the unlawful to justice in these perilous times.

'Boy's a fukin' godsend!'

Finished going through his morning ritual, DI Sark grabbed his suit jacket and hurried out of the house, not wanting or needing breakfast. There was no time. He got into his Ford, revved the engine and backed out onto the suburban street. He slammed the accelerator to the metal and lurched forward down the street onto the main road...

*

Fast asleep, at long last, Toby had made himself comfortable in his sleeping bag behind a recycling dumpster in a dark alley. There were voices in the distance, growing louder and more distinct. The small town centre was dead to the world. In a couple of hours it would awake and be bustling with shoppers and workers.

Toby eventually blinked his eyes open, having slept nine hours and was actually feeling quite refreshed. He rubbed his face and wondered how much longer this duty would take as his endurance was ebbing into thin air.

He propped himself up into a sitting position and leaned against the dumpster to keep him upright. The previous night had delivered another graphic vision of a famous actor/singer. She had been beaten to a bloody pulp after opening her front door without checking to see who it was first through the peephole. The thugs had tied her hands behind her back and left her lying face down on the living room floor while they went through her purse and desk drawers for cash. They got away with more than five hundred pounds before taking their leave. The thugs wore balaclavas and briefly discussed if they ought to leave the young star alive or dead. They used the Sellotape in the kitchen drawer to prevent her from calling out to her neighbours and left her with a concussion and traumatised.

The voices grew louder. Toby didn't have to be told that the voices were male and raucous. They came into view. Two teenagers. One pushing his bicycle, the other walking with a Yankees baseball cap on back to front.

'Hey, guys!' Toby called out.

Their heads snapped into the direction of Toby's groggy voice and he emerged from the shadows into the breaking dawn light.

'Look at this!' the boy with the baseball cap on back to front said, smiling with menace.

'Could I bother you guys to spare me a couple of quid so I can get myself a drink?'

They boys exchanged glances, turned back to Toby who looked defenceless. Already he decided that calling out to them had been a bad idea. They had no compassion whatsoever. Pleading to them would be as useless as him playing a game for Manchester United.

'Hell no!' the boy with the bike said.

'Whatcha think we are, Samaritans?' baseball cap boy said.

Toby closed his eyes in despair. 'Please guys. If you have enough to spare so I can get myself a bottle of Coke I'd be ever so grateful. Please. I don't like to ask, but as you can see, I'm cold, starving and thirsty.'

The boy with the baseball cap came towards him with a sense of bravado.

'Don't hit me, please,' Toby said. 'I'm brittle as it is.'

The boy slammed his fist into Toby's face, knocking him reeling backwards, clutching his nose.

'Fuck off!' he shouted. 'Not our fault you're a bum, is it? I got five quid on me and you ain't getting a penny.'

Blood trickled down from Toby's nose onto his lips. He staggered backwards and waved the boys off as he sat back down behind the dumpster.

The boy with the bicycle stared at Toby and his friend and silently disapproved of his mate's actions. He had a ten-pound note and had been considering getting the bum a drink in Morrisons superstore. He couldn't now because that would be going against his mate's decision.

'C'mon,' he called out. 'Let's not waste our time here. He's not worth it anyway.'

The boy with the baseball cap laughed at Toby, pivoted and then headed out of the alleyway back onto the red-bricked street with a spring in his step.

After stopping the bloodflow, Toby got to a standing position once again, slung his backpack on and walked out of the alleyway and out of the town centre, heading for the countryside where his destiny awaited him. And right now, his destiny was being cruel to him. He had run out of supplies and cash and was now running on empty. The swelling in his face puffed up his cheeks causing his eyesight to become diminished. Nevertheless, he had to make it to the farmhouse to stop his enemy from wreaking more havoc.

*

Sunlight slanted through the bedroom window onto Michael Cawthorne's face, warming and waking him simultaneously. He welcomed the warm hands of the sunshine and momentarily forgot everything that had transpired since being reunited with his son. Then it all came back to him. And the harsh reality was that his family were dead. He was the last in the chain that carried the Cawthorne name. His father had died in conflict and his mother had remarried and moved to Northampton, England.

As he blinked his eyes open, the first thing that came into his head was the fact that both he and his son were murderers.

The rage and shock of hearing that Matthew had been the one who had killed Susan Cawthorne in cold blood had sent shockwaves through his system. There was nothing else to be expected. However, the sensation and loneliness hit him as a car would going a hundred miles per hour into a brick wall.

The first thing Michael was going to do was to get out onto his land and get rid of the homeless followers and then clean the shotgun. Then he'd call the authorities and say that Matthew had gone insane and finally the pressure got too much for him which was the cause of his suicide.

Michael desperately wanted this situation to go away, leaving him alone to get his farm back in perfect working order. He had washed his hands of his son's worldly and sinister plans. Yet what really shocked Michael to the core was the fact that Matthew was able to convince such a crowd into believing and committing themselves to his malevolent plans.

Like all things, the whole situation would collapse into oblivion. The truth would eventually come out and that's what angered Michael more than anything else. He had been there for his son during these last few months, permitting him to use his land as his fortress. However, after speaking to Matthew he realised that Matthew wanted to cause anarchy. And by God, he'd managed to do that.

But there was something wrong with Matthew, Michael decided. He had been to Cefn Coed Mental Institution after killing a cat and writing evil intentions in his diary.

It all made perfect sense now…

Susan had been right not to permit him to return home after he was released. His bitterness at her refusal was uncalled for and beyond belief. To commit matricide and to still be able to live with oneself was the sign of someone evil and without conscience. It was as if someone had poisoned Matthew's mind and had driven him into a situation there would be no escaping from.

Some men were born evil…

Michael was starting to believe this more than anything else.

He wasn't evil. Susan was as far from evil as you could possibly get, but something had snapped in Matthew's psyche. Something that there would be no return from… and this was it.

Some men wanted to see the world in chaos just for kicks.

'I did the right thing,' Michael said to no one. But he was convinced he was right, and there was no guilt in him for doing what he had done.

Just like Matthew had no guilt for all he had done…

47.

THROBBING all over, young Toby departed the town centre and made his journey across the bridge on his way to Bryncoch. The sun dazzled his back, and if he hadn't been beaten badly, he might even have enjoyed the trek. Instead, blood continued to run from his nose and mouth with an acrid and tangy taste.

His ribs were killing him and caused Toby to bend at the waist. His legs were numb and would certainly bruise colourfully in the next couple of days... if he was still alive.

He knew that the world had taken a turn for the worse and his beating was the epitome of how society trampled all over the poor and downtrodden. The whole situation opened his eyes in pure amazement at how the modern world behaved. If someone wasn't making a profit or being rewarded for good work there would be resentfulness. The world centred itself around the entertainment industry.

What scared Toby the most was how Matthew had been right, at least in some ways. Had he not been a cold-blooded murderer, he might have concurred with him on some of his points. However, Matthew was a madman... with power and influence. He was a danger to society. It had cost him next to nothing to bring the homeless and desperate folks out to the farm and give them a sermon on how it was far from right what was transpiring in their nation and the whole planet and how if they wanted to survive then drastic measures needed to be taken.

But anarchy...?

Only the rioters for equality during the Black Lives Matter protests and the inept police officers using brute force to kill the freedom of speech had caused chaos. And in this chaos, Matthew had risen and taken advantage of the folks who believed him every step of the way. Matthew Cawthorne was God to them. They were making money and spending it just like the ordinary folks did every day of their lives.

Toby had to act and fast. And the only way he could achieve the end of this craziness was to get to the root of the matter. If he brought Matthew into custody his followers would scatter, having spent all their stolen money and return to the streets where they begged and pleaded for equality. In a world where rioters caused mayhem and the armed forces were treated like they were scum, Matthew had risen. Yet what the world apparently cared about more than anything else was still going on every day. If they saw a homeless person lying on the streets as he had done, they would walk right over him or worse, beat him to a pulp. All the police did was call in for an ambulance. There the victims of a narrow-minded society would receive treatment for their injuries before being sent away again, back to the streets to cope and hope that nothing unforeseen and bad would befall them again.

Now Toby knew what it felt like. Nevertheless, even in his injured self, he was fully aware of right and wrong, good and evil. Matthew had never been homeless. He had taken a stand and it had worked for all intents and purposes. Meanwhile Toby had the first-hand experience and suffered with brain trauma and broken bones, still determined to bring peace and justice back into the main front of society in an attempt to bring order to those who desired it and those who desperately required saving.

The breeze picked up as Toby walked over the bridge and his hair danced wildly. He arrived at a Burger King, and had he some money would have loved to get himself a strawberry milkshake. His stomach had shrunk in on itself like a vacuum. He couldn't enter any shops or restaurants in his physical state, anyway. If he did someone would insist that they call the emergency services. No. He couldn't allow that to happen. He was on a mission… and come hell and high water he would make sure he finished the mission and brought Matthew to justice even if it meant losing his life.

That's what he couldn't tell anyone.

Toby wondered if Annie Combs knew.

It didn't matter who knew… or more importantly did know… Toby was heading to his fate… whether it would be good or bad.

Having been beaten to a pulp and still having the strength and courage to get up and make his way to Goedre 'g Graig farm had put everything else into perspective.

Although as he hurried along as fast as his mortal self could carry him, Toby recalled his mother telling him that he might lose Anastasia in the process of this duty he felt obliged to do.

He shook his head hard in order to get rid of the thought so he could concentrate on limping across the deserted roundabout, onto another pavement and up the steep rise which slowed him down.

As he reached the zenith, a grey Peugeot 206 slowed to a halt and the driver tooted the horn.

Toby pivoted with some difficulty and then smiled his best to the middle-aged man wearing glasses and a goatee. He was being motioned to come over. Toby went and bent down to face the driver. The window wound down and the driver said, 'Jeez what the hell happened to you, friend?'

'It's the price of a divorce,' Toby said and then spat out a wad of phlegm.

The man laughed. 'Hey, c'mon!' He leaned across the passenger seat, grabbed a box of Milk Tray and dropped it on the back seat. 'Get in. Where're ya headed?'

Toby told him his destination and then hobbled around the front of the car, got in, fastened the safety harness over him and sighed heavily, only then realising how tired he actually was in making it this far already.

'Name's Clive,' the driver said as they took the highway into Rhos and down the steep slope into Pontardawe.

'Toby.'

'Seriously, what happened?'

Toby wasn't too keen on telling Clive or anyone else for that matter what had happened. However, Clive had saved him a good half an hour and some rest, so the least he could do was answer.

'I got jumped by some drunken hooligans,' he said and wiped his bloodied mouth with the sleeve of his shirt.

'You live in the countryside?' Clive asked, trying to fit the pieces together.

'Not exactly. Where're you headed?'

'Tesco.'

'That'll be fine,' Toby said, reassured that Clive wouldn't be with him for much longer and that he could get back to concentrating on bringing Matthew Cawthorne to justice once and for all.

He dearly liked Clive. However, today wasn't an ideal day to make friends. Today was a vital day that might well be his last.

Clive asked kindly if Toby would like to be dropped off further afield, but Toby said he appreciated the offer but would much rather continue the rest of his journey on foot.

The least Clive could do was get Toby a drink for his journey, and as much as he wanted to get going, the young spiritualist gratefully accepted the offer and decided it was prudent to do so. Then he thanked Clive again and headed into the small town that offered the old highway and finally onto the green pastures and towering mountains.

*

The dazzling sunshine made DI Sark narrow his eyes against the glare as he reached the top of the street. Without warning he heard something go pop. Then the car careened to the right. The rubber of the tyre was slack and keeping the vehicle straight proved to be nigh on impossible.

'God damn it!' he hissed and steered the car to the kerb, realising that he had got himself a flat. And today of all days this occurrence was the worst time for him to be in this situation.

The Mondeo clipped the kerb and rolled to a shuddering halt underneath a spruce. The detective thumped the steering wheel with his hands and forearms in vexation. If anything occurred while he sorted this new and vital problem out he would lose his temper properly... and that was something the police officer very rarely did. This was an exception. It was as though God himself was against him. Of course, nothing could be further from the truth, but he wanted to blame someone if any harm came to Toby. He had bonded with the young man and desperately wanted the very best for him after all that he had done for the law enforcement in the country.

The boy deserved a medal, DI Sark believed.

If famous actors and singers were given awards, money and fame for doing something they loved doing, then Toby ought to be given a medal made out of gold for his endeavours. He risked his life and sometimes had to sacrifice things that anyone else his age wouldn't even consider giving up for the greater good.

He applied the handbrake, killed the motor and fished out his mobile phone and dialled the RAC number. He had already used his spare tyre at the end of last year when thugs had slashed his rear tyres for being caught smoking pot and having to do community service as punishment. This was different.

'Please God, let Toby be safe.'

With that he waited while the phone rang and was eventually answered and DI Sark explained the situation to the RAC employee. He was adamant that there was a crisis he had to attend and promised to pay double for a fast service. Then he waited for assistance and breathed heavily...

*

Toby ambled with difficulty through the small town of Pontardawe drinking his bottle of Diet Coke and made progress in his journey. Clive had bought him a Monster energy can as well, which the young man had stored in his backpack. His face was swelling and he had to cover his nose due to the stink of his body odour. He had decided that whatever went down at the Cawthorne farm that today would be his last in undercover duty. He didn't care what happened more or less. Of course it would be great if he survived and got to return home to be with his mother once again. She must be worried sick and longed for him to return home so she would not have to worry anymore about where he was and what was happening.

The United Kingdom had been left shocked and wounded by this development – rich and famous folks being attacked, often killed, by masked thugs that were fulfilling Matthew Cawthorne's destiny. The young man was the same age as him and was a great talker. He made some vital points and arguments regarding the facts of the intended targets. However, had he sent his followers to rally instead of inducing anarchy, his movement might have been much harder to ignore. Instead folks were frightened to the core.

Two big star actors had been on the Graham Norton Show and by the weekend they had been shot and stabbed in their hotel by Matthew's followers. Their movies that were supposed to be released this week in cinemas had to be postponed. The male and female actors had starring roles and were young and healthy. They were in their prime.

Now their last movies would be bigger than anyone could have imagined because of their shocking and untimely deaths.

Unbeknown to anyone else, Matthew had had a meeting with one of the presidents of the exclusive society about how and why his aspirations benefited anyone. And the more it was discussed, the more the three wise men came to the conclusion that Matthew had no interest in playing fair. Instead he had killed in cold blood and then took another direction and developed his own movement to increase the crime rate by "making people equal to each other".

Before there were crooked government schemes that solved unemployment by companies employing folks without contracts as they were agency workers to make the statistics of unemployment look much better on paper while the toffs got bonuses for inventing new ways the nation could save and make more money.

No one cared about the people, Matthew had drilled into their consciousnesses. They were there simply to make up the numbers in society. The virus aftermath saw thousands and thousands out of employment and into homelessness.

Matthew had preached that the real reason for the riots, murders and increase of followers was due to the fact that his purpose was to lead hard working, downtrodden folks out into the battlefields of their great nation as a sign of things to come. Soon there were going to be more and more hungry mouths to feed unless someone (namely Matthew) took the horse by the reins and led them out of the darkness and into the light where no high official or rich businessman could ignore his movement and would have to surrender to their faults.

Toby wouldn't admit it aloud but he was deeply afraid of Matthew Cawthorne, not the person himself, but the power he had over people by preaching sermons on ways to fight back against the greedy sharks that made profit making them poor. He didn't like to admit it but perhaps Matthew Cawthorne was right. However, there was another side to Toby that became aware that the very reason the nation was in dire straits was because there were lots of protests and murders in the first instance. Matthew had added to that.

Was he being judgemental?

Maybe, he admitted.

Yet Matthew's reign as a leader resulted in murders and riots, his followers using brutal force. They used bombs and guns to destroy buildings and people who hadn't yet been affected by the biggest recession to hit the UK in more than a hundred years.

It was Toby's sole purpose to bring Matthew to justice and save those who were lost back to modern society.

And this was going to be no mean feat.

What made Toby anxious was that even if Matthew did go to prison, someone else might take over his role and continue to wreak havoc out on the streets that could no longer be controlled by the police. If that happened then they were past the point of no return and Matthew Cawthorne would have won.

He finished his Diet Coke and dropped it on the pavement. He walked with a limp and a dull, throbbing body-numbing ache for the next half hour before he came to the side of the countryside highway.

The farmhouse wasn't far now, but the young spiritualist felt his whole anatomy start to fail, like DI Sark's car. He popped open the Monster energy drink and guzzled the contents in hope that he would feel a bit more revitalised with the extra energy it offered before arriving at his destination.

Toby recalled the bus trip to the farm a couple of weeks back, but noticed big 4x4 tyre marks veering off the main highway onto the mushy field to another gate. Farther ahead was the stile he had clambered over with a lot of the other homeless folks. This rear entrance and trespassing seemed rather ominous. He reminded himself of the task at hand. So far he had touched down in the grassy pasture and used the oaks and foliage to shadow his movement beneath the rising sun.

Then he saw something that stopped him dead in his tracks… and the realisation and enormity of the risk he was taking hit him like a steam train at full speed ahead.

There before him sprawled out, face down, was a man in a brown leather jacket and denim jeans. Toby staggered backwards, absorbing the gruesome carcass of a man probably trying to escape the grounds of the Cawthorne Farmhouse. Yet there were no wounds that Toby could see. No arterial bloodstains. Instead there were lots of bodies stretched out across the land and the young spiritualist saw them all with his naked eyes. He slapped a hand over his mouth and nose in shock and to block out the smell of rotting flesh.

Already the crows had started their ample meal and disfigured the deceased whose heads looked pallid and blue.

Poisoned…

Toby had realised that Matthew or one of the more dedicated followers had used poison to contaminate the homeless that induced dire consequences.

There had to be at least twenty carcasses all sprawled out in different postures, some with their hands choking themselves. By the time they had discovered they had been poisoned fatally it was too late and in desperation some of the folks had sprinted towards the front stile and the rear horse gate, seeking help, where other non-group folks were driving past, oblivious of what had transpired.

Toby took fell to his knees, closed his eyes and asked God to give him the strength required to render Matthew Cawthorne and his father unconscious and stand sentinel until DI Sark and co. came to take action in accordance with the rules and regulations of the law.

He rose again and walked in the culvert, covering his mouth and nose against contamination and the putrid odour. Farther ahead was the farmhouse built with modern red brick and white timber panels and green shutters on the windows to block out the daylight. He breathed laboriously and hurried, keeping in a bent-over position so he could sneak up on the residents and surprise them.

The trail of the dense foliage came to an abrupt end, but before Toby emerged into broad daylight well in sight of the farmhouse, he fished out his mobile phone and selected a number. He knelt down again and welcomed the gentle breeze caressing his face softly.

'Hello?'

'It's me... Toby.'

There was a long pause. Then: 'Toby! My God! Where have you been, my boy? It's great to hear from you. I got the RAC man here repairing a flat tyre. How's things?'

'They're all dead,' Toby said, cutting to the chase, not having the time or the patience to explain his statement with long-winded detail.

'Who's dead?' DI Sark snapped.

'All of the followers here at the farm.'

'Oh shit! You have gotta be kiddin' me.'

'No... But I wish I were. He's poisoned them. I'm about to approach the house.'

'There have been riots in London over this. This cult has become infamous and famous depending on who you ask,' DI Sark said. 'The chief wants the leaders and foot soldiers to be apprehended ready for prosecution.'

'I think it's just Matthew and his father left,' Toby said. 'I need you to get me back-up. I'm gonna try and stall them before they see me and make for a quick escape.'

'Be careful, kid,' DI Sark warned. 'Your mother would kill me if anything happens to you. I'll call it in, don't you worry. I'm on my way now. Think smart and don't do anything rash.'

Toby was about to answer when his mobile made a loud *Beep, beep* noise, announcing that he had a LOW BATTERY.

The youngster peeked through the scraggly arms of the big Oak and waited for his heart to stop battering his chest walls and his breathing rate to slow so he could stay cool and calm. Then – and only then – did he move forward. As he did so he felt exposed without any protection.

Toby stared straight at the shuttered windows and knew that, being closed, they gave him a terrific advantage. He stepped forward and his trailing leg was snagged and snapped in a rusty metal contraption right round his ankle. The jagged teeth embedded themselves into his flesh and Toby cried out in agony. The mobile phone fell from his hands into the tall grass and he collapsed in a heap. The searing pain drove everything else out of his mind as quickly as it takes to flick a light switch.

His mouth was in the shape of an O and as he writhed on the ground the shutters on the first floor banged open. Then a figure appeared and Toby could not see as the pain was so much, the sun blinding him and preventing him from having sudden flashes in his eyes.

He glanced down at his right leg and gasped at how far the metal teeth had bitten into his ancle. His heart went into palpitations and the world seemed to spin all around him. The pain was overwhelming as he battled to stay conscious. The entrapment was threatening to take his ankle and foot off. He lost all feeling, and he knew without making an attempt that he did not possess the strength to pry it apart and set his leg free.

The front door flew open and Toby craned his head around and saw the father, Michael Cawthorne, hurrying towards him, wielding a double-barrelled 12-bore shotgun.

'Aw shit!'

Now Toby feared for his life.

The entrapment, meant to catch foxes, cats or rabbits, had done its job exceedingly well. Better than expected, in fact.

Toby tried to speak but all he could taste was the thick, coppery liquid of his own blood discolouring his teeth and running down his quivering chin.

'Well, well,' Michael said. 'Look what we have here. A trespasser.'

Toby flopped back in utter surrender and watched the white fluffy clouds drift by languidly. They looked great and it reminded him of the opening credits of the Simpsons TV show.

Michael came to a halt and kept his weapon hanging down by his side like a traditional gunslinger. 'And what, might I ask, are you doing trespassing on my farmland for?'

Toby didn't answer. Instead he gazed up at the azure sky, sweat beads trickling down his brow and down off his back. The day was supposed to be a scorcher, and normally Toby would have been doing something or planning to do something outside.

That thought brought back days out with his mum or more recently with his girlfriend, Anastasia. Now all of those memories and aspirations would be wiped out, obliterated by the single squeeze of Michael Cawthorne's trigger.

'You haven't answered my question,' Michael Cawthorne said nearly five minutes later.

'You poisoned all those people,' Toby said.

'No,' Michael said, shaking his head. 'Not me I'm afraid. My son's business was his own. I'm just a farmer. Did you know my son?'

'Why are you talkin' in past tense?' Toby asked, fighting against the glittery stars in his vision, trying to stay alert and focused for all he was worth.

'My son is dead...'

'You're lying.'

Michael shook his head forcefully. 'No. That son of a bitch killed his mother.'

As Toby exhaled, he coughed and a wad of thick crimson blood geyser burst from his bloodied mouth.

Matthew Cawthorne is dead?

He tried to let what Michael Cawthorne had just told him sink in and wondered why anyone would lie about such a thing as murder.

'You killed your son?' Toby spluttered, fearing Michael worse than before.

Michael nodded and grinned, somewhat proud of his endeavours.

'What about the cult?'

'What cult?'

'The cult Matthew had started.'

Michael merely shrugged and looked nonplussed. It was fair to say that he didn't give a flying monkey's about the movement Matthew Cawthorne had started.

'But you were a part of it,' Toby protested.

'Was I?'

'Yes.'

Michael lifted the weapon, aimed it at Toby who flinched, turned, and chanced a glance at Michael Cawthorne. As he did, Michael took a blast at the young man's shoulder.

Blood and bone scattered leaving Toby in shock and more horrendous pain he could have ever imagined. His left arm hung loosely with the top of the shoulder bone protruding from the torn flesh.

The deafening blast of the shotgun reverberated in Toby's head and soon he began to drift in and out of consciousness. He was in a great deal of agony and couldn't even move to relieve the pain. At that harrowing moment, Toby became acquainted with Death and although he desperately wanted to live a good, long life, the chances of that happening were very slim.

'Ready for some more?' Michael asked, laughing at his own sick humour.

'Please! Don't do this. Otherwise you'll end up like your son. He was insane,' Toby gasped, fighting for breath. 'Killing me will make things worse. Trust me on this. For your sake, put the gun down. You've already inflicted pain on me.'

'What were you gonna do if you hadn't stepped into the trap?' Michael wanted to know, seeing Toby's chest rising and falling with a great deal of respiratory problems.

Toby coughed up blood and arched his head back, preparing himself mentally for what was about to befall him on this sunny morning. He had confronted death before, but not in such a position where there had been no means of escape. These last laboured breaths were ninety-nine percent going to be his last. His eyes burned with brimming tears and his right leg had lost all feeling. His head spun and for a moment he was back on a rollercoaster of a ride, fighting to stay conscious in spite of his odds.

'Speak to me, ya son of a bitch,' Michael said, breaking Toby's reverie.

'I was gonna bring you to justice,' Toby said.

'You got some nerve…'

Toby gently nodded and Michael couldn't decipher whether or not the young lad was concurring or simply drifting in and out of consciousness. 'I guess so,' he muttered, mentally preparing himself for death and bit down on his lip to stop the compelling urge to sob. To do so would be a symbol of defeat. Failure. A weakling's way out. And now all of a sudden a new thought ignited his brain and body. If he was going to die here and now, Toby wanted to be strong and brave. He desperately wanted to go down with some gumption and fortitude. Crying and begging wasn't going to help him. However, his mother's face came to his mind's eye and Toby killed the trailing thought of his poor mother, living alone, mourning and with grief in her heart.

'Where shall I shoot you next?' Michael asked, grinning sadistically.

'Why don't you shove the barrel of that gun right up your arse? See if it fits.'

The look on Michael Cawthorne's face was one of shock and bewilderment. One second the young lad was propped up by his elbow, fighting back his tears, the next he had gone Rambo on him.

Another two minutes of silence passed and the ambience outside was not fitting for this death scenario, for the sparrows were flying again and chirpy birdsong welcomed the rising sun.

You are loved, my dearest, a voice said to Toby that didn't belong to Michael.

And this time, with the veil of death descending upon him, Toby recognised the voice as his good friend and fellow spiritualist, Annie Combs.

Annie? Is that you? I'm about to die. I hope you're out of the hospital now and making a good recovery. I'm sorry I haven't been in touch as of late, it's just that I've been up to my eyeballs with this chaotic case.

'Hey! Shit for brains!' Michael snapped, breaking a psychic conversation from here at the Cawthorne Farm and Annie's home in Skewen. 'You're daydreaming. The next place I stick this gun anywhere will be in your dirty mouth before blowing your fuckin' brains out. Think you're a wise guy, huh? Don't think you're all that tough just 'cause you got yourself a dirty mouth, 'cause it ain't gonna help your chances. I'm the one who's in charge here, not you!'

'I don't care,' Toby said and then spat out more viscous blood from his gaping, crimson mouth.

Michael raised the shotgun.

Toby inhaled sharply.

The crazy man aimed the shotgun at Toby's right leg and fired at the knee with an almighty blast that sent the phalanx of sparrows flying away somewhere quieter.

Toby saw them… and envied them.

Then he looked down and saw that his right leg was at an impossible angle. Muscle and tissue were visible and the kneecap itself was exposed, pale white.

He arched his head back and cried out, ripping handfuls of grass and soil, fully aware that before Death came to rescue him from this God-awful nightmare he would suffer beyond comprehension for trespassing, of all things.

I'm dying, Annie!

No reply.

Perhaps the elderly lady was in shock. Or she simply hadn't heard him over the blast of the shotgun.

Michael was laughing and was totally unaware that he was as insane as his son whom he had killed. The whole Cawthorne family had lost their minds. Susan Cawthorne had been spot-on when she said that she saw the evil in her son's face that would never go away when he murdered their neighbour's cat.

Matthew Cawthorne was the worst though. In the pasture claiming twenty or so carcasses and Toby's own crippled form, they had watched the world turn into chaos. The protests against crime in favour of the rich and famous were attacked by the rioters and foot soldiers of the young man who simply wanted to watch the world burn. For Matthew had an insatiable and sinister desire that couldn't be bought or changed into something lawful and far more suitable. Susan Cawthorne was right all along. She had seen the evil. She had been traumatised by it and because she refused to share her home with the madman, he had killed her.

Toby didn't know how he knew that. However, he also knew that in spite of the fact that there was no evidence it was unequivocally true, beyond a shadow of doubt.

His hearing had left him.

He opened his bloodshot eyes and could see Michael Cawthorne standing over him, shells popping out of the shotgun where a whisper of cordite air followed the disposed shells. The man reloaded his weapon and was laughing manically at his wounded prey.

He said something but Toby's mind had hit the MUTE button.

'I can't hear you,' Toby croaked, ready for death to take him into the unknown.

Michael aimed the gun at his head and closed one eye, index finger on the trigger waiting to by pulled. Then a small thwack struck Michael Cawthorne in the side of the neck and sprayed blood. The last Cawthorne tottered sideways. The shotgun fell out of his grasp and hit the overgrown grass.

Toby couldn't quite fathom what he was seeing, but the madman was struck squarely in the back. He got knocked forward before falling head first into the tall grass, paralysed...

Toby turned his head and saw a figure climbing over the stile and running across the field towards him.

The man who had saved his life was his good friend, DI Sark.

Toby collapsed back and stared up at the azure sky while the world went about its business and realised the only aspect that this was real would be the news on TV and in the newspapers. There were more dead bodies here than in a small, new cemetery...

48.

TWO MONTHS LATER

TOBY sat propped up on his bed with the window open. He had never thought he'd have the pleasure of being able to see another day, let alone a sunny one. He had just killed the TV and now relished the chirpy birdsong. He looked down at his right leg covered with a cast. He was back home. Helping the police to bring down the cult formed by Matthew Cawthorne had got him in the public eye. When he recovered fully, which was miraculous in itself, Toby was offered a lot of money for interviews for TV news and newspapers.

DI Sark had wounded Michael Cawthorne mortally and as time passed the paramedics were unable to resuscitate him. He died at the Cawthorne Farm along with his son and twenty-three followers who had been poisoned.

Toby did his utmost to avoid the news and learned to relax and let the fear subside. He had palpitations often when he had first recovered. And when he learned of Annie Combs' untimely death the day he had visited her in hospital, the distinct voice of the seasoned spiritualist on the day he too faced death, confronted by both barrels of a loaded shotgun, gave him proof that there was something after death. And if he was being honest with himself, he already believed in ghosts; but to hear one speak to him made the whole, messy matter all the more tangible. All he wanted now was to stay in his room and watch DVDs and read library books Anastasia got him whenever she visited on a daily basis.

Anastasia had openly confessed that she had kissed a boy while drunk at a party and then regretted it from that day forth. She had become overwhelmed by the police from Scotland Yard and the frenetic media exposure of her boyfriend.

Toby forgave her and started to understand how hard it must have been for his beautiful girlfriend to stay with him while he lived off the grid to get closer to the killers.

He had given the authorities a lengthy statement about his visions and voices sending him on his perilous mission to gather evidence personally and report it back to the police so they could file the case and the mass killings that had induced riots in London and Cardiff where some of the murders had taken place.

Abigail took some annual leave to be with her son while his injured leg had taken away his mobility. In the next couple of months Toby would be going back to hospital for a knee replacement and for the removal of bandages from his shoulder. His ankle had been broken in two places and was still very tender, even after the swelling had returned to its normal size.

Anastasia had been buying the newspapers with Toby's handsome face on the front pages claiming that the young spiritualist was a "Hero". He had achieved so much with his wonderful gift he and Annie had called the "Shine" and made criminals across the nation fearful. If Toby had a hunch about something unlawful and sinister, he'd bring it to the authorities' attention.

There was a light knock on the bedroom door.

Toby glanced back behind him and saw Anastasia standing on the threshold. He beckoned her to enter and take the wooden chair.

'How's my lovely, special guy doing, huh?'

'Much better when I get this operation,' he said pointing at his right leg. 'And when all this has blown over.'

'Your friend, Annie would be proud of you, do you know that?' she said and then smiled.

Toby marvelled at her beauty. She had lovely long blonde hair, crystal blue eyes and the aura of her presence made his heart flutter and a warm sensation run right through him.

'Be patient,' she said. 'Your mother's downstairs ordering a Chinese take away. A favourite of yours, apparently.'

Toby concurred that it definitely was and then opened his arms wide and accepted a hug from her. 'I love you,' Toby said.

'I love you too,' Anastasia said.

And while the pain subsided and the warm tickly sensation ran through him, Toby knew that his life would be filled with an everlasting love…

THE END

Printed in Great Britain
by Amazon